SPARKING FIRE OUT OF FATE

BRIGID KEMMERER

BLOOMSBURY
NEW YORK LONDON OXFORD NEW DELHI SYDNEY

BLOOMSBURY YA
Bloomsbury Publishing Inc., part of Bloomsbury Publishing Plc
1359 Broadway, New York, NY 10018
50 Bedford Square, London, WC1B 3DP, UK
Bloomsbury Publishing Ireland Limited, 29 Earlsfort Terrace, Dublin 2, D02 AY28, Ireland

First published in the United States of America in January 2026 by Bloomsbury YA

Library of Congress Cataloging-in-Publication Data
available upon request
ISBN 978-1-5476-1345-8 (hardcover) • ISBN 978-1-5476-1346-5 (e-book)

Book design by Jeanette Levy
Typesetting by Six Red Marbles India
Printed in the United States by Lakeside Book Company
2 4 6 8 10 9 7 5 3 1

For everyone on the Missed Deadlines Discord Server.
You helped make this book happen, and you helped
make that community happen.
I will forever be grateful to all of you.

Syhl Shallow

The Frozen River

Iishellasa Ice Forest

Briarlock

The Crystal Palace

Wildthorne Valley

N

Blackrock Plains

Emberfall
NorthLoc Hills
Valkins Valley
Ironrose Castle
Castellan Bay
Silvermoon Harbor
Rushing Bay
To the Ocean

THE ROYAL COURTS OF THE ALLIED NATIONS

SYHL SHALLOW AND **EMBERFALL**

TITLE	NAME	RESIDING IN
Queen of Syhl Shallow	Lia Mara	Syhl Shallow
King of Emberfall	Grey	Emberfall
Their Daughter	Princess Sinna Cataleha	Syhl Shallow
Queen's Chief Adviser and Sister	Nolla Verin	Syhl Shallow
Royal Physician	Noah of Disi*	Emberfall
Counsel to the King	Jacob of Disi*	Emberfall
Brother to the King	Prince Rhen	Emberfall
Princess of Disi, Rhen's Beloved	Princess Harper of Disi*	Emberfall
King's Courier	Lord Tycho of Rillisk	Emberfall

*"Disi" is not a real country, though the people of Emberfall and Syhl Shallow both believe it to be the birthplace of Princess Harper. In truth, "Disi" refers to Washington, DC. When a curse tormented Prince Rhen years ago, Harper, Noah, and Jacob were magically trapped on the grounds of Ironrose Castle in Emberfall, with no way home aside from breaking the curse . . . but that's a different story.

CHAPTER 1

NAKIIS

This fire is too hot, making my wounds ache, but I asked Igaa to smother the flames a week ago, and she refused. She claims that I summon ice in my sleep, and she wants no spark of our scraver magic to linger in the air too long. She doesn't want any risk of Xovaar or his minions finding us until I can heal enough to protect myself.

I told her not to bother. Xovaar already killed me. The death part is just taking a while.

I force my eyes open and discover the cave we share is full of sunlight, the scents of early summer filling the air. Wherever Igaa has hidden me, we must be far from any roads or houses, because I've heard little beyond the occasional drone of insects outside the cave. At night, it's crickets and cicadas, but it's bees right now. A honeysuckle bush must be nearby, because the aroma is unmistakable.

I blink again, and my eyes are slow to reopen, my vision a bit hazy around the edges. Igaa's fire isn't blazing anymore, but the summer warmth pressing in from outside the cave would melt any ice immediately anyway. I wish we had been able to reach the forests of

Iishellasa—or, at the very least, the banks of the Frozen River. Igaa could have cast me into the flowing rapids, and I would've slipped under the surface. My death would've been swift: painless and cold.

Dying here, in this miserable heat, seems to add insult to injury.

I let my eyes fall closed again. The cave is empty. Has she been gone long? I've stopped being able to measure time by a matter of minutes and hours, and now it seems that the days slip out of my grasp between my wakings. Even now, I have no idea how much time passes before my eyes open again, only that the angle of sunlight has changed. The droning bees have moved on.

A twinge of worry flickers through my head. So many of the others have already been destroyed by Xovaar and his allies. I can't lose Igaa, too.

Then again, maybe I should stop fighting. I've already lost.

The air currents change, speaking a language all their own. I might not be able to fly, but my wings twitch a little as the slightest breeze flickers across my feathers, a momentary chill breaking through the brutal heat of the day.

Magic. Alarm cracks through my chest, and my wings rustle, as if I have the strength to flee a threat.

But then I recognize the flare of power on the air, and my heart settles, my eyes falling closed in relief.

Igaa.

The scent of fresh meat strikes me at once, and then an animal carcass is unceremoniously dropped on the cave floor in front of me.

I don't move.

—I know you're awake, Igaa says, speaking her thoughts to my mind, the way we do when we're high in the air and the wind makes speech impractical. ***—Eat.***

My eyes remain closed. ***—I'm not hungry.***

A human woman might beg and cajole, but Igaa isn't human, and she's likely had quite enough of my resistance to her tending. I'm not surprised when the air currents shift again, just before her claws take hold of my chin and twist, forcing my jaw open. A second later, a scrap of raw flesh is pressed between my teeth.

I'm stronger than she is, and in another time or place, I could knock her hand away.

Right now, I can barely hold my head up.

—***Eat,*** she says again, pressing my mouth closed as if I might spit it out just to spite her.

It's tempting.

But no, the fresh blood is a bloom of copper on my tongue, and even if my brain is ready to give up, my body isn't. Against my will, my mouth automatically begins to chew.

Igaa's grip gentles. When I swallow, she presses another wet piece of flesh in behind it.

I want to resist. This all feels so futile.

But I don't.

After a few more pieces, I turn my face away, and her sharp claws press into my jaw again.

This time it draws a growl from my throat, but even that sounds pathetically weak. —***Igaa. No.***

She sighs. —***I should find your magesmith. I suspect his magic could heal this.***

She means Tycho. He's no more my magesmith than I am his scraver.

When I say nothing, Igaa adds, —***He is your friend, Nakiis. He would help you.***

I hiss. —***No. He isn't. And he wouldn't.***

I made sure of that weeks ago, when I refused to help Tycho protect that foolish king. I knew Xovaar would attack with impossible fury and kill anyone in his path. He nearly killed Tycho and I did my best to warn him away. But he didn't listen. He ran to the king's side, and the two of them nearly perished.

They *would have* perished, if I hadn't lent my magic to theirs.

But offering them my magic left me depleted, unable to defend myself when Xovaar retreated from that battle . . . and found me instead.

Igaa must have stolen a waterskin from somewhere, because she pours a bit across my lips.

—You need a magesmith, she insists.

—A magesmith cannot heal these wounds, Igaa. Enough.

—A magesmith could heal the infection.

This has become a common argument. She's right that a magesmith *could* heal the infection. The deeper wounds, both caused by a spear of Iishellasan steel, will only heal with time.

It's the infection that's going to kill me.

Her clawed hand settles against my cheek, and she swears out loud in our language, the word sounding like a clash of ice in the confines of the cave. "You are hot enough to melt the Frozen River yourself."

"Take me there," I say roughly, my spoken voice revealing my weakness. "Let's see."

She's quiet for a moment, and her fingers drift through my hair and down my neck, until her hand comes to a stop on my injured shoulder. The slight touch sends a wave of pain through my body, and I let out a breath.

"I would if I could, Nakiis," she says quietly.

I know she would—but Xovaar would find us long before we could reach the river separating Syhl Shallow from Iishellasa.

"This is hopeless," I say, the rough words barely more than a whisper. "Even if Tycho would help me, he has returned to Ironrose Castle. That is too far for you to travel alone. Not while Xovaar seeks us both."

Her fingers trail through my hair again, and my eyes fall closed. Sleep pulls at me again, the deep, dreamless sleep of illness. But her voice speaks to my mind just before I drift away.

—Tycho is not the only magesmith we know.

CHAPTER 2

CALLYN

I shouldn't be here.

The thought has been plaguing me for days, and I can't quite seem to shove it out of my head, no matter how hard I try. Lord Alek threatened to reveal my hidden magic if I didn't leave the Crystal Palace, and anyone with any common sense would've left that very night. It's no secret that magic doesn't belong in the palace. Not now. Not after everything that's happened.

But I can't seem to make myself leave.

King Grey has been gone for two weeks, and most people believe he took every scrap of magic with him. I hear the relief among the palace staff. They're glad he's gone from Syhl Shallow, thinking the absence of his magic means there won't be any further threats to the palace.

But they don't see the darker effects of his leaving, like the sorrow that began to overtake the entire palace the morning after he left. I'm not sure how many people truly miss *him*, but the change in Queen Lia Mara is profound. Morning tea is a somber affair, with the queen absently drizzling honey over her bread, while little Princess Sinna stares forlornly out at the training fields, where she used to watch her father run drills. The queen used to be occupied with advisers and courtiers all day, but of late she has begun to retire to her room after the midday meal, only to emerge hours later with red-rimmed eyes and a rough voice. By nightfall, the queen has often found the bottom of her third or fourth glass of wine, and it has not gone unnoticed among the staff. Little Sinna hasn't realized it yet, but my sister Nora has.

"Is the queen unwell?" she whispered to me yesterday, after Queen Lia Mara stumbled across the threshold into her bedroom. "She's not going to turn out like Jax's father, is she?"

The question was jolting, because I hadn't realized how much Nora noticed about my best friend's father—and how much his penchant for whiskey and ale affected his temperament. I bit my lip and stared after the queen. "No, Nora," I whispered in response. "She's just heartbroken."

The queen's sister, Verin, has no sympathy—or patience—for Lia Mara's emotion. I've heard her snapping more than once. "You have a country to rule and a daughter to raise. You are well rid of that man and his magic. You should've let me put a sword through his chest before he left."

The comment made me shiver. I wondered what Verin would do to *me* if she knew about the magic in my veins. As soon as I had the thought, I wondered what she'd do to the *queen*, who secretly shares the same talent.

Queen Lia Mara must have wondered the same thing, because she threw Verin out of her chambers.

But after that, we didn't see the queen for an entire *day*. The next morning, she looked like she hadn't slept at all.

So here I am, at the crack of dawn, two weeks after Alek demanded that I leave the palace—still here. At least I have a brief reprieve from the somberness of the royal suites, because I've been keeping up my training sessions with the army recruits. I don't really have any *friends* among the soldiers, but at least it's a distraction from the heavy grief hanging over the palace. Morning drills under the guidance of Lord Jacob might leave me a battered, sweaty mess, but it's two hours where my thoughts aren't filled with anxiety over someone else's pain.

But this morning, Jacob doesn't appear on the fields to lead drills. General Solt does.

The army recruits had been clustered in small whispering groups, which I'd been casually ignoring. I learned early on that the barracks have no shortage of gossip and drama. My sister, Nora, would probably be rapt with attention, but I don't know any of the players, and in the midst of my own drama, I can't make myself care.

But then I hear one of them murmur, "leaving the queen alone," and I snap my head around.

As soon as I do, they stop talking. The silence is sharp and sudden, like a crack of thunder.

I might train with them, but they know who I am—and they know my proximity to the queen. It's never seemed to matter, but all of a sudden, I'm keenly aware of it. Were they simply gossiping? Or was it something more?

But then General Solt appears on the fields, and the recruits snap to attention. I'm not in the army, so *I* don't, but my mother was once an officer, so I know enough to stand beside them. I can sense the unease among the others, especially since Jacob isn't here. General Solt has never come to the fields this early, and he doesn't look happy about the fact that he's here now either.

Without preamble, he says, "Tomorrow, you will join Captain Narrah's unit for midday drills. For today, run an easy five. Full gear."

His voice is tight and official, leaving no room for disobedience. "Dismissed."

An easy five. No matter how long I train, I will never get used to the way soldiers refer to a five-mile run with forty pounds of gear as if it's a light day of work. But without complaint, the recruits fall into formation and move off, their gossip forgotten.

I don't. General Solt has already begun to turn away, but I go after him. He was so severe that I'm hesitant to stop him, but I don't know what happened to Lord Jacob, and I'm not sure if I'm meant to continue joining the recruits. The king is the one who initially made the offer—and he's gone.

I grimace and jog to catch up with the man. "General?"

He turns with a fierce expression, probably ready to face a soldier who's ignoring a direct order. But then his eyes skip over my form, and I see the moment he recognizes me.

"Callyn, yes?" A hint of fondness flickers in his gaze. "Adelyn's daughter."

That takes me by surprise, because I'm not used to anyone remembering my mother. But I nod. "Yes."

He snaps his fingers and points at me. "I was supposed to find you some soldiers who served with your mother." He grimaces. "You'll have to forgive me. With the state of things—"

"Oh!" I say in surprise, remembering the promise he made weeks ago, when he said he'd locate any other soldiers who might have known my mother. That was before the scraver attacks that caused so much damage to the palace—and left so many people dead. Before the king was driven away by the people he'd sworn to protect. "Please don't apologize," I say. "Other things were more important."

"This is important, too. We all lost family. I will find them for you."

He was so prickly with the recruits that his sudden empathy takes me by surprise. I wonder who *he* lost. "Thank you, General."

He gives me a nod and begins to turn away—and I realize he thinks this is why I stopped him.

"Wait!" I say.

He turns again. "I am due in the palace," he says. He nods past me, where the recruits have already turned to specks in the distance. "And you've lost your unit."

"I'm not a soldier. I work for the queen. I was just . . . I've been training with Lord Jacob."

His eyes light with respect, and he nods. "Your mother would be proud."

Then he turns away *again.*

I start after him. "General—"

This time when he turns, his expression is exasperated.

"Sorry," I say quickly. "I just . . ." I wince. "You said that Captain Narrah would be taking over the recruits. What happened to Lord Jacob?"

A shadow falls over his expression, but only for an instant before the emotion vanishes. "The king has ordered his army to return to Emberfall, along with any remaining officials who are sworn to him." The general pauses. "They departed at midnight."

Midnight. When the king left, it was also in the middle of the night—and I didn't even know until the following day. I don't think *anyone* in the palace knew aside from the queen. I realized later that it must have been intentional, giving King Grey a long lead time before anyone even realized he was gone. I'm sure Lord Jacob was doing the same.

But it was one thing when the king *alone* left the palace. His magic has been the source of so much conflict here, and that was no secret. I witnessed the battle with the scravers that left so many people injured or dead, and I see the queen's daily pain over the fact that she placed the desires of her citizens ahead of her love for her husband. But even with the king gone, there were still Emberish citizens in the palace.

There were still Emberish soldiers barracked among the Syhl Shallow army. Many people expected them to remain—including me. A symbol of the ongoing peace between our countries.

If the king has withdrawn his people and his soldiers, that feels much more final.

That feels like a statement of something *else.*

Maybe that's what those soldiers were gossiping about. The queen is very much alone now.

I swallow thickly, then nod. "Thank you, General."

"If you intend to continue with the recruits, I will speak with Captain Narrah," he says.

"I . . ." My voice trails off. I'm not sure what to say to that. I don't know what the queen wants me to do. She's so lost to her own sorrow that she probably doesn't even know I'm down here.

But during my months in the palace, I've discovered the perfect statement for when I don't have a good answer for something and I don't want to guess wrong. I give General Solt a definitive nod. "I will speak with the queen to determine what she thinks is best."

It works with him as well as it's worked with anyone else, because he gives me a nod in return. This time, when he turns away, I turn in the opposite direction and sprint after the recruits.

By the time I complete my run, I've sweated through my tunic and breeches, and I'm envisioning a long soak in the washroom at the back of my chambers. Back in Briarlock, a warm bath was a luxury requiring buckets hauled from the well down the lane near the forge, and our only soap was made from tallow and ash. But here in the palace, the warm water seems endless, the buckets carried by well-paid servants, and the soap smells good enough to eat.

Unfortunately, when I reach the royal suites, my sister, Nora, has a tense expression on her face, and the nursery looks like a tornado rolled through it. Little Princess Sinna is nowhere to be found, but her morning tutor likely already claimed her.

"What happened?" I say to Nora.

She sighs, crouching to scoop stone tiles into her hands. They're scattered all over the floor, among broken pieces of balsam wood and a pot of spilled paint. "Sinna," she says, as if it explains everything.

It doesn't. Princess Sinna is better behaved than most four-year-olds, and I'm convinced it's because she's had courtly manners drilled into her since birth.

"I'm sorry I left you alone." I drop to a crouch to help. "Did she have a tantrum?"

"Yes."

"About what?"

"About nothing." Nora pauses, and her voice drops. "She misses her parents."

My mouth forms a line. I shouldn't be surprised.

Nora sighs again, scooping another handful of tiles into her palm. "She declared that she wants to take her pony and go find her father. She's mad that the queen won't let her."

I snort. "She's going to ride all the way to Ironrose Castle? Of course the queen won't let her."

"Well, she demanded an audience with the queen." Nora hesitates. "She's never given me a decree like a princess before. I didn't know what to do."

That's equally startling. Princess Sinna usually looks at Nora like an adopted big sister. My hands go still on the broken toys I'm picking up. "What *did* you do?"

"I told her that no one is allowed to demand an audience with the queen, but if she wants to see her when she awakens, I would make sure of it."

I glance at the closed door that leads to the queen's chambers . . . the chambers she used to share with the king. "Did that get her to calm down?"

Nora nods. "For a little while." She pauses. "But the queen did not wake. Or if she did, she hasn't come out."

I glance at the window. It took me over an hour to run five miles, and now it's reaching midmorning. The sun is blazing, the room full of light. "Not at all?"

Nora bites her lip and shakes her head.

"So Princess Sinna was unhappy," I guess.

Nora nods, then gestures emphatically to indicate the room, in complete disarray thanks to a child-size tornado.

I sigh.

"Has anyone checked on the queen?" I say.

Nora bites her lip again—then shakes her head.

I look at the door to the queen's chambers, then move across the room and press my ear to the door.

Nothing. And I'm sure Princess Sinna wasn't quiet if she caused this kind of mess.

This is why I can't leave, *Lord Alek.*

I finally move back to Nora's side and resume tidying the mess. We work together in silence until Nora whispers, "I know people were afraid of the king and his magic, but this doesn't feel better, Cally-cal."

"I know," I say. I look out the window at the training fields, where scravers attacked the king a couple of weeks ago. He only had two Emberish soldiers to stand at his side—until the queen and I emerged from the palace and lent our power to their efforts. Power that we're not supposed to have. Most people think that we're safe from the scravers now that magic has been banished from Syhl Shallow.

But every now and then, I feel the sparks and stars in my blood, and I know it's *not* gone. Not from me, and not from the queen.

After a moment, I look back at the chamber door, considering the woman trapped by her own sorrow, and the distraught child caught in the middle. I consider my country, how so many people were terrified of magic that they drove the king right out of the palace.

But now the queen is drowning in grief. Allied soldiers from Emberfall have been ordered to leave. The king is gone.

Nora is right. Nothing seems better at all.

CHAPTER 3

ALEK

I'm no stranger to being woken by nightmares.

In the past, the visions that haunted my dreams were either my sister or my mother being torn apart on a battlefield. A monster summoned by magic would swoop down from the sky, fangs and claws ripping into fragile skin, tearing them limb from limb, blood spraying in an arc to coat the faces of nearby soldiers.

The nightmares are a little ridiculous. My sister didn't even die that way. She died during an attack on King Grey, and an arrow pierced her heart.

Unfortunately, my dreams—my *nightmares*—don't seem to care about accuracy. My mother truly was torn apart by a monster on the other side of the border, and my thoughts are all too happy to connect their deaths in my mind. More than once I've woken in a cold sweat after watching them die *together*. The monsters in my dreams shift and change from night to night, taking on scales or feathers or horns—or all three at once—but they're always awful.

But this morning when a nightmare awakens me, it's not my sister or my mother being ripped to pieces by taloned hands.

It's Callyn.

I wake panting, sweat soaking the fine linen sheets on my bed. Summer heat fills the room, and the bright sunlight blazing through the window tells me it must be midmorning.

I run a hand across my face, and it comes away damp. I blindly reach for the pull cord beside my bed and give it a jerk. Somewhere, a chime rings distantly.

I shouldn't be dreaming about her. If my sleeping thoughts insist on showing me Callyn, the nightmares should be visions of her *controlling* the monster. Not being attacked by it.

Because she lied. She betrayed me. With her *magic.*

But she also saved me.

I press both hands into my face, rubbing at my eyes until I see stars. Until it hurts.

With a gasp, I jerk my hands down, and I give the cord another furious yank. I shouldn't be thinking about her anyway. She's no better than the king—and she's likely gone from the palace by now, just like he is. Grey left weeks ago, and my reports say his soldiers aren't far behind. No scraver attacks have been reported in Syhl Shallow. The king's magic is gone—and Callyn's should be, too. She's a danger to the queen, and she's a danger to the princess, so I gave her an ultimatum.

I told her to leave.

A twinge of regret flares in my chest.

Ugh. I press my fingertips into my eyes again. The room is so silent it hurts. I'm always alone, but right now, this solitude seems to have claws. I'm pressing on my eyeballs so hard that starbursts flare in my darkened vision.

"My lord?"

I startle so roughly I nearly fall out of bed. My arm knocks a bottle off my side table, and it crashes to the floor, shattering. The sound of glass skittering over the tile echoes against the walls, making my head pound immediately.

A footman stands in the doorway, unbothered.

This kind of morning is not what anyone on my staff would call *uncommon.*

"Breakfast," I say roughly.

"Yes, my lord." He pauses. "I'll send a maid to tidy the mess."

Tidy. As if I've absently left out a pair of trousers instead of scattering shards of glass everywhere.

Whatever. They're paid for discretion, so I don't mind if they extend it to *me.*

A scullery maid arrives with a broom and dustpan, followed by another servant bearing a platter of poached eggs and flaky biscuits lined with jam.

I gesture to the table in the corner, then throw back my blankets. Cautious of the broken glass, I make my way across the room, grateful for the distraction. But as I pick at the food, I can't help but think of Callyn again. We met in her bakery, and I was charmed by her independence as swiftly as I was charmed by her *food.* I don't think I ever told her that.

Maybe I should have.

The thought comes unbidden—and unwelcome.

That whole time, she had magic. She had *magic*, and she hid it.

The same kind of magic that killed my family. The same kind of magic that killed *her* family. I don't know how she could—I don't know how—I don't know why she would—

I slam the fork down, and this time I nearly break the plate. I push it away from me. My heart is pounding, and I don't know if it's anger or fear.

Anger feels more worthy, but I'm worried it's the latter. I think of my dream, and for a flicker of time, I imagine Callyn controlling those creatures, and I shudder. Betrayal lodges in my heart like a hot coal trapped behind the grate of the hearth.

I feel like such a fool. Her power surely comes from that pendant she wears around her neck. All this time, and I believed it was a ward *against* magic—not the other way around.

Another footman appears in my doorway. "Master Martyyn has delivered several messages this morning, my lord. He stated that you may wish to select the fabrics personally."

I look up in surprise. Martyyn is my personal secretary, and to anyone outside my House, he's responsible for organizing any missives regarding the shipment of fabrics and textiles.

He also secretly handles any private messages arriving from the Truthbringers.

You may wish to select the fabrics personally is a code we've used before, indicating he's received such a message.

I haven't heard that phrase in months. After the king and queen were attacked, the Truthbringers were fractured, splitting into factions: those who supported her position on the throne.

And those who didn't.

I hold out a hand to the servant. "I'll review them now."

Once he's gone, I waste no time. The letter on the top of the pile is cream-colored parchment, sealed with black-and-green wax, which is reliable because it's impossible to remelt without losing the telltale swirls that reveal whether or not a message has been tampered with. The wax has been stamped with the Truthbringer seal.

I lift my knife and slice it open.

Lord Alek,

We're pleased to report that Father has gone home for the summer season. Unfortunately, recent events have led many of *us to wonder whether the estate would be better off if Mother were gone, too. After gathering our best silver, I have discovered a way to ensure success for our family, and it is only a matter of time before everyone is safe. There are those who may be opposed, but I have always felt that the end justifies the means. Don't you agree?*

As always, your support would be appreciated.

You know how to reach me.

Karyl

Father and *Mother* are code words for King Grey and Queen Lia Mara, but I haven't received a message like this in months. For an instant, I wonder if the letter is a forgery. I haven't heard from Lady Karyl since she proved to be working against me, when she assisted in trapping the queen. Karyl isn't her real name, of course, but neither is *Lady Clarinas,* the name she went by when she worked in the palace as little Princess Sinna's governess.

She was supposed to be a spy for *me.* But someone else won her loyalty, clearly.

Honestly, it's been so long since I've heard from her that I assumed she was killed in Briarlock during the attack on the king and queen.

I read the letter again.

Recent events have led many of us to wonder whether the estate would be better off if Mother were gone, too.

Since I know the code, this letter is about as subtle as a sledgehammer. The king is gone, yet they still want to get rid of the queen.

If they want my help for *that,* they won't be getting it.

After gathering our best silver.

She's referring to the Iishellasan steel they were collecting before they battled the king in Briarlock. I wonder how much they have left . . . and what she intends to do with it.

I set down the letter and take a sip of my tea.

The next note is also sealed with black-and-green wax, and the parchment is slightly crumpled and dirty, as if it changed hands many times—or perhaps it was handled by someone who was a bit dirty himself. No Truthbringer sigil appears on this one, but then I don't expect it.

I flick my knife against the seal. This letter is written in Emberish, the handwriting barely more than scrawl—typical for a soldier in the King's Army on the other side of the border.

King Grey has arrived at Ironrose Castle. His first order was that all remaining soldiers in Syhl Shallow depart at once, to be stationed in Emberfall. He has given no further directives, but it's known that he was attacked on your soil. Tensions are high, and there are many who question whether we will return to war—and it seems there are many who would like the chance to finish what began four years ago.

I do not have direct access to the King, but I am close to those who do.

I await your orders.

This letter is not signed, but it doesn't need to be.

I know who my spies are. I pay dearly for their loyalty.

But my eyes linger on the word *war*, and I think of my mother. I think of my sister.

I think of Callyn.

Then I glance at that first letter, the one implying a threat against the queen.

Perhaps a visit to the palace is in order. I need to know what I'm dealing with.

I ignore the thump in my heart that reminds me Callyn is gone.

I ignore the pit in my stomach that worries she's *not*.

My attendant reappears, refilling my tea and adding a lump of sugar. I casually fold the letters and set them on the table.

"Will you need anything else, my lord?"

"Have my carriage brought up. I need to visit the Crystal Palace this morning." As soon as I say the words, I change my mind. Since the scraver attack, riding in a carriage is torturous. Being in a closed vehicle, where I can't see the sky, suddenly makes me feel too vulnerable. I shudder without meaning to.

"No," I say sharply. "Have my horse saddled instead. I'll ride."

She bobs a curtsy. "Yes, my lord."

But as I consider these notes and the magic that's tormented Syhl Shallow for years, a scene from that dream flares through my thoughts again. The scraver descending on Callyn, claws ripping across her flesh. I shiver.

No, as much as I hate to admit it, my true worry isn't for the queen at all. It's not even for Syhl Shallow.

It's for Callyn herself.

As head of one of the five Houses in Syhl Shallow, I'm usually admitted to the palace without question. Thanks to King Grey and his worthless little minion, Tycho, I've been greeted with suspicion and scrutiny from time to time, but today, no one even looks at me askance.

The palace is quiet and somber, however, which takes me by surprise.

When I request an audience with the queen, servants and guards exchange glances, which is uncommon.

No one says a word to *me*, however. The servants here are as discreet as my own.

To my surprise, Queen Lia Mara does not answer my summons. Instead, her younger sister, Nolla Verin, does. She strides into the salon in black training leathers, fully armed from head to toe. Her hair is in tight braids pinned to the back of her head, and the expression on her face is certainly not joy over my arrival.

That's mutual.

"Verin," I say flatly. "It seems that every time I wish to speak with the queen, I am offered you instead."

"How lucky for you," she says.

"Is it?"

Her lips purse, but I say nothing and stare at her. She stares back.

If she thinks I'm intimidated, I'm not.

As heir—and now head—of one of the Royal Houses, I've called at court since I was a boy. I've known Verin for as long as I can remember, just as I knew her mother. The former queen was ruthless and brutal and attempted to raise her daughters to be the same. Lia Mara is the elder sister, but she resisted right from the start. She has always been kind and thoughtful, and even though I'd never call her *willful*, she was certainly determined in her refusal to lead through brutality.

So instead, the old queen raised Nolla Verin to be her heir. Everyone expected the younger sister to rule, until Lia Mara claimed the crown for herself—through that same brutality she has always eschewed.

To my knowledge, the sisters have always been close, and I have never heard a single rumor spoken at court to indicate that Verin resents her sister's place on the throne.

But I remember how brutal Verin was when we were growing up, the way she could break an opponent's fingers or crush their windpipe without hesitation. The way her mother would praise her efforts every time, calling Lia Mara away from her book or whatever quiet activity she was engaged in, saying, "Why can't you be more like your sister? Nolla Verin knows what is required of a ruler."

I've often wondered how easily Verin was able to dull the edge of her ruthlessness after Lia Mara took the throne. Others have marveled at it, noting how gracious Verin must be to put her own expectations aside.

But I never marveled.

Instead, I never quite believed it.

As she stares back at me, I consider the way Verin has never fully protected the queen from these recent attacks—neither from the Truthbringers nor from the scravers.

I consider Lady Karyl and the note that was delivered this morning.

I have discovered a way to ensure success for our family, and it is only a matter of time before everyone is safe.

Could Verin be involved in this somehow? In a way, the thought seems ludicrous. She has complete access to the queen at all times. By law, she could kill Lia Mara and take the crown for herself.

As soon as I have the thought, I'm struck with another: I wonder if it's not loyalty that's stopping her, but fear of retaliation. We all saw what King Grey did during the Uprising—and I've already heard about what happened when scravers attacked him right here on the palace grounds.

If Verin killed his wife, he'd burn the world to ash until he found her.

Regardless, I can't stand here and make accusations about the queen's sister. That's a quick path to treason.

That doesn't mean I can't yank her chain. "This is boring," I say to her. I make a shooing motion toward the doorway. "Won't you be a good girl and fetch your sister?"

She doesn't move. "What do you want, Alek?"

"I'm fairly certain I've been clear about my purpose here." I glance toward the doorway. "I am seeking an audience with the queen."

"She's not receiving callers."

"The king departed weeks ago," I say. "My people tell me that his soldiers have withdrawn from Syhl Shallow. Yet the queen has not been seen."

Verin steps closer, her voice turning low and vicious. "You are not in a position to make demands, Alek. The palace was subject to a brutal attack. The queen is recovering—"

"She was injured?" My eyebrows go up.

"No."

"Then why is she recovering?"

Nolla Verin clamps her mouth shut.

This feels more like sparring than bantering—and I know the difference. Verin and I have had countless moments like this over the years. At one point my mother thought we might present a strategic couple—and on the surface, I might agree with her. I've never flinched from brutality, and Verin would never have put up with the attacks that King Grey and Queen Lia Mara have endured. Any plots against the throne would've been severely punished under her rule. If I were at her side, I certainly wouldn't have stopped her.

Verin and I are too similar, and anyone who ever envisioned a romantic pairing was fooling themselves. We're too distrustful, too ambitious, too aggressive, too unforgiving.

Neither of us should rule anything.

It shows now, because this feels like a standoff, and I know she won't back down. I won't either. A spark of aggression flickers between us, and knowing her, it'll lead to a fight. I'm glad I'm armed.

My eyes narrow. "What are you hiding?"

"Nothing. I am protecting my sister from your prying questions."

I take a step closer to her. "Are you certain?"

"I would die for Lia Mara," she says. "And I will *end* anyone who means her harm."

Right this moment, I'm not entirely sure I believe that. "Good," I say. "So will I."

She moves closer to *me*. "What do you really want, Alek?"

I want to know if magic is truly gone. I want to know if the queen is safe.

But that's not really what I want to know. That's not the root of my inquiry.

I want to know if Callyn is truly gone.

As I think the words, I discover I can't speak them. I don't want to know the answer.

I hate this part of myself. It feels like weakness. Magic *should* be banished from Syhl Shallow. If Callyn shares the king's power, she should be banished as well.

But a sliver of hope stings my heart with every beat, imagining she's still here.

A soft voice speaks from the doorway. "Nolla Verin. What are you doing?"

The voice doesn't sound familiar, so I look—and I'm shocked to discover the queen.

She's always so vibrant, with long red hair and bright eyes and a regal bearing. Queen Lia Mara seems to have endless patience, and I've seen her sit at court for hours on end, listening to the pleas and complaints of her subjects. I personally don't know how she endures it, because I'd be exasperated and ordering executions by midday, just to get everyone to shut up. But she's always tireless, spending as much time on the last person waiting for her attention as she does on the first.

Today, however, there's no vibrance. Her eyes are dull, her normally full cheeks a bit hollow. Her hair is lank and seems as though it needs a good washing. She looks as though she hasn't slept in a week.

Or more likely *two*.

"Your Majesty," I say. "Are you . . . well?"

"My husband is gone," she says evenly. "I am not well."

Verin leaves my side to join her sister. Her voice drops, but not enough that I can't hear her. "Lia Mara," she says gently, surprising me with the softness in her tone. "You should be resting."

"I am *done* resting," the queen says firmly. She looks at me. "Alek. I'm glad you are here. I need your assistance. The king has withdrawn his forces from Syhl Shallow. I have heard rumors that the people are afraid we may become embroiled in another war with Emberfall."

I wonder if she knows those same rumors are spreading on the other side of the mountain. I force my expression to remain neutral. "Will we?"

"Of course not," she says firmly. "King Grey is not—" Her voice breaks, and she goes rigid for a brief piercing moment, as if a heartbeat might shatter her to pieces. But then she clears her throat and stands strong. "The king left to *protect* Syhl Shallow. He is not my enemy."

"Yes, Your Majesty." I pause, waiting to hear what else she has to say, but her eyes flick past me, to the window overlooking the training fields. Normally there are squadrons of soldiers engaged in drills, under command of the king.

Right now, there's no one. The queen's mouth trembles the slightest bit.

I study her carefully, torn between regretful satisfaction . . . and uneasy remorse. Because the king had to go. He *had* to. I wouldn't mourn if he were dead, and I'm certainly not going to mourn the fact that he took his magic back to Emberfall.

But I'm not sure this is better. If the Truthbringers hope to eliminate the queen, they aren't going to find much resistance in the woman standing in front of me.

"Lia Mara," I say quietly, hoping her given name will break through some of the tense formality. "Tell me. How can I help you?"

It works—in a way. Her eyes lock on mine. She inhales to speak, but then her gaze settles back on her sister. "Verin," she says sharply. "Leave us."

Something in her tone makes me wonder if Lia Mara suspects her sister as well. But Verin purses her lips and obeys, striding out of the room like a soldier on a mission.

Lia Mara turns toward the door as well, her pace more sedate. "Walk with me, Alek."

I hesitate, then follow. The instant we pass the hall guards, I see them exchange a glance.

"People will talk," I say to her, dropping my voice. "You may recall I was once suspected of working with the Truthbringers myself."

I'm sure she does remember—because it was her own husband who made the accusations, after Tycho kept running his mouth. I wonder if she'll mention that, but the queen huffs a breath, scoffing. "People *always* talk."

But then she says nothing else.

After a while, I glance over. Her eyes are still red-rimmed, her frame slightly slumped. The hallways are dim and quiet, emphasizing her emotion—emotion that seems to weigh on the entire palace.

I realize I have to say *something,* so I finally offer, "Forgive me, Your Majesty. If you are seeking *comfort,* I may not be the best source."

"I'm not." She pauses, looking wistfully at a window. "There's no comfort to be found here. Not now."

"You're grieving the loss of the king."

"I'm not *grieving,*" she says sharply. "He's not *dead.*"

"Ah," I say. "Forgive me."

She's quiet for a long moment, and then she lets out a breath. "You're right, though. I am grieving. In a way."

"If it brings any comfort at all, there is a feeling of relief in the Crystal City."

She glances over at me. "Is there?"

I nod. "It was not just the Truthbringers who feared his magic."

She sighs, a sound full of regret. "I know."

"At the risk of being indelicate . . ." I pause deliberately.

"Go ahead."

"I have heard some question whether you were actually the true ruler of Syhl Shallow. That King Grey was. That you were merely his mouthpiece." I glance over, finding her lips have formed a line. "It may benefit the people to know that you are still strong without him here."

"You are speaking of force."

I shrug. "I am speaking of power."

She laughs, but there's no humor to it. "I will never be like my mother, Alek."

"No one expects you to be like your mother."

"No one *expects* it, but I certainly don't think they'd complain if I ruled with an iron fist. Not even you."

I nod, conceding. "Yes, Your Majesty."

She glances at me. "Tell me your thoughts. I wouldn't have asked you to walk with me if I didn't want to hear them."

"You are grieving. As I said before, I will be little comfort. At best, I can offer judgmental cynicism."

This time, her smile seems almost genuine. "Perhaps I *need* a dose of judgmental cynicism."

We're still strolling through the palace hallways, but just now, we're a good distance from any guards or servants. I drop my voice and say, "I do find myself wondering . . . is it possible to demonstrate strength while looking like the absence of King Grey has broken you?"

Her breath catches, and her steps falter. Perhaps another man would apologize . . . but I won't.

"I suppose I asked for that," she says breathlessly.

"You did," I say. "And you're strong enough to take it."

At that, she squares her shoulders and lifts her chin. "He ruled at my side for years, Alek. That is not a small thing to undo." She bites at her lip, and her voice drops. "But they targeted *me* to get to *him*."

She's talking about the splintered group of Truthbringers who threatened her life. The same ones Karyl is hoping I'll align with to help eliminate the queen now.

"Yes," I say carefully. "They did."

"Grey was never able to discover who was behind that plot," she says.

"Nor was I," I say.

"Before he left, Tycho indicated that the Truthbringers may have been working with these scravers to drive the king out of Syhl Shallow."

I nearly stop short. The Truthbringers couldn't be working with scravers. They couldn't be. They're trying to eradicate magic. There's no way they could be *using* it.

But I think of that line in Karyl's letter.

I have discovered a way to ensure success for our family.

No. There's no way. Karyl hated magic as much as I do. I turn to face the queen. "Impossible."

"Possible, Alek." She pauses. "The army abandoned my husband on the fields when those scravers attacked. My advisers urged me to send him out alone. I know there are still Truthbringers among the soldiers." She glances at me. "I believe *you* know it, too."

This is growing a bit too close to an accusation of treason—or maybe she's hoping for an admission. Either way, I'm not playing.

I shrug noncommittally. "I suppose there *could* be."

She smiles, and for the first time, it reaches her eyes. "So savvy, Alek."

"My loyalty, as always, is to you." I look over so she can see that I'm serious. "Not to *him*."

She gives a disgusted sigh. "You sound like Nolla Verin."

"Do I?"

"She is *overjoyed* that Grey is gone."

"I won't admit to feeling any great sorrow myself." I glance at her. "His magic endangered you and all your people. We've already lost so much."

To my surprise, her eyes well. "I know."

Please don't cry, I think, glancing at the guards stationed at a distance. People really do talk, and I'm shocked gossip about *this* hasn't been burning tongues all over the city. It's a testament to her staff that they've kept the full nature of the queen's condition a bit quiet. But if she breaks down in sobs in the middle of the hallway, it's definitely not going to give anyone the illusion of *control*.

I *tsk* lightly. "Is it time for more cynical judgment?" I say, trying to lighten the mood.

She gives a little laugh through her tears. "Please."

I reach out and give her sleeve a gentle tug. "Honestly. Who dressed you this morning? This drab frock certainly did not come out of *my* House."

Her eyes flare wide, and then she whirls on me, her tears forgotten. "Alek!" she cries, swatting my arm in feigned outrage.

"I am simply *saying*," I intone, "that if you want to look like a pillar of strength, it might be best to find some fabrics with less . . ." I let my gaze skip up and down her form. "Less *that*."

"You're incorrigible."

"Thank you."

"No wonder Callyn likes you."

I nearly stumble in the hallway. She said it so lightly, but she might as well have punched me in the face.

Callyn, I think. *Please be here.*

Immediately after the words flicker through my thoughts, I want to punch *myself* in the face.

She needs to be gone, and the magic needs to be gone with her.

Despite all that, I keep thinking of that nightmare, how instead of showing me the damage Callyn could *cause,* my brain kept showing me visions of a scraver ripping her apart. I'm not tormented by thoughts of her causing harm; I'm tormented by thoughts of harm coming to *her.* The longing in my heart isn't calling for me to drive her away; it's pushing me to ride to her rescue.

But I can't, and it's making me crazy.

Maybe I should be wearing a drab dress just like the queen.

"Alek?" Queen Lia Mara says, peering at me.

"You mentioned Callyn," I say, trying to keep any emotion from my voice—though I fail *spectacularly.* "Is she—" I have to clear my throat. "Is she still caring for Princess Sinna? I . . . I hadn't thought to ask after her."

I'm such a liar.

Worse, I *sound* like a liar.

The queen hesitates, and I know she can hear it. But she nods. "Callyn and her sister are doing a fine job keeping little Sinna busy." She sighs heavily. "As you can imagine, she misses her father."

Every word is as light as everything else she's said, but inside, I'm reeling.

She's still here. A burst of joy explodes in my heart.

But it's immediately followed by dread. The same words flicker through my brain, this time shrouded with warning.

She's still here.

As if she can read my thoughts, the queen looks over. "Why did you comc to court this morning, Alek?"

I think through every possible answer, and eventually settle on the most honest one. "Because I was worried about you."

She considers that for a long moment. "Do I have reason to be worried?"

I hear what she's asking—and I appreciate that she's given me a way to answer without implicating myself.

"Yes," I say grimly. "I believe you do."

Her breath catches, and she looks up at me. "Do you know who?" she whispers.

"No," I say.

Her expression turns sharp. "*Alek.*"

"I have no real names," I say, which is the truth. "Only suspicions."

The silence between us is suddenly very heavy. Her voice quiets. "What proof do you have?"

I think of those letters, all written in code, signed with names that lead nowhere. We were all so very careful . . . but now it leaves me with nothing tangible to give the queen. "Nothing at all."

She lets a breath out through her teeth. "You must give me something."

I consider that for a while, weighing everything that's at risk.

"The king left to protect you," I finally say. "It is good that he is gone—but I'm worried that his sudden absence has left you equally vulnerable." I hesitate. "The scravers may have left Syhl Shallow," I say quietly, "but the Truthbringers are still here."

"You're certain?"

"Yes," I say, and I keep my voice very soft. "And for now, they know you're alone."

She turns to face me, and a flicker of strength breaks through the sorrow, reminding me that she *is* the queen, and there's a reason she was able to take the throne from her vicious sister after spending all those years hiding in the corners with her books.

"Then I will send word to Ironrose Castle," the queen says, and there's a note in her voice I can't quite parse out. "I will send word to the king. He must know the risk remains."

My heart kicks. I wonder how much I'm hearing is hope that he'll return—and how much is fear that he won't. I wonder how the king will react to such a message—and how the Truthbringers will react if he attempts to come back.

But I nod, because I genuinely don't know which outcome would be worse—for her, and for Syhl Shallow. If I've learned anything in the last few years, there's a difference between what *she* wants and what her people want. "Yes, Your Majesty."

"In the meantime," she says, "you and Callyn must resume your visits among the Royal Houses."

I have to jolt myself to start walking, but my heart is pounding. Inside, I'm spinning. Part of me is rejoicing. Another part—the shameful part—wants to curl up and hide.

Callyn.

I glance at the queen and tug at my jacket. I really need to get it together. We're passing another set of guards, so I emphasize my words. "It will be a true delight to journey with Callyn again. And it is always a joy to visit the Royal Houses. I'll send word to arrange meetings within the week." I drop my voice. "What will we *really* be doing?"

The queen looks at the window. "I can't trust anyone here, Alek. You may be loyal to me, but I know your feelings about my husband. I know you played *some* role in everything that transpired here."

I inhale sharply, but she cuts me off.

"Do not lie right to my face, or you will discover *my* cynical judgment."

Her voice is so even, so pragmatic, but there's a warning in her tone. She might be the gentle sister, but even she has a limit.

Maybe Queen Lia Mara is less broken than I thought.

I close my mouth. “Yes, Your Majesty.”

“And whoever plots against me clearly still trusts *you* if you know I’m in danger. But you have no names. You have no evidence.”

I hesitate, then nod.

She turns away from the window, and this time, her eyes are clear and piercing. “Find some.”

CHAPTER 4

TYCHO

By midsummer, the grounds of Ironrose Castle are always vibrant. Watching from the window of Prince Rhen's strategy room, my eyes usually don't know where to settle. The vast gardens have exploded with color, and gold-and-red pennants flutter above every sentry stand. Sunlight gleams off the cream-colored bricks of the castle proper, too. Marble and polished brass in the outbuildings add glimmers and flashes of light when the clouds shift. When I was younger, everything here seemed magical.

That was before I learned how much harm magic had caused.

Somewhere below the window, women are gossiping as they go about their tasks, their voices high and lively like wind chimes. A broom rasps against the cobblestones. More distant, a man's laugh echoes across the grounds, followed by the high-pitched shrieks of delighted children.

Right now, none of that is a distraction. Instead, my focus is locked squarely on a building in the distance. Across the fields, smoke billows from the forge that sits near the Shield House.

Jax.

I imagine him crouched over some horse's hoof, his hammer swinging while his hair falls into his eyes—just like the day we met. My heart thumps, simply from the memory of it. He's so striking, and it's like he's not even *aware* of it. I remember when we first arrived here, how I found him walking along a path, his gleaming hair loose and unbound, his features carved in shadow. Sudden longing pulses right along with my heartbeat, and it's nearly enough to make me abandon my duties so I can gallop across the grounds to see him. It's been so long since I was *just Tycho* and he was *just Jax* and we could speak truths without the pressures of magic and royalty or the threat of treason and war weighing on us both. The sunlight carries a sense of contentment, and I'm desperate for fresh air and freedom.

Or, hell, maybe I'm just desperate to escape the tense agitation in this room.

Grey is sprawled in a chair, his heavy-lidded eyes aimed at the window as well, though his jaw is tight, and his gaze seems to be fixed on nothing.

"You've called your regiments home from Syhl Shallow, but you still haven't indicated whether we should station a small regiment at the border," Rhen is saying to his brother—though I'm not sure Grey is listening. "Currently, Syhl Shallow maintains the guard stations north of Willminton and Blind Hollow. General Ruoff has received word of minor skirmishes to the north *here*"—he taps at a map on the table, moving some figurines to represent soldier placements—"possibly related to your withdrawal of Emberish forces on the other side of the border. But without any military support in the area, we have no control over—"

He catches sight of Grey's absent expression and stops short. Silence swells in the room. One of those girls working down below the window bursts into giggles about something. A distant soldier shouts an order.

Grey doesn't move. He doesn't even appear to have noticed that Rhen stopped speaking.

"Your *Majesty*," Rhen snaps.

That gets a reaction—but barely. Grey glances his way, and his eyes narrow. "Stop it."

"I thought perhaps a reminder was in order."

"A reminder of what?" Grey's voice is rough, and he looks like he hasn't shaved in the two weeks since we got here. If I didn't know any better, I'd say he was hung over.

Honestly, he might be. I wouldn't blame him. Malin and I used to sneak bottles of liquor after we were stripped of our duties and forced to stay in Syhl Shallow. This isn't the same—not by a long shot—but Grey had to leave his wife and child to protect a country that didn't even want him there. I'm sure he's feeling just as trapped, just as isolated.

Just as hopeless.

Hell, maybe he's drunk right now. I know I would be.

"A reminder that you are king," Rhen is saying evenly. "And you have a country to rule."

Grey's frown deepens, but he goes back to looking at nothing.

Prince Rhen's eye narrows. "*Grey—*"

"Fine!" the king snaps. "Send a regiment to guard the mountain pass. Whatever you want."

His tone is sharp enough that I inwardly flinch, but Rhen holds his gaze. "This is not a time to be cavalier—"

"You *just* told me to rule," Grey growls. "Now you're going to complain when I do it?"

Prince Rhen stares back at him, then sighs and makes a note on one of the papers arranged in front of him.

Every meeting has been like this. I wish I were somewhere else. *Anywhere* else.

Well. Not *anywhere.*

I glance out the window again, reimagining Jax in the forge. This time, I wish myself into the vision. If I were there, I'd be tucking the hair out of his face while he hammered a hot shoe onto a hoof. I'd be listening to the quiet rumble of his voice as he murmured to an uneasy horse. Sudden longing swells in my chest.

But then the fantasy fractures. I imagine him frowning. Smacking my hand away. Jerking back, looking confused. Or, worse, scoffing.

All my emotion goes cold, and I look away from the window.

Because for all my longing, something between us has changed. Since the moment I returned from Syhl Shallow, everything has been different.

The worst part is that I'm not entirely sure what happened—though I'm fairly certain that whatever it is, it's my fault. I never should've been gone so long, and I should've realized it would alter things between us. But I spent so long trying to figure out a way to get back, expecting to find Jax desperate for my arrival. Instead, I arrived to discover that Jax was able to forge a path for himself here, learning the language and settling into his new role and making friends. He's always been a little defiant, a little cavalier, but while I was gone, that shifted into something new. Like confidence. Or conviction. Either way, the tense, apprehensive young man I met in Briarlock is gone.

I should be glad . . . and I am. I want him to be happy. I didn't *want* him to be longing and desperate and lonely.

But I suddenly feel like an outsider. Like I'm intruding. It's left me completely unmoored. Untethered.

And maybe a little jealous.

As I gaze out the window, the sun begins to sink toward the trees, making shadows lengthen. The dinner bells will ring soon, and Jax will be heading across the fields with his friends. He goes shooting almost every night, and I've been longing to join them since I got back.

If I'd even be welcome.

The instant I have the thought, I shove it away. It doesn't even matter. My own duties keep getting in the way regardless. I was in Hutchins Forge two days ago, I just got back from Little Cross this morning, and if Prince Rhen is arguing about Grey's reluctance to *rule*, I'm sure I'll be heading somewhere new tonight.

When we returned from Syhl Shallow, I stupidly thought I might get a brief reprieve from my duties.

Clearly, I thought wrong.

"*Tycho.*"

I snap my head around. They're both looking at me now.

Silver hell. "Forgive me," I say.

Prince Rhen drags his hand across his jaw. "I asked if you've had any contact from the scraver Nakiis."

My ever-present frown deepens, and a shard of ice seems to lodge in my chest. The last time I heard from Nakiis, he was pinning me to the ground, refusing to allow me to assist the king. Xovaar had attacked, and Nakiis was worried he'd kill me, too.

When I convinced him to let me go, I hoped he'd follow. I hoped he'd *help*.

He didn't. And I haven't seen him since.

I've started to wonder if he's dead.

After the way he tried to stop me, there's a part of me that wouldn't quite mind.

"No," I say. "Nothing."

"Good," says Rhen. "Perhaps the scravers have gone to ground."

I don't think we're that lucky. I remember how viciously Xovaar tried to kill Grey, how violently the other scravers fought on the training fields at the Crystal Palace. When the battle was done, blood and bodies were everywhere.

"The scravers believe that magesmiths stole their magic," I say.

"Xovaar wants it back—and the only way to get it is to kill us off. If the scravers have gone to ground, they won't stay there long."

The prince makes another note on his paper, spending a long moment in consideration. His gaze flicks back to the maps spread across the table, and he leans forward, gesturing toward some northern cities. "We're still hearing talk about the 'monster' returning to Emberfall. Perhaps the scravers are stoking these fears to help drive out the magesmiths. You should ride north to Gaulter to inquire about treasonous notes from the Truthbringers—or scraver attacks. Perhaps these skirmishes are related. They have a tourney there, yes? You could learn quite a bit."

I have to keep myself from sighing. Gaulter is a two-and-a-half-day ride from here—and I didn't exactly leave their tourney on good terms. I'm the one who broke their prized fighter—Nakiis—out of a cage.

But I'm not going to refuse a direct order. Not while the king is sitting there looking ready to set the world on fire. "Yes, Your Highness."

At that, Grey actually looks up. "No. Gaulter is too far. If the scravers do resurface, your magic will make you a target."

"I'm a target right here. So are you."

His frown deepens, and I wonder if the king is going to snap at me the way he just snapped at Rhen. Before he can, the prince says, "There's no need to go alone. Take some soldiers. Or some guardsmen." He pauses, his tone turning pointed. "We should not hide, Grey."

The king's expression looks like thunder, but he considers this. "Take Malin," he finally says. "He's trustworthy. Have him choose a few others, too."

There was a time when traveling with Emberish soldiers would've choked my heart with tension, but Grey is right—and Malin has more than proven himself. After he helped save the king's life, he earned a new stripe on his sleeve—and a host of new responsibilities to go with it. I've hardly seen him since I got back, but we grew close in Syhl Shallow. If I have to leave again, I wouldn't mind his company.

But . . . *Jax*. Riding to Gaulter will mean an absence of nearly a week, if not longer. If I have to keep leaving, whatever has broken between us might never recover.

I wish Noah were here. I could desperately use his counsel. I wonder if he and Jake are returning with the army regiments from Syhl Shallow.

Not like it matters, if they're sending me away for a week.

Rhen follows my gaze, and he looks out the window toward the Shield House. "Perhaps you should take Jax, too."

My eyebrows shoot up, and my head snaps around.

Back at the beginning of the summer, Jax and I curled up in the hayloft on the night before I was ordered to depart. We were tangled in some blankets spread over the hay, his eyes gleaming in the starlight. His hands were so warm and his breath was so sweet and his heart seemed to beat in time with my own. I whispered against his skin that I would be back in a matter of days.

And then I disappeared for months.

My heart gives a kick as I consider this. It pains me to admit it, but just now, I don't even know if Jax would want to *go*.

I don't even know if I want him to.

When I say nothing, Rhen adds, "Jax has *also* proven himself trustworthy—and he's earned a chance to do more than swing a hammer in the forge. I don't think he's left the grounds since he joined the soldiers on that ill-fated trip to the creek."

When half a regiment of drunk soldiers were attacked by scravers—and Jax was with them.

My jaw feels tight. When I tried to ask him about that, he brushed it off. I've heard a full report, however. Several soldiers were killed. The rest of them were close. If Jax hadn't acted quickly, more would have died. *He* might have died. He has ragged scars across his chin from the attack.

Prince Rhen glances at the king, who says nothing. But Grey's eyes are on me now. I wonder what he's thinking.

I don't like that *this* is what pulled him out of his morose reverie. A familiar tension grips my spine, reminding me of the way we faced off on the training fields in Syhl Shallow. We spent months at odds, and while we've moved past it in some ways, I know it wouldn't take much for us to end up in the same place again.

Much like the weird tension between me and Jax, I don't quite know what to do with this either. Maybe he feels the same, because he doesn't say a word.

When we're *both* silent for an eternity, Rhen sighs. "Silver hell. Find Malin, Tycho. Give him our orders, and have him select two others. Take Jax—or not. The choice is yours. You can leave at first light."

Grey is still watching me. That tension refuses to let go. I don't know if he'd see Jax as an asset—or a distraction. Like so many other moments between us, this feels like a test. I don't want to fail.

When I say nothing, Grey's eyebrows rise just a hair, and then he inhales with the weight of a commanding officer about to give an order. I brace myself, expecting him to take the choice away from me, and there's a part of me that hopes he will—even though I'll probably resent him for it.

But all he says is, "I think you've been dismissed."

That hits me like a fist, but I was a soldier long enough to know how to keep a scowl off my face. I straighten, then give him a nod. "Yes, Your Majesty." I nod to Rhen as well. "Your Highness."

But as I move through the doorway, Grey's voice calls me back. "Tycho."

I stop and turn. For the first time all afternoon, his eyes are clear, and he truly seems to see me. "Be safe."

It's only two words, but both syllables carry the weight of unspoken emotion that's different from before. It's trust, it's concern, it's regard, it's . . . *something.* A reminder that we might have been at odds, but we don't have to be now.

So I nod again. "I will," I say, and any edge has slipped out of my voice. "You too."

And then I'm gone.

Months ago, I would have been galloping across the fields, desperate to bring these orders to the forge. When Prince Rhen first told me that Jax was invited to take residence here as a blacksmith, I could barely wait a single minute before I went to tell him.

But today, I let Mercy amble through the sunlit grass as I determine what to say.

Jax, I've been ordered to leave. Rhen wants you to join us.

That sounds like I don't want him there—or like I'm only inviting him because I've been ordered to it. And Jax hates Rhen—he definitely won't want to go if he knows the prince ordered it.

Jax. I'm going to Gaulter. Would you . . . like to join me?

That sounds like I'm inviting him to a lover's tryst, not on a group mission to investigate treason.

I hate this.

Jax. I miss you.

I definitely can't say that.

"Hey," a voice calls from somewhere off to my left. "Tycho."

I glance over to see a chestnut horse peeling away from a group of soldiers that look like they're returning from patrol. As the rider canters toward me, I blink in the evening sunlight and recognize Malin's compact frame and dark hair.

A smile forces its way onto my face, breaking through my exhausted tension. I lift a hand in greeting.

"Well, well, well," I say as he draws close. I peer at the new insignia on his shoulder and whistle low, through my teeth. "Look at those stripes."

"Shut up." But I can tell he's pleased.

"Remind me—are you a commander now?" I tease. "Wait. No. A *general*?"

"I'm going to knock you off the horse."

"That sure doesn't sound like something an officer would say."

He grins. "I'm going to get a recruit to knock you off the horse."

That makes me laugh. "How is it, *Captain*?"

"More work, but I can order Seph around now, so there's that."

Sephran—his best friend. Or at least he was before we went to Syhl Shallow. But I've noticed that Sephran and Jax grew close during our absence.

Very close.

The smile must fade from my face, because Mal's gaze narrows a bit, as if he's trying to figure me out. His voice, however, is neutral. "You're in new gear yourself." He nods at my armor.

"Yeah," I say, though my new livery doesn't bring the same joy as his new stripes. For years, I wore the black of Syhl Shallow, and my armor was trimmed in silver and green. The breastplate was emblazoned with the crests of both countries, indicating my allegiance to both. Grey's own armor was similar.

But three days after we returned, the king showed up in the arena with a new breastplate. Still black, but no green, no silver. One small crest over his heart, backed with the gold and red of Emberfall alone. I opened my mouth, but he held up a hand and said, "Go see the armorer. Yours is ready, too."

His tone was so gruff that I didn't say a word. Once I got my gear, I understood. Donning the new armor felt very final. As if the division between our countries is permanent.

"Where were you headed?" Malin says.

"To look for you, actually. We've been given new orders." I tell him what Rhen and Grey said, and the reason we're being sent to Gaulter. "He said for you to choose two soldiers to join us."

"He's worried about scravers."

"He is." I hesitate, wondering how this will go over. "Prince Rhen told me to bring Jax, too."

Malin's eyebrows go up, but then he grins. "I'm sure you weren't complaining."

Weeks ago, that would've made me blush and stumble over my words. Right now, my smile vanishes.

A line appears across Malin's brow as he studies me like before. He's always been perceptive, and I sense I'm giving away too much. I wonder what he sees.

He finally speaks into my silence. "Well, if he's going, I'll pick Seph for sure. He's solid, and they get on well."

That doesn't help. Now I'm trying not to frown. Mal told me so many stories about Sephran that I thought we'd return from Syhl Shallow and we'd all become friends. He spoke with such fondness that I began to *long* for it.

But every time I see Sephran, his expression is unfriendly, his eyes ice cold as he regards me. He's *polite*, but it's a distant politeness, as if I've offended him somehow—which I can't figure out. Does he resent my position? I've encountered that before ... though he seemed friendly enough when I first met him. The change is only since I returned to Ironrose. Could he be bothered by my friendship with Malin?

I have no idea what to say, but I have to say *something*, or my lengthy silence is going to turn awkward. "Whoever you think is best," I say flatly, though I have no idea if I really mean that. I press my heels into Mercy. "I'm heading for the forge to tell Jax next."

Malin nods, then steers his horse to fall in step beside me. "I'll join you."

But as he does, Mercy slows, sensing my trepidation.

I give her another nudge, because I don't want Malin to pick up on it. "No," I say. I still have no idea how to extend this invitation. I definitely don't want to do it with Malin at my back. That feels too official. "You should head for the barracks and make your other choice. Have them pack up and see to their unit commanders. The king intends for us to leave by first light."

His eyebrows go up again, and I realize my tone has lost any hint of lighthearted banter. But Malin is a good soldier, and there's a reason he earned a new stripe on his sleeve.

"Yes, sir," he says sharply. Without another word, he gives me a salute, then whirls his horse to head south, toward the barracks.

Leaving me on my solitary path to the forge.

CHAPTER 5

JAX

In Syhl Shallow, the forge was always hot and miserable in the summer, but Emberfall is worse. By late afternoon, the heat in the air is nearly unbearable, with a cloying humidity that makes everything sticky. My forearms are always gritty with soot and grime, and any strands of hair that escape the knot at my neck end up clinging to my face. I'm lucky that I can do my work in a loose tunic and casual trousers, with nothing heavier than the leather apron I wear to hold my tools. The soldiers have it worse, with damp skin under their armor and sweat threading their hair. The horses always arrive with darkened flanks, their tails aggressively swishing at flies.

After a day of work, a unique smell clings to this end of the forge. It's not oppressive, but it's definitely . . . *pungent.*

I'm hot and tired and ready to be done, but another soldier is already leading a horse through the smoky shadows, and I swear under my breath. But then I do a double take: the animal is a deep mahogany bay with a stripe down its face.

Mercy? I snap my gaze back to the soldier, hoping for Tycho.

But no—it's not him. And the horse isn't Mercy. Just another army steed that needs new shoes.

I tether the animal to a post and sigh. I should've known better.

When Tycho was sent away to Syhl Shallow, I spent weeks hoping for any sign of him. *Months.* I'd stare at the horizon, watching for the rich brown of his mare's coat, hoping they'd come galloping over the hill. Since the day we met, I've known that his job—his *life*—is bound to the whim of the king. But that didn't stop me from lying awake every night, wishing that *tomorrow* would be the day he'd reappear. I'd imagine it constantly: he'd return with windblown cheeks and sparks in his eyes and hours' worth of stories to share. There'd be no more harassment from the soldiers who hate that I was born on the other side of the mountain, there'd be no more attacks from the vicious winged scravers that could swoop down from the sky and dismember a man in seconds.

There'd be no more loneliness weighing on my heart, no more worry tightening my chest, and no more desperation crowding every thought.

For months, I craved his presence. I thought he'd return to Ironrose Castle and my world would right itself.

But he's been back for two weeks, and nothing feels right at all.

The worst part is that I can't quite figure out *why*. The first night he returned, I invited him back to the Shield House with me, expecting to fall back into the casual ease we've always shared. But somehow that ease wasn't there anymore, replaced with an odd distance. I'd expected him to stay the night, but within an hour, our conversation became short and stilted. Awkward, like he became someone different during his months away—or maybe I did. Eventually, he claimed obligations in the castle and left.

Is it his role? I don't want to think so, but . . . maybe. Tycho isn't one to put on airs, but it's impossible to miss. Every stitch of his clothing speaks to wealth and privilege: the calfskin leather, the silver buckles, the threads in vibrant colors that I rarely see on anyone *common.* Tycho looks like exactly who he is: a young nobleman with power and influence—and access to the royal family. I'm just a blacksmith, with soot on my hands and hair in my face. That didn't seem to matter when he'd visit my forge in Briarlock, but it definitely matters *here.*

Since that first night, I've tried to shake off the new tension between us, but it seems impossible. He doesn't mean to be an intrusion, but most everyone knows who he is—especially now that the king has returned alone, withdrawing Emberish forces from Syhl Shallow. I was no stranger to village gossip when I worked in Briarlock, but this close to royalty, it's *vicious.* Every time Tycho appears in the forge, any casual conversation ceases. The nearby blacksmiths fall silent, hoping to catch a stray word they can whisper about later. Soldiers shut up and snap to attention, all icy formality—including my *friends,* like Sephran and Leo.

If Tycho were a common soldier, even one from Syhl Shallow, they wouldn't do any of that. Sephran and the others would likely invite him to come shooting, and we'd all ride out to the fields together. They'd grouse about officers or complain about their duties or share gossip from the barracks—just like they do with me.

They're sure not going to do any of that in front of the King's Courier.

I shift to the other side of the horse I'm working on, and the accompanying soldier sighs, muttering under his breath. I ignore him, because I know he's just hot and miserable. They used to grumble at *me* and knock my crutches into the dirt, but since I helped save a dozen of them from a scraver attack, a lot of the Emberish soldiers have stopped being total assholes.

A familiar voice cuts through the clanging and chattering of the forge. "Hey, Archer."

Sephran. My heart lifts a little when I hear his voice.

It shouldn't. I have to tamp that down, too.

I've got the horse's leg pinned between my knees and a heavy set of pincers in my hands, so I blow a lock of hair away from my face and look up. Despite my efforts, I can't see much higher than Sephran's scuffed boots.

"Hey," I say in return. My Emberish still isn't very good, but Sephran won't care. He doesn't speak Syssalah, so we've learned to make do. "You surprise me," I say. "Off duty?"

"Yeah. It's late."

Just as he says the words, distant bells chime, signaling a call to the mess hall—meaning there will be a mad dash for food. The soldier holding this horse knows it, too, because he swears under his breath.

I blow another lock of hair out of my eyes. "Go," I say. "You eat. I take horse to stable."

His eyebrows go up. "Yeah?" he says hopefully.

I nod, and that strand of dark hair falls right back into my face.

I clearly don't have to tell him twice, because the soldier gives the horse a pat on the shoulder, and then he's *gone.*

Sephran's boots shift through the dirt of the forge, and then, to my surprise, he reaches out to tuck that lock of hair behind my ear. It's a brief touch, just a brush of gentle fingers against my cheek, and then the shell of my ear.

But it feels like *more.*

Before Tycho returned, Sephran kissed me. It was only once, and I stopped him before it went too far—but it happened. And Sephran may have apologized, but he was angry when I told him about my secret relationship with Tycho, especially when I revealed that I was desperately longing for his return.

He left you, Jax.

When Sephran's fingers drift along my skin, my hands freeze, my tools going still against the hoof.

He notices. "Sorry," he says, though I'm not entirely sure he means that. "That looked annoying."

I hesitate, then decide to let it go. "No sorry," I say equably in my broken Emberish. "Thank you."

Since the night he kissed me, we've had a lot of moments like this one. Intimacy that's not quite *intimacy*. Touches that shouldn't feel loaded with intent or meaning . . . but suddenly do.

As I reach for my file, silence swells between us. Sephran was my first friend here, and I don't want to lose that. This doesn't have to mean anything different from the times he'd help with my archery stance or when we'd tussle and spar in the fields.

But a part of me wonders if Sephran would've done that if Tycho were standing right here.

I'm thinking not.

The silence is too much to bear, so I set the horse's leg down to reach for a fresh shoe. Using my tongs, I thrust it in the forge, burying it among the ash. "We go shooting?" I say.

"Can you?" he says, his tone a little sour. "Or do you need to check with your keeper?"

I frown at him. I'm not sure I know this word. "Keeper?"

His eyes flare in surprise, but then he scowls. "Never mind. I shouldn't have said that. Forget it."

I might not understand the word, but I'm not an idiot. I can hear his tone, and I realize this was a dig at Tycho.

The shoe in the forge is glowing red, so I yank it free roughly enough that sparks fly. "No," I say evenly, pressing the hot steel against my anvil. "Tell me, Sephran. Tell me what means."

He says nothing, but he folds his arms. Now his jaw is set.

I give him a look, then pick up my hammer and slam it against the horseshoe. The sound of ringing steel echoes through the forge, clear and solitary. The dinner bells rang, so I'm one of the few blacksmiths left. Sephran watches me in complete silence.

That sting piercing my heart refuses to stop.

Keeper. I try to figure out the word on my own. I spend an hour every morning with Mistress Elayne, my tutor, and she makes me do this all the time. I know *keep*, and considering Sephran's attitude, it's not hard to make the leap from there.

I pull the hot shoe off the anvil and thrust it into the waiting bucket of water. "Tycho is not *keeper*," I say darkly, as steam flares around me.

"I know."

I pick up the horse's hoof, still annoyed. "And I not *keeped*."

His mouth twitches, his eyes lighting with amusement. I realize I've said something wrong.

"*Tell me*," I snap.

Sephran has the decency to look contrite. "Kept." He pauses. "Not *keeped*."

That makes me scowl, though it probably shouldn't. Silence falls between us again, only interrupted by the lighter *plink-plink-plink* as I hammer the shoe onto the horse's hoof. That lock of hair falls back into my face, and I blow it angrily away.

Sephran steps forward to tuck it behind my ear again. His touch is lighter this time, but somehow more deliberate, too. My hammer freezes midstrike, because I truly don't know what to do with this. Sephran has always been kind. Always thoughtful. When I first came here, he was the only person to notice that I needed a bench to help support my weight while I was shoeing horses—and the only person who tried to remedy the problem. Are these light touches more of his usual kindness? Or something entirely different?

He sighs, and his voice drops. "I'm sorry, Jax. You just . . . you don't seem happy that he's back."

I don't know what to say to that either.

I hammer the last nail into place, then set the horse's hoof down. I pull the lead rope to slip the knot from the tether, but Sephran doesn't step back. It leaves us standing very close.

He was on duty all day, so he's still trussed up in gold-and-red-trimmed armor, every weapon buckled into place. He's a little taller than I am, and definitely broader, especially with his gear. He's got sandy hair and a ruddy, freckled complexion that usually bears an easy smile.

There's no smile now, though. His somber eyes are searching mine. "Do you understand me?" He speaks slowly and deliberately, then taps me in the center of my chest. The weight of his hand is heavy and warm, even through my tunic. "*You* are not *happy*."

I swallow, because he's not wrong. "I understand."

Movement flickers behind him, and I glance up. I recognize the blond hair, the brown eyes, the striking combination of features that nearly took my breath away on the first night I ever saw him. It's doing the same right now. My heart kicks.

"Tycho," I say in surprise.

Sephran stiffens. His gaze ices over.

Then I realize how close he is. How he was touching me. What he *just* said.

I have no idea how much Tycho heard or saw—if anything at all. His eyes flick from me to Sephran and back, and even though there's nothing between us, warmth sparks on my cheeks.

"Jax," he says. His voice isn't cold, but I'm not sure I'd call it warm. His gaze bounces between us again, settling on Sephran. "Lieutenant."

Sephran takes a step to the side, his frame rigid. An emotionless soldier, standing at attention. "My lord."

I hate this.

"You are here," I say to Tycho, trying to keep my voice light to make up for the fact that Sephran is all but staring daggers at him. "I think tomorrow."

"I rode hard so I could make it back quickly. I had to report to the king first, but—" He breaks off. "Ah, sorry." He makes a face, then begins to repeat everything in Syssalah.

"I understand you first time," I snap in Emberish.

A line appears between his eyebrows as if I've startled him. He inhales like he wants to say something, but then his mouth clamps shut. He draws back, suddenly as cool as Sephran. "I . . . forgive me."

We stand there glaring at each other for a long moment. I know he was translating for my benefit, and I should probably be grateful.

But I didn't need it. If he spent more time here, he'd know that.

You are not happy.

Yeah, no kidding.

The air has turned tense and prickly, and it doesn't help that Sephran is still standing there, watching this entire interaction. I have no doubt he can read every emotion on my face—and sadly, he can probably do it better than Tycho can.

When Tycho glances between us again, his gaze settles on Sephran for a moment longer than necessary. "I didn't mean to interrupt."

"There's no interruption," Sephran says. "Jax was just inviting me to go shooting." He pauses. "My lord."

Somehow he makes it sound like a totally different invitation. Something private. Something *intimate.*

He also says *my lord* as if he really wants to say *you asshole.*

It's my turn to stare daggers at *him.* Sephran's eyebrows go up, just a hair, his expression becoming a little daring. Any contrition is gone from his face.

Tycho's voice turns tightly formal—the way it always does when he's confronted by the soldiers. "You have duties," he says to me. "I'll find you later." He looks back at Sephran. "I believe you're due at the barracks. Captain Malin is seeking you."

Before either of us can respond, he's given me a nod, and he turns away.

Oh, this is awful.

I stride past Sephran, my step solid and sure after weeks of practice with the false foot. "Tycho," I say, catching his arm.

It's the dead heat of summer, so he's only got a light tunic under the black armor that befits his role. It leaves the bend of his elbow bare above the knife-lined bracers strapped to his forearms, and that's where my hand falls. The instant my fingertips find the warm curve of muscle, a spark rolls through me, and I can tell it does the same to him. He goes tense at once, so I'm surprised when he doesn't jerk away, and instead he turns to look at me.

For a moment, I see torment reflected in his eyes—the same exact torment I'm feeling. But he blinks and it's gone. His eyes are so cool that I almost regret touching him at all.

"Jax?" he says.

"We go shooting."

"I heard," he says evenly. "Go ahead. I won't stop you."

Clouds above. I recognize *this* Tycho—the man who'd rather pick a fight than confront a difficult emotion.

When I don't answer, he shifts to pull away.

Months ago, I would've let him go. He was the skilled nobleman, and I was the poor blacksmith. I never had a right to ask for anything.

But so much has changed since he first found me in Briarlock. I don't know if our time apart has changed him, but coming here has definitely changed *me.*

So instead of letting go, I tighten my grip and hold fast.

Belligerence flares in his expression, like he might jerk free or tussle.

That's the fight he's looking for, and anyone else would probably give it to him.

But I don't. Instead, I stroke my thumb across the warm curve of his bicep.

He stops breathing for a second, and I feel the response in his body when he exhales. He simply . . . pauses. Softens. *Waits.*

So I do it again, brushing my thumb along the slope of his skin. "Come with us," I say quietly.

The bracing tension has slipped out of his frame, and for an instant, I think he might yield. But then he frowns and glances past me. His eyes go a little cool again, and when he speaks, it's in Syssalah. "I don't think I'm invited, Jax."

I don't let go of his arm. I can almost feel his pulse, and my heart seems to seek the same rhythm.

"*I'm* inviting you," I say. "Please?"

He's frozen in place, and torment flickers in his gaze again—followed by regret. "I can't," he says. "I have orders. Prince Rhen is sending me to Gaulter for a few days, and I need to prepare. We still need to be wary of Truthbringers, and there's a concern that scravers won't stay hidden for long."

Of course. Of *course.* My heart falls. "Oh."

Sephran was right. I should've known.

And the worst part is that there seems to be no unwinding this. We'll simply continue down this path of unhappiness.

I move to let him go, but Tycho puts a hand over mine, trapping me there. His expression shifts, and he glances away. "Jax, I . . . I want . . ."

But then his voice trails off. I'm frozen in place, trapped by the space between the words.

His eyes, golden brown, find mine, and he straightens, his tone turning more formal. "I won't be going alone. Malin has been asked to assemble a small team."

Malin. Of course. They developed a closeness that took me by surprise when I first saw them together, simply because I didn't expect it.

Or maybe I just resent it. My heart seems to be growing a layer of ice that would rival the chill in Sephran's gaze.

But then Tycho adds, "Prince Rhen recommended that you join us."

For an instant, I almost can't believe I heard him correctly. "Prince Rhen wants *me* to join the soldiers?"

Tycho nods. "He said you've earned a chance to do more than swing a hammer."

My heart thumps hard in my chest. No one has *ever* offered me an opportunity to do anything more than work in a forge.

But then reality crashes down, because I'm thinking of how tense and prickly the last two weeks have been. Hell, how prickly the last few *minutes* have been.

Silence stretches between us, and I know Tycho is aware of it, too. Especially since Sephran is still at his back, watching us.

Against my will, my eyes flick to the soldier. *Captain Malin is seeking you.*

Now I understand.

Tycho follows my gaze, and I think his jaw tightens. He lets go of my hand, then steps back. "This isn't without risk. There's word of skirmishes to the north, and we have no idea where the scravers may lie in wait—to say nothing of the Truthbringers." He pauses, all cool formality. "But we've been ordered to depart by dawn. We'll meet in the courtyard before first light." Another pause. "If you want."

My heart is surging ahead. There are too many surprises here.

I'm not a soldier. I'm *not.*

But I've been asked to join them. By the *prince.* My breath catches, just for a moment. I hate Prince Rhen—and he knows it. I said it right to his face. For him to offer this, to *me* . . . I know it's significant.

But I have so many questions. Will I have to pack? What should I say to Master Garson, who runs the forge? Will I need armor? Would I ride Teddy or would we take a wagon?

But behind all the questions is a spark of emotion that I can't quite identify. Prince Rhen may have offered me the position in the forge here, but that was the same job I've always done, just in a new place.

This—*this*—is the first time in my life I've been offered something new. Something challenging.

Something *important*.

I stare right back into Tycho's brown eyes, so dark in the lantern light. All of a sudden, I don't care about the torment, I don't care about the distance between us, I don't care if the next week is prickly and tense.

All I care about is the chance to be something more.

"Yes, Tycho," I say in Emberish. "I want."

CHAPTER 6

CALLYN

I don't realize how much I miss morning drills until I don't go. The recruits I was training with have shifted to midday sessions, and that's when I'm busy with little Sinna. I still haven't seen the queen to be able to ask about alternatives—and even if I did, I'm not sure I want to bother her with something so minor.

But without any source of physical activity, I discover I'm more antsy. More agitated. I'm consumed with worry over the queen's depression, the princess's acting out, and Alek's threat to tell everyone about everything. I have nowhere to put all this energy.

When I was working in the bakery, I might have been stressed about the state of our lives, but there was no shortage of labor. Worry and anxiety never had an opportunity to consume me like this. It's hard to obsess over everyone else when sacks of flour need to be heaved into the store room, stalls need to be mucked, or pots need to be scrubbed.

Here in the Crystal Palace, my life is too easy. There's no need for heaving and mucking and scrubbing. If I'm not looking after Sinna, it seems I have two options: I can train with the soldiers . . . or I can practice embroidery and gossip with the court ladies. There's no middle ground—or if there is, I haven't discovered it.

I never thought I'd be envious of Nora's brutal afternoon training sessions with Verin, but here I am.

By the third day, I can't take the monotony. An hour before dawn, I pull on my leather trousers and lace up my boots. Then I lean over my sister's bed and deliberate between waking her gently or giving her a good shake.

She chooses that moment to snore right in my face, so I go with the latter.

Nora wakes with a start, sitting up so abruptly that she almost smacks me in the face. I have to shove her back down so I don't end up with a concussion. She thrashes against my grip.

"Nora!" I whisper fiercely. "Clouds above! It's just me!"

As soon as she hears my voice, she stops fighting. She blinks sleepy eyes up at me. "Why are you on top of me?" she demands—and she's not quiet about it at *all*. "What's wrong—"

I slap a hand over her mouth and regret this entirely.

"If you wake Sinna," I whisper through clenched teeth, "we'll never be able to do anything at all."

She breathes behind my hand for a moment, her eyes wide awake now. I let her go.

"What *are* we doing?" she finally says.

"Get your gear. Let's go spar."

Her eyebrows shoot *way* up, and her eyes skip down my form, taking in my clothes. "You want to *spar*?" she whispers. "Now?"

"Yes."

"With *me*?" she squeaks.

She sounds so excited that I regret not doing this sooner. "Sure," I whisper. "Hurry. We can probably get an hour."

She hurries.

It's so early that the hallways are nearly deserted, only a few random guards standing at their posts, their green-and-black livery matching the heraldry occasionally marking a doorway. The gold-and-red colors of Emberfall are nowhere to be seen any longer: no soldiers, no guards, no banners, nothing. Even Noah, the queen's doctor and Lord Jacob's husband, is gone. I hadn't realized how many Emberish people were always in the palace until they *weren't.*

The training arena is deserted, too, which feels unusual, though it's probably not. Without the need to share the space with other units, early morning drills are probably less necessary. When Nora and I arrive, we discover that the exterior doors to the fields are still bolted closed, and none of the lanterns or torches are lit.

"Oh," Nora breathes. "Maybe it's *too* early."

"No," I say, because I've learned that no one will mind our presence here. Soldiers can—and do—train at all hours of the day. "I don't have a key to open the doors to the fields, but we can light the torches."

In the shadows, I see her eyes widen, but I gesture for her to follow me. I have flint on my belt, and I strike it at the low torch I've seen soldiers and servants use to light the others. As the sparks glow and die in the dim, early morning air, I'm struck by a memory: Lord Tycho standing in my barn, setting a strand of hay on fire with his magic.

The same magic that flows through my veins.

For an instant, I want to try it myself. I've only ever used magic for healing: first on my own wounds, then on Alek, after he was attacked by scravers.

I glance at Nora, wondering how she'd react if she knew. King Grey's magic started the fire that killed our father. The king was defending himself and his family, but it was still magic, and still a fire. What would my sister do if she knew I could summon the same power? How would she react? Would she be afraid?

Maybe. She watched Lord Tycho heal Jax's hand, and she seemed more fascinated than wary. And she certainly had no qualms about the king and his abilities or we wouldn't be here at all.

But that's very different from discovering the same magic in her *sister*. I remember the burn of betrayal in Alek's gaze when he realized I'd used magic to save him.

I imagine seeing it in Nora's eyes, and that makes me strike the flint extra hard. But just as I do it, sparks of magic flicker in my veins.

The torch catches, flaring so brightly that I give a little *yip* and drop the flint. Nora shrieks and leaps back like I set *her* on fire.

"Hush!" I snap at her, though I'm more peeved at myself.

I walk a lap of the arena, lighting the torches I can reach. By the time I'm done, Nora is in the center, spinning in arcs with her training blade. I stop for a moment to watch her, because I keep forgetting that she's no longer a little girl. At some point a young woman slipped in to take her place.

She goes still, her eyebrows knitting together. "What on earth are you staring at?" she demands.

Well, she might not be a little girl, but she's clearly still a little sister.

"You." I draw my sword and step into the arena.

During my drills with the recruits, Lord Jacob was always relentless in his training, emphasizing that any opponent could take you by surprise, and to never underestimate anyone. One day he had an old man with a rheumy cough and a pronounced limp come lumbering onto the fields, and he asked our group who would want to fight him first. They all laughed.

No one was laughing fifteen minutes later, when the man disarmed each and every one of us.

It was a good lesson, and I'm glad I had it. Because otherwise I would have faced my sister as if I were indulging a toddler who begged me to watch her twirl. But Nora attacks like I'm an invading soldier who just threatened everything she holds dear. She's so quick, so precise, and so vicious that I backpedal a dozen steps before I remember to *block*.

"Clouds above," I pant when we break apart, circling.

"Oh, Cally-cal," she says lightly. "You don't have to let me win. Come on. *Fight.*" She swings her blade again.

I nearly choke on my breath. *Let* her win. She's hilarious. As if I'm not fighting for my life here. Nora is easily as good as the recruits I spar with—and she only started learning a few months ago!

We break apart again, and we're both panting, sweat gleaming on our faces. But Nora's expression is full of glee, as if this is the most fun she'll have all day. I might be missing the drills and exertion, but it's clear that somewhere along the line, my little sister began to *live* for this.

As soon as I have the thought, I lower my blade.

Nora frowns. "What's wrong?"

"Nothing," I say. "You're growing up."

She makes a horrific face, sticking her tongue out sideways.

It's so unexpected that I burst out laughing, and she giggles. "With such elegance and maturity," I add.

She pushes damp hair off her forehead. "I've been working hard," she says. "Do you think Mama would be proud?"

The question hits me like the broad side of a blade, and the sudden swell of emotion nearly takes my breath away. I think of our mother often when I'm training. I don't know why it never occurred to me, but I had no idea Nora was doing the same thing.

I have to clear my throat. I'm surprised to discover that my eyes feel hot. "Yeah, Nor. I do."

Then I drop my blade in the dirt and stride forward to hug her.

She hugs me back for the longest time. I still can't believe how tall she's gotten. For so long she was just my baby sister who would ramble for hours about whatever random thought entered her head. Now it's like being hugged by a peer. I don't want it to end.

Then she says, "You're not supposed to drop the blades in the arena, you know. It makes them go dull. Also, do you think we're early enough to get hot sweetcakes when we're done?"

I giggle, then kiss her on the cheek. "There's my annoying little sister."

"She's right, you know," says a male voice from behind me. "You shouldn't drop your sword."

I recognize that voice. Every drop of blood in my veins turns to ice.

Alek.

He continues, "You never know when you might need it."

I turn slowly, as if trapped in quicksand. But it's Nora, behind me, who says, "Don't worry, my lord. I still have mine."

I just thought of her as a peer, but now I want to tuck her away and keep her safe.

Instead, she moves up beside me, sword braced in front of her.

Alek's eyebrows go up. He's dressed for battle, not polite conversation. He folds his arms, and it reveals the carved muscles of his biceps, evidence of the training *he* endures. His expression is unfriendly, and his eyes lock on Nora. "Are you going to pull my hair again, *little cat*?"

He's referring to the *last* time he and Nora saw each other. Nora attacked him like a wildcat, pulling his hair and screeching in his face. Verin had to pull her off him.

I step in front of Nora, blocking her. "Get out of here, Alek."

Nora moves around my arm, shifting to stand by my side. "You don't have to protect me, Cally-cal. I have better claws this time."

Where is she getting all this confidence? I grab her arm. "*Nora.* Stop it. You are not—"

"Sure she is." Alek ducks under the arena railing, and without warning, he draws his sword.

I draw in a sharp breath, torn between diving in front of my sister and diving for my own weapon. Before I can do either, their swords meet, a clash of ringing steel in the quiet arena. Panic chokes my heart for a second, because I blink and remember Nora impaled on the blade of a soldier. She was lying in the forest, blood seeping from the wound, choking and gasping for breath.

Dying.

Blades clash again, and the image is gone. My sister is alive and well in front of me, engaged in a sword fight with my mortal enemy.

I shake myself and grab my own blade, breathless. I don't even know if we could *both* hold him off. Should I call for help? Surely there are guards within earshot.

But as soon as I straighten with my weapon in hand, I realize this isn't a battle to the death. Not really. Nora is attacking and Alek is deflecting, but he's not *retaliating*. My sister adjusts her grip and comes at him more aggressively.

This time, Alek parries and snaps his blade against hers, driving her back a step. "Easy," he says casually, as if she's not panting from the effort. "Don't lose your focus."

She makes an angry sound and comes at him again, and he does it a second time. Nora backs away, circling, looking for a new opening.

"I know all of Nolla Verin's moves," he says to her. "So you'll have to try something new."

His back is to me, his eyes tracing her movements, so I step forward and poke the end of my blade right into his back, just below the edge of his armor.

"How about this?" I say.

Alek goes still at once.

"Drop *your* sword," I say.

"I'd really rather not." He lifts his hands, however, letting the weapon hang from one.

I give him a little poke for good measure, but these are training blades, and I'd have to use real force to actually break skin.

Alek doesn't even wince. His eyes don't leave my sister. "You're very good," he says. "You need some new sparring partners so you don't trap yourself with familiar moves."

Nora wets her lips and glances between him and me.

"I'd offer now," he says, "but your sister and I have other plans."

"No, we do not," I say, reconsidering whether I want to just push this blade right into his body. I give him another jab, putting some real strength into it. He grunts and yields a step.

"Do that again," he says, "and you'll find yourself in a fight you're not ready for."

For the first time, a note of anger slips into his voice, and it's backed with a dangerous thread of warning. There once was a time when it would've made me falter.

Not anymore. I remember the way his body pressed into mine in the sunlight, how he whispered sweet nothings against my sweat-dampened skin, making me feel like the most treasured woman alive. A minute later, he was being torn apart by a scraver, his blood soaking into the soil. Two minutes later, I was using magic to save his life.

And then, three minutes later, he was looking at me with panicked betrayal and unbridled fury. He was undoing every moment of happiness I've ever found in his presence.

I grit my teeth, step forward, and jab that sword as hard as I can.

He must see it coming, because he swoops out of the way, spinning to parry, knocking my sword sideways. I'm ready for it, however, and I slam my blade right back into his. I'm gratified when his eyes flare slightly, as if he's surprised by my response. But then he retaliates, and suddenly we're fighting for *real*.

This is nothing like sparring with Nora—or with Verin, for that matter. Alek is ruthless in a different way, all brute strength and deadly precision. But it's all right. Unlike my sister, I've had a lot of different opponents among the soldiers. And I might be learning to embroider with the queen's ladies, but I still grew up on a farm, and my muscles know how to work.

Eventually, however, his skill trumps mine. He hooks my hilt, catches my ankle with his foot, and I go down. My blade goes spinning into the dirt.

I glare up at him, breathing hard. Dust from the arena floor collects along the sweat on my skin.

"Go ahead," I spit at him. "Are you going to jab at me now? Or are you just going to kill me?"

"Neither." He immediately lets me go, then straightens to sheathe his sword. "We're wasting time. The queen has asked us to continue our visits among the Royal Houses." He stands over me haughtily. "Get up. We have our orders."

I've envisioned Alek returning to the Crystal Palace for weeks, but in every imagining, he has soldiers at his back and they're dragging me through the gates in chains. I stare at him. "Really?"

"Yes."

To my left, Nora rushes forward, but Alek holds up a hand, then snaps his head around. "No more. Your sister is busy."

Something in his tone tells me his *next* fight won't be a sparring match. It'll be real.

I find my feet, wishing I didn't have just a training blade against my palm. "I'm not going *anywhere* with you," I say.

"Fine," he says. "Disobey. Ignore her orders. Run along and tell the queen you have no time for me." He glances at Nora. "Perhaps *you* would like to join me, little cat. I could introduce you to some new opponents among the Royal Houses. Your sister certainly seemed to enjoy herself during our visits."

"Alek!" I snap.

He folds his arms and raises his eyebrows. “Ah! Forgive me. Was Nora unaware of our time together?”

I’m frozen in place. Because she was *completely* unaware.

And he well knows it.

My sister’s expression has lit with surprise, and she glances between the two of us, and now she’s frowning. Her voice goes very small, and I can’t tell if she’s disappointed in me or distrustful of him. “Cally-cal?”

In that instant, I realize how very young she still is.

I grit my teeth and glare at Alek. “Nora. It’s fine. Go back to the nursery.” I heave a sigh, wanting to punch him in his triumphant face. “And when you see the queen, let her know Alek arrived, and I’m with him.”

CHAPTER 7

CALLYN

I expect a carriage, because that's the only way I've ever traveled with Alek, so I'm shocked when we don't head for the carriage house, and instead he leads me to the royal stables.

I still have no idea what he's doing here, and he hasn't said a word to me since we left Nora in the arena.

"What are we doing?" I demand.

"I'm fetching my horse." He gestures to the stable hand waiting by the doorway. "Fetch Lady Callyn's as well."

The stable hand frowns, and he looks to me in surprise. He's barely more than a boy, and he falters. "Ah . . . my lord. My lady. Forgive me, but—" He looks me up and down. He probably has no idea who I am—just like I have no idea who *he* is. I've only been here once, when Sinna wanted to show me her favorite pony.

"Alek," I say. "I don't have a horse here."

"Oh, yes." He nods to the boy. "Send word to the southern stables—"

"*No*," I snap, wondering how it's possible he made this so awkward so fast. "I mean I don't have a horse at *all*."

He looks back at me in surprise. "How is that possible?"

I glare at him. He's so *arrogant*—and this is almost humiliating. "Because I don't know how to ride? Because I'm poor? Because I didn't need a horse when I ran the bakery?" He's just staring at me, and my gaze narrows. "Should I keep going? Do you need more reasons?"

Alek sighs, then looks back to the stable hand, whose eyes are wide as saucers. "Ready a trap instead," he says.

The stable hand scurries. "Yes, my lord."

I have no idea what a *trap* is, but Alek says nothing else, so we stand there awkwardly while the stable hand outfits a horse with a gleaming leather harness, then leads the animal out of the barn. As the minutes tick on, I'm so aware of the beat of my heart, pounding hard against the inside of my ribs.

I can't separate those two moments in my head: the warm weight of his body against me, the way he held me afterward and made me feel so treasured.

And then the moment when he looked at me like the most terrifying creature to ever exist.

Against my will, tears gather behind my eyes. I hate him. *I hate him.*

Hooves clop from behind us. "Here you are, my lord."

I blink the tears away, but not quickly enough. Alek catches a glimpse of my expression, and he does a double take.

Ugh. I sniff back the tears and turn to face the stable hand. It seems that a *trap* is a small carriage, because the vehicle tethered to the horse has two wheels and a wide seat, but no doors and no cover.

Without a word, Alek offers me his hand. I reach out and take it, which is clearly another surprise, because his eyebrows shoot up, and he guides me forward.

Then I squeeze his fingers together like a bunch of twigs, and he jerks his hand away, cursing under his breath.

"Did you learn that from your little sister?" he growls under his breath.

"As a matter of fact, yes, I did."

"I should have known better," he says.

There's a rueful note in his voice that I can't quite figure out, and I peer at him curiously before I can stop myself. He glances over as he takes the reins in hand, then clucks to the horse.

"I was once a little brother," he says, as if that explains everything.

In a way, it does. His tone is light, but those first words—*I was once*—hit me harder than I expect.

Because I forgot: his sister was attacked by soldiers, just like mine. Only his sister never came home.

He's so bold and brazen that I always forget that he's lost his entire family to war and magic. Maybe the emotion over Nora never really left me, because I find myself clearing my throat again. "I'm sorry," I say, and then I immediately regret it. He's the last person in the world to deserve an apology—and I'm not even the one who brought this up.

Alek *tsks* under his breath. "Come now, Callyn, you were ready to stab me half an hour ago. Now you look like you're about to cry."

Well, that chases away the tears. "Don't worry. I'm still ready to stab you."

He chuckles as the horse draws the carriage—the *trap*, I suppose—through the gates, and we rattle over the cobblestones. But after a moment, his own emotion goes somber.

"Forgive me," he says. "I truly did not consider that you wouldn't know how to ride. My intent was not to imply weakness or poverty."

He's so frank about this that I really do think he's being genuine, and it takes the wind out of my sails a bit—but not so much that it changes my attitude about him being here. I shrug and look out at the city as we pass. "I suppose it's no surprise that a man born to privilege would forget that other people are *not*."

I expect him to bristle or spar with words, but he nods. "True enough."

"Tell me what you're doing, Alek. Are you dragging me outside the city walls to abandon my body somewhere?"

"Come now, Callyn. I certainly wouldn't undertake such a task *myself*."

I think he's being funny, but the sad thing is that it's probably also true.

He glances over. "I haven't lied to you. The queen did ask me to take you on my rounds among the nobles. While many people are pleased that the king is gone, I suspect there are some who believe the queen should be, too."

I gasp.

"You're surprised?" he says. "You yourself know the queen's life was threatened when she was captured in Briarlock."

I suppose that's accurate—but it's jarring. I've spent so much time thinking that the king is gone, so the threats about magic should be gone, too.

If the queen isn't safe, it's unfair for her to lose her husband. It's unfair for Sinna to lose her father.

Alek glances over. "As usual, I find it fascinating that you still regard me as a villain from one of your storybooks, when I've never told you anything but the truth—from the very first moment I met you."

That makes every muscle in my body go tense. I want to throw myself out of the carriage. "You *are* a villain."

"Am I? Why?"

"You just kidnapped me!"

"If I wanted to *kidnap* you, I'm sure it would take a good deal more planning and execution. I simply spoke of the queen's order and you willingly joined me."

"After *you* threatened to tell my sister about you and me," I say, seething.

"Ah." He glances away from the road, and his blue eyes are piercing. "Is that my fault, or is it your own? I certainly can't be blamed for the secrets you keep from your own sister."

My cheeks flare with heat, and I'm glad for the breeze. Oh, I hate him. I *hate* him.

I especially hate that he's right.

"I told you to take your magic and leave," he says. "You refused—or I assume you did, as you're still here. When I learned that the queen could be at risk, of course I immediately came to the palace to warn her of the danger. I was rather shocked to see her demise."

That makes me frown. I think of the queen moving through the palace like a ghost. "She's not . . . she's not in *demise*."

"Well, she certainly looks like she hasn't slept in weeks. It's no secret to anyone among the nobility that she's grieving the loss of her husband as if he's an insect-ridden corpse, and not simply sitting on his own throne—where he should've been all along."

Now I want to shove him out of the trap. "Truly, Alek, I can't imagine why *anyone* would consider you a villain."

He chuckles under his breath. "Despite your lying and deceit, I really have missed you, Callyn."

I feel the impact of that sentence like a punch to the face. "There's been no *lying and deceit*."

The smile slips off his face. He glances over, but says nothing.

His silence is sharper than a word would be, and I scowl. Fine. Maybe there's been a little deceit.

We're well away from the palace now, and the wind tugs at my hair, a welcome relief from the blazing sun. The dead heat of summer was always a challenge in the bakery. Milk would spoil and eggs would rot, and mice always got into everything. I'd sometimes try to hang supplies down the well to keep them cold, but then I discovered Jax's father was skimming from the food, so I had to stop.

I never told Jax about that. He would've been humiliated.

Thoughts of my friend make my heart give a tug. I've wanted to send him a letter for months, but so much has happened that I've never known what to say. I certainly couldn't write to him about Alek. Admitting my failures in the arena with Verin would've been humiliating, and I would've been terrified word would've gotten back to Verin herself. I might've trusted Lord Tycho with a secure message—but he and the king left so abruptly that I never had a chance to send anything at all.

I'd give anything to whisper in the bakery with him again, or to shiver around the forge. We might have been hungry and cold, but we were *friends.*

Instead, I'm stuck here with Alek.

Did I lie to him? Yes. But I had no choice. What does he think, that I could simply say, *"You know how much you hate the king's magic? Guess what I have!"*

But as the vehicle rattles along, I want to squirm in my seat. I'm remembering the moment Lord Tycho healed Jax's hand after he'd been badly burned in the forge. I had no idea Tycho had magic at all, and once he used it, I faced him with a knife and a frying pan. Jax yelled at him and chased him out of the bakery.

Was that different? Or the same?

"It wasn't deceit," I say softly now. "You made it impossible to tell you."

"How?"

I cut him a narrow glance. "You *know* how. You hate magic. You practically plotted the king's death."

"Because *his* magic endangered the queen." He pauses, glancing my way, his blue eyes piercing. "Does yours?"

I swallow, thinking of the fact that the queen has her own magic—but I can't ever share that secret. It's not mine to tell. "No. I'd never endanger her."

"I believe you already do endanger her," he says. "From what I understand, the scravers target magesmiths. It is believed that they came to the palace to attack the king." He pauses, glancing at me. "But they attacked the Crystal Palace right after *you* used your magic. What if they didn't come after the king? What if they came after you?"

"They didn't." But the words sound hollow, because I've worried about the exact same thing. I look at him. "The last time I saw you, you threatened to tell the queen about my abilities. What changed?"

He shrugs, ambivalent. "I still might. But you haven't caused her any harm, and I've decided that if you had any *real* talent, you'd have used it against me by now."

I seethe again, because I simply don't understand how he manages to defend me and insult me within the same sentence.

He glances over. "Like now. If you truly meant me harm, I'd know it."

"I'm going to knock you out of the carriage."

He flicks the reins. "If you can't ride, I rather doubt you know how to *drive*."

"I'll take my chances." I move to shove him.

I don't *really* mean it—because he's right, I have no idea how to drive—but Alek flinches. For a bare flash of time, I see shame flicker across his expression.

Then it's gone, smoothed out. Like I imagined it.

But I didn't. I know I didn't.

"I scared you," I say softly. It's almost impossible to believe, because he just faced me with a *sword*, and he wasn't intimidated at all. He even offered his hand to help me into the carriage. He doesn't quite seem intimidated, but there's still the ghost of an emotion hanging between us. "Didn't I?"

He clears his throat. "No." But he gives the tiniest little shudder, like a horse shaking off a fly.

I stare at him.

Eventually, he sighs and glances over again. "Magic killed my mother, Callyn. Magic killed my sister." His eyes return to the road. "I'm not afraid of you, but I . . ."

His voice trails off, his expression troubled.

I keep forgetting about his own losses. His manner is always so apathetic, as if death and treason were irksome and commonplace, not true tragedies.

But I realize right now I'm seeing the truth behind his mask.

Alek feels betrayed. Deeply, agonizingly betrayed.

The worst part is that I really can't blame him. I would've felt the same. I *did* feel the same, back when Tycho healed Jax. Magic has caused so much harm. It killed my mother, and even though the king was protecting his family, his magic killed my father, too.

I look back at the road. We're traveling at a good clip now, the horse trotting more swiftly than if it had the full weight of a carriage behind it. The city is behind us, the dark shadows of the woods ahead. "What's the real reason you didn't tell the queen about me?"

"I intended to, believe me. But it's become clear to me that the queen needs you here."

"She needs *me*?"

Alek nods. "If there are still people working against her, she shouldn't trust anyone." He glances over. "She needs someone who cares for her . . . not for her crown."

I inhale, intending to protest, because Queen Lia Mara is close with many in the palace. So many people demand her attention: advisers, courtiers, citizens.

But as I consider that, my protests feel hollow—and possibly untrue. Maybe there are plenty of people who imagine themselves to be close to *her*, but I've never seen the queen fall on them. In fact, the few times I've seen the queen be vulnerable have only been in front of me and Nora. When she cried over her husband, she didn't cry on her sister's shoulder . . . she cried on mine.

My heart gives a tug. She's so incredibly sad. My mouth pulls into a frown.

"Exactly," says Alek, reading my expression.

"Do you still suspect Verin?"

"Possibly," he says. "But I can't accuse the queen's sister without risking treason, and I'm not willing to do that." He pauses, and the shadows of the forest fall over us as we ride into the trees. "Yet."

Silence falls between us again. He still hasn't said where he's taking me, and it seems rather clear he's not going to. I settle back in my seat and sigh. Another cool breeze winds through the trees, ruffling the leaves overhead, a relief after the pressing heat in the city. After our bickering, I wait for tension to build between us, but . . . it doesn't.

As usual, Alek is right beside me, and somehow I can't summon the same hatred that I inevitably feel when he's *not*.

He flinched. He *flinched*.

I peer at my hands. I have a tiny scar at the tip of one finger, the remnants of an injury I acquired while repairing the barn door back at my bakery in Briarlock. When it happened, Lord Tycho offered to use magic to fix it.

I flinched, too.

I swallow. Maybe this *was* a betrayal. I made myself vulnerable to Alek, but I suppose he made himself vulnerable to me, too.

"Maybe I should have told you," I say quietly.

He nods in agreement. "Yes."

I hold my breath, weighing my next words carefully. "Do you understand why I couldn't?"

He draws a quick breath, as if he's going to be as flippant with that as he is with everything. But then he stops. His mouth forms a line. Storm clouds roll through his eyes again.

Eventually, he frowns, then turns away from the road to look at me. I hold his gaze, again startled by the turmoil I find in their depths.

But I have no idea what he was planning to say, because the horse spooks, lurching sideways. The trap rocks hard, then overturns. Wood cracks and splinters. I crash into the rocky path before I'm even aware of what's happening. Alek is shouting to the horse, pulling at my arm. Too late, I realize that the horse is scrambling in its panic, and the flipped vehicle is nearly dragged right over us. Alek shoves me out of the way at the last moment. The harness leather snaps, and the horse bolts off into the trees.

"What happened?" I say. "What spooked the horse?"

Ice-cold wind whistles down the road, making me shiver. Ice forms on the rocks around us, and I stop breathing.

A scraver drops straight out of the trees to land on the path in front of us. Wings outstretched, claws bared, black eyes glittering in the shadows.

Alek's grip is tight on my wrist. "That," he says.

CHAPTER 8

ALEK

I'm impressed at how quickly Callyn scrambles to her feet. I've seen scravers before, but my most recent experience was when they were trying to tear me to shreds. Just now, the memory of it flashes in my brain, a winged monster swooping down from the sky, claws and fangs bared. I have a sword in hand without even thinking of it, but my palm already feels slick. I tighten my grip.

But *this* scraver doesn't attack. She's landed on the road ahead of us, and her wings are half spread defensively, as if she could launch herself into the sky at a moment's notice. She's terrifying and beautiful at the same time, with gray-and-purple markings on her skin that continue onto her wings. Her hair is darker in color, though still streaked with broad strokes of gray and deep purples. It's full of tangles and hangs to her waist, and a few dried leaves are caught among the strands. She's not quite clothed, but she's not naked either. Leather is strapped to her body, and I can see sheaths for weapons, but they're all empty.

I grab Callyn's arm to put her behind me, and I'm shocked when she resists.

"What are you doing?" she grinds out. "I have magic."

Like I need a reminder. "And I have a *sword*."

The scraver still hasn't moved. "If I wanted you dead, you already would be." Her voice is light, but there's a rough quality to it, as if she doesn't speak often. Her eyes, all black, flash in my direction. "You will put your weapon away."

"No," I say. "I won't." I adjust my grip on the hilt.

A cool wind sweeps across the road, and ice forms on my sword, crawling up the length of the weapon, a slow gathering of crystals along the steel.

"Fascinating," I say, biting back a shiver. "But it's still just as sharp."

The scraver takes a step toward me, and I automatically shift, my blade lifting to defend myself. Her wings snap wide, and her lip curls, revealing the edge of her fangs. Years of training have taught me how to *see* the moment before an attack. It's a flicker of eye movement, a tightening of muscles. A shifting of weight.

I see it *now*.

To my surprise, Callyn shoves my sword arm down and steps in front of me. I nearly shove her back again, but then she turns her glare on me. "Stop. Just *stop*. I remember her."

I frown. "You *remember*—"

"Yes." Callyn looks back at the scraver, and for a moment, her voice falters. "You were in Briarlock. Right?" She hesitates, then wets her lips. "You helped my sister."

"*You* helped your sister," says the scraver. "I simply helped direct your magic."

"Why did you wreck our carriage?" I demand. "What do you want?"

"From you?" the scraver says dismissively. Bitterly cold wind whips around us, lifting her hair and stinging my cheeks. "Nothing."

"You want me?" says Callyn. She takes a step back, nearly colliding with me. "Why?"

"Nakiis is badly injured. I need your magic."

"Nakiis," Callyn whispers, like the name is unfamiliar. "Was he in Briarlock, too?"

"Yes. He helped Tycho protect your king." The scraver's head cocks to the side, and then, without warning, she leaps into the air, and she's gone.

Callyn whips around in a full circle. Her breath is still coming in clouded bursts. "What happened? Where did she go?"

But then we hear pounding hoofbeats, and a dozen soldiers come galloping through. I think they might stop when they see the broken trap lying on its side, but they don't. Callyn and I have to scramble into the trees to clear the path so we don't get trampled.

Once the soldiers are gone, I look down. Callyn has a tight grip on my forearm. Is she afraid? Or was she worried I would flag down the soldiers?

She follows my gaze, and it's as if she's surprised to find her hand there, too. Her cheeks turn pink, and she lets go. Her eyes flick to the trees and sky, looking for the scraver.

"Did the soldiers scare her off?" she murmurs.

A voice reaches our ears, but it's not like any voice I've ever heard.

—They did not scare me, magesmith. But after what Xovaar did to your king, those soldiers would shoot me out of the sky.

"Xovaar," I murmur. None of these names are familiar. I look at Callyn and realize that she might've been hiding more than just her magic. I keep my voice low. "Do you know this Xovaar? Do you know Nakiis?"

Callyn shakes her head rapidly. "I barely even know *this one*."

—My name is Igaa. As I said, I need your help.

"Why should she help you?" I call back. "Your people are attacking Syhl Shallow. Maybe those soldiers *should* shoot you out of the sky."

There's no warning aside from a few rustling leaves before I'm tackled to the ground so hard that I go skidding into the underbrush. The sword catches on a branch and slips out of my hand. Leaves and branches work their way under my armor, but if I weren't wearing any, she might've crushed my ribs. As it is, she lands on my chest, her claws gripping tight to my throat.

For an instant, all I see are her eyes, black and gleaming in the sunlight. Fear grips my heart, and I can't think. I can't *move.*

But then I hear Callyn's voice, tight with strain. "Let him go."

Igaa leans down closer, but her words are for Callyn, not me. "I don't need him. I just need *you,* magesmith."

"I'm not a magesmith." Callyn's voice is breathy but strong. "But I have his sword—and I know how to use it."

Good girl.

But Igaa doesn't move. I can feel every claw pressing into my skin. It hurts to breathe.

"Let me up," I say.

"No."

"Use the sword," I say to Callyn.

"I can kill him before you kill me," says the scraver. As if to prove it, her claws press tighter, and a sudden sting tells me she's broken the skin. I gasp, and a warm drop of blood makes its way down my neck.

"You said you need my help," says Callyn. "If you hurt him—if you hurt him at *all*—you won't get it."

At that, the scraver freezes. My heart is pounding, my head spinning. But then she abruptly shoves herself off my chest, taking to the air, landing in a tree twenty feet above. I'm left gasping in the dirt, choking on nothing, scrambling to right myself.

—We are not with the scravers who are attacking your people, she says from above. ***—Nakiis is trying to stop them.***

I sit up, rubbing a hand against my throat. "I'm not sure I believe you."

—I do not care what you believe, human.

“I’m not sure *I* believe you,” says Callyn.

—You should. Without your help, Nakiis will die. Then there will be no one to stand against Xovaar.

“One less scraver?” I say. “I’m not sure what the problem is.”

She lets out a screech that’s so shrill I can’t help but cringe. Callyn drops the sword to press her hands over her ears.

But as I hear it, the sound triggers a memory. I was seventeen years old, and my sister was still alive. We were at a court dinner in the Crystal Palace, shortly after the former queen had vowed to help Grey take the throne in Emberfall.

Queen Karis Luran had trapped a scraver named Iisak, and she kept him on a chain. After dinner, she ordered him to eviscerate a guardsman who’d disappointed her.

That scraver made a sound just like that, then attacked.

It was the most horrific thing I’d ever seen. I remember wondering if my mother had been killed by a creature just like it.

I haven’t thought of that moment in years, and the memory makes me shudder. But at the time, I was startled because Lia Mara wasn’t afraid of the creature. She seemed to trust him, and in fact, once she took the throne, she granted the scraver his freedom. She called him an ally. A *friend*.

I look up at Igaa through the branches. Her gray-and-purple coloring blends into the shadows of the branches, and as the screech dies out, I realize the sounds of the forest have gone absolutely silent. Animals hiding in the presence of a predator.

We should probably be doing the same thing. My heart won’t stop begging me to run.

But I’ve been afraid before. I know how to put away fear and move forward.

I look up at Igaa and keep my tone bored. “Are you done?”

She hisses at me.

Callyn hits me in the arm. "*Alek.*"

"You heard her. If she was going to hurt us, she would've done it already."

I think.

But I must be right, because the scraver doesn't move. Her claws are still embedded in the bark of the tree, her figure completely still, nearly lost among the foliage.

I expect her to screech at me again, but she doesn't.

—Please, she says instead, and there's a note of desperation in her silent voice. ***—I would have summoned Tycho instead, but he is too far. I cannot leave Nakiis for long.***

I consider the purpose of our mission. The queen sent us to find information about the Truthbringers. We should be conversing with the other Royal Houses, but perhaps there's another way.

My heart won't stop thrumming with wild panic, but I ignore it and look at Callyn. "Do you want to help her?"

Surprise lights in her eyes, and she drops her voice to a whisper. "She helped me save Nora." She pauses, then wets her lips. "But I don't know if we can trust them."

I study her, struck by the words—because I really don't know if I can trust *her.*

As if she realizes the same thing, Callyn sighs. "I didn't betray you, Alek."

"Hmm," I say, putting that away for later. I glance at the broken wreckage of the trap, then look back up at the scraver hiding among the branches.

"Where is Nakiis?" I say.

Igaa looks east and nods in that direction. "Five miles, perhaps." Without another word, she launches off the branch. Her wings flare wide, then snap hard, catching the wind. "I can lead you."

Five miles. I swear under my breath. “You might’ve left us the horse,” I call. Then I sheathe my sword and turn to Callyn. “Come on.”

Her eyes are wide. “*You* want me to help her?”

I shrug and start walking. “The queen sent us out to get information.” I glance over as she falls into step beside me. “Let’s go get it.”

The scraver leads us through the woods, away from the road, and I realize that the horse wouldn’t have been much help. The woods cut right into the mountainside, and the terrain is rough, thick with underbrush in some spots, fallen trees and rocks in others. I had mentally estimated that five miles would take us an hour and a half, but if it’s going to be like this the whole way, it’ll easily double that.

Callyn is panting beside me, and sweat has made a few tendrils of hair cling to her cheeks. “I’m glad I was wearing my training leathers when you found me.”

It’s the first thing she’s said in quite a while, and I can’t tell if she’s attempting to be friendly or if she’s simply uncomfortable with the silence between us. Before the horse spooked, she asked if I understood why she kept her magic a secret. I never got a chance to answer.

I don’t want to answer now.

But I have to say something, or my silence will be a different kind of response. “I suppose a gown would’ve made this quite challenging,” I agree.

“I’m surprised you’re willing to do this,” she says.

“Don’t worry. I’m second-guessing it with every step.”

That startles a soft laugh out of her. “You don’t second-guess anything.”

“I’m pleased to know I provide such an illusion of confidence, Callyn.”

She's quiet for a little while after that, until I wonder if she took my sarcasm as simple fact.

But then she says, "I really didn't mean for my magic to be a betrayal, Alek." She pauses, and her voice goes soft. "It scares me, too. I didn't know what to do with it."

That makes me glance over. I'm not sure what to say. "Does anyone else know?" I finally say.

She shakes her head.

I think of the way her sister took on a sudden look of dismay when I dared to mention our outings together, and I realize that maybe Callyn hasn't just kept this a secret from *me*. She's kept it a secret from everyone. Am I the only one who *does* know?

That loosens something inside me for some reason. It makes it less of a betrayal. It makes her actions less calculating. Something born of fear and self-protection.

Do you understand why I couldn't tell you?

All of a sudden, I do.

"Not even Nora?" I say, and my voice is a little quieter, a little less intense.

"*No.*" She takes a breath, then hesitates.

"Tell me," I say.

"Every time I want to tell her, I think about how our parents died, and I don't know how she'll take it. It's one thing to know the king has magic, or to see Tycho use it." Her voice is so soft. She looks over at me. "It's completely different to see it in her own sister. It's the same reason I couldn't tell *you*."

That tugs at my heart in a way that's unfamiliar, and I don't like it. "All that time we spent together," I say. "You knew how much I hated magic, and you pretended—"

"I wasn't pretending!" she cries, and it's so loud and sudden in the dense forest that a flock of birds explodes out of the trees overhead.

Callyn is glaring at me. "I didn't know I had it before." She swipes damp hair off her cheeks. "It wasn't until—until—"

"Until what?" I say.

"Until the battle in Briarlock. Nora was dying, and I was just . . . I was desperate." She looks ahead, trudging through the dense foliage. "Even then, I wasn't sure it was real. I thought maybe it was something else. The scravers, or Tycho, or even the king himself."

"What convinced you?" I say, and I'm genuinely curious.

Her eyes narrow ruefully. "Verin." She frowns. "She kept hurting me in the arena."

"And you'd heal yourself," I say, figuring it out.

"Yes." She frowns. "But I never did anything else! I never *wanted* to do anything else. I knew how much you hated magic, Alek. And sometimes you can be so . . . prickly."

"Prickly!"

Callyn gives me a look. "You know you're prickly."

"Callous, I'll grant," I say, musing. "Impatient." My boot slips a little, finding a rock under the branches, and I swear. "Arrogant, perhaps—"

"And you don't see how all of this qualifies you as *prickly*?"

That almost makes me smile. I missed her company, and I hate it. "Very well."

My boot finds another slick rock, and the terrain suddenly takes all our focus. We huff our way up the side of the mountain until sweat slicks the inside of my clothes and I finally abandon my jacket so I can turn my sleeves back.

When Callyn glances over, she does a double take. Her eyes linger. Not long, just for a heartbeat of time, but it's enough.

At first, my heart sparks with intrigue, and I almost smile.

But then I remember everything else between us, and the smile slips off my face. She's turned her attention back to the mountainside anyway.

"Do you really think they might have information on the Truthbringers?" she eventually says.

"I have no idea," I say. "But it's possible. Scravers have a long history with the royal families of Syhl Shallow."

Callyn snaps her head around to look at me. "They do? I didn't know that."

I nod, then gesture to the pendant at her neck, which is mostly hidden by her tunic and breastplate, aside from the thin cord. "Why do you think I know about the Iishellasan steel?"

"I . . . I don't know."

"They were once treaty bound to stay on the other side of the Frozen River," I say. "At first, magesmiths stayed with them, but they couldn't withstand the cold, so they tried to settle in Syhl Shallow. The old queen wouldn't let them, so they migrated into Emberfall." I pause. "Where they clearly wreaked havoc."

From somewhere high above, Igaa's voice calls back to us silently.

—The king of Emberfall ordered their destruction. Few survived.

Callyn turns to look at me with wide eyes. "She can hear us?" she whispers.

—Yes, magesmith. I can.

I look up and around. The scraver is well above us, her purple wings mere shadows against the sky. She's been flying lazy circles for over an hour, demonstrating the direction we're to go, but never too far ahead that we lose track. The sun at her back creates an optical illusion, because I can't quite judge her size or distance. If we didn't know any better, she could be a hawk or a falcon, soaring far overhead. If we were traveling on the road, I might glance up, but I likely wouldn't think twice.

As soon as I have the thought, I wonder if that's how they manage to travel across Syhl Shallow undetected. I wonder if that's how they managed to attack the palace.

—We once gave the magesmiths our steel as a means to share our power, she says, and it's so odd that her voice could be right beside me. ***—You wield it from within, while we draw it from the wind and sky. We were happy to share . . . for a time. But we learned that once the magic is in your blood, it cannot be taken away.***

"Can *your* magic be taken away?" Callyn says.

This time, she doesn't answer. It makes me wonder if it was really the *cold* the magesmiths couldn't stand—or if the scravers drove them out to begin with. I know what kind of tragedy unfolded in Emberfall, and apparently that was only caused by *one.*

Then again, Igaa did just say that the king of Emberfall ordered their destruction. This all happened before I was born. Were the magesmiths really *victims,* chased out of their homes again and again, constantly facing persecution . . . or were they the true monsters, stealing magic from the scravers and tormenting the citizens of two countries before they met their demise?

I inwardly scoff at the introspection. As far as I'm concerned, they're *all* monsters.

But I'm struck by the realization that if I asked the queen, she'd likely say they were all victims.

I glance at Callyn and wonder what she would think. I don't know if I'd like the answer.

We find a narrow path through the underbrush, almost stumbling onto it. Branches have been snapped, indicating we aren't the first people to come through this way.

—You are close, Igaa says. ***—Nakiis is not far.***

My heart skips a little in my chest, and I swallow. Until this moment, I hadn't quite considered that we were walking into a situation where we'd be confronted by more than one scraver—one of whom is badly injured.

Callyn glances at me. "Are you afraid?" she whispers.

Yes. "Not at all," I say.

She makes a face at me anyway. "Liar."

—Nakiis will not harm you, Igaa says.

"Stop doing that!" Callyn calls.

—He is badly injured, she adds. ***—He cannot.*** She pauses, and a vicious tone emphasizes the voice in my head. ***—It would do you well to remember that I still can.***

"Noted," I say. I stride ahead, sweat gathering on my forehead. I feel as though we're walking straight uphill now, and after another hundred feet, we're practically walking alongside sheer rock. At times, the ground off to our left seems to give way completely, offering a stunning view of the valley below.

"I didn't realize we climbed so high," says Callyn.

"I didn't either." I put out a hand to steady myself—then gasp and jerk back. The stone is ice cold.

—As I said. You are close.

My palms have gone slick, and this time it has nothing to do with the heat or the exertion. We come around a small bend in the path, and to our right is a narrow opening in the rock. It's barely a cave. In fact, it's barely anything at all. But it's a shaded gap in the side of the mountain, full of dark shadows.

Then, without warning, one of the shadows shifts. Black eyes gleam at us from the darkness, and claws shift against the ground. I freeze, my body taking on the sudden stillness of prey caught in the gaze of a predator.

This scraver doesn't move farther, but his eyes flick between us. His coloring is much darker than Igaa's, a gray so dark that he almost disappears into the shadows of the cave. Sunlight barely pierces the dimness, but when his weight shifts, silver gleams along the feathers of his wings, and then I catch a hint of fangs. When I inhale, I taste the bitter tang of old blood, with something sour on top. I can't see his injuries, but they're clearly there.

But even lying injured on the ground, he's terrifying. There's a stillness to his body that promises imminent death if we come closer. An ice-cold wind whips around us, dragging dried leaves along the ground. In this heat, it should be a relief, but I know it's this creature's magic, so it's not.

Wings rustle behind us as Igaa lands in the brush, trapping us here in the gap. Ice forms on the rock walls, melting almost instantly in the summer sunlight.

Beside me, Callyn's breath trembles, just a little. I don't know if it's the sudden chill or if it's fear, but I'm willing to bet it's both. I reach out and grab her hand.

She doesn't take her eyes off the scraver, but her body gives a little jump, as if I've startled her.

But then her fingers close around mine, gripping tight.

I want to offer reassurance. *I won't let them hurt you. You don't need to be afraid. I'll keep you safe.*

But I can't even offer that. They tore me apart the last time. Callyn had to protect *me*. She had to save *me*.

And in return, I threatened her. I drove her away.

A sudden wash of shame rolls through me—cut short when the scraver on the ground offers a low growl that seems to fill the cave. My heart stutters again.

But Igaa, behind us, says, "Spare us your threats, Nakiis. I have brought you a magesmith."

It's fascinating how much her spoken voice sounds like her silent one. Nakiis glances between the three of us, then speaks to our minds himself.

—Good, he says, and his silent voice is a low rumble, softer than I expect. ***—Let her finish me off.***

Igaa scoffs. "Go," she says. "Help him."

Callyn shuffles forward one step, but she doesn't let go of my hand. Nakiis hisses at her from the depths of the cave, and Callyn freezes. Her fingers clench so tight. So do mine.

"*No*," Nakiis growls. "Kill me or leave. I will not be trapped by another magesmith."

"I won't trap you," says Callyn, her voice breathy. "How would I even begin to—"

"*Go*," the scraver says roughly, and I can tell how badly he must be injured, because there's a weakness to his voice that steals some of the terror from the cave. Just this much conversation seems to leave him panting heavily against the ground. "Or kill me," he adds, gasping between the words. "That is all you can do here."

"I do still have my sword," I say.

The scraver's black eyes are opaque, barely gleaming in the limited light, but I watch as they shift to me.

—I remember you, he says to my thoughts, baring his fangs again. ***—You're the one who tried to kill Tycho.***

Callyn's head whips around to face me.

But I just sigh. "Which time?"

Nakiis's eyes fall closed. ***—Kill him, Igaa.***

My hand finds my sword hilt, but Callyn grabs my arm, putting herself between me and Igaa.

"Would you *stop* it?" I say.

But the other scraver hasn't even moved. She looks resigned. "Please," she says to Callyn. "Help him."

—If she is working with this man, Nakiis says, ***—I don't want her help.***

Igaa sighs. Callyn sighs. For two such different creatures, the sound is remarkably similar. As if realizing this at the same time, the two of them exchange a glance that I can't interpret.

"I'm not working with Alek," Callyn says—and there's a tone in her voice that stings, especially when she lets go of my arm.

Nakiis's black eyes center on her, and he growls again. "I told you to *leave*."

"I know," says Callyn. She exchanges that inscrutable glance with Igaa again, and then she moves forward, heedless of the growling. Her jaw is set, her eyes fiercely determined. "But guess what? I'm tired of men telling me what to do."

CHAPTER 9

CALLYN

Back in Briarlock, a fox once got trapped in a broken and splintered part of my barn wall. The wood had pierced its body, and the animal's terrified snarling spoke to something inside me, reminding me that it might be injured, but it was still a predator that could bite my hand off. Right now, the scraver's vicious growls are doing the same thing. My heart won't stop thumping against my rib cage, as if it's willing to abandon this whole venture whether I want to or not.

But as I walk toward the creature in the shadows, I realize he's only making noise. His claws have curled against the ground, and every muscle on his frame is flexed as if ready to spring. But really, he's barely lifted his head.

And then, as I get close, I catch a whiff of the infection.

That is almost worse than the growling. My insides want to recoil.

"How long have you been like this?" I whisper.

He says nothing. Somehow, his gaze turns more threatening. Against my will, my feet stop.

"Since the attack on the palace," Igaa says behind me.

That was weeks ago. I glance back at her, surprised to find that Alek has followed, waiting in the shadows. His arms are folded, but much like Nakiis, every muscle is taut and ready.

I think of that moment we were on the path and Igaa landed in front of us. He tried to jerk me behind him.

It's hard to reconcile with the man who flinched away from me when we were riding in the trap.

That's too complicated to examine right now. "What happened?"

"Xovaar came after him," she says. "He has weapons of Iishellasan steel. Nakiis cannot heal the wounds."

I touch a hand to my pendant, which is also of Iishellasan steel.

Igaa watches the motion and nods. "Yes, magesmith. Like yours."

I swallow and turn back to the injured scraver lying curled in the dirt. He hasn't stopped growling, but it's as if the effort to scare me off has worn him out, because the sound is no longer loud and threatening. Instead, it's a bit pitiful, like when that fox's threatening snarls turned to painful keening.

I stop beside him and drop to one knee, just out of reach. His claws scrape against the ground, and I freeze.

Alek must be able to see the motion, because his voice is just as low and threatening when he says, "If you hurt her, scraver, I'll rip you apart in a way that can't be healed."

My traitorous heart skips a little, and this time it has nothing to do with fear.

No, I tell my heart.

But then I remember him spinning with Nora in the arena, the way his voice was almost encouraging. I think about the joy on her face.

No. No, no, no.

My heart doesn't care. It skips again anyway.

Nakiis has given up the growling, and now he's all but panting against the ground. There isn't much light, but I'm close enough to see the wounds, and the infection seems profound. He looks like he's been stabbed in the shoulder, or maybe shot with an arrow. There's another puncture wound through his arm, and I can't entirely tell, but it looks like there's a tear in his wing.

As my eyes scan his form, I find other wounds. Claws have slashed across his abdomen, and those ridges are crusted with pus and dirt. Something impaled his thigh, too. He's wearing trousers, but the bloodstains are thick, the injury still seeping.

"Clouds above," I breathe.

"I do not want your help," he says, and these words are spoken in a plaintive whisper. "Please."

Instead of threatening, he's turned to begging.

"I know," I say. "But you definitely need it." I hesitate, my gaze skipping over the wounds again. I might have saved Alek's life, but that was nothing like this. "You should know," I begin, "I'm not very practiced in healing—"

"Keep your magic," he says. "I don't want it." But his head falls back against the ground, his eyes slipping closed.

I reach out, but my hand stops before touching him. I caught a glimpse of his fangs when he was growling, and they looked razor sharp.

—Please, Igaa says, the words carrying to my thoughts silently. Her begging is completely at odds with his. ***—Please save him.***

I take a long, slow breath, then steel my nerves and reach for his arm. When my fingers brush his skin above the injury, he flinches a little, but his eyes don't open.

"If you're going to force me," he says breathlessly, "just let the man kill me."

That makes me go still. I don't want to force him.

Igaa says something from behind me, and I don't understand the word, but it sounds like profanity. "You should have allowed Tycho to tether his magic to yours," she snarls. "Then he would still be here, and you would not be in this condition. Now you have left *him* at risk." She swears again. "He could be dead. He could be fighting Xovaar this very moment. And you will do nothing because you refuse to move past old harms."

Nakiis says nothing. He doesn't even move.

I don't know what a lot of that means—*tether his magic?*—but something in the scraver's silence makes me think he agrees.

Especially when he lets out a heavy breath and says, "Fine. Do it."

I slide my hand down his arm until I find the first swell of infection. The cave is so cold, but his dark skin is unnaturally warm, especially around the wounds. I try to summon the magic, but nothing happens.

A cool breeze swirls through the space, and I shiver. Igaa's voice speaks to my mind again. ***—You cannot force it,*** she says. ***—Have you no training?***

"No," I say. "None." I glance back. "The only time it's ever worked on other people was when I was afraid."

"Close your eyes," she says. "Think of those moments. Allow the magic to respond."

I obey, feeling a bit foolish—and a bit afraid, considering I'm not sure I should trust Nakiis. But I think of Nora bleeding in the underbrush of the forest, choking on her own blood. Dying.

My chest clenches. The memory is too hard. I don't want to think about that. The sparks and stars that usually signal magic in my blood are nowhere to be found. I shift my hand, desperate, and the scraver jerks away, making a sharp sound of pain.

"Sorry," I say quickly. "It's not working."

"Good," he hisses.

But it's not good. I can see why Igaa is so worried.

"It worked when you saved *me*," Alek says from behind me, and I realize he's come closer. "Why?"

It's a probing question, and I don't really want to answer it.

Because the truth is that I'd begun to care for him. I'd begun to *fall* for him.

But maybe thinking of that moment loosens whatever blocked my magic, because the sparks and stars flicker in my veins. As I watch, some of the infection melts away.

Under my hand, the scraver lets out a breath. Some of the tension eases out of his muscles.

"Yes," Igaa breathes from behind me. "You've found your magic."

The wound itself doesn't fully heal, but when the pus and swelling are out of the way, I can see that the puncture is half-closed—and it'll likely heal altogether now that it *can*. I shift my hand to the next injury.

I wait for Alek to make another dig, or to possibly probe for an answer to his question, which I've left unanswered. But he says nothing, so I glance back over my shoulder. He's standing in the shadows, his arms still folded. His eyes are locked on what I'm doing, and it's clear that the tension hasn't left *his* frame.

I'm so unsettled by everything between us, especially since I don't know if he's an adversary or an ally. Sometimes I think he's determined to be both.

"Scared?" I say.

A muscle twitches in his jaw, and his gaze darkens. He probably *is* scared.

But then I consider what he said *earlier*, when Nakiis was flexing those clawed fingers in the dirt.

If you hurt her, scraver, I'll rip you apart in a way that can't be healed.

It's vicious and terrible and so very Alek. He's terrified of magic. He's terrified of these creatures.

But he still came with me. He's standing there ready to fight for me.

And I don't know what to do with any of it.

So I turn my gaze back to my task and let my magic do the work.

Once I've healed as much as I can, Nakiis is asleep—or possibly unconscious. Every muscle is slack, his wings a bit splayed in the shadows. When I express concern, Igaa says, "He has been suffering for weeks. He is exhausted."

I wipe my hands on my trousers, looking past her for Alek, but I realize he's no longer in the narrow cave.

"I sent your companion to fetch water from the creek," Igaa says. "He did not go far."

"I'm surprised he came," I admit. I'm also surprised he willingly accepted a task, but I don't say that.

"Did he truly try to kill Tycho?" she says.

I hesitate, then grimace. I remember the day Jax came to my bakery to tell me what had happened between Lord Alek and Tycho—but it was the morning after Alek had also come to see me, with burns on his arms and fury in his eyes.

Did he attack? Or did he defend himself? As usual, he always seems to be the villain and the savior simultaneously.

"I don't know," I say. "But maybe." I study her. The purple and gray of her coloring is so different in the darkness of the cave, and it's fascinating. She could melt into the wall if she needed to. "What did you mean about tethering their magic?"

"A magesmith can take hold of a scraver's magic," she says. "It allows a sharing, of sorts. Nakiis would have been able to heal the damage caused by the Iishellasan steel. He would've been able to stand against Xovaar."

My eyebrows knit together. "Tycho refused?"

She shakes her head. "Nakiis was the one to refuse." She lets out a sigh, then reaches to touch the pendant that hangs over my heart. "As I said, our history with magesmiths is quite long and complicated. It is one thing to draw our magic through steel. It is quite another to take our magic directly from the source."

Her voice is grave, and I think again of the way I learned that Tycho had access to the king's magic.

"Would it make Tycho stronger than the king?" I ask softly.

"Yes." She pauses. "But Nakiis has shared his magic with a magesmith before. And once it is done, it cannot be *undone* until one of them dies. It is a trapping. An imprisonment." She glances at the sleeping scraver in the shadows. "Just as his father was trapped and imprisoned by your king."

"I remember that," Alek says, speaking from the mouth of the small cave. He sets down a bucket that sloshes lightly over the sides. "The king's scraver."

I look at him in surprise. "You do?"

He nods. "He dragged him around on a chain."

I frown a little, trying to imagine King Grey keeping a creature like this on a chain. A year ago, I would've believed it, back when I hated the king and his magic. But now that I've had a chance to know him, I struggle to reconcile this knowledge. The king is stoic and commanding, but he's also thoughtful. Reflective. *Humane.*

And even if I could imagine the king doing it, I really can't imagine Queen Lia Mara putting up with it.

I tuck this knowledge away for later. "Will he heal now?" I say to Igaa.

Her mouth forms a line, her eyes glinting in the limited light. "Perhaps," she says. "There was a time when I worried he would not survive at all."

I swipe my hands on my trousers. "Well, we've been gone for hours, and if we're going to make it back to the palace before nightfall, we're going to have to start walking."

"No," says Alek. He folds his arms, straightening to block the narrow opening of the cave. "We helped you, now you need to help us."

Beside me, Igaa hisses a breath through her teeth. "You're lucky I don't gut you."

Alek doesn't move. "Put away your fangs," he says. His eyes shift to me. "Tell her, Callyn."

I sometimes wonder if Alek would have half as much conflict if he didn't treat every conversation like a transaction. I look at Igaa. "You don't have to help us at all," I say quietly. "But the king and Tycho have been gone for weeks. If scravers intend to attack the palace again, it would help the queen to know." I wet my lips. "It would help *me* to know."

Her fangs are still bared, but she studies me. After a moment, her expression softens, and she turns for the front of the cave. "Come," she says. "Let us speak outside so Nakiis can rest."

The sun is beating down through the trees, and after the coolness of the cave, the heat smacks me in the face. I cling to the shade and lean against the sheer rock wall as Igaa speaks.

"Nakiis would not like me saying these things to you," she says. "But he is too injured to move, and if Xovaar finds us, he will kill him."

"You keep mentioning Xovaar," says Alek. "Who is he?"

Igaa hesitates, then frowns. "Before I explain *who* he is, perhaps I should start at the beginning so you can understand the *why*."

"Go ahead," I say to Igaa.

She glances at Alek. "When the scravers first struck the treaty with Syhl Shallow, they did not expect the magesmiths to follow. But they knew the power our steel offered, and we'd always been willing to share. But *sharing* turned to *stealing*. Our allies were becoming our enemies, and we were left with no choice but to make the ice forests uninhabitable for humans. But the magesmiths already had what they wanted: the secret of our steel. They eventually forged across the

Frozen River and attempted to settle in Syhl Shallow, where they could still access our magic through the steel, but without being subject to our cold." Her eyes return to mine, and I see the depths of anger there. "But your queen feared our magic, and would not allow them to remain here. The magesmiths proceeded to Emberfall—where their king eventually ordered their destruction."

"But he didn't succeed," says Alek. "Because magesmiths still exist."

"Of course," says Igaa, surprised. "As long as humans have access to our steel, magesmiths can never truly be eradicated."

My heart skips hard. "The steel," I whisper, resting my hand over my mother's pendant. The whole reason I have the magic.

The queen had access to rings, too, I think. *Rings that protected her just like Tycho. Just like my mother's pendant protected me.*

But I can't say that. I don't want Alek to know.

I let go of the pendant. "What does this have to do with Xovaar?"

"This part," she says, "has more to do with Nakiis. As the years wore on, we began to tire of the treaty. Scravers did not want to be confined to the ice forests. Our *friist*—our *king*—sought to renegotiate with your queen. She refused."

"Lia Mara?" says Alek.

"No. Her mother. Karis Luran." Igaa glances into the shadows of the cave. "She threatened destruction of any scraver who dared to enter Syhl Shallow. But Nakiis didn't believe she could capture him if he tried—and he was right."

There's a grave note in her voice that tells me there's more to this story. "What happened to him?"

"As the *friist*'s son, he wanted to prove that escape was possible. He stayed hidden, passed through your country, and made it to Emberfall, where he found a surviving magesmith named Lilith. When she offered to share their magic so they could protect each other, he agreed immediately." That grave note in her voice turns to despair. "Lilith tricked him, trapping him into her service. She used his power against him, and nearly succeeded in destroying their kingdom."

"I remember this," Alek says, and now it's his voice that's gone heavy. "She created the monster that started the war."

The same war that killed his mother and his sister.

The same war that killed *my* mother.

"Yes," says Igaa.

"How did Nakiis escape her?" I say, and my voice is a little rough.

"He didn't," says Alek. "The king had his own scraver, and they killed her."

"Yes," Igaa says. "Nakiis's father. He was our *friist*. He was killed in the conflict, and Nakiis fled." She lets out a long breath. "But he was injured, and humans found him. He was trapped again." A heavy pause. "For years, until Tycho found him and freed him."

Tycho. I swallow, hearing the emotion in her voice.

"In return," she says, "Nakiis has attempted to protect him—but he is wary of having his magic taken." She pauses. "As you can see, this has put him at a disadvantage."

Those words land like a rock thrown into a pond, spreading ripples of awareness. I feel as though I'm connecting points I never realized were related. No wonder the scravers arrived to help in Briarlock. I thought they were helping the king and queen.

But they were helping because of *Tycho*.

I think again of the day he healed Jax's hand, the gentleness in his voice as he uncurled my friend's burned fingers. I think of his kindness with Nora, or the way his skittish cat wound between his ankles after hiding from everyone else.

Of course he freed a vicious scraver. Of course he did.

Alek's voice cuts through my reverie. "None of this explains Xovaar."

Igaa's eyes shift back to him. "Our *friist* was gone, human. His son was gone. In the absence of leadership, others will rise to claim power.

In Iishellasa, that was Xovaar. When Nakiis returned to Iishellasa and said Queen Lia Mara and her magesmith king were not enforcing the treaty, he thought the other scravers would welcome the opportunity to leave the ice forests. He thought he was bringing news that we could finally be free." She pauses, then frowns. "He did not realize that Xovaar and his followers had developed a deep resentment for the magesmiths who'd taken their magic and left them trapped there so long ago."

"So they're angry," I say softly. "And that's why they're coming after the king."

"That's why they're coming after any magesmith at all."

Alek's eyes have gone a bit cold again, like he's had a new thought, and he looks back at Igaa. "Will Xovaar come after Callyn?"

Igaa nods. "He could."

"The king and Tycho are in Emberfall," Alek says. "How do we ensure that Xovaar goes after *them*?"

Ice forms on the rock wall beside us, and the bare edge of her fangs appears again. "You would commit your problems to Emberfall as well?"

He looks like she's just asked if grass is green. "Absolutely."

Quicker than thought, the scraver reaches out and clamps her clawed hand around Alek's neck. A gasping, choking sound breaks free of his throat, and a trickle of blood appears below her fingers.

"You humans are so shortsighted," she growls. "Do you not think Xovaar would turn his powers on you next, with no magesmith to keep him in check?" She leans closer, and more blood flows. "Why do you think the scravers were treaty bound to remain in Iishellasa at all?"

Alek is prying at her fingers. His face has gone a shade of white I don't want to see again.

But then he snatches a weapon from the belt at his waist, and I realize he's going to thrust it right into Igaa. I don't know which one of them I should be defending—but I know they're about to kill each other.

Without thinking about it, I tackle the scraver.

She's much lighter than I expect, and it's bizarrely like tackling little Sinna instead of a vicious creature. Her wings flare wide as if to catch her balance, snapping hard to catch the air, but I'm too close, and I slam into her side full force. For an instant, I realize that she might launch us both into the air just to drop me from above. But then we crash into the ground, rolling.

I end up on top of her, panting. I don't mean to pin her wings, but one is trapped under my knee. Just as I realize it, she swipes at me with her claws.

Before she makes contact, Alek hooks me under the arms, jerking me off her.

Then he shoves me to the side, and before I can blink, he has weapons in hand.

"Stop!" I cry—but the scraver has already leapt into the air. She takes light on a branch high above. From here, I can hear her panting.

—I gave you your information, she says. ***—Now you must help me.***

"She just helped you!" Alek snaps incredulously.

"Shut *up*," I hiss at him. I jerk free of his grip. "What do you need me to do?" I call up to her. "I can't kill Xovaar. If the king couldn't stop him, I sure can't."

She hisses back at me. "Nakiis can. With the help of a magesmith."

"He didn't even want me to heal him! He's not going to let me tether my magic or whatever—"

"I don't want *your* magic." Igaa's claws wrap around that branch, and she leans down, her balance proving just how inhuman she is. "I want you to find Tycho, Callyn. And I want you to bring him to us."

CHAPTER 10

TYCHO

The sun is barely peeking over the horizon when we gather to ride out of Ironrose, streaking the sky with shades of lavender and pink. Malin already said he would choose Sephran, so I'm not surprised when the soldier shows up in a fresh tunic with full armor, riding a dark gray gelding that stands at least a hand taller than Mercy—which sets him a good eight inches taller than me. It doesn't matter, and I *definitely* shouldn't care, but I find it annoying anyway. He and Malin arrive in the courtyard together, and their expressions are jovial . . . until Sephran's eyes fall on me. Then his expression cools, and he barely gives me a nod.

Fine. I have no idea what his problem is, but after my time in Syhl Shallow, I have a long history of working with soldiers who don't like me. I can just add him to the list.

I thought Malin might choose Kutter as the last member of our small unit, because I've heard enough stories about him, too. Then again, before Malin's promotion, Kutter actually outranked *him*. So maybe I shouldn't be surprised when an unfamiliar young man arrives with a light bay mare, no rank or insignia on his sleeves.

"This is Leo," Malin says to me. "He's a recruit."

Leo draws his horse to a perfect halt, then offers me a salute.

"At ease," I say, but I inwardly sigh. Leo looks younger than I am, and there's a brightness in his eyes that tells me he's never seen any real trouble. We already have Jax along, and despite Rhen's encouragement, I have no idea if he's ultimately going to be an asset or a liability.

"Second year?" I say to Leo.

"First year. Sir."

Silver hell. I give Malin a look.

He shrugs. "You were young once, too," he says. "Oh, wait—you're *still*—"

"All *right*," I snap, but his teasing breaks through my tension to make me smile.

He grins in response. Despite everything, I'm glad Malin is coming. He was able to keep any edge out of the air when we traveled with the king, so maybe he'll be able to do the same thing when it comes to me and Jax.

Then Jax rides into the courtyard, and the sight of him steals every thought from my head.

I recognize the horse, because I remember the first night I introduced Jax to Teddy. He seemed so surprised—and a little intimidated—at the prospect of learning to ride. But now he sits in the saddle with a casual confidence, like he's been riding all his life. I'm not used to seeing him armed, but he's got a dagger on his hip, and a bow strung across his back, a quiver buckled to the saddle behind his thigh. He's in armor, too, and it looks as new as mine: fresh black leather, gleaming silver buckles. No gold and red, because he's not an Emberish soldier—but no green either. He wears it all well enough that anyone will think twice before starting trouble, especially since the gear broadens his frame, making him take up more space in the world than I remember.

It's not just the weapons and armor, though. It's . . . it's *him*.

Beside me, Malin clears his throat *very* deliberately.

The sound gives me a jolt, and I realize I was staring, my mouth hanging half-open. I jerk my head around to glare at Malin, and his grin widens.

If we were alone, I'd smile sheepishly in return, but Sephran is watching me, too, his expression almost glacial.

I grit my teeth, glad I can fall back on training and discipline. I wasn't an officer in the Queen's Army for long, but I've been at Grey's side for years. I know how to keep emotion off my face and focus on the task at hand.

"We'll head northwest toward Wildthorne Valley," I say. I glance at the lightening sky. "We should make it to the river by dusk, and we'll camp there." I glance at Malin. "Captain, take point. Set the pace." I shift my gaze to Leo. "Recruit, you're outrider."

Responding to my tone, Malin draws up his reins, and Leo salutes me again. Even Sephran has shifted his horse to follow the formation I've set. Any icy tension has disappeared from the air. They're all soldiers, used to following orders regardless of what's going on.

But Jax isn't. He's glancing between them, a small line appearing between his eyebrows.

I frown, realizing I gave the orders in Emberish, and despite the way he snapped at me in the forge, it's clear he didn't understand *all* of that.

"Do you need me to repeat it?" I say to him in Syssalah.

The instant I say it, I regret it. My voice was sharp, the words clipped like an order.

Jax's eyes widen, and then his expression turns as cool as Sephran's—and likely as cool as mine.

"No," he says, drawing up his own reins.

I inhale tightly, wanting to undo this. I didn't mean for that to come out as a challenge, but I'm still too stirred up. But the others are already moving away, obeying. In the absence of a direct order, I think Sephran might take flank, riding beside Malin, since they're friends. Instead, he draws close to Jax as they ride out, and he's speaking low. "Look," he says, pointing ahead. "Malin—point. First. *Leader.* Yes?"

Jax is nodding, his expression easing as he puts the words together.

Sephran gestures toward the younger soldier, off to the side. "Leo—outrider. He . . . ah . . . rides out." He sounds slightly abashed, but what strikes me is that his voice is so patient—and somewhat gentle. After his clipped tone with me, it takes me by surprise. He taps under his eye, then makes a circular gesture out in front of us. "Sentry?" he says to Jax, glancing over. "Lookout?"

Jax's eyes light up with sudden comprehension. "*Outrider.* I understand."

Seeing their easy rapport makes me realize this must be a common interaction for them, and my heart gives a tug. Doesn't Jax know that I would've explained these things, too? I would've given him the words. I can also be patient and gentle.

But maybe I was gone too long. Maybe he's forgotten.

Maybe I've picked too many fights. Maybe I've proven the exact opposite.

Ahead of us, Malin kicks his horse into a canter, following my order, setting the pace.

So I draw up Mercy's reins to follow, realizing they're about to leave me behind.

The sky is clear for miles as we canter across the fields of Emberfall. If nothing else, a scraver won't be able to sneak up on us from the air. Malin's been driving a hard pace, and I'm glad. We're going too fast for much conversation, so I can lock all my complicated thoughts in my head and focus on the mission.

But Jax is *right there*, and it's killing me. After the first hour, I call for a swap with Leo, taking outrider, just because Jax's closeness is like riding too close to the sun. I'm so aware of his presence it's almost painful.

But if I thought distance would help, I was wrong. I should be watching for trouble, but my eyes keep drifting back to the group, back to *him*. He's grown into a steady rider, his hands soft on the reins, such a difference from the way he used to gasp and clutch at the reins when I first put him on Mercy. Silhouetted in the distance, he could be just another soldier, identical to the rest of our group, but I can still see the tendrils of hair that the wind keeps tugging free, and his more casual bearing that separates him from the men with military training. My heart can pick him out every time I look over.

Do you need me to repeat it?

Silver hell, I sounded like *such* an ass.

I should apologize, but I'm not sure how—or when. Since we're camping, we won't have a moment of privacy later.

Before I left Ironrose the first time, I told him that when I got back, we'd ride out to Silvermoon and spend the night under the stars. Tonight, we might be under the stars, but it's going to be an empty riverbed, not a bustling marketplace, and we're not going to be alone.

Just another promise I can't keep, I suppose.

I finally look away from the group and let my eyes search the landscape. We don't need to get slaughtered by an ambush while I'm mooning over Jax.

But this part of Emberfall is endless acres of open fields and tilled land, interspersed by the occasional dirt road. No scravers, few travelers, nothing to occupy my thoughts. Eventually the terrain grows a bit hilly, with forests and tree lines and plenty of shadows to grab my focus. But even then, Malin's competence works against me, and we reach the river when there's still a bit of light in the sky.

I sigh, returning to the group. We tether the horses along the tree line, then set about making camp. It's clear the rapport between Sephran and Jax extends to Leo, because they build a fire and set a pot of water to boil with the kind of effortless efficiency that only exists among friends. I can't help but watch as I silently strip Mercy's gear. Jax might've learned a lot of Emberish, but it's obvious that the others have learned a bit of Syssalah, too. Their conversation is a weird mix of both.

An arrow whacks me across the arm, too hard to be entirely friendly. I whip my head around. "*Ow.* Malin, what the—"

"Come on." He whacks me again. "Let's find dinner."

I scowl, but I turn to follow. We stride through the brush, moving away from the fire and the low rumble of conversation, shifting into the darkness like ghosts. We slip between the trees wordlessly, our eyes searching the shadows for prey.

Malin doesn't speak, but I know from experience that he'll be silent as an assassin until one of us puts an arrow into something. Within minutes, we hear a rustle, and I nock an arrow on the string of my bow. We wait, and eventually a shadow shifts between the trees ahead. Maybe some elk, though they tend to stick to open fields. Deer, most likely, though it seems too small.

Before I can shoot, an ice-cold breeze rolls through the trees, and I go still. Malin is frozen in place beside me, his own arrow locked against his bow. His gaze shifts to meet mine. I let out a slow breath, watching to see if it clouds in the air—usually the first clear sign of scravers.

It doesn't. The air settles, making me wonder if it wasn't very cold at all.

For a long moment, Malin doesn't move. Then his eyebrows go up, questioning. He doesn't want to spook the deer, but I know what he's asking.

I glance up at the stars, but there's too much tree cover here. I could send magic into the air to see if anything is there, but if it's scravers, they'll follow that magic right back to me. I don't want to make us a target.

In the distance, someone laughs. It's not Jax, but we're too far for me to tell if it's Leo or Sephran.

I look back at Malin and give a little shake of my head, then nod back toward where we saw the shadow.

But this time, my focus is on the feeling of the air on my skin, on the night sky above.

Nakiis, I think, wishing I could speak mind to mind the way he can. I learned how to recognize the feel of his magic, but I don't sense it now. *Is that you?*

Another breeze rustles through the woods, and my heart jumps. But this one isn't cold at all. Those shadows ahead move through the trees, finding moonlight.

Not deer or elk at all. Wild turkeys.

Beside me, Malin's bow snaps hard. A second later, I hear the punch of impact, and the surviving turkeys scatter wildly, making a racket of squawking as they scramble through underbrush and attempt to fly.

I could hit another, but there aren't many of us, and I don't want to waste the meat. I let the tension out of my bowstring, then shove my arrow back in my quiver. "Nice kill. You didn't need me."

"Nah." He scoffs and strides through the trees. "But you needed something to do."

I sigh and follow, though he probably doesn't need help carrying one wild turkey. "That obvious?"

"Only to me." He reaches the dead bird and yanks the arrow free. "Seph too. Probably. Oh, and Leo. I don't really know Jax, but I'm sure—"

"Mal."

He grins, wipes the arrow in the brush, and shoves it back in the quiver. "Trouble in paradise?"

We're alone out here, and way too far for the others to hear, but I flush anyway. "I don't know." I hesitate. "I was gone so long. Maybe . . . maybe *too* long."

He picks up the bird by the leg and begins to walk back toward camp. "I'm sure riding fifty yards away from the group made that better."

"Shut up."

He whistles low, through his teeth. "And here I thought I was babysitting the *recruit*. I didn't realize I'd have to babysit y—"

I shove him in the arm and he chuckles.

Unfortunately we've come into view of the others, and I realize they're all looking at us. Leo's eyes are on the turkey, and his expression lights up. But Sephran's gaze is still cool—especially when he leans in to murmur something. Beside him, Jax's eyes go just as cold.

I nearly stop short.

"Silver hell," Malin mutters. He gives an aggravated sigh. "Come on."

"What?" I grumble. "Why do *you* sound annoyed?"

"Because a month ago, I could just pull a flask from my saddlebags and let you all work this out."

I flick my eyes skyward. "You still can, Mal."

"No. I'm a senior officer." He jerks an arrow out of his quiver and whacks me with it again. "That means I've got to deal with it."

This time, I snatch the arrow right out of his hand. "No. You don't. It's fine. *I'm* fine."

"Hey." Malin grabs my bracer, pulling me to a stop. We're still out of earshot, but the others can see everything we're doing. I'm very aware of Jax's gaze . . . and Sephran's. Leo is staring with the unabashed curiosity of a recruit who senses trouble.

"Let me go," I say, and the words almost come out like a growl.

For a moment, he doesn't, and I wonder if *we're* going to have conflict. The weight of honor and duty flicker between us. I'm not a soldier, so Malin doesn't outrank me. But I don't really outrank him either. Our roles are too different, our sworn obligations inconsistent. He's sworn to Emberfall—but I'm sworn to the king.

"Look," he says quietly. "I know I'm not in charge of you." His eyes flick toward the camp. "But I'm in charge of *them*."

In his voice, I hear the weight of his obligation—and I hear how deeply he feels it. There's a reason Grey saw fit to award Malin this rank, and I'm seeing it right now.

Actually, I saw it ten minutes ago, when he saw my distress, then dragged me into the woods to hunt for dinner.

But I also hear the heavy implication behind his words: I can be a prick and prolong this—or I can let him do his duty and lead his men.

This isn't a reprimand, but it stings like one anyway. I exhale heavily, my jaw tight. "I'll fix it."

"Yeah?"

I nod. "Yeah."

He lets go of my arm and claps me on the shoulder. We turn back for the camp.

Once we join the others, tension tries to cling to the air, but hunger takes priority, and for the most part, the soldiers ignore me. Leo helps Sephran field dress the turkey, and when they all vote for Malin to cook the meat, I don't protest.

I actually don't say much of anything at all. Malin's words are weighing on me. I don't want to be a problem he has to deal with, and I said I'd fix it.

So I sit, I eat, I keep my mouth shut. I listen to their gossip and hide my surprise at how much Jax participates—at how much Sephran and

Leo welcome him into their circle. I keep my eyes on my food and offer nothing of my own.

But the whole time, I'm keenly aware of Jax, sitting on the other side of the fire. The light flickers off his hazel eyes, sparking in his hair, gleaming on the buckles of his armor and the few weapons he wears.

My heart gives a tug, but I dodge his gaze. I wait for him to say something. I *hope* for him to say something.

He doesn't. So I don't either.

But all night long, I feel the weight of his presence all the same.

CHAPTER 11

JAX

When I lived with Da in Briarlock, we might've been poor, but we never had occasion to sleep on the ground. Aside from my week of travel to Ironrose Castle, I haven't had much experience with a blanket and a bedroll. Since the moment we rode out of camp, I've felt Tycho's tense focus, and combined with the hard riverbed, I can't get comfortable. It's as if his anxiety is a silent companion that won't stop kneeing me in the back. As it is, I don't really drift off until the first sparks of sunlight appear on the horizon, just as the soldiers begin to wake, donning their gear and tending the horses.

From behind me, someone gives my hair a gentle tug, and for a breath of time, I think it might be Tycho. My heart gives a wary little skip, hopeful. But then Sephran says, "Time to wake up, Archer."

I turn my face into the wool of my bedroll and make an unhappy sound. I don't want to be the only one lazing around, so I throw my blankets to the side and sit up.

And there's Tycho, sitting across the fire, tying his boots. His gaze is locked on his hands, every movement sharp and precise as he pulls at his laces, snapping them sharply around each boot hook, tying them off with cool efficiency before he jerks at the leather strap to fasten the buckle overtop.

He is very deliberately not looking at me.

Just like last night, when he was *also* very deliberately not looking at me.

Everything has unraveled so quickly between us. Yesterday, I showed up in the courtyard, wearing the new armor Prince Rhen had delivered to the Shield House, my stomach dizzy with butterflies. I was wrestling with excitement and uncertainty about being included with the others, especially since I don't have a clearly defined role here. I'm not a soldier—but I'm not just a blacksmith anymore either.

But Tycho's tone was so chilly when he asked me to join them. Does he resent my presence here? Maybe. He's hardly said a word since the moment we left—and even then, he wasn't exactly friendly. He issued orders like we'd never met, and his voice was so cold. *Do you need me to repeat it?*

Then again, maybe that's my fault. I did snap at him in the forge when he offered to translate.

My heart feels twisted up in knots.

I don't realize I'm staring at him until his eyes flick up and meet mine. For an instant, his gaze *burns*. My breath nearly catches.

But then he looks away, planting his boots in the dirt to stand.

I scowl and reach for the false foot and my own boots. It takes me longer to strap everything onto my right leg, so I can't go after him. I'm not even sure I want to.

My hair is a tangled mess from sleep, and I angrily twist it into a knot, jabbing a length of steel through it to hold it in place. Then I push to my own feet and head into the woods to take care of human needs.

It's only once I'm there that I realize Tycho would've seen Sephran tug at my hair. He would've heard his comment and the warmth in his voice.

Guilt flares in my chest. Against my will, I think of the night Sephran pressed me against a tree and kissed me.

It was nothing. It *meant* nothing.

You are not happy, Sephran said. My pulse thumps, confirming that.

When I return to the fire, it's clear that I'm slower than the others. They're fully armed, their horses mostly tacked, their bedrolls put away. Only Tycho is still saddling Mercy. My own breastplate and bracers are still in the dirt beside my abandoned bedroll.

Heat flares on my cheeks, and I rush to tug the armor on.

"Hey," says Sephran. "Slow. It's all right. Here."

I look up, and he's holding out an apple, along with a chunk of cheese that looks like he broke it off a larger piece. I give him a sheepish smile. "Thank you." I shove the food in my mouth, holding the apple with my teeth while I finish buckling the armor into place.

Malin was banking the fire, but he watches this interaction, saying nothing. I can't read his expression, and I'm still not entirely sure what to make of him. I've heard a lot of fond stories from Sephran, but not as many since Malin returned from Syhl Shallow with Tycho. It's clear that his new role has caused a little friction between the two of them. Last night, when Malin tossed the wild turkey in the dirt, Sephran waited until he turned away, then leaned close to me and muttered, "I guess the new captain is too good to pluck a bird."

I don't know if they've spoken to each other this morning, but based on the current chilly silence, I'm guessing not. Clearly the tension between me and Tycho isn't the *only* conflict among our group.

My bedroll is knotted tightly, so I pick up my things and head for the horses. Despite what Sephran said, I don't want to delay them.

When I get to the tie line, I discover that Tycho has saddled Teddy for me. He's just finishing the last buckle on his bridle.

I stop short, unsure what to make of this. Is this a kindness? Or subtle reproach for taking too long?

Tycho must have heard me moving through the grass, because he looks back. I have no idea what expression is on my face, but his demeanor darkens, and he gives Teddy a pat on the neck, then moves to pass me. In silence. Again.

I catch his arm.

He goes rigid, just like at the forge, and I think he might jerk free. Everything about him is braced for a fight.

I don't give him one. "Thank you," I say softly in Emberish.

The words hit him like a blow anyway, because it seems to knock the wind right out of him. He deflates—or maybe he sags.

But it's only for a second, because his face shifts into that perfect soldier neutrality again.

"You're welcome." He hesitates. "It'll be a long day if we're to make it to Gaulter by sundown. The terrain is rough as we get closer to the mountains, and if there's been rain, it will slow us down. We might need another night on the road."

I'm frowning, trying to parse out the unfamiliar words among the ones I *do* know. But after last night, there's no way I'm asking him to translate *now*.

Tycho can surely tell, because he hesitates, studying me. A prideful part of me wants to turn away. Any softness has already been erased from his expression, and anything he says is likely to be just as abrasive.

But his brown eyes are full of sunlight, and I still haven't let him go. A hint of contrition flickers through his gaze, and then he switches to Syssalah to repeat every word. He's very fluent, but his accent is always thicker when we're in Emberfall. The low timbre of his voice is pulling at memories, making heat crawl up my neck.

My mouth opens, but I have no idea what I'm going to say. A pulse in my chest makes me wish we were alone. I'd grab hold of his armor and drag him into the woods and we could resolve everything right now.

Before I can say a thing, he pulls free of my grip. Then he claps me on the shoulder like I'm just another soldier and turns away. "Mount up," he says in Emberish. "We're burning daylight."

It's like a bucket of ice-cold water, shocking and sudden. For an instant, I can't tell if I'm grateful or annoyed. Either way, it's clear that the order wasn't just for me, because the other soldiers are swinging aboard their horses, preparing to ride out.

So I take hold of Teddy's reins and do the same.

We take the same riding positions as we did yesterday, with Malin at the front, followed by me and Sephran, with Leo riding at the back. Again, Tycho takes outrider, and sometimes he's so far that he's a blur on the horizon. I wonder if that's deliberate, as if he'd completely abandon our group if he had the option. I know he's used to making this journey on his own, and the only person who doesn't seem affected by the tension is Leo.

Regardless, Malin continues setting a hard pace, making conversation impossible—though I don't really mind today. I'm not used to this much riding, and every muscle on my frame aches. As the day wears on, the midsummer sun beats down, and I begin to hate the armor. Combined with my lack of sleep and my uncertainty about Tycho, it doesn't take any time at all for my mood to turn to shit.

By midday, Malin calls for a break, and I'm grateful. A sick, cloying scent has been following us for miles, making me wonder if an animal died nearby. It's probably rotting in the sun. The horses' flanks are all damp, and Teddy thrusts his muzzle into the water as soon as I give him a loose rein. I swing off his back to scoop a handful of water to splash over the back of my neck.

Sephran appears beside me. His freckled cheeks are flushed from the heat, his sandy hair threaded with sweat. "*Tahlas*?" he says, which means *good* in Syssalah. It's one of the first words I taught him and Leo, and it's become a common back-and-forth between us. We have a variety of responses now.

Tahlas. Men tahlas. Nah tahlas.

Good. Very good. No good.

Just now, none of those seem to fit. I grunt noncommittally and scoop another handful of cold water to splash over my neck. I'm used to the heat of the forge, but this is altogether different.

Leo appears on my other side. He's also flushed and sweating. "*Nah tahlas*," he says, scrunching up his face at either the heat or the smell. He takes a handful of water and pours it directly over his head. "Ugh. Did a whole herd of deer die out here?"

Malin must be on the other side of Sephran's horse because I see another equine muzzle splash into the stream. "Tycho is checking it out," he says, though his voice doesn't reveal any strain. "We'll break for half an hour."

"Yes, *sir*," Sephran says, his tone brisk. Somehow he manages to sound both respectful and mocking.

It's clear Leo hears the tone in his voice, because he looks uncertain for a moment, but when Sephran flicks his eyes skyward, Leo grins. Malin can't see either one of their expressions, but I think I hear him sigh.

I don't want to add to the weird undercurrent of tension between them, so I draw Teddy away from the stream. As soon as I do, however, I realize that Tycho still hasn't turned to head toward us. He's a hundred yards away, still heading northwest.

Sephran sees me looking, and the grin vanishes from his face. He snorts under his breath and mutters, "If he wants to be alone so badly, just let him go. He can ride the rest of the way by himself."

I consider all the times Tycho mentioned his solitary rides, but I can't see him abandoning our small team. He's been tense and prickly since we left, but it feels like something he wouldn't do.

My frown deepens. "Tycho not leave us," I say.

Sephran scoffs. "I feel like he's leaving even when he's here."

Well, that stings—because it's true.

From behind us, Malin snaps, "Enough."

Sephran scowls. "Yes, *sir*."

I frown, but say nothing. I don't know if that's about Sephran's feelings toward Tycho—or about the growing conflict between him and Malin. Either way, I've spent enough time around the soldiers to know when they're obeying an order—and enough time to know when they're not.

"Seriously, Seph." Malin draws closer. "Knock it off."

"I'm not doing anything."

"Yeah." The captain stops on the riverbanks, until they're staring at each other from a few feet apart. "You are."

Sephran stares back at him and says nothing. A muscle in his jaw twitches.

Seconds tick by, until Leo glances between them, and eventually glances at me. I give a tight shake of my head, because I'm not *entirely* sure what this standoff is about.

No, that's not true. The coiling pit of tension in my gut says it has nothing to do with the ranks between Sephran and Malin, and everything to do with me and Tycho.

But Sephran sneers and says, "Stay out of it. This has nothing to do with you, *Captain*."

Then again, maybe *some* of it's about rank.

Malin sighs. "Look, Seph—"

Sephran scoffs again and turns away.

Malin draws himself up. "*Lieutenant.*"

Beside me, Leo gasps. His eyes are as big as saucers. Sephran jerks to a stop, because Malin's voice was sharp. A clear order. Until this moment, his tone's been a little lazy, a little ironic. An annoyed friend.

Right now, he's an officer.

Sephran hears the change, because his gaze ices over. "Captain."

"I said, that's *enough*."

The air crackles between them, and for a moment, it's brittle, as if one wrong word will cause a fracture that can't be repaired.

Sephran snaps his reins over his horse's neck. This time, he gives a sharp salute. His eyes are focused on nothing, and his tone could cut steel. "Yes, sir."

My heart is thumping, and I expect Malin to say something to ease the tension, but he doesn't say anything. Maybe he wanted this grudging obedience. I don't know him well enough to have any idea. Instead, he turns away from the water, looking out across the field. We all watch as Tycho pulls Mercy to a halt, then dismounts. He seems to study something on the ground—but only for a minute. Then he swings aboard Mercy and canters toward us. When he's fifty yards out, he whistles and makes a loop motion with his hand.

"Mount up," says Malin, his voice as tight and sharp as before. "We're riding out now." He already has a boot in the stirrup. The others shut up and obey.

If *they're* rushing, that means I need to do the same. I swing onto Teddy, glad I didn't loosen my armor. We're all on horseback by the time Tycho reaches us, and his expression is grim.

"It's a body," he says. "A royal courier sent by the queen, based on her livery." He repeats this in Syssalah without even waiting to see if I need him to.

"Scravers?" I say.

He shakes his head and looks back at Malin. "She took an arrow through the neck."

A chill goes through me, and my pulse jumps. With all the tension and bickering, I completely forgot that there's a risk here—that there's a *reason* Tycho is traveling with soldiers.

"Does it look recent?" says Malin.

Tycho frowns. "Within a day, probably. Whoever did it stole her weapons and armor. And whatever she was carrying, obviously."

"Aren't *you* the royal courier?" says Sephran.

I hate that his voice is so sour, but if Tycho notices, he ignores it. "Not for Syhl Shallow," he says. "Not anymore." He sounds a little hollow when he says that. He looks out and around the fields. "We're too exposed." He glances at Malin. "We need a plan, Captain."

Malin's eyes widen a bit at that, but he squares his shoulders and looks at Sephran. "Lieutenant, take point. We'll head for the tree line and ride in the shadows. We're less than five miles from the Twinwatch Outpost." He nods at Tycho. "You and Jax ride abreast. Leo and I will take the back."

He says more, something about a tight formation, but I lose track of all the military words. Or maybe I stopped hearing anything after *you and Jax ride abreast.*

I give Teddy a nudge with my heels, and he moves to walk alongside Mercy. My heart is still thrumming along, trapped in the space between whatever just happened with Malin and Sephran, and whatever's going on with the dead courier. I expect the soldiers to take off at a gallop, so I'm surprised when they don't.

Tycho hasn't said a word to me, and he's all hard edges right now. But I still want to know what's going on.

"We aren't running?" I say in Syssalah.

He glances over. "No. If someone is watching for couriers, we don't want to give the impression that we're spooked—or that we're carrying something of value." He nods in the direction of where he found the body. "If we were just soldiers on patrol, we'd simply make note of it and take the information back to our superiors. We don't want to look important. We want to look *boring*." As I consider that, he adds, "Do you remember the night we met?"

It's so unexpected that my thoughts stall on the question.

Because I remember every minute of that night. The glow from the forge. Sweet Mercy blowing warm breaths against my palm. The way Tycho pulled a forged blade from the wall and spun with it, making his cloak flare. I thought he was the most beautiful man I'd ever seen. I still do.

Tycho is still talking. I force myself to focus.

"You asked why I don't travel with guards," he says. "I told you that a lone man on a horse doesn't earn much attention," he continues. "But a man trailed by guards gets plenty."

I do remember that. I glance at his rich black armor, completely different from the gold-and-red-liveried soldiers.

Rich black, just like mine. "Do you think they targeted the other courier because she's from Syhl Shallow?"

"I don't know. I didn't recognize her. But Lia Mara wouldn't send someone without substantial training. It's possible she was ambushed. Something might have happened in Syhl Shallow—or someone might have known she was coming this way."

"So we might not be a target," I say.

"It's safer to assume we are. We have no idea what kind of message she carried." He nods out at the fields. "Look sharp."

His voice has a tone of finality. I look sharp.

Wind blows across the fields, bringing relief until that sickly sweet smell grows stronger. Months ago, when Tycho and King Grey defeated the Truthbringers in Briarlock, they spent hours stripping the bodies of weapons, then dragged them down the lane to burn them. I still remember Tycho's voice, cool and practical, as he explained how dead bodies get a lot worse before they get better. It was late spring, and I remember the smell then.

It's worse now.

Too late, I discover that we're riding right past the body. I don't want to look, but morbid curiosity forces my gaze down. I can't help it. The corpse lies unnaturally twisted in the grass, and I wonder if they shot her off her horse. Scuffed marks in the turf show where a horse spooked—or maybe tried to bolt. Her tunic has been ripped open, and streaks of blood are smeared across her bare chest. By the way her body is twisted and the clothing is torn, I can't tell if they violated her, or if they were just looking for whatever she carried. I know Tycho used to carry royal missives under his armor.

I jerk my gaze up and away from the courier's chest, because I don't want to stare at her body—but the rest of her is worse. Birds have already gotten to her eyes, because the sockets are empty, leaving dark, wet gaps in her face. Flies are swarming over the wounds, and some buzz near us. I shudder and shoo them away a little too aggressively, swearing under my breath. At the front of the line, Sephran glances down dispassionately, but behind me, Leo makes a sound of disgust.

Malin speaks up from behind Tycho. He keeps his voice low. "We never figured out what happened to your safe house."

I glance at Tycho, then back at Malin. "What happen to safe house?"

"I don't know," Tycho says in Syssalah. "When we arrived, it was burned to the ground. No sign of anyone. It could've been accidental—or it could've been deliberate. A trap . . . or an ambush." He pauses, then glances back at Malin and adds in Emberish, "That's at least two days' ride from here, though."

A trap . . . or an ambush. I swallow and look around again. Wind whips through the grass, sneaking under my armor to bring another wave of relief from the heat. Tendrils of hair pull loose to stick to the sweat on my cheeks.

The wind isn't cold, but I cast my gaze up anyway, searching the sky for any sign of scravers. Nothing—not even a cloud.

I shiver anyway. The courier's body left me feeling very unsettled.

I think of that day I fought alongside the king in Briarlock. *Breathe,* he kept saying. His voice was steady and sure, as if violence was just a part of the day, as simple as drawing water from a well. But the memory of that moment brings me reassurance now, because I draw a slow breath, then let it out.

Tycho looks over, and it's as if he's remembering the same battle through different eyes. "Fate has already drawn a path beyond this moment," he says softly.

He's talking about the potential for violence, but he could be talking about *us*, too. "Let's follow it through," I say, and my voice is a little rough.

He nods, his blond hair sparking in the sunlight. "Let's follow it through."

CHAPTER 12

CALLYN

Our ride away from the palace was full of tension and bickering, so I expect our return walk to be exactly the same. But it's not. Alek strides along beside me, and to my surprise, he doesn't say much of anything at all. The sun beats down on us both, allowing sweat to gather under my gear and collect on my cheeks, though he seems as unfazed and unruffled as ever.

His silence gives me too much time to think. It was clear that he was afraid of Igaa and Nakiis, but he didn't leave me with them. If anything, he seemed prepared to *defend* me.

That doesn't really match with the man who threatened to drive me out of Syhl Shallow a few short weeks ago.

When I glance over, his blue eyes are faraway, and he seems as lost in thought as I am.

"How long do you think it's going to take us to walk back?" I say. We've been quiet so long that my voice is loud in the air.

He blinks as if startled, then casts a look up and around, then points. "I know the angle of those mountain peaks. We're a few miles north of Ustus Marsh, I think." He pats a pouch on his belt, and coins jingle. "I can hire us a carriage back to the palace from there."

Somehow he still manages to startle me with his casual *wealth.* Maybe it's visible on my face, because he casts a glance my way and frowns. "Feel free to walk if you'd rather, Callyn. My intent was not to—"

"Stop," I say, realizing that he's no more responsible for his own privileged upbringing than I am for my impoverished one. I lift a hand. "Just . . . just stop."

He obeys, falling silent. But then I'm not sure what to say. We continue striding down the path.

Eventually, I clear my throat. "What should we do about Lord Tycho?"

Alek snaps his head around. "The king's lapdog?" he practically snarls. "Why would we do anything about him at all?"

I draw back, surprised at his reaction. "Igaa said—"

"I can't speak for you, Callyn, but I am not the scravers' errand boy. I meant what I said: they can take their issues to Emberfall. The king is there. The *magic* is there. If Igaa needs Lord Tycho so badly, she can very well go find him herself."

Something in the way he says that makes me think of the day Nolla Verin first smashed a fist into my face, and the way the king healed my injuries. The king talked about his days fighting from the other side of the border, and how he came to Syhl Shallow and realized all the soldiers here were really just doing the same thing he was: following orders and fighting for what they believed was right for *their* country.

"You really think that's the solution?" I say. "To just . . . send the problems over the border where we don't have to think about them?"

"Why are they our problems to solve?"

His voice is so pragmatic that I snap back. "Because . . . because . . ."

"Because why, Callyn? Magic was driven out of Syhl Shallow *years* ago. Queen Lia Mara tried to bring it back, and her plans for peace were admirable, truly, but—"

"Driven out!" I snap. "Not solved! It doesn't help anyone to shove danger through the mountain pass. The danger is still *there*."

"I disagree. It helped Syhl Shallow—and that is the queen's primary obligation, is it not?"

"Ugh." I look back at the road and keep trudging forward. He's so impossible sometimes. "I don't know that we can call it a victory if our queen's actions put another country at risk."

"So high and mighty!" he exclaims. "Were you not on the fields beside the queen as the scravers tried to kill every magesmith they could find?"

"Yes, but—"

"And Emberfall *has* a king. He has his own magic. Queen Lia Mara is responsible for protecting her own citizens. Let him protect his."

I set my jaw. I hate how he's always so wrong about everything while also being right at the same time.

He heaves a sigh. "Again, you turn me into a villain from your storybooks, when I've only ever told you the truth, helped you succeed, and saved your life." His expression turns darkly devilish. "Considering our intimate moments together, I suppose one could also add that I've made you—"

"Don't you *dare*." My cheeks flush as I remember exactly which intimate moments he's talking about.

He grins. "—very happy?"

Heat surges up my neck. What a rake. I refuse to look at him.

This time, when he sighs, it's less performative and more genuine. "Really, Callyn. What would you have me do? Locate Tycho? He has returned to Emberfall *with the king*. Ironrose Castle is a four-day ride from here—and that's if we set a hard pace. Shall we saddle a horse you cannot ride and go galloping off across the countryside?"

"We could send a courier," I say.

"Ah, yes. And what would the message be? 'Dearest Lord Tycho, your presence is required at once to save the life of a scraver who may or may not want to kill the king. But he promises to be good.' "

"No—of course not. But—"

"But nothing! Do you not understand that the entire reason Tycho had a job at court was because the courier channels are not secure for something of international importance?" He pauses, and his voice drops. "Do you not understand why I needed to pay you and Jax to secure messages for the Truthbringers at all?"

I inhale sharply, then stop. No, I really *didn't* consider that. Even when Alek was paying me and Jax, his messages were in code.

Jax. Again, I desperately wish my friend were still here. He used to be a short walk down the lane, and we talked almost every day. Now it's been months.

"The queen could summon Lord Tycho," I say to Alek. "Surely *she* could send a secure message."

"Have you seen the queen?" he says pointedly. "Do you truly want to ask her to send a message to her absent husband asking him to send his devoted little minion back to Syhl Shallow to heal a *scraver*?" While I consider that, he adds, "Especially when the whole reason he left was to take magic *away* from the Crystal Palace?"

It's my turn to heave a sigh. "So the queen sent us out to find information, and now we can't do anything with what we *have*."

"Of course we can," he says. "We can tell her what we've learned. We can share everything that happened."

"And then what?" I say, feeling powerless.

"And then we await her orders," he says, as if it's obvious—and I suppose it is. "For she is the queen."

Somehow I forgot about Nora.

When I return to the palace with Alek, I expect to find my sister engaged with little Sinna, maybe playing games in the nursery or out in the gardens. In other words, I don't expect to find my sister at all.

Instead, when Alek and I seek the queen, we find her in the royal suites. The young princess is nowhere to be found, but Nora is sitting at the small table with the queen. She hasn't changed out of her sparring gear, and in fact weapons are still strapped to her body, making her look like a young soldier who's here to give a report, not a girl I was chiding about licking frosting off a knife a few months ago. Her hair is still in those tight braids that she's fashioned to mimic Verin's, and her face has taken on a few angles that it never used to have.

When she turns cool eyes my way, I almost feel like I need to salute.

But then she takes in Alek. If her gaze was cool when she looked at me, it turns downright frosty when she looks at him.

Alek doesn't miss it. "Your Majesty," he says, deferring to the queen first. But when he turns back to Nora, his eyes go just as cold. He folds his arms. "Look, Callyn. I'm clearly your sister's villain, too."

Nora doesn't flinch. "Verin taught me how to rip an ear right off someone's head. Want to see?"

"Nora!" I snap.

But Alek grins. "You're welcome to try."

"No," says the queen, though her tone is long-suffering, as if she's used to this kind of verbal parry from Alek—and maybe her sister. "Save your bloodshed for the arena. Not my *nursery*."

"Yes, of course." Alek gestures toward the door. "Lady Nora? After you."

She's actually getting out of her chair, so I step between them and smack him on the arm. "Both of you. Stop it." I hesitate, glancing at the queen. "You are in the presence of the *queen*."

Queen Lia Mara simply picks up her cup of tea and takes a sip.

"Honestly, Callyn, I don't mind the bickering." She pauses, and a heavy note enters her voice. "It's a bit nice to have a distraction."

That throws a pallor over the room, and it's as if we're all affected—even Alek.

The queen sighs, and it's a sound full of remorse and resignation. "Ah. There it is." She gestures to the other chairs at the table. "Sit. Both of you."

The other two chairs are across from each other, so we both end up next to my sister and the queen. Alek moves to the opposite side and sits without hesitation, and my sister almost immediately reaches for his head.

Quicker than thought, he catches her wrist. "Now, now," he says. His voice drops. "You'll have time to kill me later."

"Promise?" she says, jerking free of his grip.

He just laughs.

Queen Lia Mara takes another sip of her tea while I stare at them like they're insane.

"You mentioned villains," the queen says to Alek. "I'm not sure I believe in them."

That gets everyone's attention. It's Nora who squeaks, "You're not sure you believe in *villains*?"

The queen offers a little shrug. "No, in fact. I've come to realize that most people truly judge their own actions as decent or necessary—if not downright noble."

My eyebrows knit together. "But . . . the Truthbringers *attacked* you."

"They felt they were protecting the people of Syhl Shallow—or at least themselves." Another half shrug. "I don't agree with their methods, obviously, but it helps me to understand their motivation."

The table is silent as we consider that. The queen's eyes shift to Alek, then narrow shrewdly. "You have thoughts, Alek. I can feel it."

"Yes, Your Majesty. Of course."

But that's all he says, and then he smiles, a little too pleased with himself.

The queen smiles in return, and it breaks through some of the melancholy on her face. I don't think I ever noticed it before, but there's a tenor of . . . of *friendship* between them. As if they have a history I was never aware of until this very moment. It's not romantic, because it doesn't have that energy. But it's like that moment in the trap when Alek mentioned being a little brother. It's an awareness. An understanding. A shared loss. A depth I didn't understand.

And all of a sudden, I realize why she once told me to hear Alek out. I understand why she sent me to visit him, as if she had no worries for my safety. I know why she sent him to fetch me from the arena.

There are no tricks here, no cunning, no guile. There's just an *ease* here. Not necessarily trust, but it's the comfort of family. Of being in the presence of someone you've known all your life.

In his silence, her smile widens. "You think I'm too altruistic."

He offers half a shrug that mirrors hers. "That's fair. You often think I'm too arrogant."

I snort under my breath. He definitely is.

The queen must hear me, because she laughs lightly. "If you agree with that, Callyn, then Alek is likely right about me, too." She pauses, and the smile slips off her face. She glances at the window, and I'm not sure what about the motion is telling, but I know she's thinking of her husband. "Perhaps I *am* too altruistic."

"*I* don't think you are," Nora says.

That brings the smile back. The queen reaches across the table to give my sister's hand a squeeze. "I hope you keep thinking that. Don't let Nolla Verin's cynicism rub off on you *too* much, Nora." She glances at me. "And don't let Alek's rub off on you."

"You don't have to worry about that," I say.

"Callyn has made her feelings *quite* clear," Alek agrees.

The note in his voice makes me frown, but the queen is giving Nora's hand another squeeze, and then she sits back in her chair. "I'm certain the two of you have news to report," she says to me and Alek, "but Nora was surprised to hear that you were leaving the palace together." She pauses, and there's a weight in the sudden silence. "Your sister was concerned that you'd never said a word about your continued friendship, Callyn."

Friendship. Is that what Alek and I have?

But as the queen says the words, I realize Nora is looking at me, and her eyes are dark with censure. She really has turned the corner to become less like an annoying little sister and more like a peer.

But the look in her eyes still slices right into me, and I let out a breath.

"Nora," I begin . . . but then I don't know what else to say.

In my silence, the queen says, "I told Nora that big sisters often keep secrets to protect the people they love."

"That's true," I say, but the words feel hollow. Because I wasn't *just* protecting my sister. If I'm being wholly honest, I was protecting myself, too.

Alek is listening to this from another angle, because his eyes are on the queen. "Do you keep secrets from Verin, Your Majesty?"

Her eyes narrow. "Oh, Alek, you're not even being clever." Without waiting for a response, she turns back to me and my sister. She gives Nora a wink. "Nora knows what secrets I've kept."

My sister smiles, a bit of sunshine peeking through the storm clouds of her expression.

But then the queen looks at me. "Alek can tell me what you've learned, Callyn. I suggest you and your sister go for a walk."

Nora's smile vanishes. She looks as surprised as I feel.

But she rises from her seat at the table, so I do the same.

It's so odd to walk beside her through the palace hallways. I don't really have a destination in mind, and I don't think she does either, but it's clear that sunlight and fresh air call to her. Or maybe she's just finding a place for herself among the recruits in a way I never have. Either way, we end up striding down the stone steps to one of the many heavy wooden doors that lead out onto the training fields.

She hasn't said a word, so I finally have to break the silence. "What secrets did the queen keep from her sister?" I say.

"Oh . . . just that she was falling for a man she shouldn't have." Nora's eyes flick my way. "She didn't want her sister to know, so she kept meeting him in secret."

That's so pointed that I nearly stumble on the path. "Oh, Nora!" I exclaim. A flush crawls up my neck. "That's not what I was *doing—*"

"I'm not talking about you, Callyn. That really is the secret she kept from Verin."

My head snaps around. "Wait. Really?"

She nods, keeping her eyes forward, avoiding my gaze now. It's like she doesn't *really* want to talk to me, but Nora can't help the allure of gossip. "Apparently King Grey was first invited to Syhl Shallow to wed Nolla Verin."

"*Really*." I try to imagine the stoic, formidable king paired with the queen's fiery and vicious younger sister. In some ways, I can picture it: they're both fierce and relentless on the battlefield, and I've never seen either of them flinch from conflict. But as my mind envisions them together for anything other than *battle*, the illusion crumbles. She's too antagonistic. He's too reserved. She's relentless—and he never yields.

"Yes," says Nora. "The queen told me that after King Grey and Tycho fled Ironrose Castle, she helped them cross the border into Syhl Shallow, knowing he was supposed to marry her sister to seal the alliance between our countries. I didn't know this, but before the old queen died, *Verin* was intended to take the throne."

"That's right," I whisper. "I remember that." Years ago, Mother used to talk about the younger princess being the queen's favored. I look over. "You see why I don't trust Verin. No wonder she's such a bitter burn. There's probably a part of her that resents her sister."

"She doesn't *resent* her! She spends her whole life making sure the army is prepared to *protect* her."

"If you say so."

Nora screws up her face, offended now that I've slandered her hero. "Fine. Forget it."

I sigh. She sighs.

We walk in silence for another fifty feet. But she wants to keep gossiping. It's *killing* her.

"Clouds above, Nora. Fine. I'll build a shrine to Verin tomorrow. What happened?"

Nora glances over, her eyes flashing, eager to finish the story now. "Queen Lia Mara said she fell in love with Grey during the journey, but the alliance was more important. So she kept it from her sister in an effort to protect her."

I wait for more, but that's all she says. A bee drones past us, and I wave it away. "*And?*" I finally prompt.

"The secret eventually came out," Nora says. "She said it was quite a relief. And then Queen Lia Mara took the throne anyway."

She falls quiet again, and I wonder if she's mad at me—or if she's implying that I should be relieved that she knows something about my secrets with Alek now.

But I really don't know how I feel.

"I'm not in love with Alek," I say.

She makes a little *hmph* sound. "Are you sure?" she asks sarcastically.

"I don't know *what* I feel about him," I admit. "But . . . it's definitely not love."

That makes her peer at me. "Oh."

I scrunch up my face and heave a sigh. "And I *was* trying to protect you, Nor. I never know if I can trust him. I never know if I can believe him. Until today, I don't think I realized that the queen trusts him."

She sighs, too. "Yes, I think she does, too. She says they practically grew up together. She knows he was involved with whoever was targeting the king, but she knows he's always been on her side. She told me that when she was a girl, she was always in the corner with a book while his family kept shoving him in front of the queen, but she definitely feels some kind of kinship with him." She peers at me again. "Maybe it's a bit like you and Jax."

Jax. My heart gives a tug. I desperately wish I had a friend who could understand how much my life has changed.

But then I glance over at my sister, and consider all the secrets I've kept—and it makes me wonder if Nora is wishing for the same thing.

I let out a breath. "I'm sorry," I say. "I shouldn't have kept secrets." I hesitate. "This isn't an excuse, but I . . . I keep forgetting that you're growing up."

Maybe I've spent too much time with Alek, but I expect her to scoff or hold it against me. I should've remembered that Nora has always been quick to forgive and even quicker to forget. She hooks an arm through mine. "You can tell me everything now."

She's right.

So I reach down and rip a few blades of dried summer grass from the ground, then hold them out between my hands.

Nora frowns. "What are you—"

"I'm starting with this," I say. "Watch."

And then, as we look between my cupped hands, the blades of grass spark and sizzle with flame.

CHAPTER 13

ALEK

Once Callyn and Nora are gone, I'm pleased to realize that they took most of the tension with them. Servants silently enter the room, attending to the queen, pouring us fresh cups of tea and adding small cakes and pastries to the table. Queen Lia Mara is quiet the whole while, her gaze fixed on the training fields below, her red hair gleaming in the sunlight. It's not overly warm here in the palace, but a hint of sweat has gathered on her brow. She takes a sip of tea once the servants step away, but I notice that she hasn't touched a single pastry. She's still a bit pale, but nothing like the shell of a woman I spoke to a few days ago.

"You're looking better, Your Majesty," I say quietly.

Her eyes flick to me, and there's a hint of cynicism in their depths, like she can't tell if I'm being genuine or if I'm mocking her.

"Truly," I add.

"I'm glad to hear it, Alek."

I gesture to the platter of sweets. "You're not hungry?"

She shakes her head. "Help yourself. You've always had a fondness for chocolate."

That's true, but the only reason she knows that is because she does, too. I'm surprised she's not eating, but I'm not going to needle her about it. Not now, when her mental state still seems so precarious and so much is at risk. I ease a small piece of cake onto my plate and take a bite. The sugar all but melts on my tongue.

"Did you send word to the king?" I say. "About the lingering threats from the Truthbringers?"

"Yes," she says. "I sent word the day we spoke."

I mentally calculate. A courier likely hasn't even made it to Ironrose Castle yet. Even if the king took immediate action and determined to return to Syhl Shallow, it would take time to move troops. Even if he got on a horse by himself—which is unlikely—it would take at least another five days. Likely six.

And that's if he would consider returning. It's very possible he would deem it too dangerous. He was a massive target for the scravers when he was here. None of that has changed.

The queen's expression is a bit pained, and I know she's reflecting on all the same things.

I doubt my news about Nakiis and Xovaar is going to be very reassuring.

She clears her throat and takes another sip of tea. "What did you and Callyn discover today?"

"My *intent* was to meet with other nobles," I say. "As you ordered."

"Should I take that to mean you did not succeed?"

"Correct. We were confronted by a scraver."

The queen nearly chokes on her tea, though she's well practiced in maintaining decorum, so she dabs at her mouth with a napkin and simply sets the delicate cup on the table. "*Alek.* I cannot believe you've been here for nearly an hour and this is the first you've spoken of it."

I lift one shoulder in a casual shrug. "I was unsure how candid to be in front of Callyn's sister."

Her eyes quickly skip over my form, as if I might've been shredded by claws and she somehow didn't notice. "Tell me what happened."

I hesitate, thinking of everything I bickered about with Callyn. Lia Mara has only just begun to find her footing again. I don't want to distress her more than necessary.

In my silence, her eyes narrow. "Just *tell me*, Alek."

I obey. The queen is patient, listening carefully, and she never interrupts.

When I'm done, she says, "When Sinna and I were captured by the Truthbringers, Nakiis saved Grey's life—and later assisted us in battle." She hesitates, her gaze returning to the fields. "He tried to protect little Sinna before we even knew there was a threat." A moment of sorrow flashes across her expression, gone almost as quickly as it appeared. Her voice goes a bit husky, however. "If Nakiis requires Lord Tycho's assistance," she says, "I must do what I can to obtain it."

My eyebrows go up. "But he wants Tycho's magic."

"I assumed."

I study her for a long moment, as if we're talking about two different things. "Your Majesty—you have already sent word to the king. If you bring *magic* back to Syhl Shallow, it will lure the scravers back."

"I don't believe the scravers are gone, Alek." She takes another tiny sip of her tea. "Just like I don't believe the Truthbringers are gone. When the king returns, nothing will change."

I frown, because she's not wrong. "How did you select your new envoy?" I say, wondering if she selected a soldier, or if she pulled someone from the nobility. Considering what I know about the Truthbringers, I can't decide which would be the better option.

"I walked among the soldiers and gave a dozen of them different missives to deliver to various recipients," she says. "None of them would know their destination until they opened their orders in private. Only one was sent to Ironrose Castle."

My eyebrows go up. “And who received that one?” I say, wondering if she’ll tell me.

“Lady Elisa Ruhl,” she says. “Do you know her?”

“No.”

“She was an officer in the army,” she says. “Nolla Verin spoke for her.”

Nolla Verin again. Every time I hear her name, I genuinely wonder if she’s working to protect the queen, or if she’s determined to put her at risk for her own desires.

But maybe my doubts are obvious, because Lia Mara’s eyebrows go up. “You disapprove of my choice?”

I hesitate.

“Alek! Just tell me!”

“I . . . am unsure of your sister’s motives.”

The queen cocks her head and looks at me. “Fascinating. Nolla Verin feels the same way about you.”

I scoff. No surprise there.

But I consider this new courier, and I wonder what kind of reception she’ll find when she reaches Ironrose Castle.

The instant I have the thought, I realize what the queen just said.

When the king returns.

I study her. “Did you ask him to return?” I say softly.

Her face freezes, and she looks away.

I *tsk* under my breath. I can’t help it.

“I am your queen,” she snaps. “You will not *judge* me.”

“I’m not judging you,” I say softly—though I am. It’s likely *clear* that I am. I reach out a hand and rest it over hers. “The king left to take magic *away* from Syhl Shallow. He left to *protect* you.” I pause. “Lia Mara. What if he says no?”

She goes absolutely still. But then she pulls her hand out from under mine, putting a hand to her heart. She closes her eyes and swallows, silence weighing heavily on us both for a moment.

When her eyes open, they're clear and piercing, though her voice is barely more than a broken whisper. "The king won't say no to me."

I think of the man who faced a dozen scravers and lived to tell the tale.

The same man who faced the onslaught of a hundred Truthbringers swarming the palace.

The same man who fought off a hundred assailants with an iron bolt through his leg in Briarlock, if the stories are to be believed.

I'm pretty sure a man like that could say *no*.

But before I can say a word, the queen's expression turns shrewd, and she says, "Would *you* say no to Callyn if she asked you for something?"

My breath catches, but it's barely a fraction of a second. I'm just as practiced in hiding my emotion and maintaining control.

But Lia Mara is no fool, and she reaches out to rest a hand over *mine* this time.

I grimace, but it shifts into a frown. *Would* I say no to Callyn?

No. I probably wouldn't. I couldn't even keep my vow to force her out of the palace.

The queen's voice goes very quiet. "Surely you know she's had to care for her sister most of her life," she says. "And I'm aware of how very desperate she was in Briarlock. I saw it with my own eyes."

I swallow thickly. Guilt flickers in my chest, and I don't want it there.

Because I saw it with my own eyes, too—and I truly did what I could to help Callyn and Nora. But it's more than that. I hear an echo of that bitter desperation every time she chastises me for riding a horse or calling for a servant or even just simply having coins in a pouch on my belt.

The queen speaks into my silence. "I don't get the sense that Callyn has known many people she could trust, Alek." She pauses. "But I believe she's come to trust *you*."

I look at the window myself. "Callyn might have trusted me once," I say, musing. "But I'm not sure she does anymore. We always seem to end up at odds."

The queen smiles, and something about it is a little sad. "My husband would say that fate seems determined to bring you together."

Any other day, I'd scoff, because we don't believe in fate on this side of the mountain. But just now those words lodge in my heart, refusing to budge, no matter how cynical I feel.

The door to the nursery swings open, and Princess Sinna comes running in, breathless, her wild red curls barely tamed. "Mama!" she says. "I counted fifteen bumblebees—"

She catches sight of me and practically skids to a stop. "Oh!" she cries. "We have a guest." Without missing a beat, and as if she didn't fly into the room like a tornado, she takes hold of her skirt and drops into a perfect, courtly curtsy. "Lord Alek! Welcome to my nursery. I am honored by your . . . your . . ." Her face twists into a scowl.

"Presence," Lia Mara whispers.

"By your *presence*," Sinna says primly.

"Your Highness," I say, smiling. I stand and offer her a bow. "Thank you for your gracious welcome," I say. "Did you say *fifteen* bumblebees?"

"Yes! Do you want to play Wolf and Stone with us?"

Before I can answer, Lia Mara says, "Unfortunately, Lord Alek has business elsewhere."

My eyebrows go up. "I do?"

"Yes." She pauses, her eyes holding mine. "Your duties this morning were interrupted, were they not?"

My duties . . . to see what I could discover about the Truthbringers.

"Are you still willing to find the information I asked for?" she says.

I think of that note I received from Lady Karyl, threatening the queen.

I think of everything I discovered from the scravers.

I think of Callyn, staring up at me fiercely, challenging me at every step.

I think of the fact that the queen has called for the return of the king, and that will make everything a hundred times more complicated.

But my queen is waiting on an answer, and I'm just as powerless to tell *her* no.

"Yes, Your Majesty," I say. "I am."

CHAPTER 14

TYCHO

We left the body hours ago, but I can't shake the feeling of a target on my back, and it's clear I'm not the only one. It's a new apprehension that's overridden the tension among our group. That courier could've been killed by simple bandits, but my gut says it's bigger than that. It's the way her body was left out in the open, like someone wanted it to be found. A signal . . . or a warning. Especially since Malin was right—we never did discover who burned my safe house. The Truthbringers have caused too much harm for too long, and it's too coincidental that the first courier sent by Lia Mara would be slaughtered halfway to Ironrose Castle.

I can't stop wondering what the queen's message would've said. Is there danger in Syhl Shallow? Could the scravers have returned? Regret flares in my chest as I think of Grey languishing in Prince Rhen's strategy room, worried for his family.

I loop Mercy back around to ride parallel to Malin. Jax glances over his shoulder at me, and I have to ignore the weight of his eyes.

Instead, I keep my voice to business. "We should send word to Ironrose," I say to Malin. "The queen sent a message that was intercepted. We have no idea what she might've said."

We also don't know what we might be riding *toward*, but I don't say that. I doubt I need to. Malin considers for less than a second. "We're not far from the outpost at Twinwatch. We could have them send a courier."

I hesitate, remembering the way soldiers in Syhl Shallow turned against the king. Prince Rhen warned about unrest, and I wonder if it's spread among the army *here*. He and Grey were just talking about sending more troops to the border.

I suddenly wonder if that's the right decision . . . or the wrong one.

I'm very aware that Leo might be facing forward, but he's listening to every word we're saying. Sephran probably is, too.

"Fall back," I say to Malin. Once he does, I drop my voice and say, "We don't know who killed her. I don't want to hand a message to an army officer who might just burn it."

His eyebrows go up as he realizes what I'm saying. "You're worried about the King's Army?"

I wince. "I don't know. But *someone* knew who she was. There were spies among the army in Syhl Shallow, so it stands to reason that there would be some here, too."

He lets out a breath through his teeth. "And a soldier from either side would recognize her livery." This time, he thinks for a long moment. "Do you want to turn back?"

Yes—but also no. Our mission suddenly seems more important than ever, and I'm not sure who else Grey could trust right now.

But then I consider all the codes the Truthbringers use, and I wonder if I can use them to my advantage.

"We'll send a message from Twinwatch, but I want to get closer to the border and see what we can discover," I say. I glance up at the sky. We have another night on the road before we'll reach Gaulter. I intended to camp, but with this new knowledge about the dead courier, I want to see what kind of gossip we can hear.

"Let's get room in Willminton for the night," I say. "We can spend a little silver and find out what the people are saying." I hesitate. "In the morning, you can have one of your men take a message back to Prince Rhen with what we've found. The rest of us will continue on."

Malin nods. "I'll send Leo."

That makes my chest clench—but I agree. He's the youngest of the group, and the lowest risk. As much as I'd like to send Sephran away, just so I can be rid of his attitude and the way he keeps touching Jax, I'd rather have a skilled soldier along if we're heading into trouble.

I nod. "Well chosen. We can have him strip his livery before he goes, too."

"Yes, sir." Malin draws up his reins. "I'll let the others know."

When we reach Twinwatch, I draft a brief message while the others stand guard. I wish I had my old seal from when I rode courier so Grey would have *some* way to verify it. As it is, the message itself is suspicious as hell, and I hope he can see through the words.

Father,

Mother tried to send you a message, but she's worried you didn't receive it. It may be best to send word to let her know. I will return soon, as promised.

You'll be pleased to know I saw Hawk from Rillisk on my journey. He asked after your knee, and I assured him you had no lasting complaints.

Be well,
Tycho

Mother and *Father* were code words for the king and queen.

Hawk was the name Grey used when he was hiding in Rillisk years ago, when we first met. When he was discovered, he was shot in the knee by a guardsman who's been dead for years. Hardly *anyone* knows those details, and it's the only thing I could think to include that would be innocuous enough to ignore but would definitely convince him that this letter came from me.

I address the letter to Noah, because he should've made it to Ironrose by now. It's a risk, because I don't know for sure, but a letter to the palace physician is a lot less interesting than a missive sent directly to the *king*. A curious soldier might not even care enough to open it. Either way, this is the best I can do. I seal the note with wax, hand it to the waiting captain, and say a prayer to fate that it makes it to Grey. Then we ride out.

It's only been a day, but exhaustion is already looming.

The stop at the outpost didn't take long, but we still don't ride into Willminton until after dark. We gave up our tight formation hours ago, and by the time we ride through the city gates, we've turned into a loose pack that unconsciously breaks into two halves: me and Malin out in front, Sephran, Jax, and Leo coming up from behind. It's not intentional—at least, I don't think it is—but it *feels* deliberate.

As we ride through the streets, I expect to find a hum of tension and unease in town, with suspicious glances flicking our way at every turn. Instead, Willminton seems sleepy and disinterested, the people going about their nightly duties quietly.

"You're from up this way, aren't you?" I say to Malin, remembering a story he once told me.

He nods. "Originally, yeah. My father used to be the captain of the army outpost a few miles northwest." He gestures toward the horizon. "I used to come up here anytime I had leave."

"Not anymore?"

He shakes his head. "Not in years. They shut down the outpost after the war was over. Not much need to guard the border after that. My father was reassigned to the south, near Castellan Bay, so he and my mother had to move. It's a three-day ride, so I don't get down there as much."

Interesting. I wonder if that's why Rhen suggested sending a regiment up here. Combined with the dead courier, a shiver goes up my spine. Not just because of Truthbringers or scravers. Because I remember the war. I was only fifteen, but the world seemed to turn upside down all at once. Grey and Lia Mara hoped for a peaceful resolution, but I went from wielding a pitchfork to wearing armor in a matter of months. I knew how much dissension and hostility were growing on both sides of the border.

I worry that it's happening again, and Grey's return is simply a bandage slapped over a festering wound.

"Is it always this quiet?" I say to Malin.

"Pretty much." He grins. "I told you I spent my time shoveling manure and learning Syssalah from prisoners. You think I would've been doing that if there were anything else to do?"

I smile and intend to offer some gentle ribbing in return, but low voices behind us catch my attention. It's the other three, and whatever they're saying must be amusing, because they're laughing under their breath. The instant I glance back over my shoulder, they all go silent and stony-faced.

Well, not all of them. It's mostly Sephran. But Jax loses the smile. Leo glances between them and sobers.

I inwardly sigh. Beside me, Malin's easy manner has evaporated, a scowl replacing his smile.

A good night's sleep will probably help everyone. Maybe we'll be able to find an inn or a boarding house with private rooms.

But no. The boarding house is full, and the inn only has *one* room available. One bed, one chair, one window. A small hearth that's cold.

When I scowl about it, the innkeeper shrugs at me. "Forgive me, my lord. We're coming into the harvest season. A lot of workers have come up from the south." He pauses, jingling the coins in his palm. "A few of them might be convinced to double up for the night." Another pause. "For a price."

Silver hell. I don't want to take a room from a laborer, but I also don't want to sleep on a hard wooden floor if I don't have to. Then again, I remember a time in my life when I would've been happy to share a room if it meant an extra coin in my pocket.

I toss another two silvers at the innkeeper. "See if anyone is interested," I say. Then I ask him to make sure a fire is laid before midnight, and we head for the closest tavern—which has the advantage of being a short walk down the road.

When we push through the heavy wooden doors, we're greeted by a low hum of conversation that gradually goes quiet. If we were ignored during our walk through town, we're not ignored here. Back at the inn, Malin asked if we should leave our weapons and armor, but I was still too spooked by what happened to the courier and what we might find. But this is a sleepy town, and it's clear that five heavily armed soldiers walking into a tavern is unusual. Now that two dozen pairs of eyes have turned to stare at us, I'm regretting my choice.

But then the barkeep slaps the counter and whistles through his teeth. "Is that Gregor's boy, finally back after all these years? How's your da? Still keeping well?" Without waiting for an answer, he turns his head and calls over his shoulder to one of the barmaids. "Look here, Wenda! Your long-lost love is back."

Across the room, a young woman with waist-length copper braids and bright freckles on her cheeks lights up. "Malin!" she squeals. "You came back."

Apparently, the barkeep's recognition has relaxed the tenor of the room, because the low rumble of conversation picks up again. But beside me, Malin's cheeks are turning red. "Silver hell," he mutters under his breath.

"I guess you found a *little* time to do more than just shovel manure," I say.

"I hate you."

Then Wenda appears in front of him, all but grabbing hold of his sleeve. "So many stripes," she breathes, batting her eyelashes up at him. "You must have accomplished a lot while you were gone. But I knew you'd be back."

I clap him on the shoulder. "Go catch up with your . . . friend," I say. "We'll find a table, *Captain*."

Wenda's eyebrows go up, and her voice goes even more breathy. "*Captain.*"

Malin glares at me, but I smile and look at the others. "Come on."

But when we reach a table, I realize that this has left me with Leo, Jax, and Sephran as my companions. When we sit down, silence drops like a blanket thrown over a fire.

I think of that moment when Malin caught my arm and said he'd have to fix this, and I said I would handle it. I guess that means I have to.

So I sigh and unbuckle a pouch on my belt, withdrawing a deck of cards—though as soon as I start to shuffle, I wonder what I'll do if they refuse to play. I hate that my thoughts are so full of *doubt.* I shuffle longer than I need to.

A different barmaid stops by the table, skirts swirling around her legs. She sets a basket of crusty bread in the center of the table, along with a small pot of honey. "Ale for you boys?" she says.

"Yes," I say gratefully. "*Please.*"

Maybe I sound too desperate, because Sephran and Jax exchange a glance, though Leo gives her a smile and says, "Sure."

Jax finally looks up. "Hot tea. Please."

"Same," says Sephran.

I have no idea why that sounds significant, but it does. I should be making easy conversation with the barmaid about the goings-on in Willminton, but instead, my thoughts lock on whatever just happened between Sephran and Jax. In my silence, the barmaid gives them a nod and scurries off, leaving me with an overly shuffled deck of cards in my hands.

I need a scraver to tear through the ceiling or Truthbringers to storm through the door or even just a random patron to start a barfight, because this is brutal.

My eyes stay fixed on my hands as I deal, snapping out the requisite cards for Mules and Mares. I brace myself, ready for them to shove the cards back at me—or, worse, simply ignore them.

But no, they all pick up their hands easily, reminding me that soldiers can quite literally be in the midst of a war, but a chance to play cards or dice is always welcome.

"Mules and Mares," I say to Jax. "Do you know it?"

He inhales to answer, but Sephran says, "He knows it."

His tone is sharp, and I really don't understand what I've done to cause so much aggravation. I can feel my hackles rise.

But Jax glances at him, then back at me. "Yes, Tycho. I know it."

Something in his voice pulls the aggression out of me. Every time he speaks Emberish, it's so unexpected. It's fascinating to hear his Syssal accent curl around the words, softening every edge. I wish things weren't so rocky between us, because I long to hear it *more*.

I clear my throat and look at my cards. I have a queen and a three—a mare *and* a mule—which is a fairly good hand. I chose this game because it's slow and calculated, with several rounds of betting, and it'll be easy for Malin to join us when he's done with Wenda. But when I toss a copper on the table and glance over, Malin has actually taken a seat at the bar, and he's talking to the barkeep now. Maybe they're catching up on old times, but I know Malin pretty well by now, and I'm sure he's fishing for information.

At least one of us is getting something done.

Jax tosses a copper to match my bet, but Sephran tosses two in the middle of the table, upping the ante. Leo raises his eyebrows and lays down his cards to fold.

Sephran is staring at me boldly.

Prick, I think. I toss another copper in. Jax glances between us and does the same.

Just then, the barmaid returns with our drinks. Ale for me and Leo, tea for Jax and Sephran.

I want to drain the whole thing and ask for another.

Instead, I just lay out the next card—a three, giving me a pair—and toss out another copper. Again, Sephran raises the bet to two.

Fine. I match his bet. Jax folds, leaving me and Sephran in the game.

I lay out another card. This time it's a queen, giving me two pair. My heart skips a little. The only way Sephran could beat me is if he had two queens or two threes in his hand, which is unlikely. Then again, he's been betting hard the whole time, so maybe he feels confident.

All right, then. He can prove it. I toss a silver onto the table.

"Whoa!" Leo whistles through his teeth. "Big money."

Sephran has gone still, and he's staring at that coin. For a moment,

I feel triumphant, thinking I've called his bluff, and now he'll fold. But then he scowls, still considering, and I realize the full impact of what Leo meant.

Betting a silver would mean risking a lot of money for a soldier, especially since he's already bet a handful of coppers. Meanwhile, I've been tossing down coins like they don't matter. Now *I'm* the one who looks like a prick.

Regret curls in my gut. I might have a good hand, but I didn't intend to shame him.

"Wait," I say, reaching out. "I'll take it back—"

Sephran knocks my hand away, the movement quick and aggressive. "Don't you dare."

"Fine," I snap. "Then call my bet or fold your cards."

He stares at that silver again, biting his lip. Then he swears under his breath and folds. When he tosses them down, they're faceup.

He did have two threes. If I'd had two queens, I would've beaten him, but I didn't. He could've won.

I frown, but he's already looking away, sitting back in his chair, ignoring me. Mules and Mares is a betting game—a *bluffing* game—but it doesn't feel like I've won anything at all. Instead, it feels like I bullied him into it.

I hate this, and we've only played one hand. I shuffle all the cards back into my hands, skimming them across each other to start a new deck. While I deal, Malin makes his way over, carrying a stein of ale.

He drops down onto the bench beside me as if he's completely unaware of any tension. "Mules and Mares?" he says. "Deal me in."

I do automatically, but I barely want to play myself anymore.

While I flip the cards onto the table, he drops his voice. "I talked to the barkeep. He said a lot of people are worried about the *creature* returning to Emberfall, but no one has seen anything in weeks. So I don't think they've had any scraver attacks."

"Good," I say absently. My attention is completely focused on Jax, who's leaned close to Sephran to say something low enough that I can't hear. A strand of hair has escaped the knot at the back of his neck, and I desperately want to reach out and tuck it back, the way I once would have.

The thought reminds me of the way I saw Sephran tug his hair nonchalantly this morning, and a spark of agitation rolls through me. I suddenly don't regret playing that silver at all.

"There are a lot of mixed feelings about the king, though," Malin continues. "It seems like some of the Truthbringer rhetoric has made the rounds."

That gets my attention, and my hands go still on my cards. "What does that mean?"

He shrugs a little. "They're wary of his magic. They're worried he could summon another monster to terrorize the country."

Leo goes a little pale, his eyes widening. "Could he do that?"

I shake my head. "No," I scoff, because the last thing Grey needs is his own soldiers thinking he's a potential threat.

But Grey could. I know he could. I've seen it.

Malin's eyes flick my way, and I know he hears the lie.

"Did you get the sense that any Truthbringers are here?" I say to him so we can move away from the king's magic.

"No," he says. "Not in Willminton. But Wenda said she's heard some gossip from Gaulter, because her sister lives over there. There's apparently a tourney there that draws people from miles away, and they've been seeing a lot of people from Syhl Shallow. She said they show up with silver to spare."

Huh. That's surprising. People from Syhl Shallow tend to have a disdainful view of Emberfall, especially among the nobility, so I can't really see them spending a lot of coin at a tourney. Gaulter is also the same city where I originally found Nakiis in a cage. Maybe that's significant.

And if it is, I wonder if we're potentially walking right into a hotbed of Truthbringers. Anyone carrying a bunch of silver is sure to be armed, and likely backed by guards. Lord Alek used to travel with two or three, and he himself wore as many weapons as a soldier.

"Do you still want me to take a message back to Ironrose Castle?" Leo says, glancing between us. "Or should I stay with you?" I can tell from his tone that he's hoping for the latter.

Malin glances at me. "Gaulter is another full day's ride, right?"

"If we leave at daybreak, we'll be lucky to make it by dinner." I hesitate, thinking. I hate to lose a soldier, and I already sent a coded message. But I still have no way to be *sure* the king will get it—and I didn't know about Truthbringers possibly gathering in Gaulter.

Just as I'm wondering if I could somehow send another message in code, Jax says, "In Gaulter, we will not be far from . . . from Crystal Palace." He says the words carefully, glancing between us, so I can't tell if he's unsure of the words or the distance. But then he adds, "And you can deliver message to queen." He hesitates. "Yes?"

"Yes," I say slowly, because it's not a terrible idea. We're closer to the Crystal Palace even here. I just don't know what's happening in Syhl Shallow, and crossing the border right now feels like a risk.

Then again *all* of this feels like a risk. It's the whole reason Rhen sent me with a small team at all.

Sephran is looking across the table at Malin. "Maybe our *captain* has an idea."

Malin flicks his eyes skyward. "Knock it off."

Sephran offers him a halfhearted salute and practically rolls his eyes in return. "Yes, sir."

"I said, *knock it off*." Mal's voice grows sharp, turning it into an order, and I watch the words land. Sephran draws himself up as belligerence and betrayal march across his expression.

I'd enjoy it if I hadn't just shamed him into laying down his cards.

"Yes, *sir*," Sephran says, and this time his voice is as tight and formal as mine is when I'm unhappy.

Then they just stare at each other, as if this is a standoff on a battlefield instead of a sticky table in the middle of a tavern.

Leo clears his throat. "So . . . um . . . am I going back to Ironrose? Or continuing on?"

Malin breaks the staring match and looks at him. "We'll continue on. Depending on what we discover in Gaulter, we'll send you back from there—or press on for the Crystal Palace." He looks to me for confirmation, and his voice is just as clipped. "Agreed?"

"Agreed," I say.

"Good," says Malin. He takes a hearty swig of his ale.

After that mess, so do I.

But then I realize Jax is watching me, his hazel-green eyes glinting in the light of the lanterns strung about the tavern, and I set down the stein. His eyes don't leave mine, but he picks up his mug of tea, blows steam off the top, and takes a sip.

Beside him, Sephran does the same thing.

CHAPTER 15

TYCHO

We're given a second room, which is a blessing—at first. After the tension in the tavern, I'm not sure *anyone* would've found sleep if we'd been trapped in shared quarters all night long. But then it occurs to me that we're going to have to divvy up the two spaces, and it simply serves to amplify the growing friction among all of us. It's clear Sephran doesn't want to room with Malin—and I doubt he wants to spend any time at all with me. I have no idea where Jax's preferences would fall, but I hate the thought of our clear division continuing. Poor Leo probably doesn't care, but I'm sure he's not ignorant to any of it.

So, in an effort to escape everything, I take first watch.

The innkeeper spoke true, and most of the rooms are occupied by men and women who've been hired for the harvest season. Unlike the tavern, which was still bustling when we left, the inn's sitting room was empty when we returned, everyone gone to bed or gone home. It's after midnight, so the main door is barred now, the desk abandoned. The clerk left a lantern burning low, but I sense that it's only because I'd taken a post near the front door and he didn't want to leave me in complete darkness. I'll have to toss another coin his way when we leave in the morning.

The thought reminds me of the way I bet that silver during the card game. I've spent too much time playing among officers and noblemen, so I forgot that throwing down a coin so casually would indicate an arrogance I don't truly feel.

The worst part is that it's not unlike the way Alek behaves.

As soon as I think it, I internally recoil. I resent the idea that I am anything like him at all. But this awareness leaves a bitter taste in my mouth that refuses to go away. I probably drank too much ale earlier, and that's not helping.

But the instant I have *that* thought, I remember the mugs full of tea that Jax and Sephran chose for some inexplicable reason.

Ugh. Maybe fresh air would help. I should walk a patrol anyway. I push off from the wall, pull my bow off my shoulder, and unlatch the door.

Once I'm outside, however, the air doesn't feel fresh at all. Heat still clings to the shadows, humidity making everything sticky. It's usually cooler this far north, but summer seems to have settled over Emberfall with a vengeance I can't escape.

Maybe it's a stroke of luck. Scravers hate the heat.

I can't say I'm much of a fan myself. Back when I worked in the tourney with Grey, we were two hundred miles south of here, and summers were downright miserable. I still remember the night old Worwick, the man who ran the place, showed up with a scraver in a cage. The creature was half dead from exhaustion and dehydration.

Iisak. My heart gives a tug, and I have to shrug it off. My friend has been dead for years.

I wonder what he would think of everything that's happened. Iisak wanted to find his son so desperately—and then when he did, he died to protect him.

This trail of thoughts is going nowhere. I have no idea where Nakiis is, and I have no idea what Iisak would think of any of this. He was always friendly, always fatherly, always kind and thoughtful in a way that Nakiis is . . . *not.*

But maybe that's not Nakiis's fault. He had his reasons for being wary of others.

Just like I do, I suppose.

These memories cling, and I try to shake them off. I walk a loop around the inn, letting the tiniest hint of my magic seep into the ground, seeking any sign of an enemy. When I'm near the back quarter, I check the stable. As I ease down the aisle as quietly as I can, the sleeping horses barely pay me any notice, with the exception of Mercy, who offers me a low nicker, hoping for a caramel. Of course I give her one. She presses her warm muzzle against my jaw, the heat of her breath sneaking along my throat to whisper under my armor. I pat her on the neck and move on.

But there's nothing. No sign of danger, no magic in the air, no whisper of sound to carry on the night sky. Nothing at all.

It should be a relief, and it *is*, but it's also a disappointment. I'd kill for a distraction.

When I cross the dark stretch of ground between the stable and the inn, a cool breeze whips between the buildings. The light shifts, revealing movement in the shadows. A person in the darkness.

Before I can think, I have an arrow nocked, the string drawn tight.

"Tycho!" The figure lifts its hands. "*Tycho.* It's me."

I freeze, then carefully loosen the bow, lowering the weapon to my side. "Jax," I breathe, because it *is* him, the shadows still cloaking him in the moonlight, though the stars find a tiny gleam in his eyes. His armor is gone, leaving him in a tunic and loose trousers. He's lucky I didn't shoot him. "Thank fate," I whisper.

"I not mean to scare you," he says.

"What are you *doing*?" I snap—and because I *was* scared, the words come out ten times sharper than I intend.

He looks a bit affronted, and honestly, I can't blame him.

"Looking for you," he says, his voice equally sharp. "What else?"

That makes me feel like an idiot. I jam the arrow back in my quiver and hang the bow over my shoulder. "Fine," I say. "Come on. I'm on watch."

Without waiting, I turn and head for the front of the inn. Jax falls in step beside me.

He walks with a slight unevenness due to the false foot, but it's more of a heavy step than a limp. It's fascinating to me that he's grown so used to it that he was able to abandon his crutches entirely. I still don't know the story of how it even happened. Did Rhen order it? Was it one of the soldiers?

Much like that little moment over the tea or the thickness of his accent when he speaks the language here, it serves as a reminder that Jax has built a life for himself that I know nothing about. Even now, we're speaking Emberish and I hardly even realized it.

As we turn the corner to come back around to the front side of the inn, there's more light. A lone lantern hangs over the doorway, the wick trimmed low. Down the road, the tavern hasn't closed up shop yet, because light spills through the windows. The voices of men and women carry on the night air, but they're faint. A horse is trotting somewhere in the distance because I can hear the clopping from here, though the road is empty all the way down the lane.

I don't know what Jax wants or why he was looking for me, but this echoing silence emphasizes just how vast the distance is between us.

"Can we sit?" he finally says. "Or you need to stand?"

I can't figure out his tone, and the defensive part of my brain wants it to be salty, antagonistic. But honestly, it just sounds like a question. I have to clear my throat so I don't snap at him again. "We can sit."

He doesn't wait for me, and he drops onto the top step that leads into the inn. As soon as he does, it invites the question of how close or how far *I* should sit, and I hate that my thoughts are so twisted up in deliberation and calculation when everything used to feel so easy.

Was it easy? Or did I just imagine it was?

Maybe he reads something in my shadowed expression because he sighs. "Tycho," he says quietly. "Sit. Just sit."

I don't know how he always does this, but a note in his voice loosens something inside me, tugging at an old memory. It was the first night we spent together, when every fiber of my being was drawn tighter than a bowstring. He was so patient and so careful in a way that unwound my worries and let me confess all my deeply buried truths.

And just like that, the low, easy timbre of his voice unwinds me now, because I drop to sit on the step beside him. Unexpected emotion swells to fill my chest and clog my throat. I can't breathe. I can't speak. I can't *see*. I press the heels of my hands into my eyes and hold my breath, because allowing anything else is going to turn me into a puddle in the dirt.

Eventually, my lungs are screaming, and I let out my breath in a rush. When I do, words fall out of my mouth. "I'm sorry," I say. "I'm sorry." The words are so broken that I can't even tell if he understands them. I switch to Syssalah anyway. "Jax, I'm so sorry." Then my voice catches, and I have to hold my breath again. My hands are pressing into my eyes so hard that it hurts, and my insides are clenched so tight I don't know how my heart is continuing to function.

For a moment there's nothing but silence, and then I hear him sigh again, a soft sound against the night. But he shifts on the step, and suddenly his hip is against my hip, his thigh against my thigh, his calf against my calf. His hand falls on my knee, and then, to my absolute shock, his head falls against my shoulder.

"Tycho," he breathes.

It's too much. The clenching in my chest stops my heart altogether. My lungs refuse to function. But I put a hand over his and hold it there like it's the only thing anchoring us both to the world.

Then he murmurs, "You're supposed to be keeping watch."

If *anything* could break through my emotion, it's that. I swear and jerk my hand away from my eyes, trying to focus.

Jax gives my knee a gentle squeeze, and I feel it all the way through my body. Any hope of focus is gone.

But he lifts his head from my shoulder and lets go, pulling his hand away.

I reach out and snatch it back, winding my fingers around his, pulling his hand to the center of my chest like a treasure.

He doesn't resist, but I can't look at him now. A part of me feels as though I've taken something that doesn't belong to me. My eyes are still hot, but I scan the darkness for danger, doing my duty. I hate that I broke down. A familiar belligerence has set up camp in my chest, like I'm waiting for him to jerk away, for that same tension to settle between us.

But he doesn't jerk away. His hand is so warm within my grip, his fingers loosely wrapped around my own.

I finally turn and look at him, and that's my undoing. His hair is loose over one shoulder, his hazel-green eyes so dark in the starlight, his face so close.

My breath catches again, and I have to let his hand go so I can give my eyes another frustrated swipe. I swear under my breath. It's humiliating that he's so calm and I'm practically . . . dissolving.

"Forgive me," I say, and it sounds like I'm speaking through gravel. "I didn't mean to . . ." I search for the right words, but none exist in *either* language. "Ah . . . completely unravel."

Jax looks out at the night and shakes his head slightly. "I did it plenty while you were gone."

Well, that just makes me feel *worse*. "Silver hell, Jax. I'm *sorry—*"

"Stop. I know." He glances over. "I'm sorry, too."

"You haven't done anything to apologize for. It's me. All me." As I say the words, I feel the truth of them so deeply. I'm the one who keeps leaving.

Jax says nothing for the longest moment, and he eventually looks at me. His voice is so quiet. "It's not *all* you."

Something in the words forces me still. Another cool breeze winds down the road, and I almost shiver. That happened the last time we sat in the darkness, so I glance up at the sky, thinking of scravers.

But there's no dangerous magic here. Just me and Jax and the weight of everything unspoken between us.

I want to grab his hand back and pull it against my heart and leave it that way. But if all my conflict with the king has taught me anything, keeping wounds hidden just lets them deepen and fester until they're nearly impossible to heal.

"Tell me," I say softly.

He stares out at the darkness again, his jaw set. His leg is still pressed into mine, and I can feel his sudden tension, the weight of words *he* isn't ready to say.

I reach out and take his hand again, pressing it over my knee, holding it there. "Please," I say.

He lets out a breath, and in the sound, I hear frustration. "It's not . . . it's not *fair*," he says. "You're beholden to the king. None of this is your fault. Not really."

I frown. "None of what—"

"I was *angry*, Tycho." He finally looks at me, and his eyes are full of fire. "I was lonely and homesick and you were just—you were *gone*. And then you came back and you were gone *again*. Every time!"

I swallow. "I know. I'm sorry—"

"*Stop*. I don't want you to be sorry. Like I said, it's not your fault. I just—I want—I want—" He jerks free of my grip and runs both hands back through his hair.

"Tell me," I say more firmly. "Tell me what you want."

"But why?" He scoffs. "It doesn't matter. I don't have any right to want anything."

"You *do*."

"Tycho, I *can't* want anything from the King's Courier—"

"Silver hell, Jax!" My own anger finally flares. "Just *tell me*."

"Fine." His eyes blaze into mine. "Stop leaving me. That's what I want. I want you to stop *leaving* me."

He might as well have punched me in the gut. Air leaves my lungs in a rush. I look back at the night and run a hand over my jaw.

We're both rigid, not touching now, staring into the darkness. Back where we started. The King's Courier, always alone, always beholden to someone else's needs. The poor blacksmith, always left behind.

But as I sit there and breathe, I realize that's not quite accurate. At least not anymore.

We're literally sitting here proving it.

I turn my head and look at him, then reach up to wind a finger through a lock of his hair. He looks so angry that I think he might punch me for *real*, but I give his hair a gentle tug, and it has the same effect on him that his voice has on me. The anger melts off his face. His eyes soften.

"I didn't leave you," I say softly. "This time, you came along."

He gives a little jerk, his eyes flaring wide, as if he's struck by that.

I wind another lock of hair, letting it slide between my fingers like a satin ribbon. "While I was gone, you learned to ride, to shoot, to speak Emberish. To *walk*, Jax. No one can leave you behind. *No one*. Never again."

He flushes, and I can even see it in the shadows. "I can't speak Emberish. Not yet."

I give him a look, and his flush deepens. "Well," he adds, "*you* taught me how to shoot."

"Not like you are now. I've seen you on the fields."

His eyes flick up to meet mine. "Yeah?"

"I can't keep my eyes off you." I wind another lock, letting my thumb graze his cheek this time. He leans into my touch, so I do it again. When my fingers brush his mouth, his lips part, and something inside me clenches tight.

"You're supposed to be keeping watch," he whispers.

"*Damn* it," I snap, jerking my hand down, turning my head to look out at the night.

But he moves closer, until we're pressed together again, his hand against my knee, his head falling against my shoulder. Down the road, a man laughs heartily, his voice booming, then choking off as his silhouetted form practically falls out of the tavern. A series of girlish giggles follow. Beside me, Jax shifts his weight a little, and then his breath falls on my neck, his hand sliding away from my knee to the inside of my thigh.

My breath catches at once. "You just told me to keep watch," I growl under my breath.

"Yes," he breathes against me. "Do that." His hand slides higher up my thigh just as his mouth closes on the skin below my ear, and fire spreads through my veins. Truthbringers could flood the street, and I'd sit right here, trapped by the feel of his hand. A low sound pulls free of my throat, and I reach up, catching another lock of his hair, giving it a harder tug this time.

As soon as I do it, a memory smacks me in the face: Sephran doing the same thing to him this morning. *Time to wake up, Archer.*

That throws an icy dart right in the center of all my warmth.

"Jax," I whisper, and he clenches his fingers into the muscle of my thigh in a way that nearly makes me forget everything I wanted to say. Especially when his tongue finds the skin of my neck.

"Why—why—" I inhale deeply and force my thoughts to organize. "Why does Sephran hate me?"

He goes still so abruptly that it feels profound. His hands are heavy against me, but it's like he's frozen. I draw back to look at him, and he straightens, pulling his hands back into his lap. My eyebrows knit together.

Jax frowns, then looks down. When he speaks, his voice is small. "Sephran doesn't *hate* you."

"Jax."

"He *doesn't*." Then he grimaces. Exhales. "Well . . ."

"But . . . why? I know he's upset about Malin's rank, but that's not my doing."

"No." Jax is quiet for a moment. "Though . . . maybe that's some of it." He hesitates. "Sephran has been a good friend. I was so . . ." His voice goes soft. "*Alone.* I was so alone. I don't know if this makes sense, but he . . . he saw it. He saw my sadness."

That tugs at me and makes me think of Malin, who saw *my* sadness. "It makes sense," I say. "But . . . why does he hate me?"

Jax's eyes glitter in the darkness, and his mouth twists. I watch him battle with what to say.

And in his silence, I think of the hair tug this morning. That quiet tone when Sephran speaks to him. The way he carefully translated after I was so sharp, or the way he said *same* when Jax ordered tea.

The way Jax went so still when I mentioned his name.

"Ah," I say softly, drawing back farther. Something inside me curls into a painful knot. "He's not *just* a friend."

"*No*," Jax says sharply. "Tycho. Stop. He *is* a friend."

Maybe I'm a complete idiot, but this is a conversation I didn't see coming—and now that it's here, I'm reevaluating every moment, every glance, every *word*. "He touched your hair. He ordered the tea."

"We had . . . we had a misunderstanding." Jax draws a frustrated breath. "He wanted more, but I didn't."

I've instinctively pulled away, but Jax grabs my arm, and his grip is tight, his fingers digging in. "*Tycho.*" His eyes are dark with censure, holding mine. "Sephran was a friend when I had *no one*. He was here when you were *not*."

That hits me like another blow.

In his voice, I hear the depth of his pain. I see a shadow of how difficult those months must have been.

The worst part is that I understand it. I remember my first months in Syhl Shallow, when no one trusted me. I didn't speak the language, and I had no friends. I was miserable and lonely and scared, and I spent every moment I could hiding in the infirmary with Noah.

He was here when you were not.

And now Sephran resents me for it.

It doesn't take the sting out of it, but it shifts. Changes. A dull ache instead of a stab.

Until I fixate on the rest of what Jax said. I tilt my head and peer at him in the shadows. "What do you mean, you had a *misunderstanding*?"

He's pulled his legs up to sit cross-legged on the step, and now he's fidgeting with his bootlaces, his expression fully in shadow.

My heart feels like it's plummeting through my chest, but there's nothing to catch it. I cannot believe the sheer spectrum of emotions I've gone through in the last fifteen minutes. I let a breath out through my teeth and stare back at the darkened road again. I don't know what to say. I don't know what I *want* to say.

Honestly, I don't know if I have a right to say anything at all.

Because I did leave. It wasn't my fault, but it wasn't his either.

I think of something Prince Rhen said to me months ago, when I challenged him to sparring in the arena.

Maybe it's time to leave old wounds behind.

Maybe it's time to leave new ones behind, too. Jax changed in so many ways while I was gone, but so did I.

Jax inhales to speak, but I reach up and rest my fingers against his mouth. "Whatever happened—Jax, you don't need to—"

He takes hold of my wrist and pulls my hand down. "*Stop.*" Despite the shadows, his gaze locks on mine. For a moment, he holds his breath, but then he says, "Sephran thought his feelings were returned. They weren't."

That catches my heart, setting it back into place, though it's not as secure as it was before. "Not at all?"

"No. Well . . ." Jax hesitates, then shrugs a little. "No. Just—"

He is *killing* me. I just said he didn't have to tell me, but now I'm going to evaporate if he doesn't keep talking.

"What?" I say desperately.

"Maybe I was curious," he admits. "Because you were gone so long without word. I began to wonder if you were ever coming back. I began to wonder if I was meant to be lonely forever, which felt . . . deeply unfair."

I clench my jaw and look away. All of that was Grey's doing. It was deeply unfair to both of us.

Anger flickers through my chest. So much for letting go of old wounds.

Jax reaches up and catches my chin, dragging my gaze back. "What I'm saying is that I wasn't . . . I wasn't curious about Sephran." He swallows, and his eyes are somehow full of sorrow and hope at the same time. "I was curious about what it would be like to stop missing you."

That's so profoundly sad that I reach up and take hold of his hand, then pull it to my heart. "Forgive me," I whisper.

"Tycho." He shakes his head slightly. "It wasn't your fault."

I let out a breath, then pull his hand to my mouth to kiss his knuckles. "It wasn't yours either."

His lips part, his eyes sparkling in the fading lantern light. This hasn't solved *everything*, but the tension between us seems to have drifted away on the night air. Something broke between us, but in a good way. Or maybe . . . maybe something broke *within* us. Something that needed to break. We're not a soldier and a civilian. We're not even a noble and a commoner. Instead of facing each other as King's Courier and blacksmith, I feel like we're truly on equal footing for the first time.

Then he brushes a thumb across the back of my hand, and a low pulse flares through my body. "How much longer do you have to keep watch?" he murmurs.

Malin speaks from behind us. "Until about right now."

Jax and I snap apart, and I swear. "Silver hell, Mal."

I expect him to laugh under his breath, or maybe offer some good-natured ribbing in return, but he doesn't. He just offers a displeased grunt. "I'll take over," he says gruffly. "Any problems?"

"Ah . . . no," I say.

He jerks his head toward the inn and drops onto the step as if Jax and I weren't just sharing a moment. "Get some sleep," he says tersely, his eyes on the darkness.

I wonder if he's annoyed at the way he found me. Grey would've lost his mind if he'd come to relieve me from watch and discovered me whispering with Jax. I open my mouth to apologize, but before I can, Malin glances over. "Sorry," he says, his voice suddenly contrite. "It's been a long day." He hesitates. "Spar in the morning?"

That's a habit we started on our first ride to Syhl Shallow. I nod. "Sure."

He nods, then glances at Jax. "You too. Get some sleep." He hesitates, then flicks his eyebrows at me. "*Real* sleep."

I smack him on the back of the head as we move away. Appropriately chastised, we leave a foot of space between us.

But the instant we reach the inn, Jax grabs hold of my armor and drags me into the shadowed depths of the vestibule. My shoulders hit the wall, and before I can react, he presses his mouth to mine and slips a hand along my waist, finding the gap in my armor. A gasp bursts from my lips, and I suddenly want to throw every coin I have at the innkeeper to find a private room for a few hours.

But then he lets go, well before I'm ready. I try to pull him back, but he puts a finger against my mouth and shakes his head. "We *should* get some sleep," he whispers.

I nod, still dazed. "You're right."

As he starts to pull away, I catch his tunic anyway, pulling him close. This time it's my hand finding his waist, my fingers tangling in his hair. He flushes in the shadows. "*Tycho.*"

"No. Listen." I tug him closer, then lean in, speaking right to his skin. "You don't have to be left behind, Jax. You don't have to be *alone*. Never again."

He looks into my eyes, then gives my hand a squeeze. "You too."

My breath catches. But then he gives me one last, quick kiss, and he lets go of my hand. "Good night. I'll room with Sephran so you don't kill each other."

That gives my heart a tug, but not like it would have yesterday.

But as I climb the stairs a minute later, I consider Malin's terse aggravation. Jax and I might have resolved things between *us*, but my friend is still fighting a battle with a man he once considered his best friend.

I stop at the top of the stairs, hesitating with my hand on the banister. Jax and I aren't the only ones struggling with loneliness on this journey.

So I turn back around and head outside to keep watch with my friend.

CHAPTER 16

ALEK

A new letter is waiting for me when I return to my House. I recognize Lady Karyl's handwriting before I've even fully unfolded the missive. For a moment, a bolt of alarm pierces my chest. Could she know I was asked to investigate the Truthbringers? I think of the guards lining the hallways the other day. We were careful, but listening ears are everywhere—I know that as well as anyone. And just this afternoon, Little Sinna came bursting into the room right when we were discussing the scravers. Someone at the palace may have overheard our conversation then, too. A tutor, maybe. Or one of the servants.

Again, I think of the queen's sister, trying to figure out where she could fit into all of this. Lady Karyl worked in the palace for a short time, hired as a governess for little Sinna. Could she have aligned herself with Verin while she was there? It feels unlikely—but a chill washes through me because it also feels *possible.*

There are too many questions and not enough answers. I tear open the letter.

Lord Alek,

The days grow warm as I await your response. We've been discussing Mother quite often lately. If you'd like to be a part of the conversation, you can find me in the south part of the city this evening, just near the bowyer's shop. I have a new friend I'd like you to meet.

If you don't show, I will assume your interest in our family has waned.

We will be forced to act accordingly.

-K

Well, that's not subtle. I don't know if that's a threat against me or against the queen, but neither is ideal. My eyes flick to the top of the letter, looking for a date, but there's none.

I call to the servant in the hall. "When was this delivered?"

"This morning, my lord."

Evening isn't far off. The south part of the city isn't far either, but much like the way *Mother* refers to the queen, Karyl's named location is another false clue. *South part of the city* has always referred to Bexcona, a small town located at a crossroads northwest of the Crystal City, not far from the Frozen River that separates Syhl Shallow from Iishellasa. The *bowyer's shop* is a reference to a large tree with a branch that bends in an arc like the curve of a bow. I've met her there before.

The air is still warm from the day, but another chill rolls through me. The river won't be frozen at this time of year, and the current clearly hasn't trapped the scravers on the other side as our childhood stories used to claim. But after what happened with Igaa and Nakiis—to say nothing of the scravers who attacked me and Callyn weeks ago—I don't want to go anywhere near Iishellasa.

But I sigh and grit my teeth, because what I *must* do rarely aligns with what I *want* to do.

"Send word to the stables," I call to the servant waiting for my orders. "Tell them I'll need a fresh horse."

The horizon is aglow with red and yellow as I gallop along the road, heading north. This is often my favorite part of the day in the summertime, when the effect of the sun through the trees makes it look like the mountain could be on fire. The horse's neck is slick with sweat, with every breath bringing a rhythmic little snort. I hate driving the animal so hard, but that last line of Karyl's letter keeps flashing in my thoughts. If she was willing to kidnap the queen in order to kill the king, I have no doubt she has mercenaries she can send after me. Like anyone else, I have guards protecting my House, but there's been too much double-crossing in the last few months. I'm not sure who to trust.

As the horse's hooves pound against the turf and the sun continues to set, I keep thinking of Callyn. Should I have returned to bring her with me? It would've taken hours, which feels reckless—and I'm not sure I want to reveal her to Karyl. Callyn feels like a point of vulnerability I don't need to expose.

But I wonder if this will feel like a betrayal. I never told her about the first letter.

And Lady Karyl represents everything I've done wrong in my efforts to protect Syhl Shallow and the queen. I don't want to reveal any of that to Callyn.

So I ride on, my heart pounding in time with the horse's hoofbeats.

I reach Bexcona just as the sun fully sinks below the horizon, painting the sky with streaks of red and purple, dousing the illusory flames beyond the trees. Dark clouds hang in the distance, promising rain tomorrow, but only bringing humidity now. I let the horse walk, and the animal's head hangs low, its sides heaving from the effort. If I want to return home tonight, I'll have to hire a carriage or pay to swap out for a fresh mount before I head back to the Crystal City.

The thought strikes me: maybe I should find a fresh horse *now*. An exhausted horse won't be the best means of escape if I need it.

I hate that I'm already thinking of escape.

But I shake it off. Karyl sent the summons, and I'm appearing as demanded. I've never given her a reason to think she can't trust me.

Though . . . she did plot against the queen without me. Lia Mara was never meant to be bait for the king.

That nagging worry in the back of my mind begins to poke at me harder.

When I reach the banks of the Frozen River, a cool breeze whips off the water to dry my sweat. The horse pricks its ears and nickers at the sight of the flowing water, so I swing off the animal's back, leading it to the edge. It's so hot that I can't help but crouch to pull a handful of water to my own lips. Then I take a handful and drizzle it over the back of my neck. When it trickles down my shoulders, sneaking under my armor, it's such a relief from the heat of the day that I immediately want to do it again.

But when I lift another handful of water from the river, it crystalizes in my hand. The ice forms so quickly that my skin stings. Sudden panic grips my chest, and cloudy breath bursts from my lungs as I try to fling the ice away.

I'm shocked when it gives without effort, ripping free from my hand to shatter the layer of ice that's suddenly formed along the riverbanks. The horse snorts in alarm, pawing at the swiftly forming crystals, trying to break through to the water below.

Rapid clouds of breath are blooming in front of my face, and I shiver. This time I can't tell if it's the cold or if it's the sudden burst of adrenaline. I whip around, my hand going for my sword. Grabbing the hilt feels like seizing an icicle, and I gasp, but I have the blade half drawn before I'm fully upright.

But there's no scraver behind me. Just Lady Karyl.

My eyes skip to the sky anyway, then the trees. I'm still breathing hard, and it's wild to watch my breath cloud in air that was nearly vibrating with heat a few minutes ago. But still—no scravers. Just an ordinary middle-aged woman I've seen a hundred times before. Fine clothes, elegant braids pinned to her head, noble stature. Her only unique feature is the mismatched color of her eyes: one brown, one blue.

But *she* doesn't have magic, so there has to be a scraver here. I finish drawing my weapon, and ice crawls along the blade, forming a vivid snowflake pattern that might be enchanting in any other circumstance.

Karyl *tsks*. "You look a bit panicked, Alek."

Well . . . maybe. It's been a long day.

But what's more startling is that *she's* not panicking. I remember the queen suggesting that the Truthbringers could've been working with the scravers, but I simply didn't want to believe it. I don't want to believe it *now*. I set my jaw and look up and around again. "Where is it?" I say.

"Keeping out of sight," she says. "Xovaar has grown tired of humans trying to kill him."

Xovaar. My heart stutters, and I fight to keep any hint of emotion off my face. "You're working with a scraver, Karyl?"

"I find it suits my needs," she says. "As I said in my letter, we gathered our best silver, and I discovered it was a lot more useful than I expected."

I swallow, my eyes continuing to search the trees. I don't know what that means, and I can't figure it out. But she's using our code, so I do the same. I bite back a shiver and say, "Your letter said you had plans to send Mother away. Is this scraver helping you?"

"In a way. He wants to reclaim his magic from the magesmiths. I want the magic gone from Syhl Shallow. I've made him my ally . . . for now. It was much easier than I expected. Had I known, we could've killed the king months ago in Briarlock."

My eyes flick to the trees again, wishing I could follow. "How?"

"By using the scravers, of course." She pauses. "I'm surprised you came. I was beginning to wonder if you were having second thoughts about your loyalty to the cause."

I need to play this very carefully, especially if Karyl has a scraver here and they're working together. The ice on my sword melts in the shadows, then immediately re-forms. The hilt is so cold my palm stings.

I give a short laugh—then worry it sounds a bit strained. "I've always been loyal to the cause."

"We were counting on your assistance when we took the queen, and you were nowhere to be found."

"I was in Emberfall," I say haughtily. "With the *king*. I had no idea you were making a move on the queen or I would've made myself available to you."

I'm lying through my teeth, and I hope it's not obvious.

She walks toward me. "Are you available to me now?"

I offer half a shrug, indifferent. "I can be."

"You *can* be," she says, sneering. "You're always so careful to protect yourself. Is that *why* you were in Emberfall with the king?"

A cold wind blows past me, kicking up droplets from the swiftly moving river. I don't want to shiver again, but I can't help it. The horse gives a slight tug at the reins, and I realize I'm a bit trapped here with my back to the water.

I need to stop thinking of this like an attack.

I step away from the banks anyway, moving forward so I'm on level ground as I face her. "I'm careful to protect the best interests of my *country*."

A whispering voice finds my thought, but it's not really something I can *hear*.

—He was not among those fighting on the fields.

I hate the way they can do this, because there's something so unnatural to it. I want to put my hands over my ears anyway. Even without sound, the words feel like they're coming from the right. I whip my head around, searching the trees for the scraver.

I spot him *there*, just near the upper branches of an oak tree. Xovaar has deep reddish wings and hair, and he blends with the brown and green of the tree effortlessly. He's at a distance, so I can't make out too much of his features, but the evening starlight glints on *something*. He's probably wearing weapons.

Against my will, I think of the scraver that attacked me and Callyn. The way its claws tore into me. The sound of its screech in the sunlight. It was a hot day, just like this one.

My mouth goes dry.

Another blast of cold wind blows past me, and I realize ice is forming on the buckles of my armor.

I'm better with a sword than I am with a bow, but my hands suddenly itch for an arrow.

"I was called here as an ally," I call to him, and I'm pleased that I can hold a note of disdain, even as my heart hammers in my chest.

Unfortunately, he can, too.

—I can smell your fear from here.

Lady Karyl smiles. "Are you afraid, Alek?"

"The scravers eviscerated more than fifty soldiers on the training fields," I say. "Are you *not*?"

"Xovaar and I have come to . . ." She hesitates and looks to the trees. "An agreement."

"There was a time when you wouldn't have negotiated with a scraver," I say. "As I recall, you believed they were under the king's control."

"I have discovered that they were not under his control," she says. "But now, aside from a few . . . shall we say, *stragglers*, these scravers share our goals. This one in particular shares my intent, and the others bend to his will."

Stragglers. I wonder if she's talking about Nakiis and Igaa. I cast another glance at the scraver in the trees, but he doesn't move. "And what goal is that?"

"I just told you." She laughs darkly. "To remove magic from Syhl Shallow, by whatever means possible."

"Magic has already been driven out of Syhl Shallow. The king is gone."

—The king is not the only one with magic, says the scraver. ***—I was on those fields. There were many magesmiths there that day. More than two, for certain.***

His voice in my head makes my skin crawl, and the fact that Lady Karyl is working with him feels almost like a bigger threat to Syhl Shallow than Grey ever was. I spare a moment to thank fate that the queen sent word to the king, begging him to return.

"Lord Jacob has already gone back to Emberfall," I say casually, as if they're worried about nothing and I can't understand the drama. "Lord Tycho is gone. So is the healer Noah. Who else could there be? We'll drive them out, too."

Lady Karyl frowns, her voice thickening with disgust. "His wife, perhaps? Why else do you think we've been targeting the queen?"

That nearly stops me in my tracks. "You think the *queen* shares his magic?"

"Why would she not?" Karyl says. "Why would the king share his power with others in his circle yet not his *wife*?"

"The queen lost a child!" I say desperately. "If she had magic, why would she not prevent such a thing?"

That seems to throw Karyl, because she's frozen in place, her brow furrowing. But it's only for a moment, and her expression smooths over. "Again, we aren't certain. Regardless of her abilities, the queen has a soft heart for magic—and it's clear that other magesmiths were there that day. Whoever they are, it's likely she allowed it. She cannot remain on the throne."

They plan to replace the queen? My thoughts are spinning. This was never—*never*—a part of my discussions with the Truthbringers. Our goal has always been to protect the queen.

"So what are you proposing?" I say, swiftly calculating in my head. It's been several days since the queen sent word to King Grey in Emberfall. If he agreed to return—which is still a big *if*—it would be at least another few days before he would arrive.

"We have already taken steps to cut off her contact with the king. We failed to stop the King's Courier last spring, but we've been more successful this time."

I go still. *More successful.*

"Oh?" I say carefully.

A smile spreads across her face. "Do you know," she says, "that in her missive, she was *begging* her husband to return? Our queen, so desperate for a man to stand at her side." The smile disappears as quickly as it formed. "It's no wonder she's destined to fall."

"You killed her courier," I breathe.

"It wasn't even a challenge. We cannot have the king returning to Syhl Shallow, of course, and when he fails to respond to her request, it will further encourage the division between them."

My heart won't stop pounding. If Karyl and the Truthbringers killed the courier, it means the king has no idea of what's happening here. It means there's no hope of assistance from across the border.

My eyes flick toward that tree, where the scraver is waiting, his taloned fingers wrapped around a branch. He bares his fangs at me, and my breath forms a thin cloud.

It means we'll be facing this scraver and his allies alone.

It means we'll be facing the Truthbringers *alone.*

"Are you insane?" I demand. "The queen will know, and our operations will be uncovered. She'll receive word—"

"Not for weeks," Karyl says, waving a hand. "And even then, I have friends in the palace, securing things from within." Her eyes narrow. "Such little faith. I thought I could count you among those friends."

Friends. Plural. A bolt of ice slides right through my heart. Could Nolla Verin be working with Karyl? When Lia Mara was kidnapped, Verin was left at the Crystal Palace, completely unharmed.

Even this afternoon, Verin wasn't in the nursery with us, but she definitely would've been told that I returned to the palace with Callyn—and she probably would have heard that I met with the queen privately afterward. It's entirely possible that Queen Lia Mara would have told Verin everything I reported about the scravers, right down to summoning Tycho from Emberfall.

And now Karyl is working with a scraver. Did I leave the queen in a more precarious position than she started in? At least there's no way Nolla Verin could have informed Lady Karyl of that by now.

I clear my throat, trying to figure out how to play this, but there is absolutely no clear path. "Of course I am your friend," I say. I look between her and the scraver again. "But this . . . this is unexpected. How can you trust him, Karyl? *How?* What if you remove the king and queen from power and he takes it for himself?"

Her eyes flash. "He cannot."

The scraver's claws flex on the branch, and I frown. "He cannot?"

"No." She smiles again. "As I said, gathering their steel worked in our favor. I figured out how to harness their magic—and how to master control."

She says it so callously, and for all my arrogance, something in me recoils. I think of all the reasons Nakiis claimed to be afraid of Tycho—and then of Callyn. I remember what Igaa said, how the magesmiths once used their steel to access the scravers' magic.

Sharing turned to stealing.

I swallow thickly and glance between them again. I have no idea how she did it, but Karyl must have figured out the same thing.

Magic by itself is terrifying. Magic in the hands of the Truthbringers is somehow worse.

"What do you need from me?" I say, and my voice is almost a rasp. I'm afraid, and I can't even hide it.

"You've always had the queen's ear," says Lady Karyl. "You're right—she did lose a child. So find out who else in the palace has access to the king's magic." She waves a hand. "Once we know who they are, we can eradicate them."

My heart stumbles, and I swallow to hide it. "And what will *you* be doing?"

"The same thing I've been doing for weeks. Gathering allies on both sides of the border. In fact, I have somewhere to be tomorrow night." She stoops to pick up a dried leaf from the ground, then holds it up. "I have plans to put in motion."

The skin on my forehead gathers into a frown. "*Plans*, my lady?"

As I watch, ice forms on the leaf, and my frown deepens, because it's no different from the scraver magic that I've already seen. "There are more scravers here?" I say, searching the trees again.

"No, Alek." She smiles furtively. "You see, the king isn't the only one who can share his power. The magesmiths and the scravers were once great allies. Weren't they, Xovaar?"

For the first time, the scraver doesn't answer. His black eyes stare down at me, and I can't read anything in them.

Karyl doesn't seem to need an answer. "There are ways to drive a magesmith out of hiding," she says. "Sometimes it takes a full-scale attack—but sometimes it just takes a little spark."

The leaf in her hand bursts into flame.

Even though she just warned me, I'm not ready. I gasp and stumble back. "Karyl. Do the others—do the others know—"

"They know," she says. The firelight flickers off her cheeks, painting shadows in the hollows under her eyes. "And they know this is a means to an end. I have secured a scraver's power."

I think of how many Truthbringers have shared a distaste for magic with me. "And the others are in agreement with this?" I say.

"Yes. They are ready to reclaim Syhl Shallow. The scravers are ready to reclaim their magic. Together, we can find and eliminate every last one of them, and then I will give the power back."

"Together," I echo, though I'm barely listening. My heart won't stop pounding, and my thoughts are racing. I'm planning how to get to Callyn without them knowing. I'm planning for how I'm going to get her out of the Crystal Palace.

I just don't know where to take her. Or *when*.

What did Karyl just say? She has to be somewhere tomorrow night? Would Xovaar go with her? Is that an opportunity? Or just an opportunity for everything to go wrong?

My pulse jumps. There are too many variables. Karyl has magic, and the king is gone. I have no defense against any of this.

I look back at the scraver, sitting on that branch, his razor-sharp talons gripping tight.

—Yes, says Xovaar, but somehow the word is hollow. ***—Together. And then she will return our magic to us.***

Well, if all I have is wit and arrogance, it's going to have to do.

My sword is still in my hand, but I wipe the gathered frost against my boot, then thrust it into the sheath. "Fine," I say, but this time, my voice is level. "I'll find your magesmiths."

"Good," says Lady Karyl. "It's time for you to prove which side you're on."

CHAPTER 17

JAX

When we ride out the next morning, the sky is overcast, heavy with unshed rain. The darker skies haven't brought any relief from the heat, however. I can't believe I spent years wishing I could have a chance to wear armor like a soldier. Now that I've spent two days sweating under the weight of leather and steel, I just want to leave it all behind.

Sephran was asleep when I slipped into the room last night, and when I woke hours later, Leo was in his place on the pallet beside me. The younger soldier was snoring away, the room flooded with sunlight, so I shoved him awake, worried we overslept. By the time we dressed and headed downstairs, the horses were saddled and ready. Tycho, Malin, and Sephran stood alongside, not speaking, their expressions stony.

I might have resolved things with Tycho, but it's clear no one else resolved anything at all.

We aren't riding as far today, and endless acres of crops force us to stick to the King's Highway instead of traversing the open fields we galloped across earlier. The roadway is crowded with workers and travelers going about their early morning duties, so we keep the horses at a walk and break into pairs again: Tycho and Malin at the front, then me and Sephran, with Leo holding the back. At my side, Sephran has been unusually quiet, but I'm not sure how much I can pry, especially when we're riding in such a tight formation. His expression seems permanently fixed in a glower, and I can't tell if he's more annoyed by Tycho or by Malin.

To his credit, Tycho has been coolly professional since the moment he handed me Teddy's reins. I don't know if he's worried about discretion since we're sharing such close quarters, or if he's trying not to stoke the tension with Sephran any higher than it already is. Maybe both. But before he turned away, he let his fingers stroke a line across my arm in a way that made me shiver, and I haven't been able to stop thinking about it. He's riding right in front of me, and every time I glance away, my gaze is called back by something new: the sun gleaming on the gold of his hair, the way his back narrows into his waist, the sway of his body as he moves with the horse.

Last night he pulled my hand to his chest like something to be cherished. Like he'd never let go. I almost melted into a puddle right there.

No one can leave you behind. No one. Never again.

The words lit me up inside, a glow that refuses to dim. If I don't stop thinking about this, I'll melt right off this horse.

Then I glance at Sephran. His eyes are shadowed with exhaustion, but his whole frame is tense. I don't think he's said more than ten words to me all morning.

I shouldn't feel guilty, but I do.

"Did you sleep?" I ask in Emberish.

He lifts one shoulder in a tense shrug. "I'm fine."

"You not talk?"

His head jerks in my direction. "I said I'm *fine*."

He's never snapped at me. My eyebrows go up. Malin looks back over his shoulder. "What's wrong?"

Sephran heaves a breath. "Nothing." He leaves a long pause, and his eyes flash with rancor. "*Sir.*"

Malin's eyes narrow, and I expect him to give Sephran a sharp order, the way he did during the card game. Instead, his voice drops. "Quit being such a prick, Seph."

Sephran draws up his reins, and the horse prances, responding to his tension. "Why don't *you* suck my—"

"*Hey.*" Tycho whips his head around. "Both of you. Knock it off."

Two middle-aged men are leading a pair of mules past us with a cart full of baled straw. They must hear the warning in his tone, because one nudges the other, and their mules seem to slow. They glance over with clear interest, one of them craning his neck around.

A group of arguing soldiers would've been high entertainment back in Briarlock, and I'm sure it's no different here.

Sephran's gaze shifts to Tycho. His tone turns as cold as steel, each word as sharp as a dagger. "Yes, my lord."

A young woman with a basket of vegetables is walking from the opposite direction, and one of the men with the mules leans close to murmur a few words to her. Her eyes widen, and we suddenly have her attention, too.

Malin has drawn a sharp breath, and he looks ready to breathe fire. Tycho reaches out to grab his forearm. "Ride on," he says.

Beside me, Sephran's horse jerks at the reins again, prancing sideways until he nearly collides with Teddy. "No," Sephran says. "Maybe we should just put an end to this right now."

Another woman on the road has joined the others. They've all come to a stop, and we're beginning to attract more attention. I think I hear one of the men say something about fetching the enforcers.

I have no idea what would happen if a group of uniformed soldiers started brawling in the middle of the road, but I doubt it would end well for any of us.

"*Ride on*," Tycho says, and the sharp note in his voice reminds me he used to be an officer, too. "Both of you. *Now*."

For an instant, the tension seems tangible, like a wire binding us all together—a wire that won't snap without bloodshed. Sephran and Malin are still glaring at each other, and beneath the exhaustion and fury, I see the real basis for all of it: regret and resentment.

Last night, I said that Sephran saw my sadness. Just now, I realize I'm seeing *his*.

I pull an arrow from my quiver and poke Sephran in the arm with it. "Ride on," I say quietly, echoing Tycho. "Ride on, Sephran."

He snaps his head around like he's going to fight with *me* next, but I just raise my eyebrows at him.

Sephran gives a disgusted sigh. "Fine."

Malin turns forward and gives his horse a nudge with his heels. "Fine."

The men with the mules and the woman with the vegetables quickly look away, busying themselves with their own duties.

From behind us, Leo mutters, "Silver hell," almost under his breath. "What *was* that?"

No one answers him. But once we're moving, Tycho glances back at me. He has enough sense to stay silent, but his eyebrows lift, just a bit, in question. *All good?*

I nod slightly, but I'm really not sure. I truly thought that was going to end in a fight—and that's the last thing we need right now. Not after the queen's messenger was executed. Not with scravers lying in wait. We have no idea what we'll face in the next town, and whether we'll have to press on for the Crystal Palace—where soldiers from Emberfall may not be welcome at all.

But Tycho turns to face forward, and we ride on.

By the time we ride into Gaulter, the heat and humidity have been weighing on us all day, and everyone is too tired to fight anymore. Tycho and Malin set out to secure lodging for the horses at the local livery, leaving me and Leo to walk to the nearest boarding house with Sephran. He hasn't said much since he almost picked that fight on the road, but this is the first time they've been separated all day. Once Malin is out of earshot, it's like Sephran visibly *deflates*.

"Finally," he says.

"You are so angry at him," I say.

"Not just Mal." He cuts a glance in my direction. "Both of them."

Oh. I hadn't really considered that. I frown.

"Mal and I were recruits together," he says. "We came up together, reached lieutenant together—" He breaks off and sighs, then scrubs a hand through his hair. His cheeks are so red from the sun. "This is stupid. It doesn't matter."

"Yes," I say. "It matter."

"No. It doesn't. Come on. Hopefully we can get some private rooms this time." He jerks a hand toward Leo, who's gazing down the road toward some serving girls who are sweeping the steps out in front of a bakery. When they notice his attention, they stop what they're doing to blush and giggle.

He doesn't seem to mind the attention, but Sephran whistles through his teeth and barks, "Leo!"

The younger soldier whips around, his expression aggrieved. The girls giggle again. Sephran softens his tone, but only a bit. "Let's go."

Gaulter is larger than the previous town, and we're relieved to discover that the boarding house *does* have single rooms available. Sephran slides coins across the counter and asks the clerk if extra firewood can be laid out. Then we head to the tavern to wait for Tycho and Malin. When we're sitting in a corner, it's like the remaining tension leaks out of Sephran's frame. He all but wilts in his chair.

He runs a finger along the edge of the table as a barmaid heads in our direction. "I might need real ale tonight."

"Me too," I say, though I'm not sure if I mean that. But Sephran looks like he needs an ally.

Leo grins. "I'm in."

When the barmaid brings the ale, it's ice cold, and I'm startled since it's so blisteringly hot outside. I gulp twice as much as I normally would.

She smiles at my reaction. "We hang the jugs down the well," she says. "Can I bring you boys anything else?"

"Dinner," says Sephran.

"We should wait," I say to him. "For Mal and Tycho."

His eyebrows flick skyward, and he takes a long swallow of ale. "Whatever."

The barmaid startles at my voice, then looks at me more closely. "You . . . you're from Syhl Shallow."

"Yes." I wince, realizing how thick my accent must sound to people who aren't used to it. We're closer to the border here, but I have no way of knowing if that means attitudes about my country are better or worse. So many people hated me in the palace that I wonder if I'm going to run into problems here, too. I try to enunciate. "I . . . sorry," I say. "My Emberish is . . . not good. Not yet."

"Oh! No, it's fine." She glances from me to Sephran and Leo and then back. Her smile turns furtive, and her voice drops. "I didn't know Emberish soldiers were here for the meeting, too. I don't speak Syssalah, but I'd heard—well." She pats me on the shoulder and leans in a little, as if we're all in on a secret. "When you're ready, dinner will be on the house, gentlemen. You're among friends."

I blink, puzzled, but she's already stepping away. For a moment, I can't tell if my confusion is because I didn't understand the words or if I don't understand the situation.

When I look at Sephran and Leo, they're both staring after her, equally nonplussed. "Help me," I say to them softly. "I not understand."

Sephran hesitates. For the first time all day, his expression isn't twisted up with angst and fury, and instead his eyes are lit with a hint of curiosity. "I'm not sure I understand either. She said there's a meeting." When I frown at this word, Sephran gestures in a circle around the table. "Like . . . *meet.* People meet together. A meeting."

"People from Syhl Shallow?" I guess. But then I frown. "Here? In Emberfall?"

"Maybe." He glances after her again, then scans the rest of the patrons in the tavern. It's still somewhat early, so the place isn't crowded. When Sephran looks back at me, he sighs, and for an instant, bitterness returns to his expression. "But I think we're going to need to wait to talk to the other two about this."

We don't have to wait long. Tycho and Malin come striding into the tavern while our steins are still half full. They both look tense and drawn, and for a brief moment, I'm reminded of the brittle tension that dogged me and Tycho for most of the journey. But his eyes shift my way and he smiles, and suddenly it's like I imagined any tension at all.

The rest of the world might be hanging by a thread, but he and I aren't at odds.

For now.

The thought hits me quick and hard, and I shove it away before it can fully take root. We have more important things to worry about anyway.

When they join us at the table, Tycho and Malin sit on opposite sides of me. It's obvious that Sephran is ready for Mal to pick a fight—and Leo is sitting here ready to watch. The bracing apprehension in the air is simply that thick.

So I attempt to slice through it before any aggression can truly form. "Tell them," I say to Sephran. "Tell them what she said."

That gets Malin's attention. "What who said?"

Sephran's gaze goes dark, but he repeats what we heard from the barmaid. When he gets to the part about a *meeting,* Malin and Tycho exchange a glance, and I can tell they're thinking of everything we heard from Wenda in the last town, about how nobility shows up at the tourney here, ready with silver to spend. I think of that slain courier again, wondering if that is somehow related to all of this.

While they consider, Sephran looks across the table at me. "Maybe you really *could* be here for that meeting."

My eyebrows go up. "Me?"

"Yeah. You are from Syhl Shallow. You'd know what they're saying at least." Before I can respond, his eyes narrow, and he glares at Malin. "I mean . . . if I'm allowed to make suggestions before our captain."

"You're allowed," Malin says, but he doesn't sound annoyed. He sounds like he's actually considering this.

"But I am no—I no—I *not—*" I break off, frustrated, tripping over my words because I have too much to say and not enough of the language to do it. I look to Tycho and switch to Syssalah. "I'm not from one of the Royal Houses. I'm not even born of the nobility. No one would believe it." I pat the pouch on my belt, and it rattles with a handful of coppers. "I don't even have silver to spend."

Malin must have understood most of what I said, because he looks to Tycho. "*You* have silver," he says in Emberish. He gives us both more of an appraising look. "And you're both in black armor."

I didn't consider that. Tycho and I are clad in the same black armor that the king's guard wears here in Emberfall—but it's not unlike the army livery worn on the other side of the border. It's not trimmed in the green and silver of Syhl Shallow's royal crest, but I doubt a barmaid in Gaulter would even notice that.

I glance at the windows at the front of the tavern. It's nearing dusk. I doubt *anyone* would notice it in the shadows. Back when I was shoeing horses in the shadows of a forge, I certainly wouldn't.

Tycho runs a hand across his jaw. "We still don't know who's *here.* Even if we pretend to be soldiers, someone from the Royal Houses might recognize me." He hesitates, considering. "Lesser nobles probably wouldn't, but . . . well, it's a risk."

"The barmaid is coming back," Leo says under his breath, warning in his tone.

Sephran and Malin exchange a glance, and in that one look, there's a spark of their old camaraderie. I've heard no shortage of stories about the pranks and hijinks they used to pull together, and I realize I'm seeing a flicker of it now.

Malin kicks Tycho under the table. "Speak Syssalah," he hisses. "Now."

Tycho gives him an aggrieved look, then turns to me. "So," he drawls. "How much longer do you think we're going to have before these two punch each other?"

That's so unexpected that it startles a smile out of me. "You think it's just going to be a punch?"

He scoffs. "I think it'll *start* with a punch."

Malin kicks him under the table again just as the barmaid steps up between him and Leo.

My smile widens. "Malin understands a lot more Syssalah than I remember," I say to Tycho.

He shrugs. "Our time in Syhl Shallow gave him a lot of practice." His gaze turns a little wicked. "He was all over Nolla Verin."

I was in the middle of taking a sip of my ale, but this makes me choke. "The sister to the *queen*?"

Tycho nods. "They kept trying to kill each other. For Verin, that's practically a love letter."

The barmaid turns to him. "I'm so sorry," she says, her cheeks turning pink. She speaks slowly and clearly. "As I told your friend, I don't speak Syssalah. But . . . ah . . ." She bites at her lip, waiting to see if he comprehends.

"I understand your words," Tycho says with such a thick Syssal accent that I almost choke on my ale again. "I speak some Emberish."

"Clouds above," I mutter. "That's terrible. Is that what I sound like?"

Tycho is still looking at the barmaid. "Ale for me, too, if you please," he says, his fake accent thickening further, which makes me grin. But then he glances at me and switches to Syssalah. "No," he says earnestly. "When you speak in any language, it's beautiful."

That catches me off guard, and a flush crawls up my neck. Tycho isn't teasing now, and he said it so plainly that it knocked the smile off my face. Honestly, it almost knocked me out of the chair.

Tycho's cheeks turn a little pink, but his brown eyes hold mine.

I have no idea how he erased three months of angst and longing and anger and uncertainty in twelve hours.

The barmaid is speaking now, but I'm barely listening. "I'll bring food quickly so you can make it to the tourney before dark," she's saying.

That makes Tycho look up. "The tourney?" he says—and it's clear he almost forgot his accent, because he tacks it on halfway through the word.

She nods. "For . . . the *meeting*," she says quietly, glancing at me.

"Ah. Yes." I nod briskly, as if we're all in on a secret, and I look to Tycho. "The tourney," I say in Syssalah, as if he needed me to translate.

His eyebrows go up. "Ah," he says. "The *tourney*." He offers her a grateful smile, and the barmaid nods helpfully, then rushes off.

Tycho turns back to me. A light sparks in his eye, and he adds, "You make a rather good spy, Master Jax."

Heat flares on my cheeks, and I have to take another sip of my ale. I cannot *believe* he ever told me he was bad at courtship.

Malin kicks him under the table again. "Maybe it was better when you two were fighting."

"We were never fighting," he says without looking away from me.

There's heat in his voice, but he adds that ridiculous Syssal accent again, so it startles another laugh out of me.

This time Sephran glances between us, and his gaze darkens. It's like his annoyance at Malin has eased now that they share a goal, but his annoyance at Tycho has returned with full force.

The smile falls off my face, and I take a sip of my ale. By the time the barmaid returns with drinks for Malin and Tycho, the table has gone stony silent.

Leo glances among all of us. "Does anyone want to play cards?" he ventures.

"*No,*" Sephran and Tycho say at the same time.

Leo cringes a little. "Silver hell," he mutters.

Malin takes a long draw from his stein, then looks from me to Tycho. "So you'll go to this *meeting*. See who's there. See what they're saying." He pauses, running a hand across his jaw. "If they ask why you were sitting with us, say we served together on the other side. We're on leave, but we share your sentiments about the king, so we were curious."

I glance from him to Tycho. "What . . . *sentiments*?"

When Tycho translates, I shake my head quickly. "No—what sentiments are we sharing?"

Malin drops his voice. "Probably Truthbringer sentiments."

"That you hate magic," says Leo.

"And the king," adds Sephran.

Malin exchanges a glance with Tycho, and for the first time a flicker of concern crosses his expression. "Not just that you hate him," he says. "Not if it's really the Truthbringers."

I look to Tycho, unsure if I'm following.

His brown eyes meet mine, and this time there's no heat there at all. "That we want him dead."

CHAPTER 18

TYCHO

By the time the sun sets, we have a weak plan that's full of holes. I've been to Gaulter's tourney before, and I first battled Nakiis right in the middle of the arena, so I don't just have to worry about Syhl Shallow's nobility. It's been months, so I doubt I'd be recognized by any of the regular citizens, but Journ, the man who runs the tourney, would definitely remember me. We worked together when I was young.

Malin, Sephran, and Leo are going to walk the crowd and attend as spectators. Some of that is part of our original mission: to see what kind of gossip they'll hear in the stands. But some of it is outright caution. If I'm recognized, or if this "meeting" goes badly in any way, I don't want to have to fight my way out alone.

I hate that the sun hasn't fully set, and I'm already thinking about this ending in a battle.

"You're very quiet," Jax says as we wind through shadowed alleys toward the tourney. We're alone again, because we don't want to be seen with the soldiers now, but there's a part of me that wishes we'd kept the others with us. I can't shake the feeling that we're being watched, that there's magic in the air, that something is *off* about Gaulter that I haven't yet figured out.

But maybe none of that is true. Maybe I'm just hot and tired and anxious.

"Tycho?"

"Sorry." The air is so humid and still, and despite the heavy clouds, it hasn't rained all day. I'd give anything for a breeze. "I was just thinking of everything that could go wrong."

"Oh, good. I thought maybe you were worried."

His tone makes me smile, and I glance over. Jax has re-pinned his hair in a tight knot at the back of his neck, and he's wearing a few more weapons than before, adding to the illusion of a soldier. No sword, because it's weight he doesn't need if he doesn't have the skill to use it, but a longer dagger hangs from his belt, and two knives are strapped to his thigh. I left my quiver with Mercy's gear, but he's got his buckled over one shoulder, his bow crisscrossed over the other. A faint sheen of sweat glints on any exposed skin, revealing the curved muscle of his forearms, the first slope of his biceps, the way his neck disappears into his tunic.

I didn't realize it until now, but it's more than just the armor broadening his frame. It's just . . . it's just *him*. Likely from the months of training with the soldiers. Or maybe months of eating better food than whatever he and his father were able to scrape together—which I know wasn't much.

"What?" he says, and I realize I'm staring.

I jerk my eyes forward. "Sorry," I say again, but now I'm tongue-tied, flustered. "I was just—I mean you—you look—" I break off and make the mistake of glancing over, and his eyes are dark and beguiling, making me wish we could go anywhere else and do anything else. I swear under my breath.

"I look . . . ?" he prompts, but there's a hint of mischief in his voice.

I shake my head and keep my eyes on the alley. "You changed so much, Jax."

He bumps me with his shoulder, and when I look over, he smiles. "You changed, too."

I was in the midst of smiling back, but this takes me by surprise. "Yeah?"

He nods—and he clearly wants to torment me, because he says *nothing*.

"How?" I demand.

His expression twists a little, as if he needs to consider that. "I'm not sure how to explain it. Less . . . something. More . . . something else."

"Oh. Well." My eyes flick skyward.

He bumps me with his shoulder again. This time he gives me a stronger *push*, so I shove him back. It's playful, but Jax has never backed away from a little rough-and-tumble. Neither have I, so for a second, we scuffle in the alley. But when his fingers brush my arm, there's a different intent to the touch.

"Don't start *that*," I warn. "We'll never make it to the tourney."

He must agree, because he sighs regretfully and hooks his thumbs in his weapons belt and faces forward. After a while, he says, "It's not quite *confidence*. You've always been confident." His tone is musing, so I keep my mouth shut, because now I'm curious. But after a moment, he says nothing, and I glance over.

"Tell me," I say.

He shakes his head a little. "I'm really not sure."

"Jax, you are *killing* me."

He grins. "Is that the tourney?"

We've turned a corner, and he's right. The tourney is just ahead. The building is larger than I remember, and it's early enough that people are milling about in all directions. We'll be able to lose ourselves in the crowd easily enough—though a Syssal accent will be obvious as soon as we speak. My heart gives a little kick. I don't usually play the role of a *spy*, and my thoughts keep whispering about the million ways this evening could unravel.

But Jax is by my side, and he just called me confident. My heart is thrumming with pride, too. I don't want to prove him wrong.

"That's it," I say briskly. "Let's go."

When I was here last winter, the tourney was crowded yet tolerable. Now that it's the dead heat of summer, the space is packed and stifling. As Jax and I move among the people, I have no idea how we'll find a meeting at all. I have no idea how we'll find *anyone*. An hour ago I was thinking about escape, but now I'm more worried about getting trampled.

Jax presses close, and at first I thought it might be a necessity from the dense crowds, but when his hand brushes mine, he grips my fingers for the barest second. I'm not sure what about the motion catches my attention, but I glance over. His expression is steady and cool, but his eyes are flicking from face to face, and a bead of sweat rolls down his forehead.

"Doing all right?" I murmur in Syssalah.

"It's so many people," he says. "I've never been anywhere like this." He shakes himself a little. "Was it like this when you were young? At your tourney in Rillisk?"

I grimace, then nod. "Yeah—but I could hide in the stables."

He looks over at me when I say that. Jax knows my history—and everything I ever had to hide from.

"With Grey?" he says, and his voice is so low I can barely hear him over the crowd. But he's right—and as soon as he says it, the memories flare. I'm suddenly fifteen again, feeling the press of unfamiliar people all around me, smelling the tang of spilled ale that's gone sour in the heat, hearing the low rumble of slurred voices that meant people wouldn't be thinking clearly. The man who ran the tourney in Rillisk was known to take a coin for pretty much anything, and I remember the spike of fear in my heart the first time I heard someone ask, "How much for an hour with the boy?"

I wait for that same spike of fear to find me now, because it always does when these memories invade my mind. Sparks and stars always flicker in my blood, my magic responding to the burst of panic.

But for the first time, there's no fear. Because I'm not fifteen, I'm nearly twenty. And I'm not hungry and hiding in the shadows, I'm strapped full of weapons and backed by soldiers. I don't need to hide behind the king anymore. I don't need to hide behind anyone at all.

Maybe this is what Jax meant when he said that I've changed.

I look into his hazel-green eyes and nod. "Yes. With Grey." I brush my hand against his, and this time, I give *his* fingers a squeeze. "Come on," I say, tugging him toward the outer wall. "Let's see if we can head toward the weapons rooms. We'll never learn anything this way."

He follows as I tug him through the crowd. Once we pass the narrow walkway that leads into the stands, the press of people thins out somewhat. The vendor stalls are back here, craftsmen and tradesmen calling their wares. I recognize a girl selling small painted figurines from the last time I was here, and I give her stand a wide berth.

The whole time, I listen carefully for Syssalah, and I look for signs of wealth and nobility. Unfortunately, all I hear is Emberish. All I see are sweat-stained tunics and dusty boots. The only coins that spark in the light are copper.

No one mentions a meeting, or the Truthbringers, or even the king.

I heave a sigh and look at Jax. "Nothing yet," I say to him.

He frowns. "Maybe the meeting isn't here?"

I shake my head a little. “The barmaid seemed so—”

I break off as a little scuffle erupts to our left. A boy of ten or eleven is shoving between people, and a middle-aged woman sourly grabs for his tunic.

“Come back here!” she snaps irascibly.

The boy slips past her, all but falling over his own feet as he tries to weave through the shifting crowd. “Sorry! Sorry!” he calls over his shoulder. “I’m late for the stables, madame—whoa!”

A man sidesteps to get out of his way, but clearly not quickly enough. The boy trips over the man’s leg and stumbles forward, trying to catch himself before he goes sailing into the dirt. When the woman shouts, “Stop him! Someone needs to give that young man a good lashing!” the boy abruptly changes direction and whirls, digging in his heels to bolt.

But instead of finding an opening, he slams right into Jax—who stumbles into *me*.

Luckily, the boy’s slight enough that he doesn’t send us all to the ground. I manage to steady Jax and grab hold of the boy’s arm, keeping him upright. He recoils instantly, spinning away from me, trying to jerk free like a lassoed horse. His teeth are gritted, his eyes wild. He looks over his shoulder like he can’t decide who’s the greater danger: the woman shouting about a “good lashing” or the armed man who’s got him by the wrist.

“*Easy*,” Jax says. He casts a disdainful glance in the woman’s direction. “We not hurt you.”

The boy ignores him, jerking at my grip again, and I realize we’re earning attention I don’t want. But just as I’m about to let him go, I freeze, recognition dawning.

I *know* this boy. He watched me let Nakiis out of a cage.

As he tries to twist free of the grip I have on his arm, I say, “Bailey?”

The sound of his name makes him startle, and he whips his head around, breathless. His eyes search my face for the longest moment, and then his eyebrows go up. "*You*," he whispers.

I nod. "Me." I glance up, past him. That woman is fighting her way through the crowd, shouting about putting him in his place, that he must be a thief. I remember the patrons like this. Based on the look on her face, she's ready to raise hell, just because an overworked boy was too busy to look where he was going. Bailey follows my gaze and cringes.

"She's coming this way," I murmur to him quickly. "I'll get you out of here. Fight me. Now."

Bailey isn't as quick on the uptake as Jax was earlier. His eyes flare wide, and he glances between the two of us, wetting his lips. I remember the last time I met him, one of the tourney's champions tried to backhand him into the wall. Just now, the boy doesn't look ready to be a co-conspirator. He looks like he can't decide whether to bolt or cower.

But Jax understands, and he moves closer, putting himself between Bailey and the woman. He gives Bailey a little shove on the arm, pushing him toward me. "*Fight*," he urges under his breath, his tone light. "We help you."

The woman has almost made her way through the crowd, and I give her a sharp nod. "Don't worry," I call to her, letting a stern note slip into my tone, almost forgetting my Syssal accent. "We take care of this one."

Some of the men nearby snicker knowingly, though one says, "Eh, he's just a boy. Go easy." But that's *all* he says.

It reminds me how it was when *I* was young, tearing through the crowds of an arena. They're all too eager to get a cold drink and a good seat, and all too willing to turn a blind eye and let soldiers—or anyone else—do whatever they want to the help.

Bailey still hasn't moved, so without waiting for a response, I turn away, tugging him after me as if we really are going to give him a good lashing.

Maybe I'm too convincing, because he finally *does* fight, twisting against my hold and trying to jerk free. I grip tight because I can't tell if he's playing along, but he's thrashing like a tethered animal. Then he swings a fist at the base of my rib cage, right at the gap in the armor.

"Silver hell, kid." We're definitely not working together here. I grunt and drag him between the gathering patrons. "I'm trying to help—"

He kicks me in the side of the knee. It's so unexpected that I stumble and my grip goes slack. It's enough time for him to twist free, but Jax catches him before he can dart off.

Bailey wrenches against his hold, too. "Let me *go*," he growls. An undercurrent of fear clings to his words, and I realize Bailey thinks we really *are* dragging him into the shadows to beat the piss out of him.

Unfortunately we've drawn too much attention now, and I can't let him go without drawing more. We're nearing a narrow alleyway that leads back outside, but it's so tight that it's not a practical exit—or entrance. I glance at Jax and jerk my head in that direction, and we tug the boy into the tiny gap. From the smell, it seems like it's mostly used by drunk patrons who need a place to relieve themselves, but it's quiet and empty, and we're away from the press and bustle of the tourney.

Once we're alone, Bailey's eyes shoot from me and Jax to the ends of the narrow space. He's breathing hard, and I'm half expecting him to try to punch me again.

Instead, he stomps on Jax's right foot.

Jax doesn't even flinch, because it's the false foot. He gives an aggrieved sigh, and his eyebrows go up. Bailey recoils a little, startled.

Jax looks at me. "Who is this?" he says in Syssalah. "Why did we grab him?"

The boy draws a sharp breath when he hears the foreign language, glancing between us again. "I'm not interfering with the meeting," he says in a rush. "I never said anything to anyone. The champions just need to get their horses out—"

"Relax," I say. "We're not trapping you here." I give a significant glance back toward the tourney. "I truly *was* trying to get you away from the woman calling for a lashing."

At that, Bailey blanches a little, and then he swallows. "You're the one who freed Journ's scraver. All the rumors said the king could control them, so I thought maybe that's why you let him . . ." His voice trails off as he glances down at my blank armor. His eyes widen fractionally when he sees that I'm not bearing the dual crests of Emberfall and Syhl Shallow anymore. His voice drops to a hushed whisper. "You no longer serve the king," he says. "Then why . . . why did you come back?"

I don't correct him. Instead, I touch a hand to his chin and tip his gaze back up. "What do you know about the meeting?"

"I know the Truthbringers oppose the king's return." He glances at Jax. "You spoke Syssalah. You're with *them*."

"Yes," Jax says. "I am from Syhl Shallow." His voice has such a cool assurance that it's a little startling—because it lets all of Bailey's assumptions hang in the air without confirmation or denial. It's like the way he immediately picked up on Malin's trickery in front of the barmaid, or the way he figured out that I was trying to separate Bailey from the crowd. I told him earlier that he makes a good spy, and I meant it—but seeing his easy competence in action is a little uncanny.

But then I remember that he was conning Lord Alek out of silver and passing notes of treason for the Truthbringers for *months* when we first met. The whole time, I never had a clue.

I've known the truth for a while now, but I haven't examined it from this angle, and the awareness pricks at me in a way I'm not expecting. It's intriguing—and a little frightening. I'm not entirely sure I like it.

Bailey is studying me in the shadows. "You're a Truthbringer," he says. A line appears between his eyebrows as if he can't quite figure me out. "Is *that* why you let the scraver go? You've been working with them all along?"

"If you can't tell us about the meeting, then we have to get moving, Bailey." I nod back toward the tourney. "Are you going to find any more trouble in the crowds?"

I meant for that to be a prelude to letting him go, but the boy must hear it as a veiled threat. He cringes a little, then shakes his head rapidly. "No," he says in a rush, like we're going to *make* trouble if he says the wrong thing. "No, my lord. I won't say anything."

All of a sudden, I'm reminded of the time I showed up at Jax's forge to apologize and bring him apple tarts, but he was wound up like a steel spring, thinking I was only there to beat the hell out of him.

The memory makes me want to send Bailey on his way right this very second, with a pocket full of coins for his trouble. But he's so keyed up and anxious that a part of me worries he's going to run right to Journ and tell him I'm here.

Jax must read the emotion as it crosses my face, because he speaks low in Syssalah. "He clearly knows about the meeting. Maybe he could lead us there."

"He's afraid of them," I say. "He could also ruin our cover."

Bailey's gaze bounces back and forth between us—though it's clear he doesn't understand, and that scares him, too.

"He's afraid of *us*, too," Jax says. A dark light sparks in his eye, and for one intense moment, he reminds me of Grey. The king doesn't revel in the darkest parts of soldiering, but he'll do what he has to when the need arises. The morning he confronted Jax in the shadows of his forge, Grey was ready to turn him into a sniveling pile of broken bones in order to get the answers we needed. For half a second, I wonder if Jax expects me to treat Bailey the same way.

Worse, I wonder if he might do it himself.

But Jax blinks, and the dark look is gone. "Make it so he's not," he says softly. He gives my arm a gentle nudge. "You're good at that."

I consider that, then turn back toward Bailey, holding his gaze. "When I freed the scraver . . . did you really keep it a secret?"

He nods vigorously. "I did! I swear to you, I did! I thought Master Journ was going to turn me out when I wouldn't say anything, but he didn't."

That sounds so earnest that I almost smile. "Good." I hesitate, hoping I'm not making the wrong choice here. "Can you keep another one?"

He inhales sharply, but before he says a word, I dip a hand in the pouch at my waist and withdraw five silvers.

Bailey's eyes go wide as dinner plates. "Y-yes. Yes, my lord."

"I'm not a Truthbringer," I say quietly. My eyes flick toward Jax. "He's not either."

"But . . . you're here for their meeting." Bailey's face twists as he processes this information. Realization dawns. "If you're not a Truthbringer, then who do you spy for?" he says, his voice lit with sudden intrigue. "The king?" His eyes skip down to my black armor. "Or . . . the queen?"

"That depends on what we find out," I say, and his eyes shoot wide again.

A roar goes up from the tourney crowd, which means too much time has passed since we dragged him back here. The first matches must be starting. Bailey looks worriedly toward the end of the narrow tunnel, and I'm sure he's very late for his duties now.

Jax automatically shifts, prepared to block his path, and the boy clenches his jaw. I wonder if he's going to aim a kick at Jax's knee next.

"Bailey," I say urgently. "It's important that no one knows I've been here before. If you're asked what happened, don't tell anyone you saw me. Just say some Syssal soldiers roughed you up and let you go when the tourney started. That's it." I jingle the coins. "Can I trust you?"

That gets his attention. He nods vigorously again, so I hold out my hand, dropping two silvers into his palm.

He frowns, closing his fingers around the coins. "What about the rest?"

I hesitate, weighing my options, wondering how much I can trust a kid—and realizing that even if I do, it's still not the most reckless part of our plan.

"If you want the other three," I say, "you have to earn it."

His eyes finally narrow. Maybe there's a little savvy practicality in there after all. "How?"

"You need to show us how to find the meeting."

He glances between us again. This must not be what he was expecting, because his mouth twists worriedly, and again he looks toward the end of the tunnel. Whatever Truthbringers have assembled here must be very intimidating.

Then again, I consider the way I first met him. I consider the way he fought to escape us.

Maybe everyone is.

His eyes are still tight with concern, but he says, "All right. I'll show you."

I let out a breath. "Good."

He puts out his empty hand, his expression shifting into determination. "But it's going to cost you six."

I almost choke on my breath, but Jax grins, then laughs softly. "I like this kid."

"*Six*," I mutter. "Honestly." I scowl and fish more coins out of my pouch.

Bailey still has a hand outstretched, but before I let go of the coins, Jax reaches out, closing his fingers around mine. He looks at Bailey and loses the smile. "Two first," he says in Emberish. "The rest when we get to *meeting*."

Bailey blinks at him in surprise, but then his expression sharpens. "Four first."

"Three." Jax takes a step closer, until standing turns to looming. His voice drops, that dark look returning to his eye. "And if you lie, we take back."

Bailey blanches again, and for a moment, he looks like he wants to throw all the coins back at us and be done with this altogether. But he gathers his mettle and gives a sharp nod. "D-done."

Jax lets go of my hand. "Pay him."

I sigh, wondering if this is a mistake. But I drop three coins in the boy's palm.

Bailey wastes no time. His fingers close around the silver, and without a backward glance, he bolts.

We weave through the tourney crowds again, but the press of people isn't as thick now that the arena competitions have begun. Bailey is small and nimble, darting between people well ahead of us. I lose track of him a few times, and I swear under my breath, but then he'll pop out from behind a vendor's stall or from behind a wooden post. Every now and again, the crowd in the arena will roar or groan, interspersed with wild clapping or the stomping of boots on the risers. There must be a sword fight now because the clash of steel echoes over everything.

I haven't seen Malin, Sephran, or Leo at all. A twinge of worry tugs at my heart.

"This is probably a mistake," I say to Jax.

"Probably," he agrees.

We've walked halfway around the tourney now, and I'm beginning to wonder where Bailey is leading us. But eventually we near the stables, because the scent of hay and horse sweat begins to overwhelm the reek of spoiled ale and the smoked beef of the food stalls.

And then, right there, a cold breeze whips through the air. It's brisk and sudden and gone so quickly that I almost wonder if I imagined it.

My magic recognizes it, however. *A scraver.*

I nearly stop short in the aisle. It takes everything I have to keep the sparks and stars from surging in my blood, sending my own magic flaring wide to find the source.

Jax grabs my arm. "Did you feel that?"

"Yeah."

"Is it—"

"Yes." I peer after Bailey, but he's still bounding ahead, his brown hair nearly disappearing in the crowd. If we lose the boy, I'll figure out a new plan, but right now, we need to wait. I need to *know*.

Jax searches my expression. I stand and listen to the sounds from the arena, feeling the heavy humidity in the air pressing down. There were dozens of scravers attacking the Crystal Palace last month, and there were rumors of others attacking in Emberfall. Ironrose Castle was braced for scraver attacks—would word have reached Gaulter? Would they have known to be wary?

But then darker thoughts curl through my head. I remember the way they kept Nakiis on a chain, making him fight battle after battle. I've seen the worst parts of humanity. I know what people are capable of when they feel righteous. Could Journ have another scraver here? Would the people of Gaulter be all too happy to have another scraver that they could torment in the arena, after all the scravers had done?

As we stand there, another cold breeze whips past us, lifting a tendril of Jax's hair.

He's watching my face so carefully. "Is it Nakiis?" he says softly.

"No," I say—and I'm surprised at the second pulse of worry in my heart. I haven't seen or heard from Nakiis since that day the king was attacked. "But I don't recognize the magic at all. There were so many scravers attacking the Crystal Palace. I have no idea who it is."

I glance after Bailey, but the boy is gone.

Silver hell. I frown. I heave a sigh and run a rough hand through my hair. Maybe this is all pointless.

Jax gives my arm a tug. "Come on. He went that way."

I yield to his touch, because he's right, we should keep moving. There are mysteries to solve, and I don't have anywhere near enough clues yet. But as we stride among the people again, his hand gives my arm a quick squeeze.

I look over, and Jax gives me a smile. "It's not *all* bad," he says.

There's a note in his voice that I remember from when I was a recruit, that naive eagerness for adventure that's eventually whittled away by the grimness of reality. My cynical side wants to scoff, because experience tells me we'll probably finish the night in a worse place than we started. But Jax has faced his own dose of reality, and more than once. It's a big part of why Prince Rhen sent him along at all.

So I just say, "Tell me if you still think that in an hour."

I expect him to scowl, because that's all *I* feel like doing. Instead, he laughs. Then, to my absolute shock, he hooks an arm around my neck and pulls me close. It's brotherly, soldierly—but also shockingly intimate, because a moment later, I feel the warmth of his breath against my cheek. For an instant I think he's going to kiss me right there in the walkway of the tourney, and I'm shocked at how abruptly my entire mind forgets literally *everything* I'm supposed to care about. There's only Jax and the weight of his arm against my neck.

"As long as we're together in an hour," he says against my jaw, "I'll still think it."

My heart pounds. If I turn my head, our lips will meet.

Bailey pops up out of absolutely *nowhere.* "What are you *doing*?" he demands. "I thought I lost you."

I jump a mile and almost shout. He's lucky I don't draw a dagger.

Jax is laughing under his breath again. He's let me go, and I don't even know when that happened. "Go," he says to Bailey, more sternly. "We follow."

"No," I say, trying to make my thoughts focus. I catch Bailey's sleeve. "Stop." I lean in and drop my voice. "Does Journ have another scraver?" I say.

He startles almost as hard as I just did—and then he cringes, his eyes skipping away. "No?"

"Don't lie to me. There's a scraver here. I can tell."

"I'm not lying." He wets his lips. "It's not Journ's."

"Then whose?"

He looks between us. "Don't you know? It's here with the Truthbringers."

CHAPTER 19

JAX

Earlier, I told Tycho that he'd changed, and I'm seeing the proof right now. As I told him, it's not confidence. It's a shift in his bearing. A difference in his composure. An equilibrium where before he always seemed like he couldn't *quite* find his footing.

When we first met, I didn't want to lie to him about Alek and the Truthbringers, but I had no choice. And even though I didn't *want* to do it, a part of me knew I could get away with it. Tycho has a generosity of spirit that's easy to exploit—which is probably why so many people have taken advantage of him. Despite everything he's been through, he was too earnest, too honest, too trusting.

But there's an edge to him now. Hard-won, like a blade forged in a fire that's not quite hot enough. It might not be pretty, but it's sharp, and that's all that matters.

Something about that makes me sad.

But it also makes me proud.

Tycho has a firm grip on Bailey's sleeve, and he jerks him a little closer, keeping his voice low. "The Truthbringers have a *scraver?*"

Bailey is staring up at him, his eyes wide and panicked. "I haven't seen it," he says, his head shaking vigorously. "But—but—"

"But what?" Tycho demands. "Do they have it in a cage like Nakiis?"

"Like *what*?" Bailey frowns, then wets his lips. "What . . . what's a *Nakiis*—"

"The other one Journ had," Tycho says impatiently.

"No. It—it—"

"Hey!" a man from one of the vendor stalls shouts from a ways down. He's peering through the thinning crowd. "What are you two doing to that boy?"

Tycho straightens, loosening his grip. Bailey immediately jerks free and *bolts*. He ducks between patrons and slips between planks in the wall.

Coins or not, I don't think he'll be reappearing.

"Silver hell," Tycho mutters. "I think we really scared him off that time." He looks up toward the man who shouted, and he affects that same terrible Syssal accent he used in the tavern. "He try to pocket my coins," he calls back.

"Now boy gone," I call to the vendor. "You pay us what he stole?"

The man's eyes flare wide in surprise, but then he grunts and turns away, busying himself with his wares.

Tycho snorts, but he runs a hand across the back of his neck. "We should keep moving," he murmurs in Syssalah.

"Are you worried about the scraver?"

"Yes. If I use any magic, it will sense me." He hesitates. "It's possible it already has."

"Can it recognize you, the way you can recognize them?"

He grimaces. "I'm not sure. But maybe—especially if it's one of the ones I fought before."

Another cold breeze swirls through the crowd, and this time it seems to linger. People around us shiver and look around in wonder, because the motionless heat was stifling.

"Is it looking for you?" I say.

"I don't know. Maybe."

I scan the surrounding people, looking for any sign of the other soldiers, but Malin, Sephran, and Leo aren't anywhere in sight. I wish I knew if that was good or bad or simply irrelevant. Could they have been captured by the Truthbringers already? Or are they just among the crowd somewhere else in the tourney?

But then I realize I might be asking the wrong questions.

"What happens if the scraver finds you?" I say, and my tone is grim.

"They want to kill anyone with magic, so it probably wouldn't be a joyful interaction. At the Crystal Palace, Grey and I could barely hold them off, even with Malin's help."

And right now, he's only got me by his side. I wonder if he's regretting that.

"Should we leave?" I say. "Wait for the others and regroup?"

He considers that, then winces. "I don't want to run when we're so close. Whatever we find, we can report to Grey . . . or to Lia Mara. If we leave now, we might not get another chance." He gestures ahead. "There can't be much tourney left. The crowds are thinner here. We have to be close."

My pulse skips a little bit, and I nod. But then Tycho looks over sharply. "Jax, if *you* want to leave, you can—"

"Oh, stop," I say. "I'm not leaving you." It's my turn to wince. "I'm just sorry I'm not one of the soldiers."

He bumps me with his shoulder. "Could've fooled me."

The warmth in his voice makes me look up, and I'm startled by the sudden glow in my heart. I nudge him back. "*Focus*," I say with a grin. "We might be dead in five minutes."

"*That's* the spirit," he says.

But then we turn a corner and realize we've reached the end of the tourney. There's nothing here. Just a wide-open door that leads to the grounds behind the massive arena. We're greeted by nothing more than starlight and tree trunks. Over in the shadows, a man is urinating against the side of the building.

Tycho lets out a breath. "I don't understand."

As soon as he says it, another cold breeze slips through the warm night air, winding around us before whistling along the edge of the building.

I inhale sharply. "The wind. It has to be close—"

Tycho slaps a hand over my mouth, then shakes his head fiercely. He taps his ear, then makes a revolving gesture with his hand, indicating the air around us. Finally, he taps a finger over his lips and mimes, *Shh.*

For a moment, I don't understand, but then I remember all the storybooks I used to read with Callyn when we were children. Every story featuring a scraver talked about their ability to wield the wind and sky with magic—but also their preternatural hearing.

I nod, and he drops his hand, letting me go.

The man finishes his business against the wall, and he yanks at the cord on his trousers. Tycho and I are rigid and silent, and I have no idea what the man thinks, but he barely gives us a passing glance as he heads back into the tourney.

"Windy tonight," he mutters as he goes by. Tycho just nods.

Once the man is gone, Tycho gestures toward the woods, but before he moves, he reaches out and tugs at the bow strung over my shoulder, then raises his eyebrows.

Oh. Yes. I suppose it would help to remember I'm armed. I grab my bow and yank it over my head, then tuck a few arrows against my palm for good measure. Then we head into the cloaking darkness of the trees.

Tycho is so silent that he could be an assassin. I don't know if it's army training or if it's just a natural vigilance, but the bare shuffle of my false foot moving through the underbrush seems very loud. Then again, so does the pounding of my heart. My brain is all too happy to remind me of the other scraver attacks I've survived. I still have wide scars across my jaw from the last time.

I don't want any more.

Another cool breeze swirls through the trees, and I shiver. I can't sense the magic the way Tycho can, but there's something so unnatural about it right now, with the heavy heat of summer bearing down on top of us. My hand has gone a bit slick on the bow, and I adjust my grip. Beside me, Tycho already has a hand on the hilt of his sword.

Then we hear the voices, and we both slow.

First, it's a man. ". . . is already here in Emberfall. The magic has left Syhl Shallow, but it could return. I've heard rumors that the queen is desperate for him to come back."

He's speaking in clear Emberish, with a thick, cultured accent—the way Prince Rhen speaks Syssalah. Like he's learned from books and a tutor instead of sheer desperation. I'm guessing he's of the nobility in Syhl Shallow.

A woman responds in kind. "While the queen sits on the throne," she says, "the risk of magic returning exists."

Another man cries out, and the lack of an accent says he's from this side of the border. "Well, we don't want him here either. We've already had enough problems with magic."

Beside me, Tycho has gone absolutely still.

A second woman speaks, her voice slower, more thoughtful, though there's an edge to her tone. "I have heard from my spies that the king's forces at Ironrose Castle aren't as fortified as they could be, as the king has been slow and distracted since returning. Perhaps while the king and queen are separated, we have an opportunity to resolve things in a way that will satisfy everyone."

Something about her voice sounds familiar, but I can't quite place it since she's speaking in Emberish.

"Just how are you going to do that?" another man calls.

In the shadows, I look at Tycho. My heart beats so hard that it's painful inside my chest.

He lifts a hand and gestures for us to move closer, then taps under his eye and points.

I think I understand. He wants to *see* who these people are.

Silently, he shifts between the trees, and I do my best to mimic his movements. I can't move like a ghost the way he can, however, and I wince every time my foot makes a slight drag through the pine needles and dried leaves littering the ground.

Ahead, a few torches are lit, because I spot the glow among the trees. The forest is too dense, so I can't make out any individual faces from here, but this "meeting" seems to be much more like a crowd. As my eyes scan the shadowed moonlight, I estimate at least thirty people standing in the woods.

A torch shifts, and I change that estimate to forty.

No, *fifty*. Maybe more. I swallow.

This isn't a meeting. This is a mob.

Then the woman says, "Xovaar, shall we show them how effectively we can resolve our difficulties?"

Tycho freezes, his hand grabbing my forearm, making us both stop short. That icy breeze whips between the trees again, lifting his hair and making us both shiver. Suddenly the tree trunks around us glisten in the moonlight, ice crawling along the wood before melting in the heat.

Then I hear the scraver's voice, though it's not a sound at all. It's words carried on the air, spoken right to my mind.

—We are not alone.

For an instant, panic clogs my thoughts, and I can't move. If we run, a scraver will be able to chase us—and so will everyone else waiting in this clearing. What if they have soldiers? Guards? I doubt I can outrun fifty people. I definitely can't outrun an arrow.

And that's if I can even run at all. I've grown comfortable walking on this false foot, but running takes a lot more coordination. If I don't land exactly right, the spot where my leg meets the wood sometimes slips or buckles, and I end up in a heap on the ground.

Boots swish through the underbrush. Someone is coming toward us. My eyes flash to Tycho's.

Run? I mouth.

He shakes his head and mouths two words back. *Kiss me.*

That cuts through my panic. There is absolutely no way I interpreted that correctly.

But then he grabs hold of my armor and presses his mouth to mine.

The kiss is aggressive and unexpected, and I inhale sharply ... before almost immediately melting right into him. Especially when he reaches up and tugs the pin that keeps my hair in a knot. My hair tumbles loose around my shoulders, and he buries a hand in the strands, tugging tight.

My bow hits the ground. The arrows fall a second later. I suddenly can't remember what we're even supposed to be running *from.*

"Shove me up against a tree," he murmurs, his breath hot against my skin. Before I can process that, he hooks his fingers in my armor again, then steps back, slamming himself into a tree. I have to reach up and brace a hand against the trunk so he doesn't yank me right off my feet.

"What are you—"

"Hush." Then he kisses me *again.*

My thoughts are trapped in a weird space between awareness of the Truthbringer meeting, fear for my life, and the fact that I would be fine if I died *right here.*

A man speaks from behind us, and his voice is a low growl of sound. "What are you two doing back here?"

Tycho draws back a little, and his face is cloaked in shadow from the trees. When he speaks, his tone is full of annoyance, and he's still using that ridiculous accent. "What does it look like?"

"Well, go find somewhere else to do . . . *that*." The man sounds equally annoyed.

Tycho sighs reluctantly. "I'm pretty sure we were here first—" But then his eyes shift past me, and I feel a sudden change in his body. Every muscle on his frame goes tense, all at once. Then he ducks his head a bit, almost pressing it against mine.

I have no idea if it's safe to speak. *What?* I want to demand. *What is it?*

"You were not here first," a woman says from behind me. It's the one from earlier, with the voice I can't quite place. She's closer now, and I start to turn, because I want to see her face.

But Tycho gives my hair a tug, and there's something significant in the motion. His eyes return to mine, and he looks like he's seen a ghost. "Fine," he says to her, though his eyes are locked on my own. Another cold breeze whips through the trees, and this time it makes me shiver. Is the scraver there? Is it right behind me?

"Come on," Tycho says, taking hold of my wrist. His gaze is piercing, but his voice is somehow calm. "We'll find somewhere else."

I search his gaze, wondering what I'm missing. "Sure," I say, trying to mimic his annoyance. "Whatever you want."

When he gives my wrist a tug, I follow. Curiosity gets the better of me, however, and when I duck to grab my bow from the ground, I look over my shoulder. A chill rolls through my body, because I'm terrified I'm about to lock eyes with a scraver just waiting to rip my throat out.

But there's no scraver, despite the icy wind.

Instead, there's the woman whose voice I didn't recognize: Lady Karyl.

The very first person who hired me to carry notes of treason against the king.

And the same woman who planned the first attack on the queen.

We plunge back into the tourney, and Tycho eventually lets go of my wrist to take hold of my hand. He hasn't said a word, so I haven't either. The crowd is still roaring in the arena, but my heartbeat overpowers it all. I have no idea how much the scravers can hear, and I doubt they can hear *anything* over the sounds of this crowd, but I don't want to be the one to break our silence.

The next time the crowd goes wild with cheers and clapping, Tycho glances at me. His voice is so quiet that I can barely hear him. "Did you see her?"

"Lady Karyl? Yeah."

He shakes his head. "Her name was Lady Clarinas—or at least that's the name she gave when the queen hired her to be Sinna's governess."

That nearly stops me in my tracks. I knew Lady Karyl—or Lady Clarinas—was involved in the first attack on the queen, but I had no idea she'd been in the palace itself. "She was Princess Sinna's *governess*?"

"Yes." His expression twists. "The scraver Nakiis knew she was bad, too—or at least I think he did. He tried to lead Sinna away." He frowns, a deeper sadness darkening his eyes. "That's what led to the queen eventually losing the baby."

And that's why the king left Syhl Shallow at all. To give the queen and his daughter a chance at safety. I give Tycho's hand a squeeze. "They're plotting against the king and queen again."

"Yes." He hesitates. "I wonder if the queen knows. I wonder if that's why she sent a courier."

An urgency rings under every word, but it's completely at odds with his unhurried pace. "Then why aren't we *running*?"

Tycho scowls. "If we go tearing out of here, that scraver *will* hear it. We don't need him chasing us." He pauses. "We'll leave quietly and make a plan. I wish we'd had one more minute to hear what they were planning. We might have to split up and send word in both directions."

"Have you seen him before?" I say. "Xov—"

"*Don't* say his name." He casts a glance over his shoulder, as if the scraver might have followed us into the crowds. "I have no idea how much he can hear." He winces a little. "I'm trying to stay calm so my magic doesn't flare."

"That was a smart trick, in the woods." I hesitate. "Do you think she might have recognized us?"

He considers that for a minute. "No one came after us—and there were definitely enough of them to cause trouble. I never spoke with her directly, and I only ever saw her once. I doubt she'd expect either of us to be *here*." He bumps me with his shoulder. "And you're walking."

That's true. "So maybe we're safe."

He hooks an arm around my neck, exactly the way I did to him earlier. It lights a fire in my gut that reminds me of the way he tugged me against the tree. "And together," he whispers.

My heart does a flip in my chest. Again, I wish we could find a room and forget everything we're supposed to be doing.

But then Leo appears in the crowd. His eyes are searching every face, his expression tight and drawn.

Tycho spots him the instant I do. "Leo," he calls sharply.

I expect the young soldier to look relieved when he spots us, but instead, concern washes across his expression. He cuts through the people to join us.

"I've been looking for you all over," he says.

"What's wrong?" says Tycho.

"It's Mal and Sephran."

"Are they in trouble?"

"No." Leo grimaces. "For a while, they were fine, but then we couldn't find you, so we headed for the stables, and they couldn't decide what to do, so then they—"

"Leo! What's happening *now*?"

"They're fighting."

Tycho sighs, then swears under his breath. "Show me."

We hear Sephran and Malin before we see them—and considering the noise of the tourney, that's saying something. They're on the far side of the stables, and I have no idea how long they've been fighting, but they're rolling in the dirt, fists swinging.

"At least they're not in the middle of the crowd," Tycho says, sighing. He strides forward. "Mal," he growls. "We need to get out of here. We don't have time for this."

Malin shoves Sephran onto his back, then draws a fist to punch him. "Oh, he's had it coming for *days*—"

Tycho grabs hold of his arm before Malin can swing, and they grapple for a minute.

"Let him do it!" Sephran snaps. "Just let him—"

"Shut *up*," Tycho says. He drags Malin back, and Leo rushes forward to help him. Together they're able to drag him off Sephran.

"I'm fine!" Mal snarls. "I'm *fine*. Let me go."

Suddenly free, Sephran finds his feet. "No. Hold him so I can finish this." He strides forward, fist swinging.

"*Stop*," I say. "Sephran, *stop*." I surge forward to block him, but on my false foot, I'm not as fast as the others were. He's midswing, and I go for his arm, the way Tycho just did to Malin.

But I'm too slow—or maybe he's too fast. Instead of slamming a fist into Malin, his arm slams right into my throat.

Stars explode in my vision. The pain is sudden and shocking. I don't realize I'm falling until I hit the ground. I hear them shouting my name, but I don't know who it is. Tycho? Sephran? I can't quite focus.

And then I realize I can't breathe.

"Jax. *Jax.*" Tycho's voice. He sounds distant. "Jax, open your eyes."

I open them—and all I see are flares of light. I try to inhale, but my body doesn't want to work.

"What's wrong?" someone cries. "What did I do? Did I break his neck?"

That is Sephran.

I'm scrabbling at my neck, clawing at my skin. I'm being choked by fire.

"You crushed his windpipe," says Leo. He sounds horrified. I don't even know the word *windpipe*, but I can guess.

"Get the horses. All of you." Any panic is gone from Tycho's voice, replaced with the sharp tone of an order. "*Now.*"

They must obey, because boots shuffle through the dirt.

Tycho's hand falls against my throat, and I barely feel it. I barely feel anything.

Then I feel the prickling fire of his magic, gone in an instant as the injury heals. As soon as I can inhale, I'm choking on my breath, desperate for air. Suddenly Tycho is staring down at me in the moonlight, his warm brown eyes full of concern.

"Better?" he says softly.

I nod, gasping.

"Good." He sighs and runs a hand down his face, then snaps his head up as an icy wind whips around us, lifting dried leaves and debris from the ground. "Come on." He grabs hold of my hand and begins to pull me upright before I'm ready.

"Why—" I gasp. "Why did you need the horses?"

"Because I used magic, and they felt it." He looks around again, then gives me a firmer tug. "Which means we need to run."

CHAPTER 20

CALLYN

It's well after midnight, but I'm lying awake, troubled by too many thoughts to count.

Alek never returned this morning.

At first I assumed he was simply busy with House duties. But when midday passed and he didn't appear at court, I began to worry, especially when the queen asked when I intended to go on his rounds with him. I admitted that there'd been no word, and I didn't miss the sudden tight set to her eyes, as if she was worried.

So am I.

Outside the window, clouds block the moon, but the room is flooded with silvery light anyway. It's been too hot and humid for a fire, so no embers linger in the hearth. It's almost too hot to *sleep.*

In the bed beside mine, Nora isn't having any problems. She's been lightly snoring for hours, and I get the sense that she thinks we've resolved everything and she's going to be right by my side the next time I go anywhere with Alek. But if that's the case, she's got another think coming. She's only thirteen years old, and she's not a soldier. She's not a spy. She's hardly even a *nanny*.

But then I consider that I wasn't much older than Nora when Mother died—and I wasn't much older than *that* when Father died. I was left to run the bakery and care for a little sister without any help at all. Just a friend down the lane who was every bit as desperate as I was.

I have to shove these memories away. I did what I had to do—and Nora shouldn't have to be a part of any of this. She can stay here in the palace, where she's safe.

But is she safe? After that walk in the gardens, I can't stop thinking about Verin—and the way she's become my sister's role model. When I revealed my suspicions and worries, Nora seemed determined to prove Verin's innocence. Knowing my sister, she'll walk right up to Verin and tell her I've made accusations of treason. It's possible she already has.

I sigh. I'm never going to sleep at this rate.

Maybe that's a good thing, because someone is coming through the door.

I freeze in my bed, going absolutely still. The door doesn't make a sound, but I watch as it begins to ease forward in the shadows. My heart suddenly feels like it's going to rocket out of my chest.

But then I realize I'm being foolish. It's got to be Princess Sinna, awake and sneaking around. I have no idea how she slipped past the guards at the entrance to the royal suites, but I do know it wouldn't be the first time.

I slip out from under my covers and put a stern expression on my face. In the other bed, Nora keeps snoring away. I creep over to the door and grab hold of the handle.

"You little sneaky sneak," I whisper as I give it a yank, jerking the door wide. "Got you!"

But it's not a four-year-old princess. It's a man in the shadows.

I give a little *yip* of alarm, then try to slam the door on his hand. "Nora!" I cry. My heart is in my throat. "Nora, there's a—"

A hand slaps over my mouth, and the man wrestles his way into the room. "Callyn!" he snarls in an aggravated whisper. "What is *wrong* with you? It's me!"

Alek.

My thundering heartbeat won't settle, and he shoves the door closed behind him. He's still in the clothes he wore yesterday, right down to the weapons and armor, though he looks a little rough-and-ready, which I've *never* seen. A dusting of beard growth coats his chin, and his hair is a bit sweat-slicked along the temples. Exhaustion clings to his eyes, too, like he's lived all the days of the week in the last twenty-four hours.

"What are you doing here?" I demand in a hushed voice. "How did you get into the palace?"

"I'm the lord of the Fifth House," he whispers back, his tone full of arrogance. "I'm *allowed* in the palace."

"You're not allowed in my chambers!"

Nora's bedclothes rustle, and then she sits up, rubbing her eyes in the moonlight. "Is someone here?" she mumbles.

"No," I snap, annoyed. "No one at all. Go back to sleep." I move to shove him back out the door.

"Cally-cal," Nora says sleepily. "What is he *doing* here?"

"I have no idea. But he's being inappropriate, and he needs to come back tomorrow." I wrench at the grip on my wrist, then nod toward the door. "*Go.*"

"You could be dead by tomorrow," Alek says. His tone is low and full of urgency. "You need to leave."

I go still, frozen in place. "What?"

Behind me, Nora says the same thing. "*What?*"

"You need to *leave*," he says again. "I've brought my carriage. You can—"

"I didn't leave the first time you told me to," I snarl. "What makes you think I'm going to leave *now*?"

"I'm not the one threatening you this time, Callyn."

Nora climbs out of bed to stand beside me. "Then who's threatening her?"

She sounds so fierce that I regret thinking she would've talked the scravers to death.

Alek glances at Nora, and he hesitates.

"Just tell her," I say. "She knows everything."

He sighs. "I've seen Lady Karyl," he says. "She is working with the scraver Xovaar." He moves closer to me. His eyes catch a glint of light from somewhere and glitter menacingly. "He's sensed the magic in the palace. I don't know how long you have, but he's rather determined to seek it out."

My breath catches. He's talking about *my* magic.

Alek nods as the full weight of his words sinks in. "He and Karyl had a meeting elsewhere tonight, so I had to bide my time in Bexcona until it was safe to come to you. I was worried they would follow me back to the Crystal City, and I couldn't risk them seeing me sneak you out of the palace. But this is the *only* time I know they are elsewhere. The only time I know you can leave without them seeing."

Nora reaches out to wind her fingers through mine. When she was younger, she used to do this when she was afraid, but just now she gives my hand a firm squeeze of reassurance.

"I can't just *leave*," I say.

"You must." He pauses, his tone grim. "They're coming for your magic, Callyn. They're too close. Your presence here endangers the queen."

"No," I say. "She endangers herself." Maybe this isn't my secret to tell, but all of this has gotten too big, and I can't carry it by myself anymore. My voice hitches, but I square my shoulders. "If they're coming for anyone with magic, she's at risk, too."

Alek goes absolutely still. Nora gasps and slaps a hand over her mouth.

"So," I say grimly. "If anyone with magic needs to get out of the palace, we need to bring her with us."

It's the middle of the night, and I certainly don't have unfettered access to the queen, so at first, I'm not sure how we're going to convince her to leave.

Nora says, "What about Nolla Verin?"

I frown. "No."

She scowls. "She is not the queen's enemy! You don't know—"

"*No*," Alek says, and his tone is more final. "*You* don't know, Nora." He hesitates, his eyes meeting mine. "I don't know who Karyl is working with, but I am unsure we can trust the queen's sister. At the very least, she has the strongest motive in the kingdom for usurping her. Perhaps she means well, but too many seeds of doubt have been sown. Of anyone in the palace, she could keep us trapped here most effectively. We'd be lost before we began."

Nora huffs, then lets out that breath, defeated. But then she screws up her face and says, "Well, what about Sinna?"

I bite my lip and consider that. We *do* have access to the nursery. But Princess Sinna is four years old, and I'm not sure she's up to sneaking into her mother's bedroom and convincing her to leave.

Then again, she's the only option we have. The guards aren't going to let me in. And Alek may have access to the palace, but they're not even going to let *him* in.

But they'll let her daughter in.

When I creep into the nursery, I murmur to the guard that Sinna was having difficulty falling asleep earlier, and I want to check on her. Once I'm inside, I ease onto the little girl's bed and rub her back.

She sits up at once, nearly clocking me in the face.

"Cally-cal!" she says brightly. "Is it time to play?" Without waiting for an answer, she squints at the window. "But it's still so dark. You always tell me we can't play until I can see the sun. Is this a game—"

"Yes!" I say desperately. "Yes, it's a new game."

She twists up her face. "How do we play in the dark?"

"You need to see if you can find your mama."

"But that's an *easy* game."

I try to think quickly. "Oh, but you haven't heard the best part. You have to convince her to come to my bedroom without the guards knowing. Do you think you can do that?"

Her face lights up. "Oh, yes. I can go through the fireplace."

"The *fireplace*! No, Sinna, you can't—"

"But I can! Mama told me she did it once, when she met Da. I've done it before! But Mama says only when the hearth is cold. Watch."

She throws off the bedclothes and scurries to the stone hearth, which *is* cold at this time of year. At first, I have no idea what she means, but then she crawls right past the grating and into the embers scattered along the stone.

"Sinna!" I hiss—just before she disappears.

I dart after her, but I can't see how she even *did* that—or where she went. I put my hands on the stone and lean in, but it's too dark.

"Sinna," I call again, but I'm met with absolute silence. "*Sinna.*"

Nothing.

I ease onto the ledge of the hearth, feeling the grit of ash and soot under my knees.

And then, to my absolute shock, the shadows of the hearth shift, and then it's not Sinna in front of me, it's the queen.

My breath catches in my throat, and I stumble back, nearly falling over my own feet. The queen's sleeping shift is flecked with black stains from the hearth, but she steps through, followed by her daughter.

"How—" I begin. "What—"

"I told you!" Sinna chirps.

"Quietly," the queen whispers. "You said Callyn told you we need to play a game." She looks at me pointedly. "Is this similar to the game I once had to play in your barn?"

I swallow thickly, remembering the day I first met the queen. She'd been kidnapped by the Truthbringers, brutalized and locked in my barn with little Sinna. She pretended it was a game then, too.

"Yes, Your Majesty," I say softly.

She nods. "Tell me."

I glance at Sinna. "Lord Alek has learned that the scravers have sensed magic in the palace." I pause. "And they may be coming to eradicate it."

She stares at me. I stare back at her.

For months, I've known the queen has magic. She's *known* that I know. But she's refused to acknowledge it, so I've done my best to accommodate her wishes.

But I think of that moment when I finally told my sister the truth. I think of that moment when I finally revealed the queen's secret. Instead of leaving me weak and vulnerable, admitting the truth finally allowed me to help figure out a way to move forward.

"Does he know?" she whispers.

I hesitate, then nod. "He was coming to rescue me. But once I knew the reason, I had to tell you."

She puts a hand over her mouth, and for a moment, her fingers tremble. Then she says, "Alek despises magic. Does he intend to drive me out like my husband? Or is this another trick like—"

"What? No!" I step closer to her and drop my voice. "Alek is loyal." I pause. "And so am I."

Her eyes search mine. "Why did you tell Sinna to evade the guards?"

Sinna pipes up beside us. "It was part of our game, Mama!"

"That's right!" I whisper brightly. But then I bite my lip and look back at the queen. "I considered it. But . . . the guards have been implicated. They didn't stop your—" I break off, glancing at little Sinna, who's watching us both with wide eyes. "They didn't stop the *game* last time." I hesitate, thinking of our moments during the scravers' attack on the palace, when her advisers and guards were urging her to send the king out into the melee. "Neither did your sister," I add softly. "I wasn't sure who could be trusted."

For the longest time, the queen is completely silent, regarding me. I wish I could read her thoughts, because I have no idea what she could be thinking. Her breathing has a slight tremor, and I realize she's wary of *me*. I suddenly consider how all of this must look: sneaking into her room, using Sinna as a ploy, revealing her magic to Alek. She could easily call for guards right this second and have us all hauled off to the stone prison for conspiring against her.

But the queen eventually scoops up her daughter, situating the little girl on her hip. "Alek warned me about the Truthbringers days ago," she says. There's no tremor in her breath now. "I sent word to the king."

"You did?"

"Yes. But it's too soon for him to return. Where is Alek now?"

"In my chambers," I say. "With Nora—if she hasn't killed him yet." I grimace. "But I'm not sure how to sneak you past the guards—"

"Oh, don't worry about that," she says. She heads for the hearth on the opposite side of the nursery. "I never should've shown Sinna, because I've regretted this little trick since that day she escaped from the palace. But I'll show *you*."

"We're going through the fireplace?" I squeak.

"I told you!" says little Sinna.

"Yes," says the queen. "Verin and I used to sneak past Mother when we were little." She draws up the skirts of her sleeping shift and crawls into darkness with her daughter.

For a breath of time, I stare after them. Then, hoping I'm not leading us all into danger, I hitch up my sleeping gown and do the same thing.

CHAPTER 21

CALLYN

I expect it to be difficult to sneak past the guards, but Queen Lia Mara is shockingly good at getting out of the palace without being seen. Once we joined Alek and Nora in my chambers, we all dressed in riding clothes from my wardrobe. Only Sinna is still in her nightdress. Now the queen is leading us through the darkness, and we slip through unlit hearths and servant passages and down hidden stairways until I completely lose track of which way we're going, especially when our twists and turns seem counterintuitive. Luckily, the queen seems to know every step, every tunnel, and every door.

"How do you remember all of this?" I murmur to her, a little breathless after we sidle along a narrow passage in complete darkness, Sinna between us, gripping our hands with her tiny fingers. Nora is right behind me, gripping my hand just as tightly.

Alek is behind her, the only one not part of our little chain, probably because Nora would break his fingers before she'd consider holding *his* hand.

"Admittedly," the queen whispers, "I don't remember *all* of it."

"That's reassuring, Your Majesty," Alek says from the back of the line.

"Hush, you," she says—but she doesn't sound too upset about it.

"Mama taught me how to *sneak*," Sinna says in a musical little whisper.

"I know," I say. "I'm glad you didn't know about *these* passages or I never would've found you."

"Believe me," says the queen with a sigh, "I already know I'm going to regret this." She stops short. "Be silent through here. We're near the main atrium, and sound carries."

We ease along in complete silence. I try to inhale as shallowly as I can, as if distant guards might be able to hear even that.

But after another hundred feet, the queen lets out a relieved breath. "We're safer here," she says. "This is the last servant tunnel. It comes out along the wall by the dungeon, and we'll have to watch for a guard patrol, but we should have a few minutes to escape."

A guard patrol. I don't even want to *think* about what a guard patrol might do to us if they found us sneaking around in the dark.

Then again, we're with the queen—though she's in plain clothing, her hair in a loose braid. We all seem a little rough and harried, even Alek. What would the guards believe?

And what if they're working with the Truthbringers?

I still have so many questions for Alek, but I can't ask him like *this*. He clearly thinks everyone in the palace is a potential threat.

"Are these the paths you and the king used?" Nora whispers from behind me, her soft voice full of intrigue. "For your trysts?"

"Nora!" I admonish.

But the queen laughs lightly under her breath.

"What's a tryst?" says Sinna.

"A meeting," I say promptly.

The queen laughs again. "I'm so glad you're here, Callyn."

My cheeks warm immediately, and I'm startled by the sudden burst of warmth in my chest. "Thank you, Your Majesty." I hesitate. "I'm glad, too."

"Where are we going to go?" Nora asks. "Are we just going to walk through the Crystal City?"

"I have a carriage waiting," says Alek.

Of course he does.

Once we make it off the palace grounds, it's easier to breathe. No guards wait around every corner, ready to pounce on anything suspicious. True to his word, Alek does have a carriage, the horses tethered not far off the road. There's no footman or driver, but I'm still a little shocked when he climbs up onto the driver's seat on his own.

"Feel free to join me," he says, and there's a note in his voice that says he doesn't expect me to do anything of the sort. The queen, Sinna, and Nora are already slipping into the carriage, but I take hold of the rail along the front of the carriage and yank myself up to sit beside him.

Alek glances at me in surprise, but he doesn't say anything. He just snaps the whip, and the horses leap forward.

My heart still hasn't settled, and I can't tell what's louder: my thundering pulse, or the steady pounding of the horses' hooves on the cobblestones.

Eventually, the silence is too much for me to bear. I shiver despite the warmth in the air. I don't want to be snippy, but I'm still too tense and my voice comes out sharper than I intend. "I'm shocked you didn't have a full staff waiting."

He glances over. "I try not to put my staff at risk, Callyn. They have no part in this."

That steals some of my ire. "Sorry. I'm just worried someone is going to come after us."

"They will," he says gravely. "Eventually."

I let out a breath and gesture at the trotting horses. "Shouldn't we be . . . I don't know . . . *galloping*?"

"Galloping with a carriage would draw more attention at this hour." Despite the words, he chirps to the horses and gives the reins a twitch, and the animals immediately lengthen their stride. "It's also pitch-dark, and I'd rather not slam into a tree while the queen is in my care."

I shiver again. There are always too many things to worry about.

"Do you really think scravers might come after us?" I say.

"Yes."

He says it without hesitation, and I glance over. "You're full of reassurance tonight," I say dryly.

When Alek says nothing, I frown, studying him. His expression is drawn and tired, but there's a tension that I haven't seen before. "Did anything else happen?" I say carefully. "With Xovaar?"

He shakes his head a little, and then *he* is the one who shudders. "All I wanted was to eradicate magic from Syhl Shallow. I wanted to protect the queen." He hesitates. "I wanted to protect *you*."

I swallow, not sure what to say.

He doesn't give me a chance anyway. He glances over. "Now it seems I've brought danger right to our door."

"You're helping us escape," I say.

He huffs a laugh. "That remains to be seen."

"Are we returning to your House?" I say. "How do you plan to keep the queen hidden?"

He looks over in surprise. "*My* House? No. Of course not. That's the first place Karyl would seek me out. If the queen were to vanish, the guards would begin by questioning all of the Royal Houses—and so would the Truthbringers."

I turn that around in my head for a minute, and I hate that my immediate realization is cynical. My eyes narrow, because I suddenly can't stop thinking about the queen's wariness when she appeared through the hearth with little Sinna. All of a sudden, I'm worried that he's tricked me again. "This isn't just a convenient way to get me and the queen out of the way so you and the Truthbringers can claim the throne, is it?"

Alek glances over—but again, he says nothing. It's too dark for me to read much of his expression, so I have no idea what kind of impact those words are having.

After a moment, he sighs. "Callyn, I spend hours alone with the queen on a regular basis. If I wanted to get her *out of the way*, I could've done it a lot more easily than *this*." The horses have begun to slow, so he gives another twitch of the rein. His voice quiets. "The same goes for you."

As usual, he's right. Yet I still sit here every time, unsure if I can trust him.

"Fine," I say. "Then where are we going?"

"I'm taking you across the border," he says. "Into Emberfall."

I almost choke on my breath. "Emberfall!" I hiss. "Does the queen know?"

"I have no idea," he says. "But we need to flee, and if you all have magic, you'll be better protected if you're with the king."

"But the queen sent for the king!" I say. "What if he's already gone—"

"Her courier is dead." Alek's eyes are so dark. A note in his voice makes my heart give a clench. Even in the shadows, I can see the dusting of red that's grown to coat his jaw. His eyes look a bit hollow, too.

"Dead," I echo, my voice a bare whisper.

"Yes," he murmurs. His gaze hasn't left mine, and I see the worry there. "Ambushed, according to Karyl. The king isn't coming. So I intend to take you to him."

I stare at him. *The king isn't coming.*

"You need to watch the road," I finally say.

He snorts and looks back at the road, though there's not much to see. The weight in his silence presses into both of us until it's hard to breathe. He hates magic so much—and now he's risking his life to protect me. To protect the queen.

And in a way, to protect the king.

A minute ago, I all but accused him of treason.

"Alek," I say. "I—"

"We shouldn't talk," he says, his voice flat. "If there are scravers about, they'll hear us."

I clamp my mouth shut.

Less than ten seconds later, I open it again. "Alek. Truly. I'm—"

"Hush," he says, like I'm an errant child.

"Don't tell me to—"

A screech splits the night, the sound making me cringe involuntarily. One of the horses spooks into the other, making the carriage sway and totter wildly until Alek grabs hold of the reins, getting the animals under control. Sharp, panicked screams sound from the carriage.

Another scraver shriek pierces the sky.

Alek swears under his breath. "Under the seat," he hisses at me. "I have crossbows stashed."

I'm barely listening to him, my eyes searching the sky overhead. I only see the moon between the trees—until a dark shape soars in front of it.

"Callyn!" Alek snaps. He gives me a good shake, and I realize I've grabbed hold of his arm. "The crossbows!"

"Right," I say. "Right." I duck and reach under the seat, scrabbling for anything that might feel like a weapon.

"Got them!" I cry victoriously. I straighten, simultaneously holding one out to him and trying to get my hand on the trigger of another.

Before I can do anything at all, wings block out the moon, a body slams into me, and I go tumbling out of the carriage.

I cry out in surprise. The collision is so sharp that the crossbows go flying, and I completely lose track of which way they go. The fall somehow seems *eternal*, because I haven't hit the ground yet. Am I going to die? Is this like drowning, where the actual *death* seems to take forever, because your entire life flashes before your eyes?

But no, nothing is flashing before my eyes.

I'm just falling in slow motion.

The pale scraver practically glows in the moonlight now that she's so close to me. I realize her claws have dug into my waist and my shoulder, and her wings have snapped wide behind her, slowing my descent.

Igaa? I think. And then we hit the ground.

We don't crash, but that doesn't mean the landing is *soft*, especially since Igaa lands right on my chest. I have no armor, and her claws have definitely broken the skin in a few places. Her knees press right into my rib cage, and I know I'm going to have deep bruises tomorrow.

Then her claws find my throat, digging in immediately. My breath catches.

"Please," I gasp.

She leans down so close that her black eyes glitter above mine, and I wonder if this will be the last thing I ever see.

"You were to fetch Tycho," she says.

I wheeze a breath. "Something came up."

"Cally-cal!" Nora calls—and I'm shocked that there's no panic in her voice, just determination. "Callyn!" She swears, using a word I've only heard from the soldiers. "Alek! Find those crossbows."

"Please," I gasp to Igaa. Between the claws at my neck and the weight on my chest, it's becoming hard to breathe. "We're—we're running—"

"I heard you," she growls right into my face. "I know where you're going."

"Please," I say again. "Running—from—Xovaar—"

The name has the effect I hoped. She snaps back, looking up at the sky. A cold breeze whips around us both, and I don't know if it's *her* magic or if another scraver has arrived.

"Let my sister go," Nora calls. She sounds so fierce, and it's a surprise every time. "Let her go or I'll *shoot* you."

"No," Alek calls. "I will."

The scraver shrieks again, and I cringe, clenching my eyes shut at the sound.

But it's the queen who speaks through the tension, her voice clear and full of authority. "*No*," she says. "Lay down the crossbows. Both of you. This scraver saved your life, Nora."

I'm still gasping under the weight of the scraver, so I have no idea how Nora receives this news. But Igaa is no longer shrieking, and Alek and Nora aren't issuing threats, so I'm hopeful that *something* is changing.

"Please," I whisper again.

Igaa leans down close again. "You were to find Tycho," she says. "Nakiis needs him."

"We're going to Emberfall," I rasp. "We *will* find him."

But it sounds like a lie, even to myself.

"No," she growls. "You are *running*. You are leaving him to die."

I inhale sharply—because she's right. We *are* running. And I have no way to convince her otherwise.

"Are you talking about Nakiis?" says the queen. She sounds closer, but I can't see past the scraver to know for sure.

"Yes," Igaa hisses.

"We *are* running," the queen confirms. "But if Nakiis needs our help, we can bring him along."

CHAPTER 22

TYCHO

Wind blasts through the woods behind us, an icy kiss on the back of my neck as we gallop north. A piercing shriek splits the night air, and Mercy spooks a little underneath me, skittering sideways on the trail, colliding with Jax's horse and nearly unseating us both.

I swear and check the reins, straightening her out. Her ears flatten back, and her tail lashes, showing her agitation, but she obeys.

"Are you all right?" I call to him.

"Yeah," Jax calls back, but his fingers are wound into his horse's mane, gripping for dear life. Luckily Teddy is older, and so steady that a scraver could probably land directly on his back and he wouldn't break pace.

Another shriek splits the air overhead, and behind me, Sephran swears—or maybe it's Leo. I can barely hear over the sound of the scraver and Mercy's hoofbeats.

Wind rushes through the woods like a hurricane, causing branches to crack and fall. Mercy spooks again, but this time I've got a tighter grip on the reins and she can't go far. Jax glances over, his eyes full of determination, his hair streaming out behind him. His fear is evident, though: his jaw is clenched, and his knuckles have turned white.

"Don't let up!" Malin calls from somewhere behind us. "They aren't far behind!"

My heart skips, and Mercy jerks against my hold as if she understands him. "Steady," I murmur to her, but I'm not just talking to the horse. I'm talking to Jax, too. Hell, I'm talking to myself.

Because we might be able to outrun whoever is behind us, but we can't outrun a flying scraver. I don't even know if there are more than one. Right now, our only advantage is the dense tree cover, but that won't last forever, and it's as hazardous as it is protective. One wrong step and we could slam right into a tree.

A voice speaks to my mind. ***—I can follow you, magesmith.***

"Yeah, yeah," I mutter. "Tell me something I don't know."

—Your horses can't run forever, he adds.

No kidding.

"He's right," Sephran calls from behind us. "What's the plan?"

I have no idea, but I do know I'm not going to shout it into the air. "He'll hear anything you say," I call over my shoulder. At some point I'm going to have to reckon with everything that just happened between Sephran and Malin, but this is not that point. "So shut up."

Mostly because I need to *think*.

A snap and whistle sounds from behind me, followed by a crack of wood. A second later, it happens again.

"Silver hell!" Leo snaps. "Was that a crossbow?"

It happens a third time, and one of them cries out behind me.

If we stop, we're dead. "Who's hit?" I shout.

"Clipped me," Sephran calls back.

Good, I think. "Stay low!" I snap. "They can't see in the dark."

The scraver's voice comes from above. ***—I can.***

I grit my teeth and fight for a plan—but I've got nothing.

Jax glances over again. "We're going to run out of woods," he says. He's already breathing hard from the exertion—another reminder that he's not a soldier. He might have been training with them in his free time, but that doesn't mean he was ready for days of riding without a break. It doesn't mean he was ready for us to run for our lives.

I wish I knew how many were following us, and how many guards and soldiers are among them—though it might not matter. Violence has long been glorified on the other side of the mountain. Even the wealthiest noble knows how to fight.

As if we could fight off a crowd of that size either way. There are only five of us, and there were *dozens* of them.

Then Jax looks over again. "Magic?" he calls.

I don't know what he means, but then he flicks his eyes skyward before glancing back at me. "He already knows you used it."

Meaning I could use it again.

Aside from the one time Alek tried to kill me, I've never used magic in battle. I know Grey can repel an enemy when fighting one-on-one, and he once made an entire courtyard full of people collapse at once. I don't know how much power or focus it would take to accomplish either option—and I've never tried.

But I do know how to start a fire.

"Hold the line," I call to Jax. "Straight out—don't stop."

Then I don't wait for a response. I simply sit deep in the saddle, brace with my heels, and cue Mercy to whirl. We're galloping hard, but we run drills often, and she drops her haunches to slow, skidding in the dirt. Behind me, Malin and Sephran shout and swear as they veer to avoid us, but I can't worry about them now. We've got too many people behind us and a scraver overhead.

Before Mercy even comes to a stop, I'm swinging down from the saddle, grabbing hold of her breastplate, and landing in a run to absorb the impact. As soon as I'm on the ground, Mercy prances in a tight circle around me, clearly done with these maneuvers. Fifty yards back, horses are crashing through the woods, and I know I only have seconds. Sparks and stars are already flaring in my vision. I'm so used to tamping them down, rejecting any hint of magic to keep it all hidden.

This time, I let it flare like a bonfire. The magic surges in my blood, light filling my eyes until it's nearly impossible to see.

Calling a flame was one of the first skills Grey ever taught me. The intent was for basic survival—a fire can keep you warm and cook a meal.

But fire can also repel an enemy. It worked on Alek once, and I feel rather certain it'll work on everyone following us.

I drop to touch the dried underbrush around my feet and let the magic surge. Fire bursts around my feet, and Mercy blows hard through her nostrils, jerking back to the end of the reins.

"Steady," I say, more confident now, touching another spot and pouring more magic into the ground, this time willing it out, in a line through the trees.

For an instant, I don't think it'll be enough. My heartbeat keeps pounding, and I feel like I can't catch my breath. Magic always seems reluctant when I need it most, and I try to force myself to relax.

—Found you, the scraver says, just as he sounds an earsplitting screech that makes every hair on my skin stand up. I'm not going to be fast enough.

A man shouts from the other side of the flames. "He's there! The magesmith!"

Silver hell. I think of Jax and the others. If this doesn't work, they're dead.

I close my eyes and try to shake off the panic. But then the magic finally gives, sudden flames bursting off the ground, surging high and wide, a wall of flame jetting off in two directions. Mercy spooks again, dragging me back. I dig in my heels and gasp, trying to hold fast, but the rein snaps, and her bridle gives.

Her hooves dig into the turf as she bolts away, and I can feel my magic *lurch* as she leaves me. Flames surround me, filling the air with smoke that instantly obscures the stars and makes it hard to breathe. Now it's more than just a wall. From the other side of the flames, men and women shout. Horses scream and whinny as they encounter the fire, and I cringe—then cough, as smoke fills my lungs. The fire is suddenly *everywhere*, as if the entire forest is on fire. The heat is intense, and sweat drips into my eyes. I blink and I'm surrounded.

I turn and run, though it's like the fire wants to follow. Flames lick around my boots, rushing through the underbrush as I sprint through the smoke-filled woods. My lungs are screaming now, and I've somehow lost the path.

And I'm alone.

Oh, Mercy. I need you.

But at the same time, I'm glad I sent the others to safety. I'm glad my mare ran. They're safe.

And the human Truthbringers are panicked, though some are finding a way around the flames. Hopefully I've created enough of a distraction that my soldiers can gain distance to get to safety.

Fire grabs for my boots, for my trousers. I can't remember the last time I could draw a good breath. I'm disoriented, and I'm suddenly worried I've turned around, that I'm heading back into the flames.

Without warning, a cold wind swoops between the trees, making the flames flicker and spread farther. The scraver shrieks overhead, and then his voice comes right to my ears.

—I'm not afraid of your fire, little magesmith.

Another blast of wind blows the smoke back and away from me, bringing immediate relief—until I realize that the scraver is swooping down through the trees, claws and fangs bared.

My eyes are still burning, and I can barely see, but his wings are wide and such a rich red they'd match the color of the flames. My right hand finds my sword automatically, my left hand drawing a dagger without thought—though I'm not going to be fast enough. At least I can try to take him out before he rips me apart. I swing my blades up and brace for impact.

But then his body jerks midair, and the resulting screech isn't one of warning, it's pain and rage. His flight cuts short, and he crashes into the smoldering underbrush fifteen feet away.

Swip. Swip.

I hear the arrows before I see the archer. The scraver screams again. Somewhere behind me, men are shouting, finding a way around the flames that are surging in the absence of the scraver's magic. Smoke fills the air again, and I cough.

"Tycho!"

Jax's voice. I whip around, but I can barely see him through the haze. I can't tell if my eyes are blurry from the fires or if I've inhaled so much smoke that everything is dizzy.

Then something hits my left shoulder, *hard*. It feels like a punch, with a burn like acid. I stumble to my knees, and my dagger goes skipping into the fiery underbrush. I'm so dazed by the smoke and the pain that my head cracks into a tree. I fight for equilibrium, trying to whirl, to face this new assailant.

But there's no one.

The crossbows. I've been hit.

I reach for the bolt, but it's buried in my shoulder, and I can't see anything. I can't *breathe*.

But then Jax is there, appearing through the smoke and flames like

I conjured him out of the air. He's got his bow in one hand, Teddy's reins drawn up tight in the other.

"Get up," he says breathlessly. "Get *on*. I don't know if I killed it, but I hear them coming."

I'm able to find my feet, but when I reach for the saddle's cantle, my shoulder screams at me. I'm dizzy again, pain stealing my breath in an entirely different way. But Jax throws the bow over his shoulder, then grabs hold of my good arm and *pulls*. Awkwardly, I swing onto Teddy's back behind him. My breaths are coming too fast, and it's like I'm keening with every exhale.

"Grab hold of me," he says.

I cough hard, but I grab Jax around the waist with my good arm. I wish I could reach that crossbow bolt. Did they set it on fire? The pain is like something alive, and my vision swims. I don't know if it's the smoke, or the fact that I cracked my head into the tree, but neither is helping me right now. "Go," I choke out. "Go."

His weight shifts, and Teddy leaps forward. I grip tight and press my face against Jax's armor. He smells like sweat and leather and *Jax*, and my breathing almost hitches. That was too close.

It's *still* close.

Because I don't know where Mercy is. I don't know what happened to the others. I don't know if Xovaar survived.

But Jax rode back through the flames to find me.

Not just to find me. To save my *life*.

"Thank you," I say. "Jax—*thank* you."

He puts a hand over mine where it rests along his waist, and he gives my fingers a squeeze. "Always, Tycho. Always."

For much of the day, the pressing heat in the air felt like a weight I couldn't escape. But getting away from the raging fire in the woods is such a relief that the summer night air feels like a cool balm against my cheeks.

My shoulder won't stop burning, and it feels like a white-hot steel poker has been driven into my body. I've been shot before, but it's never ached like burning acid was injected directly into my bones. Combined with the awkward way we're riding double, the pain keeps making me want to pass out. I've been trying to summon magic to heal it, but I can't heal around a bolt from a crossbow—if that's even what this is. I'm desperately hoping it's not tipped with poison.

The instant I have the thought, my head spins, and I'm worried I'm going to vomit down the back of Jax's armor.

"Tycho. *Tycho.*"

It's too late. I'm falling.

No. Wait. Someone caught me. I'm half on the horse, half off. Jax grunts with strain. His horse sidesteps, trying to accommodate for my slide.

"Help me, damn it," Jax growls, and I think he's talking to me.

"Sorry," I slur. "Sorry—"

"No—not you. Seph, give dagger belt." His voice is harried, impatient. "Give *now*. Help. Tie to me."

Then I'm shoved upright again, and I practically faceplant into Jax's back. It jars my shoulder, and I cry out. They ignore me. A belt is strung around my waist, jerking tight, pinning me to Jax.

Leo speaks, and his voice sounds distant. "Should we pull that out of his shoulder?"

"Not yet." That's Malin. "We need to move."

"Please," I murmur against Jax's back, but he doesn't respond. The horse leaps forward, and I try not to fall off again. My fingers are slick with sweat, but I try to grip at his armor as the horse runs.

Every now and again, his hand presses over mine. "Almost there," he'll say.

But it's meaningless. Almost *where*? It'll take days to make it back to Ironrose—and we're more than half a day's ride from the Crystal Palace. And that's not even considering the fact that his horse carries two.

I think of my brave mare, pushed past any common courage by a scraver in the air and a fire all around us. I don't even know if she made it out of the woods. A pulse of worry joins the ache in my shoulder and the pounding in my head.

"Mercy?" I murmur.

I don't think Jax will answer, but he says, "Malin has her. His horse took two in the hip."

"Oh," I say, and my breath hitches. "Oh, sweet Mercy."

Jax gives my hand another squeeze. My heart gives another lurch.

Then the pain in my head takes over, and darkness swallows me up.

When I wake, I'm facedown in bed. My head aches like I'm hung over, but it's nothing compared to the brutal fire that seems to have replaced my shoulder joint. I have no idea where I am, but I'm not in chains and I'm not dead, so at least I've got that going for me.

I blink hazy eyes and try to figure out where I am. The room is dim and full of shadows, and I'm facing a wall I don't recognize—though it seems vaguely familiar. The air smells musty, but the bedding beneath my head is soft and clean. I try to move, and every muscle on my frame protests. Or maybe that's just the ache in my head. My shoulder and chest seem tightly bound, and it takes me a moment to realize I'm bandaged. A low sound comes out of my throat, and it's so raspy that I wonder how long it's been since I've had a drop of water.

That's enough to force me to lift my head to turn and face the other way.

And then, all at once, awareness snaps into place. This is Jax's bedroom. Or . . . it was. We're at his old forge. The window is partially boarded over, and a few sheets have been thrown over the furniture. Dust motes hang in the air, caught in the shafts of moonlight.

Jax himself is asleep in a chair, his upper body half collapsed on the end of the bed, his hair a mess of wild tangles. Dried blood is in streaks and stains all over him. On his cheek, on his tunic, on his hands where they lie against the mattress.

Blood. Maybe he's not actually *asleep*. I nearly sit up in alarm, but my body instantly protests.

"Jax," I croak out, bracing my good hand against the mattress. "*Jax*."

He wakes with a start, nearly sliding out of the chair before realizing he was already half out of it. When he rights himself, he chokes on his breath and stares at me. Then he exhales like he's been bearing the weight of the world for hours, and he's finally able to set it down.

"You're awake," he says—and there's a note in his voice that tells me he was worried I wouldn't.

"I'm awake," I say, and it still sounds like I'm speaking through gravel. My gaze narrows. "But you're hurt. Where are you—"

"You think *I'm* hurt?" He huffs a laugh without any humor, then glances down at his bloodstained forearms. "No, Tycho. All this is *yours*."

I stare at him for a solid minute, but then I have to put my head back down. I clench my eyes closed, wishing the pain in my head would go away. "What about the others?"

"They're fine. Sleeping." He frowns. "We lost Malin's horse, and Sephran's is lame. Malin intends to send Leo on to the Crystal Palace at dawn, so long as there's no sign of the Truthbringers."

My thoughts don't want to process all that. "Mercy?" I press.

"She's fine," he says, his voice gentling a bit. "I swear it. So is Teddy. They're tethered in Callyn's old barn."

A little of the tightness around my heart eases. "What . . . what happened?"

He runs a hand down his face. "I don't know for sure. They didn't chase us long—though I don't know if that was because of the fire or because we shot the scraver and they were worried about your magic. You had a pretty bad hit to the head, though. We didn't even know about *that* until we got here. It was so dark, and the arrow wound was so much worse—"

"Hit to the head?" I reach for my head, and I'm surprised when I find hair that's matted and sticky—with blood, presumably—but no pain when I press along my scalp.

Jax nods, then shifts so he's sitting beside me. "Just here." He runs a hand along my hair, and just that light touch makes me shiver. Then he says, "It bled a lot—but just as Malin was talking about field sutures, it began to close over."

"Magic," I murmur. That's happened before—when my magic flared to keep me alive, even without my conscious awareness.

"Yeah," says Jax.

I brace my hand against the mattress again, but my whole body feels like it's been trampled by a horse, and I let out a breath.

"Do you need to get out of bed?" he says.

I'll need to attend to human needs soon, but I'm not sure I can manage it yet. I shake my head, and I'm glad when the room doesn't spin—but the movement makes my skull pound. I desperately want to call magic to see what else I can heal, but I'm too worried about Xovaar and the rest of the Truthbringers that were on our tail.

For now, I just want to sit up, and that alone seems insurmountable. "Just—water?" I whisper. "Please."

"Yeah. Of course." He disappears, but only for a moment, returning with a dripping stein. I'm so thirsty I can almost *smell* it. "Here," he says. "I'll help you sit up."

"No," I rasp. "I can do it." But when I push against the mattress again, my head pounds so badly that I just want to lie down. Sparks and stars flicker in my blood, my magic eager to repair whatever it can, and I do my best to tamp it down.

If a scraver attacked us right now, I wouldn't be able to fight at all. I can still see Xovaar descending through the smoke, ready to tear me apart.

Too close.

Without a word, Jax crawls onto the bed beside me. Almost before I'm ready, he loops an arm around my chest under the bandages. It pulls a little whimper from my throat, but he tugs me upright anyway, then eases me against the headboard, holding me there loosely. It leaves me leaning against him, gasping a little from the effort. Sweat blooms on my forehead, and I clench my jaw shut so I don't make another sound. But despite the pain in my body, I am acutely aware of the warmth of his arm against the bare skin of my back. I can feel each individual finger where his hand rests against my waist.

When he picks up the stein and holds it to my lips, I feel helpless and ashamed.

This thirst is brutal, though. I close my eyes and drink.

As soon as I'm done, he sets it aside. His voice is still low. "Do you want me to stay? Or should I let you go?"

I put a hand over his as if I could trap him here. Then I turn my head to look at him, my eyes taking in the bloodstains scattered along his face and clothing. *My* bloodstains.

He saved my life.

I can't believe I ever wondered if he would be a liability on this journey.

"Stay," I murmur.

"All right." He shifts a little, settling against me, and silence falls between us. Outside the window, thunder rumbles somewhere in the distance. All the pressing heat and humidity were sure to lead to a storm, so I suppose I shouldn't be surprised.

I'm sure there are things I should be *doing*, and I have so many questions, but just now, my thoughts are content to drift as I feel the warm weight of Jax's body against mine.

Though I'd enjoy it a lot more if my shoulder weren't insisting that a hot coal must be buried in the joint. I think I have an old kit full of tinctures and powders from Noah in my pack, but I've never used any of them. Thanks to magic, I've never had to.

I shift my weight, trying to get more comfortable, but that only makes it worse. When I utter a little sound without meaning to, Jax moves again, setting me a bit more upright, then taking a pillow to wedge under my arm. I don't expect it to make a difference, but it does.

"You're a rather good nurse," I say.

"I got a lot of practice from taking care of Da when he drank himself sick." That nearly makes me frown, but then he adds, "At least you didn't wet the bed."

"You're welcome."

He laughs—but he sobers quickly. "Why didn't your magic heal your shoulder like your head?"

I lift a hand to my temple. "I don't know if it healed my head all the way. It's still pounding."

He grimaces. "That might be the sleeping ether. When we dug the bolt out of your shoulder—it was bad. You were barely yourself. You were fighting Malin, Leo was trying to hold you down . . . luckily Seph had a bottle in his pack."

Sleeping ether. No wonder my head is pounding.

But then I realize what he said. "When you *dug* the bolt out of my shoulder?" I echo.

He nods. "It was a steel bolt with spikes along the sides. Malin says they must have shot it from a crossbow." Another grimace. "It was hell getting it out."

I'm fascinated—and a little disgusted. My stomach rolls, and those sparks flicker in my blood again. I have to close my eyes for a moment. "Was the arrow tipped in Iishellasan steel?" I say.

"I don't know. Here." He pulls away from me, and my eyes snap open, but Jax only reaches down beside the bed, coming back up with a long steel rod that's vaguely shaped like an arrow—but definitely isn't. The bolt is easily two feet long, with a barbed point, plus a dozen angled "thorns" along the shaft. It's clearly designed to do a lot of damage to whatever it finds. I'm shocked they got it out of my shoulder at *all*.

The entire length is stained with my blood.

"Silver hell," I say.

"Yeah."

I take it from him, and I'm surprised at the weight. It's more vicious than any weapon I've ever seen—and considering my time in the Syhl Shallow army, that's saying something.

But it's definitely Iishellasan steel. I wonder where the Truthbringers got it—and how many they have left.

Last spring, Jax's father had similar weapons. He shot me and the king—but it wasn't anything like this. If I'd taken this bolt to the heart or the head, all the magic in the world wouldn't have helped me survive.

My thoughts are suddenly a bit clearer. Maybe it's the awareness that we're still in danger, and more than I expected if they have weapons like this.

And then I think of another reason the Truthbringers might have let us go.

I'm not the primary target.

Perhaps while the king and queen are separated, we have an opportunity to resolve things in a way that will satisfy everyone.

My heart pounds for an entirely new reason. I wish I could climb on Mercy right now, but I know I'm in no shape for this kind of ride. "You said Malin was sending Leo to the Crystal Palace?" I say. "To alert the queen?"

Jax nods, then glances at the window. "At first light."

Just as he says it, another roll of thunder carries across the sky. I shake my head. "Go. Stop him."

He's already extracting himself from the bed. "Why?"

"That meeting was in *Emberfall.* They killed the queen's courier to stop her from bringing a message to Grey." I hold up the steel arrow. "And this *is* Iishellasan steel. Magic can't heal any damage it causes."

His eyes go from me to the bolt and back.

"Jax, if they're armed with weapons like this, they're not on their way to attack the queen." I touch a finger to one of the barbs. It's razor sharp, and blood wells on my fingertip. I hold it up to show him. "Someone needs to warn *the king.*"

CHAPTER 23

ALEK

This day has grown too long, and I've been desperate for a hot meal and a soft bed for hours.

Unfortunately, it's the middle of the night, and I'm loading a half-conscious scraver into my carriage. Our journey is going to end in a country I loathe, in the presence of men I can't stand. I'm exhausted and hungry, and my clothing feels stiff and tacky with two days of dried sweat. If there's any relief here, it's that the creatures' magic has dropped the temperature by a good ten degrees—though even that comes with a price. Igaa watches our efforts, and I have no doubt she's ready to rip out my throat if I do anything suspicious. She might've been growling at Callyn, but it's no secret that I'm the one who hates magic here.

When the queen agreed to have us help the scraver, my immediate reaction was to wonder *how* we'd do such a thing. Nakiis wasn't exactly willing when Callyn tried to help him. But maybe his efforts to fight us yesterday stole the last of his will, because he was barely conscious as Callyn and I carried him through the woods, and even now, his eyes barely flicker open as we ease him onto the carriage floor.

The whole time, Nora asks a thousand questions and the young princess chatters from where she clings to the queen, but Callyn and I have been completely silent since the moment we were bickering in the carriage. I have no idea what emotions are behind *her* reticence, but it seems that any path we choose to follow always ends this way, with both of us at odds.

The only distraction is the fact that we're spending so much time doing *this,* when we should be crossing the border into Emberfall by now.

I swipe sweat from my forehead, feeling a swell of exhaustion. I hardly slept last night, desperate to ride back to the Crystal City to warn the queen—though I knew I had to wait until nightfall. Now I feel as though I haven't slept in days. Dawn can't be far off, and I'm not sure how much longer I can stay awake. Callyn can't drive the horses, which means Nora likely can't either. I have no doubt that Lia Mara can, but I'm reluctant to have the queen out in the open while I sleep in the carriage.

If I even could. Injured or not, the idea of being trapped inside a carriage with a scraver still makes me want to shudder. When Igaa brought Callyn to the ground, it took everything I had to keep from filling her back with bolts from the crossbow.

Once Nakiis is loaded in the carriage, Igaa doesn't say a word. Her pale purple wings snap wide, and she leaps into the air.

—Go, she says. ***—Now.***

I roll my eyes at the order, but I climb up onto the driver's seat.

I'm actually shocked when Callyn reclaims her spot beside me. A spark of anger flared in my heart when she accused me of treason, and it seems determined to burn. I almost ask her to get down and ride in the carriage. At this point, I might prefer Nora, even though she'd likely spend the rest of the journey yanking on my ears and trying to break my fingers.

Hell, maybe that would be better. It would keep me awake.

"Alek?"

I look over to find that Callyn is staring at me, and I realize I'm just sitting here.

I run a hand down my face and sigh, then chirp to the horses and snap the reins. "*Lord* Alek," I say sourly, even though I don't really mean it. I just hate the way she persists in getting under my skin at every turn.

"I'm sorry," she says quietly.

For a moment, I think she's apologizing for neglecting my title. But the weight in her voice tells me it's more.

"It's fine," I say flatly. "You've made your feelings clear, and more than once. I'm the fool for continuing to think otherwise."

"You have to admit that you make it hard to trust you."

I scoff. "Do I? I've only ever spoken the truth to you."

When she looks over, it's too dark to see her expression clearly, but her eyes might as well be a lit match, because her gaze captures mine. "You might tell the truth, but it's rarely the *whole* truth, and you know it."

That stings like a dart.

Because she's right.

I look back at the shadowed road and twitch the reins at the horses. Overhead, Igaa loops back and forth, occasionally crossing over the moon. She's very high, and if I didn't know any better, I wouldn't give the creature a second glance. I have no idea what would happen if Xovaar headed back this way, and I doubt I want to find out.

As the horses trot on, I'm painfully aware of the tension between me and Callyn, and I have no idea how to undo it. There are so many more important things to worry about anyway.

But the tension is here and now, and despite everything, I want to fix it.

"I was raised at court," I say to Callyn, and my voice is rough and low. "I know you've only been here for a few short months, but surely you've already discovered the backstabbing and doublespeak that's part of living in the palace. Gossip is everywhere, and knowledge is often traded like an asset. In an environment like that, *truth* becomes what you make it, not necessarily what *is*." I hesitate. "You're right that I reveal information in a calculated way. But it's . . . it's *not* . . ." I break off and sigh.

She's quiet, waiting, but I'm not sure how to proceed. She's patient, however, and I eventually grimace. "I was going to say it's not intentional, but that's not precisely true. Even this conversation is evidence of it. You must understand that when you've been raised to balance and measure every word you speak, this kind of strategic discourse becomes as commonplace as breathing." I glance over. "At court, any vulnerability is a weakness to be exploited. Any admission of truth becomes a weapon that can be used against you." I shrug a little. "In my experience, it's safer to be the weapon first."

She frowns, but her eyes don't leave the road. For the longest time, there's only the sound of the hoofbeats clopping along the path.

When she finally looks over, her voice is as quiet as mine was. "I wish you'd talk to me like that more often."

"Like what?"

"Like . . . a friend." Her eyes are dark pools, gleaming in the moonlight. "Instead of an opponent."

"Ah," I say coolly. "Like a *friend*." I twitch the reins again.

She shifts closer to me, and the warmth of her body presses into mine, all the way from knee to shoulder. Her hand falls on my knee, and I lose track of every thought in my head.

"Do it again," she murmurs, and then she gives my knee a gentle squeeze.

My brain is completely fixated on the location of her hand, so I have no idea what action bears repeating. When she says *do it again*, every suggestion my brain offers involves a lot less clothing.

Then she says, "Talk to me, *Lord Alek*."

I huff a breath that's half laughter, half surprise. "What should I say, *Lady Callyn*?"

"Is that why you're so close to the queen?" she says—and it's not at all what I expect her to say, so it grabs my attention. "The way you were raised at court?"

I'm not sure what to say. "Her Majesty is . . . well. I—ah—"

Her hand squeezes my knee again. "It's clear you're closer than you let on."

"Is it? How?"

"Because Queen Lia Mara trusts you. It's the only reason *I* keep giving you second chances."

I look over in surprise. "Does she?"

"Isn't it obvious?" she says. "Look at where we are!"

Well. I suppose there's that.

Callyn gives me a nudge with her shoulder. "So tell me."

I think back to my childhood, remembering all the times I wished I could hide in the corner like the less-favored princess.

"Lia Mara always had a book in her hands," I say. My words are slow, because I've never talked about this with anyone. It's not a secret, because there was never anything between us, but this part of my youth *feels* like a secret. "She was always in the corners, in the shadows. Always left alone. Truly, I envied her. My mother kept pushing me at Nolla Verin, because it was clear that she was destined for the throne. If Mother hadn't died in the war—and if Karis Luran had kept the throne—I'm sure our union would've been seen as a rather strategic partnership. But it would've been rude to ignore Lia Mara, so I was allowed to cling to the shadows from time to time. By then, I'd learned the ways of life at court, so we could never be truly *close*. But we were companions, of a sort. We'd share books from time to time. She'd tell me about her favorite stories—and I'd share mine."

For a moment, I'm lost in the memory, remembering how Lia Mara used to love the romance in her stories. One book was quite racy, and when I teased her about it, she smacked me on the knuckles with the spine—then blushed so red that her younger sister scurried over to ask what we were talking about.

"I used to do that with Jax," Callyn says, and her tone is musing in a way that tells me she's lost in memories, too. "We'd curl up in the corner of the bakery when it was cold, or sit around his forge during the summer months when he was busy. Nora used to beg us to read the kissing scenes out loud." She pauses, then looks at me in the shadows. "It's so odd to think that we were probably all doing the same thing at the same time. You living your life in the Crystal City, and me living mine in Briarlock."

I'm struck by that. Overhead, Igaa soars across the moon, plunging the path into darkness again. A cold breeze whips between the trees, a relief and an assault simultaneously.

Callyn shivers and presses closer. It'll likely be too hot in a moment, but for right now, I don't mind at all.

But then she says, "You can't drive all night."

She's probably right. I feel ready to pitch sideways off this seat right *now*. "I can try," I say.

"Well, the rest of us can't *ride* all night," she says. "Sinna is going to need to stop to eat before long."

"Indeed. And the palace guard will likely be after us by then."

She shivers again, but this time I know it's not the cold. "We should find an inn. Or a tavern. Or—"

"If you think I am willing to take the queen of Syhl Shallow into a tavern unguarded while a half-dead *scraver* bleeds all over my carriage, you are sadly mistaken. I was prepared to protect *you*—not a carriage full of liabilities."

A voice comes to us through the air, and this time it's not Igaa.

—I am not bleeding all over your carriage, human. And I did not ask for your help.

—I did, Igaa calls from above. ***—They are taking us to Tycho.***

"I'll just drive straight through without stopping," I say. "Four days shouldn't be a problem at all."

—Good, Igaa says, ignoring my sarcasm.

I sigh and drag a hand back through my hair. Callyn is right—we can't ride like this forever. We'll have to stop before long.

I look over at her, trying to ignore the fact that she's still leaning against me. "Our best bet is to go to ground after daybreak and travel at night," I say. "But we need to put more distance between ourselves and the palace—or we need a way to send guards in the opposite direction. They'll be able to cover a lot of ground between here and the border. We need somewhere to hide."

Callyn sighs. "With a four-year-old, no less."

Just as she says it, thunder rolls in the distance.

Perfect, I think. *Just what we need.* At least a rainstorm will obstruct our tracks and make any search effort difficult.

We fall silent again, both thinking. I know Tycho had safe houses along his route as King's Courier, but I don't know them all—and I have no idea if they were truly *safe.* We definitely can't take a carriage over the mountain, so we're going to have to stay relatively close to the main road—which will also mean riding through the guard station, again with a queen and scraver in my carriage. If they demand to search my things, we'll be caught for sure. There's another mountain pass farther west that's not well guarded, but that would add ten miles to our journey and keep us on this side of the border.

Another peal of thunder rumbles across the sky, and I sigh heavily, then rub at my eyes.

I'm so tired. There's so much at risk.

And there's nowhere to go.

"How much farther can you drive this carriage?" Callyn says, her voice low.

"Apparently I'm supposed to drive it all the way to Ironrose Castle."

"Alek. Truly."

I think of the truths I just shared, how it seemed to dissolve the tension between us. I look over and make my voice equally quiet. "A few hours, maybe." I hesitate. "Why?"

Callyn looks over, biting her lip. "Well . . . there's one place we could go."

CHAPTER 24

TYCHO

By daybreak, the effects of the sleeping ether have worn off, so my head is finally clear. It's well and truly storming now, lightning flickering through the sky outside the hastily boarded windows of Jax's small house. My shoulder aches like the bolt is still buried in the joint, but I found my herbs and tinctures from Noah and dumped half of them into a cup of tea. That was enough to take the edge off the pain—and it's so effective that I wish I'd rationed some of it. I have no idea when I'll get more.

I still haven't seen anyone but Jax, and I can't tell if the others are avoiding me, or if they're simply sitting sentry to make sure scravers and Truthbringers aren't coming after us. Either way, there's a part of me that's glad. I haven't forgotten that Malin and Sephran were fighting instead of backing us up.

I haven't forgotten the way Sephran's fist cracked right into Jax's throat.

Every time I think about *that*, my shoulders go tight and I start to wonder if I should go looking for trouble.

But I don't. I'm in no shape to fight anyone at all.

Instead, I'm writing a new letter to Grey and Rhen, using one of Jax's kohl pencils from the forge. I've moved into the main part of the house to sit at the dusty kitchen table so *he* could finally get some sleep. I have no idea if my first missive might've reached the king, but I'm more sure of Leo's loyalty than a random army courier, so I'm more open about what we've discovered, though I still keep details sparse. As I write, the sound of the pencil scratching along the parchment is drowned out by the rain rattling against the roof, and I inwardly cringe. This weather will slow the Truthbringers, but it'll make travel slow and difficult for Leo, too.

It's not until I'm finally done and folding the letter that Malin appears in the doorway to the house, rapping his knuckles lightly on the frame. I glance at him, but say nothing.

He must take that as an invitation, because he steps across the threshold. I might have been right about him sitting sentry, because his hair is threaded with rain, the leather of his armor glistening with water droplets. Even in the shadows, his eyes are clearly heavy with exhaustion, and he's got a pretty deep scrape across his jaw that someone stitched together with field sutures. It's an angry red, and I have no doubt it'll leave a brutal scar.

I wonder if he got that in the fight with Sephran, or if he got hurt while we were trying to escape.

Not like it matters. We wouldn't have been running like hell if they'd been doing their job instead of scuffling in the dirt.

I tell myself not to care. We're down two horses thanks to their antics, which limits our options. And Malin might have a scar, but I can barely lift my arm.

His eyes skip down my form, lingering on the bandage at my shoulder. There's still blood in my hair, but I haven't had any desire to look in a mirror, so I wonder how bad I look. "Tycho," he begins, his voice low. "Jax said you were—"

"Captain," I say brusquely, cutting him off. "I've finished the letter for your recruit."

He nearly snaps to attention when he hears my tone, but he *must* be tired, because he almost immediately deflates. "Come on," he says with a sigh. "Please. Don't . . . don't do *that*."

As soon as I hear that tired note in his voice, it tugs at me—because I remember feeling the exact same way during every single standoff with Grey.

If anything could steal some of my bitterness, it's that.

"I'm sorry," he adds. His mouth twists. "Really."

And that.

I think of Jax telling me how long it took them to dig that spike out of my shoulder. I frown, then look away. "*You* lectured *me* about this, Mal."

"I know." He hesitates. "Trust me, I *know*. And I should've left it alone. Seph just . . . he wouldn't *stop*." A flare of anger washes across his expression. "If it wasn't about you and Jax, it was about me and him. The whole time we were trying to follow you through the tourney, he wouldn't shut up. Every ten seconds, another dig. And then we lost you in the crowd and we couldn't find you anywhere. *Then* he started blaming me—"

"I get it."

Malin scowls. "I shouldn't have let it happen."

I go to shrug, but I stop halfway through because it hurts so much. I do my best to swallow the pain, then say, "Well. I ended up punching the king when *I* was mad, so I'm not in any position to point fingers."

His eyebrows go way up. "You never told me that."

It's my turn to grimace, because these are memories I'm not proud of. "Twice."

A roguish spark lights in his eye, and he says, "Between you and me, he deserved it."

Despite everything, that makes me smile. "Yeah. He did." I hesitate, then finish folding the letter, which is awkward one-handed. "Where is Sephran now?"

That roguish spark in his eye darkens just a bit. "As soon as it started pouring, I made him take the sentry post. Do you still intend to send Leo back to Ironrose?"

I nod. "The king needs to know. As soon as possible." I glance at the doorway. The rain is so heavy that it's a wall of gray just past the overhang. "If the Truthbringers left last night, they're already ahead of him."

"Yeah, but they were injured, too. And it'll take time to move that many people." He gestures. "Give me a slip of that parchment. I'll give him orders to swap out for a new mount in each city." Without waiting for an answer, he drops into the chair across from me and picks up the kohl pencil I was using.

The slice across his jaw looks even worse up close. "Jax didn't tell me you were injured," I say as he writes.

"I don't even know what got me," he says without looking up. "It might've been a bolt like yours."

If so, that was a near miss. An inch lower, and it would've gone right through his throat. No magesmith would've been able to fix *that.*

In my silence, he looks up. "If you're sending Leo back alone, what are *we* doing?"

It's a good question—and despite thinking about it for the last hour, I don't have a good answer. My primary goal in sending Leo is a matter of speed. That leaves four of us—and only two horses. Briarlock is a tiny town, but we're miles away from the center of it. Even if we could find more horses—questionable at best—I can't decide if it would be more prudent to ride on to the Crystal Palace, or if we should turn back and follow Leo.

As usual, I'm torn between two countries.

Then again, maybe it doesn't matter. It hurts to sit in a chair. If I set off on horseback, this shoulder won't handle it well. And in a fight, I'd be worthless.

I have no idea what we'd find at the Crystal Palace, anyway. Xovaar sensed my magic last night. Could he find me again? And what if the Truthbringers are taking their weapons to go after the king—while the scravers are coming after me? Would I be leading them right back to the queen? Right when the king isn't there to help protect her?

"So the plan is crystal clear, huh?" says Malin.

I run a hand across my face. I'm sure I look as exhausted as he does. "The king is usually the one with the plans. I just follow orders."

I think of Grey sitting in Rhen's strategy room, the way his gaze finally cleared and he really looked at me. *Be safe.*

I wish he were here to give orders right now.

Across from me, Malin looks like he wishes the same thing.

Outside, lightning flickers in the window. A few moments later, thunder cracks *hard,* and we both jump. Almost immediately, a man gives a sharp shout of alarm.

Malin smirks. "I guess that one scared Seph."

Good, I think. But then there's another shout, followed by a higher-pitched voice crying out in dismay.

Followed by the screech of a scraver.

Malin and I scrape out of our chairs at the same time. I'm immediately hit by a wave of dizziness, but Mal is already out the door. I stumble out behind him, realizing too late that I have no weapons and no armor, and I will be absolutely *useless* in a scraver fight.

But we don't find Xovaar and the other Truthbringers in the lane, we find Lord Alek driving a carriage. Callyn is on the seat beside him. Overhead, a scraver screeches again, and I'm shocked to recognize Igaa, Nakiis's frequent companion. The rain has turned ice cold, stinging my cheeks.

Sephran stands alone, a nocked arrow drawn taut on his bow,

blocking them from going farther. "You *will not pass*!" he's shouting in the downpour.

I have no idea what *any* of them are doing here, but a small, dark part of my heart finds one brief moment to hope Alek keeps driving that carriage right over Sephran.

No, not really.

Well, maybe a little.

I might not even need to wish for that, because Igaa changes course in the air, and she seems ready to dive through the sky to tackle him.

Sephran is already shifting to shoot *her*, so I shout, "Igaa! No!"

She banks midair, but Sephran shoots anyway. For a moment, I think we'll have a repeat of the night when Malin shot Nakiis, but the arrow barely misses. Igaa sails past him to land in front of *me*, skidding a little in the mud.

"Tycho," she says. "We have found you."

I can't tell if I'm still dazed or if this is really happening. I shiver in the rain, which feels like sleet as it hits my skin. "Were you looking?"

"Yes," she says. "I have brought Nakiis. He needs your help."

I can barely process that, because behind her, Sephran is already nocking another arrow. "Hold!" I snap at him. "Igaa is not my enemy." But then I glance past *him* to see Alek and Callyn climbing down from the carriage. The rain continues to pour down, soaking all of us. I have *no* idea what to make of any of this.

"Is that the girl from the palace?" Mal says, peering through the rain. He's got a hand on the hilt of his sword, but he hasn't drawn a weapon.

Behind us, feet shuffle against the wood floor of the house, and then I hear Jax's sleepy voice. "I heard shouting," he says. "What—what's—" He breaks off as he stops beside me. "A scraver," he says in a rush.

"A friend," I say quickly, but Jax is already looking past Igaa toward the carriage.

"*Cal?*" he says in surprise.

Callyn was accepting a hand down from the carriage from Alek, but upon hearing his voice, she turns in surprise. "Jax? Jax!" She immediately starts sprinting through the rain toward us.

At that, the carriage door is flung open, and Nora bursts out. "Jax?" she cries. "Jax, it's you!" Then she's running through the rain, too.

"What is happening?" Malin says beside me.

But a second later, the carriage door bounces open, and suddenly little Sinna is bounding through the rain, too. "Me too!" she's calling. "I want to see!"

Despite all their joy at seeing each other, dread has already begun to fill my heart. There are no guards, no soldiers. No royal entourage. It's barely dawn, and we're four hours away from the palace.

Something happened.

As soon as I have the thought, another traveler descends from the carriage, stepping out into the rain. Alek has offered his hand to her as well, but she's waving him off.

I haven't seen the queen since the day the scravers attacked, and the tension between her and the king was no secret to anyone in the Crystal Palace. When Grey made his decision to leave, I never had an opportunity to say goodbye. I have no idea how the queen feels about my part in any of it, but without a thought, I'm striding through the rain to reach her. My boots are unlaced, and the mud drags at each step, but I don't care.

As soon as she sees me, she does the same. "Tycho," she says in surprise—and if I didn't know any better, I'd say her voice broke on the second syllable.

It's Sinna who reaches me first, though. She practically tackles me, throwing her little arms around my waist in a way that reminds me that my body has had better days. But then the queen is right behind her, and she wraps her arms around me. I can feel her desperation and despair, and they're so potent that I bite back the hiss of pain when she unknowingly jars my shoulder.

"Tycho," she says again, and this time I'm sure her voice breaks. There's so much guarded relief in her tone that I can't quite figure it out. "Oh, Tycho. Is he here? Is he with you?"

And then I do figure it out, and my heart breaks a little.

Again, I think of Grey, sitting lost and lonely in the castle.

"No," I say, and her breath catches. "I'm sorry. Lia Mara, I'm sorry."

Her breath catches again, and her eyes stare up into mine, pleading, as if I might change my answer.

"Forgive me," I gasp. Her grip on my arms is *agony*, and much like with Jax, I make a small sound of pain. "Please. Let—"

She jerks back at once. "You're hurt."

Just as I say it, Lord Alek has stepped up beside her. The expression on his face is sheer exhaustion—but also disdain. If I'd been standing in Sephran's place, I have no doubt Alek would have run *me* over.

"What happened to you?" he says, and there's a scornful note in his voice that tells me he's sorry my injury wasn't worse. "What are you doing here?"

The ice-cold rain on my cheeks feels suitable as I glare back at him. *I hate you, too,* I think. If I had a weapon, I'd use it.

But there are bigger issues at stake, so I jerk my gaze away from him to give the queen a nod. "I have much to report, Your Majesty."

My voice is still a bit breathy, but she must hear the importance in my tone. Despite the rain turning her hair into a sodden rope, despite the fact that she was very nearly just crying on my shoulder, she stands a bit straighter. "I do too."

But then a gust of wind grabs hold of the carriage door, making it snap back against the wall, the wood cracking loudly. An ink-dark wing spills through the opening, a lone feather falling loose to land in the mud below.

I freeze in place, remembering what Igaa just said, and how I haven't had a moment to put it together until now.

I have brought Nakiis. He needs your help.

I step past the queen, my boots sinking into the mud with each step. By the time I reach the carriage, the rain has frozen to the walls, making the vehicle glisten in the dim light. Thunder cracks overhead again, lightning splitting the sky.

But my eyes are only on Nakiis, who's sprawled on the floor of the carriage, his wings splayed crookedly. Blood mats the feathers of his wings in a few spots, and I see bruising, darker spots against the gray of his skin. He smells vaguely of infection, but he looks broken.

Or maybe dead.

"Nakiis," I say softly.

His coal-black eyes flutter open. "Magesmith," he says, and the word is full of pain: half gasp, half growl. He might be hurt, but his tone is still thick with the ironic drawl I've grown used to. "Well met."

Injured or not, I have no idea how to feel about him being here. There's a part of me that wants to slam the door on him and leave him out in the cold, like he did the king weeks ago. I still have no idea whether Nakiis is an ally or an adversary, but he certainly doesn't seem like a *friend*.

But as his eyes find mine, it's clear he wonders the same thing about me—especially as he's lying here, wounded and defenseless and desperate. Much like the night we first met, when he'd been trapped and tormented, with no one left to trust.

It makes me think of all the ways I've been in the same position.

It makes me think of all the ways vulnerability has been used against *me*.

So I reach out a hand and rest it over his. Despite the wind and the rain and the feel of his magic in the air, his skin is still warm, and it reminds me of his father, who *was* my friend.

"Well met, Nakiis," I say, and there's not a hint of irony in my tone. Just sorrow and mercy. "Well met."

CHAPTER 25

JAX

After I spent so many months in Emberfall, it's odd to find myself sitting on a milking stool in Callyn's old barn as if we were just here yesterday. The animals are gone, of course, and much like the forge, a faint layer of dust clings to everything, but the deeper scents of old hay and manure haven't dissipated. If anything, the heat and the rain have filled the space with an earthy aroma that reminds me of the stables back at Ironrose at the end of a hot day. It's not *bad*, but it's certainly not great.

It's also the absolute last place I could've imagined a grouping like this.

Callyn and Nora are sharing a bale of hay to my left. Nora seems to have grown three inches since I saw her last, along with a sharper jawline and a new resolve to her gaze. Now she's the same height as her sister, and if she hadn't tackled me with a hug, I'm not entirely sure I would've recognized her. Callyn has changed, too, though her differences are more subtle—and I haven't decided if I like them. She's always been a bit wounded and wary, but there's a new edge that wasn't there before.

Though it's possible I'm just annoyed to discover that she's attached to Lord Alek again, who's standing just to her left, glowering from the shadows. It's been months, but I haven't forgotten the way he tormented me and attacked Tycho. Every time I look in his direction, my jaw tightens, my fingers wanting to curl into fists. He's probably lucky I don't have a weapon—though I have enough adrenaline surging through my veins to knock him flat.

He doesn't seem to care. Since they arrived, Alek hasn't looked at me *once*.

In a way, it's making me *angrier*.

Tycho told Malin to carry the wounded scraver in here, and I was startled when Callyn jumped in to help. Now Nakiis is lying on an old quilt over a thin layer of straw off to the side of the room. The other one—*Igaa?*—stands over him, looking ready to claw out the heart of anyone who dares to come near.

The queen herself has all but collapsed on another bale of hay, the young princess curled up beside her. When they first climbed out of the carriage, the little girl was full of energy, but now her eyes keep flickering toward sleep.

Tycho stands near them both, leaning against one of the support posts, but I really wish he'd sit down. His shoulder wound has bled through the bandages, and the rain soaked his tunic to his chest, making the bloodstain spread. He looks too pale, but his jaw is set, his eyes clear. It hasn't escaped my notice that he's *also* glaring at Lord Alek, and it's probably good that he's not armed either.

He's holding his wounded arm against his abdomen, though. I hope he doesn't pick a fight he can't finish. It was bad enough watching the first time.

Once everyone was under cover, they shared information: Tycho revealing everything that happened in Emberfall, the queen revealing the challenges on this side of the border. I thought the queen might be upset to hear that her courier was killed, but maybe she's grown used to bad news, or maybe she expected it along with everything else that's happened. Once they were done, Callyn shared the way she and Alek were confronted by Igaa, and how she did her best to help Nakiis—though he's clearly still in bad shape. In turn, Alek explained about his confrontation with Lady Karyl—and the fact that she's borrowed magic from the scravers herself. A ripple of shock traveled through the group when we heard that Lady Karyl was able to travel so far in such a short time, but then Igaa spoke from the side of the room.

"If Xovaar has shared his magic," she said, "this Lady Karyl can travel *quite* far." She looked at Tycho. "Nakiis did the same for you, did he not?"

"He did," Tycho said.

"How far?" said the queen.

"Twenty miles." Tycho snapped his fingers. "Like *that*." He looked at Igaa. "Can you do that? Can you return me to Ironrose Castle?"

"That much magic would send a flare into the sky and make this spot a target," she said. "And I doubt I could manage it even if I wanted to." She glanced at the scraver by her feet, then bared her fangs. Ice formed on the posts beside her. "I will not leave him."

Sephran and Leo are the only two who aren't here. Malin gave Leo orders to depart at once with the letter Tycho drafted to the king, and he took off on horseback almost immediately. He then ordered Sephran to sit sentry at the end of the lane. I expected my friend to be bitter and annoyed to be excluded, the way he's been for days, but for the first time, there wasn't an ounce of rebellion in his voice when he said, "Yes, sir."

He *also* hasn't looked at me all morning, but unlike Lord Alek, I think Sephran is simply ashamed.

After Sephran is gone, the queen turns to Malin, takes in the bars on his sleeve, and briskly says in Emberish, "If the Truthbringers are planning an attack, then we must take action. You, Captain, will ride to the Crystal Palace. You will ask to speak with—"

"Forgive me, Your Majesty," Malin says, smoothly cutting her off. His tone is cool, but his expression is genuinely penitent. "I am sworn to Emberfall, and to King Grey." He pauses. "I am not under your command."

Half the people in the room suck in a breath. Alek surges forward. "You are speaking to the *queen*—"

"The king has returned to Emberfall," Malin says evenly. "She is not *my* queen."

Off to my left, Callyn's and Nora's eyes are bouncing back and forth. I wonder how much of the Emberish they can follow.

"*Insolence*," Alek snaps. He takes another step forward, and Malin draws himself up. Immediately, Tycho straightens, pushing away from the beam he was leaning against. The tension in the room triples.

Clouds above. I'm on my feet without even thinking about it, my hands already curling into fists.

"Jax!" Callyn hisses in surprise, but I ignore it. There was a time when I would have backed down from Lord Alek, but those days are well behind me.

For the first time, he seems to notice that he might be outnumbered, because he falters slightly. But it's only for a second, once he evaluates his opponents. Only Malin is armed, and Tycho is clearly injured. Alek's gaze narrows, and his hand falls on the hilt of his sword.

"Enough." Queen Lia Mara holds up a hand, and we all freeze. Her voice is quiet and sure, but her eyes haven't left Malin. The queen seems genuinely struck by what he said, because a flare of annoyance washes over her face, followed by a swell of anger, and finally regret. But then she turns to Tycho—one of the few who didn't seem shocked at Malin's response. "If he is not under my command, is he under yours?"

"Not really, no." When her eyes flare wide, Tycho gives half a shrug with his good shoulder. "He's an army captain. His orders came from Grey himself."

"And my orders," says Malin, "are to protect the King's Courier."

Alek's hand finds the hilt of his sword again. "Maybe we should remove your obstacle, then."

Yes, I'm definitely going to punch him in the face. I take half a step forward.

"*Jax*," cries Callyn, as if she can't believe I'm even a part of this.

"*Enough*," says the queen. She lets out a breath, and it's a sound full of sorrow. "I know my husband. I know he would agree with your actions, Captain." She glances at Alek. "You will be civil, Alek."

"Yes, Your Majesty." He's scowling, but he obeys, taking a step back.

Callyn leans toward me, but she glances between us. "What are they saying?" she whispers. "Do you know?"

I'm shocked to realize that I *do* know—and until this very moment, I didn't quite realize they were only speaking in Emberish. But before I can answer, Alek turns to her and mutters in Syssalah, "The captain is refusing to obey the queen's order. She intended to send him back to the Crystal Palace."

Callyn's eyes widen, but Nora shoots up from her spot on the hay bale. "I'll go!" she says. "Your Majesty, I can return—"

"Nora!" cries Callyn. She grabs her sister's arm as if she'll yank her back onto the hay bale. "You can't—"

"Yes, I can! Your Majesty, I can—"

"You can't even *ride*," Callyn growls.

"Of course I can. I've been learning with Verin."

That seems to draw Callyn up short.

Little Sinna sits up in the straw. "Princess Nora is leaving?"

The queen strokes her hair. "No. Not yet." She looks at Nora. "Though I am grateful for your offer, Nora, I'm not willing to send you off alone." She glances toward the scravers in the shadows, continuing in Syssalah. "We've all been awake all night. None of my people are in any shape to go riding back to the Crystal Palace."

"We've been awake all night, too," says Tycho. He glances at Malin, then back at the queen. "None of us are in any shape to take on the Truthbringers right now, especially if they're working with scravers and they have weapons of Iishellasan steel."

"I'm fine," Alek snaps.

"So am I," Malin says darkly, making it clear that he's understood every word.

I fold my arms. "Me too."

This time Alek doesn't falter, but he finally looks at me, and his eyes are coolly assessing. In his gaze I can see that he's remembering every interaction we've ever had.

Good. So am I.

Nora hops up from the hay bale again. "Me too," she says, though her tone is more gleeful than threatening.

Little Sinna starts to sit up. "Me too!"

The queen sighs, then evaluates everyone in the barn. After the longest minute, she runs a hand down her face, and her shoulders droop. I barely know the queen beyond the time we spent together in Briarlock months ago, but her exhaustion is clear, and it's obvious that Malin's declaration has rattled her.

"We came here to rest and recover," I say. "Maybe we should still do that."

"And while we rest," the queen says, "these Truthbringers and scravers ride toward my husband, intent on his death." She looks at Tycho. "You said they may have a head start?"

He hesitates, then nods. "I don't know that they would have set off for Ironrose *immediately*, because they were injured, too—but I also don't know how many scravers and soldiers they had at their disposal." He pauses. "To say nothing of those weapons."

She looks to Malin. “Can your soldier beat them there?”

Before he can answer, Igaa speaks from the corner. “A human on horseback will not beat a scraver in the sky.”

The queen grimaces. Her face nearly crumples.

Tycho takes a step toward her. “Lia Mara,” he says softly. “The king is not defenseless.”

“He barely survived the last time,” she says, and her voice breaks. “He needed your help.” She takes a gasping breath. “He needed *my* help.” Another breath. “And now we’re stuck *here*.”

Those words hang over the room. Because if Leo can’t make it back to Ironrose ahead of them, then this half-injured crew with too few horses definitely can’t.

“Could we summon the scravers and Truthbringers *here*?” I say. “Draw them away from the king?”

Lord Alek scoffs. “So they can kill *us*?”

“Are you volunteering?” I say.

His eyes flare in surprise. Maybe he thought I’d still be the blacksmith who used to cower in front of a powerful lord, but that Jax is gone. Alek takes a threatening step toward me, and I stiffen—but Tycho steps out in front of him. He might be injured, but right this moment, he looks like he could take on an army barehanded.

“If you ever touch him again,” he says icily, “I will break every bone in your body.” I’ve never heard him sound so vicious, and it makes me shiver. Especially when he adds, “Then I’ll heal you so I can do it *twice*.”

Alek inhales like he wants to retort, but the little princess gasps. “Tycho!” she cries. “Why would you be so mean?” And then she bursts into tears, clinging to her mother.

“Because he deserves it,” Tycho snaps.

“Don’t worry, Your Highness,” Alek says to the little girl. “He couldn’t hurt me if he tried.”

"*Enough!*" the queen snaps. "This fighting is useless." She looks between Alek and Tycho. "And it will *cease*."

Neither of them says a word. They're simply glowering.

The queen sighs and looks at me. "We couldn't outrun scravers either, Jax."

Callyn looks back and forth between us. "But we have magic *here*." She looks toward Igaa and Nakiis. "Could we summon them somehow?"

The scraver's eyes gleam in the darkness. "If Nakiis shares his magic with Tycho, the others would know it immediately." She pauses. "It would heal some of the damage from their wounds—and it would also strengthen their magic. It would be like a beacon in the sky, summoning them."

For the first time, the queen looks thoughtful. "Do they have any weaknesses?" she says. "Could we lay a trap?"

But Alek says, "No. What kind of trap would you lay?" He sneers. "Lady Karyl has magic. Who knows what others have accepted it as well—or how many scravers this Xovaar has at his disposal. According to your story, you have *one* weapon that can stop them."

As soon as he says it, I think of the rod of Iishellasan steel that pierced Tycho's shoulder. Immediately, a solution snaps into place in my head. I've never believed in fate, but all of a sudden, taking shelter at the forge seems predestined.

"We only have one weapon *for now*," I say.

The queen frowns, but Tycho's head snaps around. He meets my eyes, and he smiles. "For now," he agrees.

"What?" says Callyn, looking between us. "What does that mean?"

"We have a bar of Iishellasan steel," I say, lifting one shoulder in a shrug. "So if we just need to make more weapons . . ."

Tycho's smile widens. "Then it's a good thing we have a blacksmith."

CHAPTER 26

CALLYN

Somehow, I'm back in my bed in the bakery, and I can't quite make myself believe it. It's not that I never expected to come back here. It's more that I never expected Alek to be lying right beside me.

Across the hall, Nora is asleep in her own room, little Sinna curled up beside *her*. I checked on them an hour ago, and the princess had her hands wrapped around Nora's arm so tightly, as if my sister were a full-grown doll.

I offered my bed to the queen, but she declined, choosing instead to follow Tycho and Jax back to the forge, where my friend intends to get to work. The familiar *plink-plink-plink* of his hammer is a sound that's deeply embedded in my consciousness. I'd hoped to have an opportunity to reunite with my best friend, because so much about him has changed, but it seems that we're on opposite sides again, at least in a small way.

I saw how he looked at Alek.

I also saw how Alek talked to *him*.

As usual, my thoughts are a mess. Even now, we're in bed together, but we're not *in bed* together. We just have a lot of people who need sleep, and not a lot of areas to do it. Two feet of space exists between us. Honestly, we were closer in the carriage.

"You should be asleep."

His voice is a low rumble, barely audible over the sound of the rain on the roof. I look over. "So should you."

"What troubles you, Callyn?"

"Ah . . . literally everything? What troubles *you*?"

He doesn't smile. If anything, his frown deepens. "Their plan is so . . . reckless."

He sounds so aggravated. I study him in the shadows. Beard growth covers his jaw now, and his hair is a tufted mess from the rain. He stripped his armor a while ago, so now he's in a loose tunic and trousers, but they're damp and rumpled from the downpour. I don't think I've ever seen him quite this unkempt.

"If you're worried about it," I say, "maybe you should be in the forge helping them."

He scoffs. "Helping them with what? Making arrows? Lining the edge of my sword with their steel?"

"Yes . . . ? Those actually sound like phenomenal ideas."

"Callyn. Tycho has two soldiers and a lazy blacksmith—"

"He's not lazy," I say hotly.

Alek continues, unperturbed. "The queen only has you and me. The Truthbringers killed her courier. No help is coming. We have no army, no guards, no *defense*, yet they intend to summon the Truthbringers and the scravers *here*. The king barely survived the first attack, and he had a field of soldiers. We have almost no one."

"You've forgotten Nora," I say. "The queen has her, too."

"Ah, yes, the key to surviving the battle! Your *sister*."

I shove him in the shoulder. "Stop being such an ass."

"I'm being a realist."

I sigh, because he's right as usual. "I know."

We lapse into silence again, and something about it reminds me of our time together in the carriage. I think of the way he finally began to share his true thoughts with me when we were alone in the darkness, compared with how he spoke to Jax and Tycho in the barn—or even the way he's speaking to me *now.* I wonder if things between us will always be like this: sharp and brittle, with any softness hidden behind shards of glass.

But then his voice quiets to a murmur, and he says, "Truly, I understand why she's doing it."

For a moment, I'm not entirely sure I heard him correctly. I look over again, staring into his eyes. "You do?"

He nods. "The king sacrificed himself to protect her. So now she's going to sacrifice herself for him."

As soon as he says it, I hear the truth of it. Of course that's what she's doing. Of *course.* No wonder she didn't protest when Alek said we needed to go to Emberfall. No wonder she was so eager to take Nakiis to find Tycho. It has nothing to do with helping the scravers or hiding our magic. It has nothing to do with Lady Karyl or the Truthbringers. It has nothing to do with any of this. Not really.

It has everything to do with the king, and how desperately she misses him.

I can't believe I didn't see it earlier. I've been seeing her pain for weeks, how badly she's been suffering.

No wonder she crawled through fireplaces and evaded the guards.

"She loves him," Alek says. Then his voice takes on his usual cynicism. "I don't know *why*, mind you, because the man has the personality of a plank of wood—"

"Alek."

He falls silent, looking back at me, and I reach out to put a hand against his cheek. His jaw is prickly, and I drag my thumb across it, barely grazing his bottom lip. He seems to stop breathing, his eyes so intent on mine.

"You're so disheveled," I say flatly, because I know it'll make him crazy.

He nearly sits straight up in bed. "I am not *disheveled*—"

I rap him on the hand, like he's a child. "Hush, you'll wake the princess."

Alek clamps his mouth shut, then drops his voice. "Fine. But I am *not*—"

"Downright unkempt," I add. "I thought your House was known for style and—"

He puts a hand over my mouth. "Stop, before you truly offend me."

I laugh softly behind his fingers. But then *his* thumb brushes across my lip, and it's my turn to stop breathing. When he leans down to kiss me, it's not the swift surety I've always felt before from him. There's a question. An inquiry.

So I kiss him back, and I'm struck by the fact that it's . . . *gentle*. Not that he's ever been forceful or demanding in his intimacy. Just that he's always so arrogant. This almost feels vulnerable.

When he draws back an inch, I almost grab hold of his tunic and pull him closer.

But then he traces a warm finger over my lip and says, "Callyn, as lovely as you are, I have spent far too many hours on a horse for me to be a suitable bed partner."

It's so unexpected that I burst out laughing. "Aww," I say with feigned sympathy, stroking a hand down his chest. "Are you a bit sore—"

"No!" he snaps in a fierce whisper. "I am *filthy*."

He's so outraged about his state of being that it just makes me laugh harder. "I can't possibly think of any other man who'd put cleanliness above—"

"Callyn."

He sounds so stern that I curl in on myself, trying not to giggle so loud. I'm sure it's stress, but I don't care. He's just so *ridiculous.*

But then he strokes a hand along my hair, and it's so gentle and soothing that it steals every bit of laughter from my body. I blink and stare at him, my body gone completely still.

"I'm very sorry for the way I treated you," he says softly. "I regret every word."

I'm frozen in place, because I can't imagine any possible way I heard him properly. "Pardon?" I say.

He flicks his eyes skyward and taps me on the nose. "Go to sleep. We're going to war in a few hours."

I take hold of his hand. "No. Say it again."

He goes still. "I know I hurt you, and I'm sorry." His fingers wrap around mine. "If I could undo it, I would."

There was a time when that would've been enough to unwind everything that's happened between us, but not now. But as I consider the way he sat beside me on the carriage and revealed shadows of his past that I don't think he's ever shared with anyone, I wonder if we've begun to forge a new path.

So I give his fingers a squeeze. "You still can," I say.

A light sparks in his eye, and he leans in to brush his lips against mine. Very soft, very chaste, but it sends fire through my veins anyway, especially when he smiles. "I'll try."

CHAPTER 27

TYCHO

Despite Jax's idea, it took him a while to get the forge set up, especially when we headed back to his workshop with the queen and discovered one crucial problem.

"I took most of my tools to Emberfall," he said with a scowl. "I forgot."

I thought we'd have to scrap everything right then and there. The queen's immediate dismay was visible.

But Jax looked around the workshop and said, "Wait. Some of Da's old things must be under here somewhere." He dug through dusty piles of iron and wood until it all began to stick to his damp skin. Eventually he emerged with a hammer and a pair of pincers, blowing dust and grit off the metal.

The queen looked a bit dubious, and she glanced at me worriedly. We could clearly see that the hammer seemed crooked, and the pincers were rusty.

Jax saw her glance and smiled. "Don't worry," he said. "It won't take long to make new ones."

Sure enough, within minutes, he fashioned a new hammer like it was nothing. Now, we're standing back and watching as he crafts a new pair of pincers, too. The rain is rattling on the roof overhead, and we're all exhausted, but there's something peaceful about the rhythmic smacking of his hammer, the scent of the smoke. Jax moves with careful precision, and I remember the way he used to shift around with benches and ropes to help him maneuver without his crutches.

Now that he has the false foot, he doesn't need any of it. He was always quick and efficient, but this is a new level. I can't take my eyes off him.

Lia Mara must notice me staring, because she bumps me in the arm, then leans in to whisper, "He's a useful one, isn't he?"

"Yeah," I say, thinking of everything we'd been through over the last few days. "He is."

"I knew it." She leans in again and drops her voice. "I kept telling Grey to leave you alone about him. But you know how he is."

That makes me snap my head around. Until this moment, I had no idea that Grey and Lia Mara had discussed me and Jax. When she and Grey separated, I hardly spoke to Lia Mara at all.

"You did?" I say.

"Tycho! Of course!" She bumps me in the arm again.

My expression must reveal that there's no *of course* about it, because she frowns and looks away, then sighs.

"I keep thinking our challenges are simply our *own*," she says. "But they're not, are they?"

I turn those words around in my head, then frown. "I don't know what you mean."

"For so long, my conflict with Grey seemed . . . very private. Very solitary. Something that affected us. *Only* us." She pauses and looks up at me. "But it wasn't."

I shake my head.

She sighs. Jax's hammer swings. *Plink-plink-plink.*

"How is he?" she finally asks.

"Grey?" I say, like it needs clarification.

She nods, biting her lip.

"Absolutely destroyed," I say. "Like his world is ending."

She swats me on the arm.

I raise my eyebrows. "I spoke true."

"Oh." Her face falls.

And then, without warning, her face absolutely *crumples.*

I let out a breath. "Lia Mara," I whisper.

Without warning, she falls against me. It's mostly against my good shoulder, so I keep from making a sound.

Jax must sense that something has happened, because he looks up to discover the queen sobbing on my shoulder.

All good? he mouths.

I have no idea how to answer that, so I give a halfhearted gesture.

His eyes narrow and shift to my injury, which has well and truly soaked through my tunic at this point. It's become a pulsing burn that's impossible to ignore, but because it's constant, I can push the pain aside.

Or maybe that's just the herbs I added to my tea earlier.

He stops hammering and disappears into the house, though.

At the absence of sound, Lia Mara straightens. "Forgive me," she says, swiping at her cheeks. "I shouldn't be so . . . so . . ."

"Human?" I say.

She smiles through her tears. "You're so kind, Tycho." She swipes at her face again. "I'm never this emotional. I feel like I haven't slept in days."

Jax reappears. He has a belt and a kerchief. "You should sleep while you can, Your Majesty," he says. He offers the kerchief to the queen, then gestures at my arm. "Here. I meant to fashion you a sling this morning."

As Lia Mara dabs at her eyes, she looks at me over Jax's shoulder.

Very useful, she mouths.

He's very close, tugging the strap of leather around my neck, his fingers deftly wrapping it around my forearm to keep my arm immobile. Against my will, I blush.

Especially since he looks up, his hazel-green eyes meeting mine from an inch away. "Good?" he murmurs.

Silver hell, how I wish we weren't about to start a war.

"Good," I whisper.

He gives the strap one last tug for good measure. If Lia Mara weren't standing right there, I'd hook my fingers in his tunic and pull him close.

But she is. So I don't.

"Go," he says. "Find the queen a bed." He nods toward the door to the house. "You're just distracting me out here."

That makes my blush burn hotter, and when I look up, Lia Mara's eyes are twinkling. I suppose that's better than sobbing on my shoulder. But I see that her expression is drawn, her eyes red-rimmed, her hair lank where it hangs over her shoulder.

She's likely more exhausted than I am, and that's saying something.

"Come on," I say gently. "You can't fight the Truthbringers if you haven't slept in days."

After I show her to Jax's room, she takes a seat on the side of the bed, but she makes no attempt to move any farther than that. She stares at the window.

"Should I stay?" I say.

She shakes her head—but a tear falls down her cheek anyway.

Then she says, "Am I making a mistake, Tycho?"

I draw a breath, then hesitate—but I suppose that's answer enough.

The queen presses a hand to her eyes. Her shoulders shake, but she doesn't make a sound.

After a moment, I cross the room to sit beside her. She immediately grabs hold of my hand.

Her own is trembling, so I grip tight. Then we sit, and we breathe, and we both try not to think of what's at stake.

If we were in the palace, I would never be this close to her. We've been friends for years, but she's been the queen for so long that there's always been a bit of distance between us, just by virtue of her position—and mine.

When I was fifteen, when Grey and I so desperately needed to escape Ironrose Castle, it was Lia Mara who offered sanctuary. She risked everything to do it.

She's risking everything *now*—because she loves him so very much.

If we don't try to summon the scravers here with our magic, Karyl and Xovaar will go after Grey. I know they will. I can *feel* it. He's the most vulnerable right now, and they know it—especially since they know I'm *not there*. And if they can take out Grey, it's only a matter of time before they can eliminate the rest of us, one by one. It's the only reason they didn't come after me when we fled the tourney.

But if we summon Xovaar and the other scravers here, we won't survive. I can feel that, too. We're too badly outnumbered. If we're lucky, we'll take some of them out, but we won't win.

Months ago, when they first came after the king and queen, I thought we were lost. I was right here in this very forge, and Grey shouted to me, *Tycho. If they've taken the royal family, they've taken Syhl Shallow.*

Grey left to protect his family, and instead it seems he's put both kingdoms at risk.

If we bring the battle here, we'll be giving Grey time to prepare.

While possibly sacrificing ourselves.

And maybe that's the best we can do.

"It's not a mistake," I say to her. My voice is low and quiet. "There is no easy choice here."

"I'm going to give Sinna to Nora," she whispers. "I'm going to send them away." Her breath hitches. "I can't . . . I can't let them use my daughter against me again. I can't watch them do that to Nora. Does that sound weak, Tycho?"

She's talking about the first attack, the way they put a blade to Sinna's neck—and the way a Truthbringer thrust a sword right through Nora's body. "No," I say. "It sounds like you're protecting the children."

The queen looks into my eyes. "Do you trust him, Tycho? Will he help us protect my husband?"

She means Nakiis. As always, when it comes to *trust,* I have no idea where I stand with the scraver.

But that would be the wrong thing to say in the face of all her emotion. I give her hand a squeeze. "He's just as desperate as we are," I say roughly.

It's not really an answer to her question, but it seems to settle her, even if only a little.

"Jax was right," I say softly. "You really *should* sleep."

"Fine," she says, and she must be exhausted, because she does lie down. "But only for an hour or so. We can't let them gain too much ground."

I nod. "I'll see to it."

When I'm by the door, she calls me back. "Tycho."

I stop and turn, remembering how I found her on the night they lost the baby. Her skirts were stained with blood, and her eyes were red-rimmed, just like this.

"Your Majesty," I say.

"I'm so grateful for your friendship."

The words tug at my heart. "And I'm grateful for yours." Then I close the door behind me.

When I return to the workshop, Jax is pulling the steel bolt from the forge. The end is glowing brightly, and he lays it against the anvil, then smacks it sharply with his hammer. Sweat gleams on his brow and threads his hair, but he's intent, focused. As I watch, the end of the bolt flattens. He makes a notch with the sharp end of his hammer, and without missing a beat, he snaps it off. I'm transfixed.

Jax doesn't glance up, but he says, "Tycho. You should sleep, too."

"No. I need to relieve Mal and Sephran so they can get some rest. I'll take sentry for a while."

At that, he looks at me like I'm crazy. "Your arm is in a sling."

"I can still use a sword." *Probably.*

He gives me a look, then uses his pincers to heat the smaller piece. As it begins to glow, he says, "As soon as I'm done with these arrowheads, wait until you see what I do to your throwing knives."

That makes me grin. I run a hand over the back of my neck. "Ah, Jax."

I can't tell if he blushes or if it's just the heat from the forge, but I highly suspect it's both. "Keep smiling like that and I'll make you a whole armory."

That nearly puts me over the edge, because I suddenly want to forget the queen exists so I can drag him into the house where we can share the bed.

"*Go*," he says firmly. "I'm not the only one who needs to be useful." He scowls. "And Mal and Seph probably *do* need a break."

"Not yet," I say, and his eyebrows go up. I reach out and run a finger across his jaw, then tuck a piece of hair behind his ear. Just as his eyes begin to soften, I let go. "I don't mean *that*," I say, and he laughs under his breath. "But there's something else I need to do first."

The rain is keeping the worst of the heat away, but I'm soaked by the time I reach the barn, so I'm not a fan of the trade-off. Noah's herbs seem to be wearing off, too, because my shoulder is on fire again. I ease through the heavy wooden doors.

Nakiis is exactly where we left him before, curled in a heap in the shadowed corner, but Igaa is nowhere to be seen. I sweep my eyes along the rafters, wondering if she took a higher spot, but she's gone.

When I look back at Nakiis, his dark eyes have opened, watching *me*. A cool breeze comes from nowhere to make me shiver. As I watch, ice forms on some of the posts near him.

He doesn't move, but his shoulder muscles have gone taut, his clawed fingers flexed against the ground.

I wonder if he's afraid.

After everything we've been through, that makes me a bit sad. But I suppose I can't blame him.

I grab one of the milking stools and drag it close to him, though I stop about ten feet away because it's clear he's anxious. "Where's Igaa?"

"Keeping watch," he says.

"Is she going to come rip my throat out?" I say, and I'm only half kidding.

"No," he says. "She expects that I will share my power with you."

"Everyone expects that," I say, and it's true. It's the basis for their entire plan to stop Xovaar. I think it's the only reason the queen was willing to fall asleep. This plan has given her some vague sense of hope that we can protect her husband.

His eyes don't leave mine. Outside, the rain pours down, trapping us in this cocoon of sound.

"But not you," he finally says. "You do not expect this."

It's not a question. It's a statement. As if he already knows.

Because I *don't* expect this. He's had many opportunities to share his power with me. Every time, he's withdrawn. I don't know what's worse, whether it's his fear of Xovaar or his fear of being trapped by a magesmith, but it doesn't matter. Either way, his fear is an obstacle he can't overcome. Fear might control him, but I can't let it control me anymore.

"No," I say to him. "I don't."

"Yet you allow the others to have false hope?"

"It's not false hope," I say.

He bares his fangs at me, his claws digging into the straw. "You cannot force me to do this."

"I'm not forcing you to do anything," I say—and despite everything, my voice is soft, because I mean every word. "I intend to ask Igaa."

For one silent, piercing moment, his sudden rage is like the moment between a lightning strike and a clap of thunder. He doesn't move, but the temperature in the barn drops twenty degrees. Thirty. Forty.

I shiver and tuck my good arm against my abdomen.

Finally, he speaks through the air, and as usual, it's not a sound, but somehow it's so loud that it hurts.

—She. Will. Not. Do. This.

I cringe, but I keep my seat on the stool. "She will," I say. "I think she will."

—No.

"Yes. Because she loves you, Nakiis. She loves you, and she wants to stop Xovaar. And so do *we*."

—You cannot stop him. Her magic is not strong enough. You will call them here, and they will destroy you.

"Is *that* what you're afraid of, or are you afraid that binding my magic to hers will allow me to *control* her?"

He makes a sound full of rage and tries to surge off the ground, but it's clear he's really hurt, because his arms and legs give out, his wings flickering limply against the straw. He collapses there, panting. The ice that's formed on the posts and the walls begins to melt in the summer heat.

"So this is how you will trap me," he says, and his spoken voice is ragged. "This is how you will *trick* me."

"I'm not trapping you," I say, and a spark of anger colors my voice. "I'm doing whatever I can to protect as many people as I can."

He says nothing. He just breathes against the ground like he hates me, his claws flexed like he really would tear out my throat if he could.

In a flash, I remember the moment I lay in the dirt at Grey's feet, right after I went after him for keeping me in Syhl Shallow.

I was furious at him for all the same reasons: trapping me there, forcing my hand, keeping me away from Jax. It felt spiteful. It felt *deliberate.*

When he said he was just trying to protect me, I didn't believe him.

But I suddenly understand why he did it. It's the same reason we're all doing *this*. Protection. Loyalty. Love.

"I'm doing the best I can," I say quietly. "Please, Nakiis. You once made me swear to help you—"

"Not like this," he growls.

"Fine," I say, because Mal and Sephran truly do need to be relieved, and we only have a matter of hours before we need to act. "Stay here. I'll ask Igaa, and she can decide."

From outside the barn, her magical voice carries on the air.

—I already have.

Nakiis turns his face to the straw, looking away from me. His eyes clench closed.

I rise from the stool and head for the doors.

He doesn't say a word, and I don't look back.

CHAPTER 28

ALEK

I've barely slept in days, but we're probably going to be dead in a matter of hours, so I imagine I can put it off a little longer. Callyn is finally sound asleep, so I brush a kiss along her temple and slip out of the dusty bakery. The rain has eased off a bit, turning to a drizzle from a gray sky. It's turned the lane into a pit of mud stretching all the way back to the forge. Jax has been hammering for an hour, and maybe that's why I can't sleep. I honestly have no idea what could be taking all this time. That bolt wasn't *that* big.

Clouds block the sun, but they don't block the heat, making for a miserable day. If the Truthbringers come, they'll practically be able to take us unawares. My eyes scan the landscape, looking for Tycho, but I only see those two Emberish soldiers sitting sentry at the end of the lane. Now that it's summer, the trees are lush and green, so I can't see much beyond them, and I definitely can't see very far into the forest. My lip curls, because they should be walking a patrol instead of just sitting there, and I'm ready to walk out and give them a piece of my mind. Just as I'm about to step away from the bakery, one of them salutes the other, then heads into the trees himself.

Good.

No. Not good. I don't know who I'm fooling. He's one man. I myself used to travel with two guards. I know what kind of skilled warriors will be among the Truthbringers. Tycho's soldiers could be the best in the whole army and it won't matter. They can't hold off dozens of armed men backed by scravers and magic.

I hate everything about this.

On the other side of the mountain, they'd likely say I deserve this ending, that fate brought this outcome to my doorstep for plotting against the king.

Luckily I don't believe in fate.

I sigh and make my way up the lane to the forge.

I'm forty feet away when Jax notices me. He doesn't look up, but he goes completely still for one spare second, and then his hammer resumes the rhythmic motion. Even at this distance, tension crackles between us. Earlier, in the barn, I could tell he wanted to take a swing at me.

Good. He can try. We'll see how he feels about my sword.

He's ignoring me now, so I don't break my stride. When I'm ten feet away, he makes absolutely no acknowledgment of my presence, but it's clear he knows I'm here.

"Where is the queen?" I call over the clanging of his hammer. "I need to speak with her."

He completely ignores me.

I don't have time for this. I stride forward, stopping when I'm on the other side of his anvil. He stops hammering, but he still doesn't look at me, instead turning to thrust the small piece of metal back into the flames. He pulls at the bellows, and sparks fly, smoke billowing into the air. It's so hot in here, I don't know how he can stand it. Sweat blooms on my forehead immediately.

"I asked you a question," I snap. "Where is the *queen*?"

He yanks the iron out of the fire, then turns for the anvil. His movement is faster than I'm ready for, the glowing steel held out in front of him as he swings it wide.

I jerk back without meaning to, and he smirks, making me wonder if that was deliberate. But he just smacks the metal against his anvil and starts hammering again.

I don't care if we're outnumbered. I'm going to stab him.

No. I can't. At least not until the weapons are done.

I inhale sharply through my teeth, but he glances up. "She's *sleeping*," he says, as if I'm an idiot for not figuring that out myself. He looks back at his task and starts swinging again. *Plink-plink-plink.* "So shut up."

Ire swells to fill my chest, and I can't imagine why Lady Karyl ever agreed to leave a note with this man. If fate exists, maybe it's been foretold that I should shove him into the forge.

"If the queen is sleeping," I grind out, "then where is Tycho?"

"I'm right here."

He speaks from right behind me, and I jump a little. They're both so different from what I remember, and it's putting me off balance. Tycho and I have never liked each other, but in my eyes, he's always been like a kitten swiping with its claws from the shadows beside a lion. Powerless on his own, but an adversary couldn't strike back without risking the wrath of the bigger predator.

But now it's like he's grown his own set of fangs. His eyes shift past me to Jax. "Did he touch you?"

I remember what he said in the barn about breaking every bone, and I immediately bristle, ready for a fight I don't want. But I glance at the weeping wound on his shoulder, and my eyes narrow. Tycho is pale, his eyes shadowed with a combination of exhaustion and bruising.

"And what would you do if I did?" I say.

His expression darkens further, but Jax looks up without a break from his hammering. "He didn't touch me," he says flatly. "I told you before, no one wants to mess with hot iron."

With that, he turns away from the anvil to thrust the small piece of metal into a waiting bucket of water. A bit of steam rises, and then he tosses the tiny steel onto the table.

It's only then that I realize he's fashioned a narrow arrowhead. Several of them are already lying on the table, waiting to be strung into arrows.

"Good." Tycho's brown eyes shift back to me. He might be injured, but there's enough fury in his gaze that a lesser man might back down.

I don't.

"What do you want?" he says. "If you're here to cause trouble, you're just wasting time—"

"I'm not." I nearly feel my lip curling as I consider this next part, but I say, "I came to talk to you. We should have a plan."

He stares at me for a solid ten seconds. "*You* want to make a plan with *me*."

"Your soldier has already declared he will not act on the order of the queen—"

"And he shouldn't. Would *you* obey Grey's order?"

"That is beside the point—"

"What *is* your point?"

"If you'd shut up for a moment," I growl, "I'd tell you."

He clamps his mouth shut and glares. Beside us, Jax glances up, but then he thrusts the shortened length of Iishellasan steel into the fire and pulls at the bellows again.

"If you're both going to be in here," he says, "start sharpening those."

He nods at a pile of odds and ends toward the other end of the table. "There should be a whetstone or two under there."

For a moment, neither of us moves, but then Tycho shifts past me, moving scraps of wood and lengths of dried leather until he unearths a few dusty stones. He takes two in one hand and brings them back.

He sets one on the table in front of him, and then, without warning, he flings the other one at me.

I swear and scramble to catch it. But because he immediately gets to work one-handed, I do the same. For a little while, the workshop is full of sounds: Jax and his hammer, and us with steel against stone.

But I'm glad for the work, because there's something settling in this. Maybe it's just because I'm *doing* something. An hour ago, Callyn chastised me for not doing exactly this, and maybe I should've taken it more seriously.

Eventually, Tycho says, "Alek. What were your thoughts?"

If he said it belligerently, I'd throw this whetstone back at him, but he sounds fairly genuine, so I keep my eyes on my work. "You're injured, but you have two soldiers. Are they capable?"

"Yes." Tycho glances at the blacksmith. "And Jax. He's got killer aim." He pauses, glancing past me down the lane. "And I've seen Callyn swing a sword."

"So have I." I set down the first sharpened arrowhead. "But she's never fought in a battle."

"She was in a battle right here," Jax says coolly.

I want to scoff, but Tycho looks at him. "But she didn't fight," he says quietly. "There's a difference."

I wait for Jax to argue, but he doesn't. He hesitates, and then he nods.

"You stopped the Truthbringers here once before," I say. "How did you do it?"

"We got lucky," he says. "And they didn't have a scraver lending magic from their side."

"But still," I press. "How?"

"The king and I stood our ground from here," says Jax. "I took out as many as I could with a bow, and he used his sword for any who got past. Tycho set a fire in the woods to trap them in the lane."

I look between the two of them, waiting for more, but that's all he says.

"That's it?" I say.

Tycho nods. "Nakiis showed up with Igaa and some others, and they were able to help in the end, but for the most part . . . that's it."

I look down the lane toward Callyn's barn again. "Does he have more scravers who can help?"

Tycho shakes his head. "I don't think so. Not since Xovaar started terrorizing everyone." He sets down an arrowhead and picks up another. "You saw what Nakiis looked like." He gestures at his own shoulder. "You see what *I* look like. Do you blame them?"

"No." I finish my second and reach for a third. "So that's our advantage," I say. "High ground?"

"Yep," says Tycho.

"And because Lady Karyl has bonded with this Xovaar, she can heal any injuries more efficiently?"

"Yep."

"And our entire armed force consists of"—I quickly count—"seven people?"

"Ah . . . yep."

"Well, that's a piss-poor plan."

Tycho picks up his next arrowhead. "You can always leave if you don't like it."

I bristle again, and I have to remind myself of Callyn's words in the carriage, about the way I set myself up as an opponent. It's just so difficult to see the world through any other view.

"I came to you to discuss a way to succeed," I say tightly. "Not to flee."

His hand goes still against the whetstone, and then he nods. "That's true. You did." He pauses, then looks at me. "Forgive me."

This might be the first time Tycho has ever offered me a genuine apology, and it's so freely given that I'm nearly knocked sideways. I almost have to clear my throat. "The road is muddy, so that will slow the Truthbringers on foot."

"It'll slow us, too," Tycho says, and a lot of the rancor has slipped out of his voice. "But it won't slow the scravers."

From down the lane, Igaa's magical voice speaks to us. ***—The rain will. Our magic brings the ice, which makes it difficult to fly.***

I raise my eyebrows. "That's something."

Tycho considers this for a while. "In Emberfall, the magesmith who trapped Prince Rhen for years was able to use magic to reverse an entire season." He raises his voice. "Igaa, if you share your magic, could we somehow gain more time to assemble a larger force here?"

—You need more powerful magic than mine, she says. ***—And you were not raised as a magesmith. You lack the skill for such a thing, do you not?***

Tycho swears under his breath.

"Neither was Karyl," I say. "So any magic she can use will be similarly limited."

He lets out a breath. "There's that, at least."

"It's too wet for fire," says Jax. "You won't be able to use that against them again."

"Well, they can't use it against *us*."

"So we're back to more practical defenses," I say. "No magic."

We all fall silent again, thinking. Jax tosses another arrowhead onto the table, then looks dubiously at the rest of the bolt. "I'm going to melt a small stretch of this," he says. "We should test whether coating the edge of your blades will have the same effect."

—It will, Igaa says. ***—Iishellasan steel is quite potent.***

I glance at the arrowheads on the table. I'm genuinely shocked at how quickly he made this many. Maybe I shouldn't have called him lazy.

Even still, there don't seem to be anywhere near enough. "We're limited to twenty arrows?" I say.

"I don't have a lot of steel to work with," says Jax. "We have a lot of blades to coat."

"And regular arrows will still work," Tycho says. "But it'll be a lot harder to kill a scraver."

"Fine," I say. "Regular arrows or not—how many do we have at *all*?"

He looks right back at me, and the expression in his eyes tells me it's not going to be enough. "Fewer than forty. We lost a lot in the fight last night, and I wasn't sending Leo off without a full quiver."

This time *I* swear.

Jax ignores me and thrusts the bolt back into the fire. While it's heating, he looks toward the lane, then does a double take. "Cal," he says.

I turn in surprise. She's trudging up the lane, her hair pinned in twin braids like when I first met her.

I stand automatically. "Callyn," I say softly.

"You left," she says, and I can't read *anything* from her voice, whether it's dismay or anger or uncertainty.

"I couldn't sleep," I say, and I realize I sound regretful. "I didn't want to disturb you." I'm *very* aware of Tycho and Jax at my back, and I hate that they're hearing this conversation and very likely judging it. But I also don't want to ruin this course of honesty that's opened between us. I hesitate, uncertain, then say, "You told me it would be a *phenomenal idea* to help make weapons, so . . ."

Her eyes flick past me, to the table. "So you were," she says softly.

"And he was only an ass for the first five minutes," Tycho offers.

I whip around. "You are in the presence of a *lady*—"

"A lady who's used the word before," Callyn says dryly. "Tell me what you're doing. I can help."

"Sharpening arrowheads," says Tycho. He nods toward the table. "We have a few shafts. Alek can show you how to string the ones that are done."

She steps close to me, and I'm gratified when her hand brushes mine, and she automatically threads her fingers between my own without saying a word. She surveys the table. "Is this all we can make?"

Jax nods. "I need the rest of the steel for the blades." He pulls the shortened bar out of the fire, then hammers another piece off the end, then drops it in a stone bowl that he sets back in the fire.

As Callyn watches him, she puts her hand over her heart.

No, not her heart. Her pendant.

Her *mother's* pendant. The one made of Iishellasan steel.

I don't know if the others notice, but I do. Callyn's eyes meet mine, and she swallows.

She expects me to tell her to give it up—I can tell. A day ago, maybe I would have. I don't know.

Just now, I put a hand over hers, pressing the pendant into her skin. Then I lean down and brush a kiss against her lips before letting go. "Come on," I say, scooping up a handful of the sharpened arrowheads. "I'll show you how to string the arrows."

Her breath trembles a bit, and her hand doesn't move from the pendant, but then she shakes herself and follows me.

"It's been a while since the war," Tycho says, "but Grey once said something about how it doesn't take an army to defeat an army." He pauses, reaching for one of the last arrowheads. "And the Truthbringers don't *have* a whole army. Not really. The magic is going to call them here, but it doesn't have to be like last time. We don't have to be waiting out in the open. We *shouldn't* be waiting out in the open—because it'll be too easy for the scravers to take us out from above."

"So we should just hide in the bakery?" asks Callyn.

Tycho's hands go still. "Yes." He looks at Jax. "And the forge."

"So we lie in wait," I say. "And kill them as they come through."

Beside me, Callyn's breath catches, just a little, and I remember what we said about *battle.*

Then she says, "If we're going to lure them into the houses, where are we going to hide Sinna?" she says.

"The queen is going to send her away," says Tycho. When Callyn's eyes flare wide, he adds, "With Nora."

Callyn goes still.

Tycho says, "Do you think she'll be willing?"

"Yes." Her voice breaks. "I'm so glad she's sending them away." She swipes away a tear before it can fall.

I exchange a glance with Tycho. Again, this might be the first time I've ever shared a moment of understanding with him. But before I even say a word, he echoes my thoughts by gently saying, "Callyn. You can leave with them."

Beside me, she startles. "What? No. I'm not leaving." This time she really does swipe away a tear, but her expression turns fierce. "I just wanted to make sure I could keep my sister safe. Nora might not leave if I told her to, but she'll want to protect Sinna, and she'll obey the queen."

"I'm glad to hear it," says the queen. She steps through the doorway into the workshop.

She looks just as exhausted as she did an hour ago, but her expression is more settled. More determined.

Tycho stands. "Your Majesty. We've determined a plan."

"I'm glad to hear that, too."

Jax uses a pair of tongs to shift the stone bowl in the fire, and the molten steel glows red in the light. "Tycho. Give me a blade."

Tycho draws the dagger at his right hip and holds it out. Jax uses his tongs to press the glowing Iishellasan steel against the end of his dagger, then uses pincers to clip off the excess. Moving quickly, he hammers the steel around the tip, flattening it along the edge until it's a thin layer along the point. As the metal cools, it turns gray against the gleaming silver of the weapon. Jax thrusts it into the bucket of water like he did the arrowheads.

When he pulls it out, he shakes it off. "Here," he says. "See if that'll sharpen well."

Tycho obeys, and for a minute, we all watch, listening to the sound of his blade scraping against the whetstone.

Only Jax continues to work, because he's already snapping off another piece. "Give me one of yours," he says, and it takes me a second to realize he's talking to *me*.

"Oh," I say, startled. "Here."

My dagger is wider, but Jax quickly adapts, swiftly taking extra steel from the bowl to coat both edges, hammering it into place until it's flattening along the edge and ready to be dunked in the water. Then he holds mine out as well.

Tycho pulls his off the whetstone and holds it up to the light. "Looks sharp," he says. He presses a thumb to the blade, and blood wells almost instantly. "*Feels* sharp."

"Good," Jax says absently, as if he expected nothing less.

"Can you heal it?" asks the queen, her voice hushed.

Tycho's gaze goes a bit distant, and then he shakes his head. "No. It works."

More assured now, I put my own blade against the whetstone.

"It won't hold forever," Jax says. "But it would take too long to blend the steel in the blades—and I'm not sure if that would work." He gestures to me again. "Give me your sword." Without waiting, he looks to Tycho, then swipes sweat off his forehead. "Leave yours, too, then call Mal and Seph in so I can do theirs. I'm not sure how much I'll have left, but I'll do my best."

Tycho gives him a nod, then strips his weapons, awkwardly laying them on the table. Callyn is following my lead with the shafts and arrowheads, but she watches Tycho disarm, her eyes flicking from person to person, eventually landing on Jax.

Her hand falls back over her mother's pendant.

She doesn't want to. I know it. She lost her mother in the war—just like I lost mine. Unlike me, she doesn't have much left. It's one pendant, and it's not much steel at all. Hardly anything. At best, it'll offer an extra edge to one sword. Maybe two.

But as I watch, she puts down the arrow, and she reaches behind her neck to untie the leather that holds the pendant in place. "Jax." She holds out the pendant, and the steel gleams in the light. "You can use this, too."

CHAPTER 29

CALLYN

My sister, as expected, is eager to follow the queen's order.

"You are to obey Princess Nora," the queen says sternly to her daughter, tears gleaming in her eyes. "No sneaking. Do you understand me? We want to make sure we win our game."

"Yes, Mama."

The queen sweeps the little girl into her arms, then presses a long kiss to her forehead. While she's doing that, I turn to my sister, who's already astride Jax's horse, Teddy.

"He's steady and capable," Tycho said when he led him out of the barn, "and the best one for an inexperienced rider."

Nora nodded, her eyes as clear and focused as if she were being sent into battle.

I sure hope she's not.

Just now, I look up at her. She's got a sword on one hip and a dagger on the other, along with the training armor she wore out of the palace—the same armor she's been wearing in her sessions with Verin. It won't hold up to a determined swordsman, but it'll stop an arrow, and we can't ask the soldiers to give up theirs. For now it's the best we have.

The queen has told Nora not to return to the palace. We still don't know who's involved—which means we don't know who we can trust. "It's past daybreak," the queen said. "Soon, they'll discover I'm gone, if they haven't already. If there are Truthbringers in the palace, I don't want to think of what they'll do to you and Sinna to get to me."

"What about Verin?" said Nora. "What if we could get to her?"

For a moment, the queen looked stricken, and I consider how many times we've wondered whether Nolla Verin was loyal. "I don't . . . I don't know."

My sister nodded fiercely. "Don't worry, Your Majesty. I'll keep Princess Sinna safe."

"Don't stray far from the road," I murmur now so the princess won't hear. Before we moved to the Crystal Palace, Nora had rarely left Briarlock. "You don't want to get lost in the woods." My throat feels thick, and I swallow tightly. "If you're questioned, say you're wearing your mother's old gear from the war. You're playing a game with your sister."

She nods. "Don't worry, Cally-cal."

Cally-cal. Oh, Nora. I try not to think about the fact that I might never hear my sister say that again.

The queen passes little Sinna up to her, and Nora situates the princess in front of her, somewhat wedged between the pommel and her lap.

"Here," says Tycho, handing over a length of fabric. "Tie this around your waists so you don't have to worry about her falling." As my sister does that, he unhooks a pouch from his belt and holds that out, too. "This is all the silver I have," he says. "But those are Emberish coins, so you'll have to be careful where you spend it, or people might question you."

Nora nods sagely, for all the world looking like a soldier taking orders from a commanding officer.

Alek must overhear, because he strides down from where he was standing with the soldiers, discussing the plans for the day. "Take mine, too," he says. "Then you'll have funds you can spend on either side of the border if you need to."

Nora goes a little pale at that, and I can tell that she hasn't considered crossing the border with the princess until this very moment.

"I don't speak Emberish," she whispers, and her voice trembles, just a bit.

"I do!" Sinna chirps. "I can teach you!"

A tear blooms in my sister's eye, as if she's only just now understanding everything at risk. For an instant I want to leap onto the horse behind her, because this is insane.

But I don't want to leave the queen—and Nora swipes that tear away immediately anyway.

"Tuck the money under your armor," Alek says briskly.

"And if you need to spend it," says Tycho, "draw it out a coin at a time so no one ever knows how much you have."

Nora's eyes widen further, but she nods, tucking the pouches under her breastplate, then buckling it securely.

Alek takes a step forward. "And if you stop at a tavern—"

"I think that's enough warnings," says the queen. She pushes past Alek to look up at my sister, putting a hand on her knee. "Hide out until it's safe," the queen says softly. "Don't come back here."

Nora nods. "Yes, Your Majesty." Then she looks at me. "I love you, Cally-cal."

Without waiting for an answer, she gives the horse a swift kick, and they're off.

My breath catches in my throat. "I love you, too," I say, but the words only come out as a whisper.

My sister is the only family I have left, and I just sent her away.

I'm the only family *she* has left, and I just sent her away.

I gave Jax that pendant. I should've given it to my sister.

The queen reaches out and grips my hand. Her eyes are glittering, too. I draw a shuddering breath and look at her.

Before I can say anything, she says, "They'll be safe. Nora will make sure of it. I know she will."

That almost makes me burst into tears—but there's no time for emotion now. We have to act before the Truthbringers get too far.

The queen is already turning to Tycho. "I'm worried we've waited too long."

He nods, then looks to the others. "Find your places to hide. We don't know how long it'll be."

Igaa's voice carries through the trees. ***—For the humans, it may be slow.*** She pauses. ***—For Xovaar and the scravers, it will be quick.***

I don't know if that's good news or bad news. But either way, we've been given our orders, so I move.

CHAPTER 30

TYCHO

After hearing Jax's hammer for more than an hour, the sudden silence in the lane between the bakery and the forge is shocking. I don't think it's ever been this quiet anytime I've been here—and that counts the spring afternoon I spent with Jax and Grey, stripping weapons and armor off the dead bodies of Truthbringers.

If there's any spot of relief, the rain has mostly stopped, leaving only the occasional droplet of water to fall from a branch. The remaining humidity hangs in the air like a cloak to weigh on me as I head for the barn. The sun seems to be trying to break through the clouds overhead, but it's a losing battle for now.

I hope that's not an omen.

Then again, we have a handful of fighters and barely more than a handful of arrows. It probably is.

When I ease into the barn, Mercy nickers to me from where we've tethered the horses, and I wish I had a caramel to give her. Malin tacked the remaining horses earlier so they'd be saddled and ready in the event we needed them, but ever since Alek mentioned fire, I've been worried the Truthbringers would set the barn ablaze as soon as they got here. *Sweet Mercy.* My fingers are itching to strip her gear and set her loose.

But I have more important things to do. Instead of heading for Mercy, I head for the shadowed corner where Igaa stands over Nakiis.

He doesn't even look at me.

Fine.

"Are you ready?" I say to her.

"Yes," she says.

"No," says Nakiis.

I ignore him completely. "Tell me what to do."

"I said *no*," Nakiis growls. A cool breeze stirs up the straw littering the floor of the barn, and ice begins to form on the exposed steel.

"Sit," Igaa says to me, ignoring him. "Allow your magic to find the air."

I sit and close my eyes. At first, it's hard to find my magic, because I've spent days trying to tamp it down to prevent discovery. But every inch of my body aches, and my shoulder flares with pain every time I inhale, so as soon as I relax, the sparks and stars surge in my blood.

"More," says Igaa, and I hear her shift in the straw. "You need to allow the magic to leave yourself. Send it into the air, where it can find mine."

"*No*," Nakiis says. "*Stop this.*"

"No," I say.

"It's never going to work," he says bitterly. "Not like this."

"Hush," says Igaa, and I gasp and open my eyes, because her voice is right against my ear. "Focus on your magic."

The wind in the room picks up, sending straw swirling across the ground. On the other side of the barn, the horses shift anxiously, and Mercy nickers again. Those sparks and stars in my blood settle a bit, withdrawing.

"Try again," Igaa says patiently.

I close my eyes and try to relax, but Nakiis growls again. "Maybe I should just kill you so you can't do this."

This is clearly just posturing, so I don't even look at him. "You'd have to get off the floor first."

It was a mistake to close my eyes, because I don't see the attack coming. Nakiis is weak, but my injuries put us on equal footing. I'm shoved back against the ground before I realize it's happening, and his claws dig right through my tunic and pierce the skin of my upper arms, pinioning me in place.

His wings are crookedly splayed behind him, and my vision is clouded with a haze of pain and magic. I'm trying to struggle, but one arm is still tied to my body with Jax's makeshift splint, and the other is trapped by Nakiis's claws.

He leans down, until we're almost sharing breath. "Would you like to repeat that?"

I wince and try to swallow my pain. "In truth," I gasp, "you've smelled better, Nakiis."

Igaa stands over him, though she looks more like a disapproving schoolmistress than a fierce creature who's going to come to my aid anytime soon. "Let him up, Nakiis." Even her voice is mildly apathetic.

He doesn't. Instead, his claws dig deeper into my arms, and it pulls a sound from my throat.

I don't want to beg him to stop, but everything hurts. Those sparks and stars are stealing my vision again.

"Now," I gasp. "Igaa, now. Even if he kills me—"

"*No.*" Nakiis lets go of my left arm, but the relief is short-lived, because he drives his claws right under the bandage, grabbing fabric and flesh.

Then he digs in and pulls.

"*Please,*" I cry, and I hate myself for it. I don't know if I'm begging him or if I'm begging her.

I do feel like an idiot.

"If you want it, then take it from me. I'm not letting you do this to her."

The pain is overwhelming. I can't see. It's possible I can't hear and his words are only reaching my brain through his magic. My stomach gives a heave, because it feels like he's going to rip my arm right out of its socket. I'm curling in on myself involuntarily. I wish I could call for Callyn or the queen. If Nakiis kills me, maybe one of them can merge their magic with Igaa somehow.

They wouldn't be strong enough.

The thought comes to me unbidden, and I hate it. This plan was destined to fail from the start, but I didn't expect it to fail so quickly.

I'm so cold. The wind is blasting every bit of exposed skin it can find, and my blood seems to be turning to ice when it pulses out of the wound on my shoulder. Nakiis's voice is low and vicious in my mind.

—Where's your magic now, Tycho? You fight so valiantly to save everyone else, but you have nothing left for yourself?

I can't speak. My throat won't work. Maybe he's ripped that out, too. My entire vision is overtaken with vivid stars, bright white in the dimness of the barn.

—Where is your pride? Where is your fight?

His hand shifts again, and I realize I can still *feel,* because something in my shoulder *gives.* I choke on a sound, and the taste of blood coats my tongue.

The air is colder, and I hear Mercy nicker. Nakiis's magic is in the air now, because I can feel it brushing against my senses, the way he once taught me to feel it.

I hate it. I hate *him.* I imagine shoving him away, and those sparks of magic seem to flare in the air, sending the wind swirling away for the barest moment.

"If you want to give me your magic," I rage, panting, "then *give it to me*."

—No, he says. ***—Don't you understand yet? The magic has always been ours. If you truly want it, it must be taken.***

No. I don't understand. I don't understand any of this. My thoughts are too full of pain.

—Why do you think I hated her so much? Why do you think Xovaar hates magesmiths so much?

Only then does it click into place. Nakiis hated the first magesmith who trapped him. It's the whole reason he's resisted doing this at all. It's the whole reason he didn't want me to trap Igaa.

And this is what Xovaar has been after this whole time: a reclaiming of their magic—because magesmiths have stolen it to use it against them.

If you truly want it, it must be taken.

Now I understand. No wonder he hates it. No wonder he's been so afraid.

And I don't *want* to take it. It's . . . it's a *violation.*

I've had too much taken from me. I don't ever want to do that to another creature. Especially not one who doesn't want to give it to me.

Not even while he's ripping out my shoulder.

"I can't," I gasp. "I won't. Just—just let me go. I—I can't—"

—You must. Or he will kill your king, and then he will come for you.

I don't understand. Does he want me to? Or does he hate me for this? The ice seems to be forming its way into my shoulder. "Nakiis—"

—Tycho, you must take it. You must. Please. You must.

Even as he says the words, my magic is finding his in the air like strands weaving together.

But my thoughts are fading. The stars are flickering and going dim.

Nakiis shakes me. My head smacks the ground, and my arm flops limply. He presses those fanged teeth right against my ear. "Everyone here is counting on you, Tycho. Even me. If you won't defend yourself, then defend *them*."

Everyone here is counting on you.

I think of Jax, forgoing sleep to work in the forge so we'd have more effective weapons. I think of Lia Mara, willing to sacrifice herself so Grey has a chance to survive. I think of young Nora, riding off with little Sinna tied in front of her.

I think of Nakiis, who dragged his broken body off the floor to spare Igaa any violation of sharing her magic.

Unfortunately, I don't know what to do.

But maybe he just told me.

You fight so valiantly to save everyone else, but you have nothing left for yourself?

I thought he was mocking me—but he wasn't. Maybe he was truly asking me.

Again, I let my magic scatter into the air, until my vision goes white again. But this time, when I sense the tendrils of his power in the air, I don't push it away, I try to grab hold. At first, the wind swirls away, and I realize what he meant about *taking* it. But I dig deep, thinking of everything he's sacrificed, of everything *I've* sacrificed. I think of my parents. Of my siblings. Of the way Grey pulled me out of the shadows in that tourney and put a sword in my hands.

And somehow, I find a well of strength in my gut, because I surge against Nakiis's hold, flipping him onto his back at the same time as my magic seems to grab hold of his.

For one blazing, furious instant, I almost lose hold of it. I can't tell if I'm losing consciousness or if the magic is just too overwhelming, but it's like trying to grab sunlight or sound—there's nothing *tangible.*

But just as power begins to drift away, I throw all my effort at it. All of my will.

The day Grey and I rode recklessly across the fields to rescue Lia Mara, he was pouring magic into the sky just like this. Nakiis found me that night, and he was shocked that Grey sent all of his magic out of his body like a beacon. Then, I didn't fully understand, but now I do. I can sense my magic, like a living thing outside my body, weaving through the air to mesh with the scraver's.

And just like that, I get it. My magic lives in my blood. I had to work to learn how to send it *out*: to start a fire, to heal a wound. But Nakiis's scraver magic is *always* in the air, always outside his body, always there to be taken. I didn't have to wait for him to agree—I could've taken it at any time, if I'd known. So could Grey. So could any of us.

No wonder he was always so wary. No wonder he was always so afraid of being trapped by a magesmith.

No wonder they all fled, that very first day they helped us in Briarlock.

The wind is roaring around us, biting at my skin, tearing at my hair. My lips feel chapped, and my fingers are numb. I can't feel my shoulder anymore. I can't feel anything.

I'm sorry, I think. But I call my magic back to myself, dragging the magic of the wind and sky right along with it.

Dragging *his* magic with it.

The power hits me all at once, and I'm not ready for it. It's ice flowing through my veins, it's gale force winds making me breathe. It's a relief and an assault all at once, a power so fierce it's trying to escape. My body feels like a blizzard is stuck inside my skin, desperate to get out.

Nakiis's voice finds me. "Breathe, Tycho. This magic is not meant to be kept within you."

I exhale, and I didn't realize I was holding my breath. The air that comes out of my lungs is like a winter wind as it passes across my lips, and I shiver.

Then I look down at Nakiis. My arm has fully come out of the sling, and I'm pinning him to the ground, his wings splayed crookedly in the snow beneath him.

Snow.

My breath catches, and I look past him. An inch of snow coats everything in the barn: the straw, the equipment, the horses. Icicles hang from the rafters above, already dripping in the summer heat. As I watch, Mercy shakes herself, and snowflakes shudder free, drifting to the ground.

And my magic—my magic still feels like something alive in my veins telling me I could run a hundred miles or burn a hundred buildings or start a hundred wars. Telling me I could *fly.* The power was always there before, but this is altogether different. It's terrifying. It's exhilarating.

It's familiar, too, because I recognize that it's *Nakiis's* magic of the wind and sky bound to the sparks and stars in my blood. I can feel it with every pulse of my heartbeat. I give the magic a little *push,* and wind swirls through the space, blowing some of the snow and making his feathers ruffle.

Oh.

When I look back down, Nakiis is staring up at me, his eyes so dark. The sling has gone loose around my neck, and my tunic is a shredded ruin, but the pain in my shoulder is gone.

Part of me wants to let him go—but another part of me is vividly aware of the way he just tore me apart.

"How did you do that?" I demand. "How am I healed?" I flick my eyes over *his* wounds, which aren't. "Why aren't you?"

"The steel of their weapon only touched you briefly." He pauses. "I had to tear away the flesh it touched so you could heal what remained."

"Oh." Just the memory of it causes my stomach to roll again, and I almost have to close my eyes. "Should I . . . do that to you?" As I say it, however, I remember that Jax already coated my weapons with Iishellasan steel. I couldn't do it even if I wanted to.

Nakiis shakes his head anyway. "It has been too long. My wounds are set." He pauses. "You are the one who must fight when Xovaar comes." A light sparks in his eye, a hint of his ironic humor. "But by all means, make yourself comfortable."

It's the same thing I said to him once. I swear and scramble off him. The snow has already gone soft, but there's enough of it that it hasn't fully melted yet.

"Go," he says. "Find your armor. If Xovaar sensed our magic, he and the others will not be long."

If.

But I nod, then shove to my feet. My bow and my breastplate are back at the forge because I couldn't use them. But I need them now.

"Your magic . . . ," I begin.

"Our magic," he says, and there's a note in his voice that I don't like.

"Nakiis." I frown. "I don't want it. You can have it back. We just needed to summon Xovaar—"

"You can't give it back, Tycho. My magic is carried within your body now. We are bound until you die—or until I do." He closes his eyes. "Go. You don't have much time. If he has another magesmith, he can travel far in seconds."

I inhale sharply, but he blasts me with his magical voice, which is so much louder now that we're bound.

—Go!

"Silver hell," I mutter. I head for the double doors.

But once I'm there, I do look back this time. Igaa has moved close to him again, and she's crouched down in the snowy straw. As I watch, she pulls his head into her lap.

I suddenly realize why he did it. He saw no other way to protect *her.*

This suddenly feels too intimate, and I slip through the doors as silently as I'm able.

Once I'm out, I stop short. It wasn't just the interior of the barn coated in snow. It's . . . everything. The entire lane, the bakery, the trees, the forge in the distance. It's melting swiftly in the midsummer heat, because drops are already falling from the trees, but the snow itself evokes the first time I came here, the way I first talked to Jax in the lantern light of his forge. The air was so sharp and cold, and I found him so intriguing. I'd spent so much of my life guarding my emotions that it was the first time I'd ever felt a true pull of attraction for someone else. The feeling was so new and raw that I wasn't sure what to do with it.

I know what to do with it now, but as usual, something else requires my attention.

I shake off the memories and stride forward, feeling the slush-covered mud grab at my boots with every step. Wind swirls around me as I walk, and it takes me a minute to realize that it's not Nakiis's magic causing the wind anymore. It's . . . it's *mine.* After so long without using my power, I expect it to feel sluggish again, but sparks and stars flare in my blood almost without me thinking about it, and the wind picks up. Without warning, the temperature begins to drop. Clouds shift across the sky, and a new round of snowflakes fall.

I shiver, trying not to stare—but I'm not dressed for this.

When I reach the forge, I turn for the door to the house, but a shadow in the far corner shifts, and I jump, my hand automatically going for my blade.

My magic responds simultaneously, and frigid wind blasts through the space, icicles forming *everywhere.*

"Tycho," says Jax, pulling free of the shadows.

My heart is still pounding. "Jax." The wind settles. "You have *got* to stop doing that."

His eyes fix on my shoulder, and then he looks out and around. "We could hear the wind—we thought it was going to blow the buildings down." He hesitates. "I know you said to stay in the house, but I didn't—I couldn't—" He makes a face. "Well, I knew I could watch from here."

There's so much emotion hiding among those words. "Jax," I say softly.

His eyes shift back to my shoulder. "The magic fixed you."

I nod. "I need my breastplate and my bow." This time I hesitate, because it feels like so many things are unsaid, and there's not enough time to say them. "Before Xovaar gets here."

Just as I say it, a new wind swirls through the forge, and this time I have nothing to do with it.

I immediately go rigid, then rush for where my things are shoved against the work bench. Jax sees my sudden movement and yanks the bow over his head, pinning two arrows in his palm like he's been a soldier all his life. Without a thought, I have the breastplate strapped to my chest, and I grab my quiver and join him in the shadowed corner.

We both have a nocked arrow now, but we're shoulder to shoulder, knee to knee, just like the night we finally realized we were on equal ground. It seems fitting somehow that we're having this standoff right here in his forge.

Beside me, his breathing is steady, his eyes clear and focused on the lane.

He's as ready as I am.

A bit of snow falls again, and I look down at the barn. I wonder if I should've made an attempt to hide Nakiis and Igaa somewhere else. Somewhere *better*. When she pulled his head into her lap, there was something so tender about it. Guilt is still tugging at me about everything that happened between me and Nakiis, the way he forced me to bind my magic to his. I know he hated it—and Igaa was willing. *He* knew she was willing. It didn't have to be this way.

But then I consider what he said.

We are bound until you die—or until I do.

And I suddenly realize Nakiis doesn't expect Xovaar to come here to kill me.

He expects the scraver to finish what he clearly already started.

Nakiis expects Xovaar to follow this trail of magic to kill *him.*

CHAPTER 31

JAX

It's midsummer, but the lane between the bakery and the forge are white with the snowdrifts we normally see by the winter solstice. Ice and snow are dripping everywhere, melting in the warmth of the sun, but every now and again, Tycho will adjust his position or shift his weight, and a strong gust of wind will blast through, carrying the taste of snow.

"Is that you?" I whisper.

"I don't quite know," he whispers back.

I wet my lips as the wind blasts past us again. "Can you control it?"

"I don't know that either."

Well, that's reassuring.

When Tycho was down in the barn, I heard him cry out, and it took everything I had not to leave my post in the forge. It was bad enough that I left Da's bedroom to hide in the corner out here.

But I had to wait. I had to see.

The storm clouds swept across the sky unnaturally fast, and the cold descended in a way that made me want to hide. When the snow began to fall, it was so frightening because it was so *wrong*.

And then when Tycho emerged, he was the same, yet altogether different. When he walked up the lane, the snow seemed to follow him. Even now, there's an aura to his being that wasn't there before. I've seen him heal wounds in seconds before, and I've seen him start a fire, so it's more than that. I've never been *aware* of the magic before. He's pressed against me, and the weight of his body is as warm as it ever was, but it's not like sitting beside a sunbeam. This is like sitting beside a bolt of lightning.

Tycho looks over at me. Again, the wind swirls. Snow falls. And I just stare at him.

"What?" he whispers.

"I . . . don't know."

But then I see it. Flecks of gray in the brown of his eyes, a narrow ring of bluish white around the pupil. Like the ice is *inside* him.

My breath catches, and I have to look away.

We fall into silence again, waiting. But as we sit, I can't quite relax. It's still Tycho—only now he's put a target on his back. He's not even doing anything, and this level of power is terrifying.

I wonder if the others would notice, too, or if it's only because I've come to know him so well. But they're all tucked away in their assigned spaces. Callyn is in the bakery with Alek and Malin. They've each taken a room, and they're hiding in the hopes that they can attack from behind if the Truthbringers go for Tycho and his magic, waiting farther down the lane. Sephran and the queen are hidden in the depths of my house, both heavily armed, with Tycho and me posted out here as a first line of defense to protect the queen.

But so far, there's been no sign of anyone. Just the wind and the snow. Tycho said Nakiis healed his arm, and I thought for sure the scraver might come out of the barn to stand sentry with us, but he didn't.

I wonder how long we have to wait—or if they're coming at all. My stomach has been begging for food for hours now, but we've been gone for months, so there was little here to scavenge. We went through the supplies in our packs *hours* ago.

The worst part of me wonders if we waited too long. Maybe this display of magic wasn't a lure at all. Maybe the Truthbringers have already gone too far, and we're wasting our time.

A new gust of wind slithers through the forge, and there's nothing really *different* about this one, but Tycho stiffens beside me.

I inhale to ask, but he shakes his head brusquely, so I clamp my mouth shut. He's got an arrow nocked, the string drawn a bit taut, but he's not aiming at anything yet.

We've got a clear view down the lane. There's nothing *to* aim at.

He cuts a glance at me, then nods toward the side of the workshop.

I nod in return, then move across the space, while he goes in the opposite direction, heading for the door of the house. I immediately understand why—we can see more of the space down the lane.

There's still nothing to see.

But that gust of icy wind wraps around us again, stinging my eyes and making me cringe. I wince and search the lane for invaders.

Tycho snaps his fingers, and I look over. He points toward the sky.

At first I have no idea what he's pointing at. There are just a few birds against the heavy clouds.

Then my heart thumps hard in my chest.

Those aren't birds.

I tighten my grip on the bow, drawing the string a bit tighter. Nothing is close enough to shoot. I know my range, and I can't hit anything closer than a hundred yards with any kind of accuracy. We have a limited number of arrows, too. I have six tipped with Iishellasan steel, and ten tipped with regular iron. Tycho has the same.

I look back at the clouds. At least a dozen scravers are dark shapes against the sky.

A dozen. We have no idea how many Truthbringers are coming.

I glance across the workshop again. Tycho holds up a closed fist and shakes his head.

I don't know all their military symbols, but I know this one. *Don't shoot.*

My heart keeps pounding, begging me to disobey. The scravers are growing closer now, becoming larger shapes against the sky, with wings in various colors. I remember my awe when they came to Briarlock once before, descending from the sky in the midst of our battle against the Truthbringers. But then, they came to help.

This time feels very different.

Ice is forming along the exposed iron in the forge, crystals crawling along my anvil and tools. As I watch, flecks of ice appear on my bow, too.

When I exhale, it comes out in a stream of white, and I shiver.

I glance across the workshop, and Tycho shakes his head again.

It's so odd to think I was right here months ago, a different bow in my hands, the king offering a litany of instructions—mostly warnings of what *not* to do.

Don't waste your arrows. Take time to aim. Don't wait to see if your arrow strikes true. Either it does or it doesn't. Find your next shot.

Don't forget to breathe.

I need that last reminder right now, because I have to force air into my lungs. Every muscle on my frame is as taut as this bowstring. The scravers are close enough for me to take a shot, and my fingers are itching to loose an arrow. I could take down two of them right now—I know I could.

But when I glance across the workshop, Tycho doesn't even look my way. He gives one sharp, fierce shake of his head.

I understand why. The instant I shoot one arrow, they'll know where we are.

I can take down two, but we can't take them *all.*

The voice that carries on the wind is familiar, but there's a flicker of power behind it that hurts my head when I hear it.

—We know you're here, little magesmith.

My heart skips. It must be Xovaar. I heard him last night.

If he's flying, he clearly healed the damage I caused. Is Karyl with him? Did Xovaar make her more powerful in the way Tycho is more powerful?

The scravers swoop wide, changing direction, looping to circle back over the trees behind the barn. My heart stumbles, not understanding—but then I realize that this is exactly what we hoped for. We're under cover, and the winged creatures *don't* know where we are.

Yet.

—Karyl isn't far behind, the scraver continues. ***—We'll flush you out.***

This is our plan. This is exactly what we wanted. Lure them here, yet hide in the buildings where they don't have the advantage of flight and weather.

The scravers begin to fly out of my range of vision, and my heart trips and falls again. I nearly inch forward, out of the shadows, but I have to force myself still. I can't look. I can't *move.* These creatures have such keen senses, and even the slightest motion will draw their focus.

But the scravers circle around the barn to where I can see them again, several of them dropping to land on the roof. One of them shrieks, the sound splitting the air. Another one shrieks more loudly, and I wince.

I wonder if they can sense Nakiis and Igaa inside.

Just as I have the thought, the wind kicks up wildly, snow spinning from the sky. In any other situation, I'd be fascinated at the way snow is falling on a summer day, and I'd be begging him to make it happen over and over again. But just now, I know it's Tycho, and I know his magic is responding to the scravers closing in on Nakiis.

Despite everything, I know he sees him as a friend—or at least something close.

Despite *all* of this, I know he wants to protect him.

As soon as the wind swirls with his power, the scravers sense it. They're off the roof and soaring this way.

Tycho swears under his breath. "I'm sorry, Jax. I'm sorry. I'm sorry—"

"No sorry," I say. "We're together, remember?"

And then I can't say anything else.

All I can do is shoot.

CHAPTER 32

CALLYN

When I hear the scravers shriek, my heart gives a little jump, and I almost make a sound. I press a hand over my mouth and hold my breath. Tycho warned us all that they have exceptional hearing, and I don't want to be the one who gives us away.

How long has it been since Nora rode off with Sinna? Ten minutes? An hour? Somehow it seems like they just left while also feeling like I've been hiding in the bakery for hours. I hope they're well away.

Would the scravers have noticed her running through the forest? Would they have paid attention? Nora has no magic of her own—but what about little Sinna? She's the king's child. What if they sensed it?

And what about this snow? How far does it stretch? How deep does it run? Could Nora get stuck with the princess somewhere?

I do know she'd be disappointed that she's not seeing all this snow in the *house*.

Cally-cal, she'd be saying, her voice as bright as chimes. *It's snowing in my* bedroom.

Well, it *was* snowing in her bedroom. Now it's melting, though snowflakes began drifting through the air again the instant the scravers started shrieking. As I watch, ice forms on the door hinges, spreading along the steel. The next time a scraver shrieks, it sounds like it's right on the other side of the shutters.

My heart skips, and I put a hand over my chest, feeling for Mother's pendant—which isn't there anymore.

I swallow. I should've given it to my sister. It protected me once. Maybe it could've protected her.

Then again, perhaps that's selfish.

Or is it? Like Alek said, we have almost no hope of surviving any of this.

Another shriek cuts through my spiraling thoughts, and I check my weapons for the fifteenth time—though I force myself to leave them in their sheaths. I trained with Lord Jacob for months, and that was one of his first lessons.

Don't draw a blade until you need it. Don't waste your grip strength.

I barely knew him, but I wish Lord Jacob were here now. I wish the whole *army* was here.

But as soon as I have the thought, I feel like such a coward. I've trained with the recruits for months. I have a dagger edged with Iishellasan steel. I have a sword tipped with the same. I might not know how to shoot, but I know how to *move,* and I know how to *fight.*

At the same time, I'm not an idiot. There's a reason Alek and Malin are hiding in the bakery downstairs, while I've been told—ordered?—to take shelter in one of the upstairs bedrooms.

They don't expect me to help.

I keep thinking of the disdain in Alek's voice when he said, *Ah, yes, the key to surviving the battle! Your sister.*

He held me so tenderly in bed, but Alek is nothing if not practical. He might have praised my sister's abilities in the arena, but he knows exactly how far her skills would take her in a *real* fight. I'm sure he doesn't feel all that different about me.

And he's probably not wrong. My heart is so loud I can't hear anything else. When I shiver, I can't decide if it's really cold or if I'm just afraid. The room is full of snow, but a bead of sweat trickles down my back.

Another scraver shrieks. Should we be moving? Should we be taking action? I can't hear a sound from downstairs, so I hold my position.

But is that a mistake? I have no idea.

Automatically, I put a hand over my heart again, and I'm still surprised that the pendant is gone, even though I just did the same thing.

But this time, my hand freezes in place. I'm not sure what sparks it, but all of a sudden, I can't help but think that Mother must have had moments just like this one. She once trained with recruits, long before she ever set foot in battle—until one day, when she finally had to fight.

She must have been afraid, too. She must have thought of my father, or me, or Nora.

She must have wished to be anywhere else.

For the first time, it settles something inside me. This isn't about avenging her or impressing her or failing her or disgusting her.

Because she's not here. *I* am.

The instant I have the thought, a scraver shrieks right on the other side of the shutters, and I bite back a cry, but I can't help the gasp that escapes my lips. The wood rattles hard, and I press my shoulders into the wall. My hands find the hilts of my weapons.

I'm torn between shouting for Alek and Malin and holding my breath, because I don't know what this means. I can't tell if it's trying to break in, or if it's simply taken roost in the tree outside.

Either way, were we really so stupid to think scravers were only going to come in *through the front door*?

Another shriek, and this time the creature slams into the shutters, claws scrabbling at the wood. My windows are only so strong, and they can barely keep out the winter wind. They're definitely not going to hold fast against determined scravers.

I inhale sharply and yank those blades just as the shutters rip wide and glass shatters inward. Wind blasts into the room, swirling the snow in every direction. And it's not one, but *two* scravers that crash through the gap, bringing splintered wood and shards of ice with them. They surge at me before I have time to react—and then I'm suddenly glad for the months of training.

Because without a thought, my body *moves*, my sword swinging in an arc, my dagger thrusting. Sparks and stars have flared in my blood, reminding me of all those times I healed someone. Only this time, the magic is lending strength and speed to my skill. As if they can sense it, one of the scravers screeches so loudly that my ears hurt, and the other one regroups to attack me from the side. But this is just like all those lessons with Lord Jacob and the other recruits, only with magic. *Spin. Thrust. Parry.*

My sword meets resistance for the first time, and I almost falter—but then I hear Jacob's voice in my head, telling me to follow through. I shove hard. The scraver shrieks in my face, fangs snapping toward my throat, wind screaming into the room to tear at my hair.

—Magesmith, it hisses, right to my ears.

I cringe away, but that's all it takes for me to lose track of the other one. It's coming at me from the left, and I don't have enough time to pull my sword free. I go to swing my dagger, but this one swipes with its claws. I try to jerk my arm out of the way, but I know I'm not going to be quick enough.

But then an arrow appears in its throat, and its head snaps back, wings splaying wildly as it scrabbles for its neck, trying to rip the arrow free. For an instant, I can only stare.

"Stab it!" Alek shouts from behind me. "Don't let it break the arrow!"

Right, right. The first one is still fighting against the sword embedded in its body, so I let go of the hilt and drive my dagger into the chest of this one. I slam it home so fiercely that the creature stumbles backward and crashes into the floor of my old bedroom, blood spraying.

Behind me, Malin is suddenly there, pulling my sword free of the first, using his booted foot to shove the scraver off the blade. Then Alek is pulling the arrow out of the neck of the one he shot. Blood and viscera cling to the tip, and I wait for my stomach to roll, but it doesn't. My vision flickers, though, just a little.

Wind keeps whipping through the window, and the shrieks outside haven't stopped.

Alek wipes the bloodied arrow on his trousers and shoves it back in his quiver. His eyes are harder than I've ever seen them. Malin hands me my sword, then moves closer to the window, staying off to the side so he's not visible through the gap.

Desperately curious, I start to follow, but just as I begin to move, the Emberish soldier shakes his head. He snaps his fingers, then points at both of us in turn, then points back at the stairs.

To my surprise, Alek nods, then grabs hold of the bracer at my forearm, tugging me with him. His fingers press into my wrist for one quick second, and I feel the emotion in his grip. I swallow and attempt to wipe my blades on my trousers the way he did, and the scraver blood soaks right through the fabric. *This* time my stomach rolls. But I swallow thickly and shove the weapons back into their sheaths. When we reach the stairs, Malin goes first, and then Alek sends me after him.

Malin leads down the stairs, stopping midway to listen. From here, I can see the front window, and there's nothing but snow outside, wind blowing fast and hard like the kinds of storms that come down from the mountains in late winter. The shrieking of the scravers is getting lost in the howling of the wind, and my heart pounds to consider that these creatures might've been in the trees in the past and we never knew it.

They were supposed to be friendly. They were supposed to be magical. They were supposed to be helpful.

But I remember what Nakiis said about how Xovaar wanted what was taken. Maybe they *were* friendly, but they're not anymore.

I wish I could give it back. I wish we could *all* give it back.

Once we're down in the bakery, the sound of the howling wind is lessened. We all exchange glances, and Malin finally peers out the window.

"No humans," he says in Syssalah, and his voice is very soft, but his Emberish accent is thick. "Six scravers on the barn, but I can't see the forge. Three in the air. Maybe more."

"But none here," Alek murmurs. The wind keeps whistling upstairs, but no further shrieking.

The scravers have gone after Tycho—and Nakiis.

But if they've gone for the forge, that means they're also going after Jax and the queen.

My breathing feels so tight and shallow.

We're alone—and there are dozens of scravers out there. Even if we can somehow defeat them, there are Truthbringers coming along behind them.

But Malin and Alek have been at war before, because their expressions are fierce, revealing no weakness or hesitation. I try to school mine to match.

That way, when Malin nods toward the back of the bakery, indicating the next part of our plan, I can nod.

Jax, I think. *We're coming.*

My breath shakes for one bare second, and then I tack on one more thought.

Please be alive.

CHAPTER 33

TYCHO

At first, the forge felt like a good hiding place, because the deep corners and shadowed overhang kept us out of sight. Jax and the king once held the high ground from here, and they were able to fend off the Truthbringers as they came up the narrow lane, while I used my magic to set the woods on fire, fighting traitorous soldiers from behind.

But today's battle is different. *High ground* doesn't matter when your opponents can fly.

My magic is wild and unpredictable, too. The wind and snow swirl around us like a blizzard. Power is everywhere—in the air, in my veins, in my *breath*—but I'm unpracticed with this much of it. It's like trying to ride a wild stallion in the middle of a hurricane. I have no idea how to control any of this. Out of desperation, I try to call for fire, hoping to catch the trees around us so the scravers don't have quite as much room to travel. But when I try to summon a flame the way I'd light a campfire, lightning blasts from the sky to pierce the snow and scorch the ground in front of the forge, resulting in a tremendous thundercrack that shakes the ground and makes Jax fall backward.

If nothing else, it makes the scravers retreat for a minute.

"Sorry!" I call to Jax. He's six feet away from me, and at some point, a scraver must have gotten close enough to take a swipe at his arm. Blood soaks his sleeve all the way down to his bracer, but it hasn't affected his aim. Despite the strong winds, Jax has a singular focus, and I don't think he's missed once.

But in our brief reprieve, I can see that his quiver is empty. His chest is heaving from the exertion, and only two arrows are left in his palm.

"Don't be sorry!" he calls, scrambling back onto his feet. "Do it again!"

I do. This time the lightning bolt strikes a tree, and the upper branches explode in a rain of twigs and leaves and shards of wood that spray everywhere. We duck back under cover, but the scravers screech again and take flight, going higher into the air to escape the falling debris, though I know it won't last. Jax and I are both breathing hard, the wind still blowing snow everywhere.

I cast a quick look down the lane, peering through the weather. I haven't seen Malin or anyone from the bakery, so I have no idea if they're fighting their own battles or if they even know a fight has begun—though there's no way they haven't heard this screeching. If these scravers get past me and Jax, however, it's only a matter of time before they take on Sephran—and the queen.

Then I realize scravers are ripping apart the doors to the barn.

They're going after Nakiis and Igaa.

Wind blasts around me, and I try for another lightning strike, wondering if I can aim for the barn.

It works—kind of. I hit the barn itself. Wood explodes outward in the snow, but that's all I can see before the scravers attacking *us* swoop down for yet another attack.

Swip. Swip. Jax shoots those two arrows in rapid succession. One strikes a scraver square in the chest, and the creature jerks midair, then falls to the ground, screeching. The other one banks, dodging the arrow and snatching it out of the air.

Then it dives right for me, fangs bared, the steel-tipped arrow held straight out in front of it. We're both out of arrows, and I think Jax shouts, but I'm too focused on the sparks of magic in my eyes and the sword in my hand.

But I don't have to swing. An arrow catches it right in the neck, and the scraver cants sideways, then crashes into the forge, landing in a crumpled heap on the other side of Jax's anvil.

I'm panting, but I look up to find Sephran in the doorway, a bow in his hands, the queen right behind him.

"Good?" he says.

"Yeah," I say, a little dazed.

Beyond him, the air erupts with sound as more scravers fill the sky. Some are attacking the barn, and some are heading for us. More than ten. Dozens, maybe.

We're never going to be able to handle them all. The wind is howling, their screeching so shrill my heart keeps stuttering, wanting to panic.

Stars burst in my vision, and wind blasts around us, my magic responding to my emotion.

"I'm out," Jax calls, but I already knew. He has blades in hand, and I see his fingers flex on the hilts. I have no idea how skilled he is with a dagger, but I guess we're all going to find out.

"I have four," says Sephran, already lining up a shot, a second arrow pinned in his palm.

I think of lightning, and the sky flashes as a bolt cracks down to the earth, barely clipping a few branches that fall in a spray of sparks and flames. Sephran swears and scrambles back against the doorway, but the scravers aren't frightened this time. Two dive at once, one aiming straight for Jax, the other aiming for Sephran. He shoots, but the wind is too wild, and he's not as good as Jax. The arrow narrowly misses.

But then a throwing blade comes from behind, slicing right into one of the scravers' wings, quickly followed by another. The scraver shrieks and falls, just as another blade flies, trailed by an arrow that goes right into the chest of the second scraver.

Across the forge, Sephran looks up, and his eyes light with surprise, and then he grins. For days, they've been at odds, but just now, true relief washes across his expression.

I know that look of camaraderie when a soldier sees a friend in the thick of battle. I don't even need the snow to clear to see who's coming up the lane. Before I know it, I find myself smiling, too.

Mal, Alek, and Callyn have arrived.

CHAPTER 34

ALEK

I don't know what these idiots are smiling at, because we're never going to survive this. If it were in my nature to surrender, I would've laid down my sword half an hour ago. I've got a shallow scrape across my shoulder, a deeper one under my ribs, and my head is pounding like I've been up all night drinking.

I *wish* that's what I was up all night doing.

Hell, I wish I could do it right now.

Instead, I'm swinging a sword at a winged monster who clearly wants me dead, and I'm desperately trying to cover Callyn's left side in addition to my own. She keeps leaving herself open, and I'm terrified they're going to rip her in half when she's not looking. She's strong and capable with a blade, but she's still too inexperienced. If she were facing a swordsman instead of fangs and claws, she'd have a sword buried in her ribs already.

There are just too many of them. These stupid Emberish soldiers must be out of arrows, because no one is shooting, and now we're all relying on daggers and swords. A scraver lets out a shriek right beside my ear, and I spin automatically, already stabbing, and my blade drives right into its chest, just as claws clamp down on my arm.

I'm glad for the bracer. It hurts, but it doesn't break the skin. The creature collapses to the ground, and I jerk the blade free.

Almost immediately, another one tackles me. The impact sends me to the ground, and I go skidding through the snow. Grit and dirt scrape along the back of my head, getting under my armor.

Fangs are coming for my throat, and it's like a repeat of that moment in the sunlight with Callyn. It's going to tear me apart.

But then I hear a shriek of rage, and this one is purely human. Callyn's sword drives right into the creature's rib cage. Its grip immediately goes slack.

She's panting as she stares down at me, her chest heaving, breath leaving her mouth in short, clouded bursts. A note in every exhale tells me she's riding a line between panic and determination. It won't take much to make her yield.

Blood is in a spray across the front of her tunic, and she's got a line of red down the side of her arm that could be hers or could be a scraver's. Half her hair has come loose from her braid, and her eyes are a little wild.

I smile up at her like we're just lying in a field, staring at the stars. "That was *exceptional*," I say. "Do it again."

She huffs a laugh—but she yanks that blade free and swings just in time to drive it right into the next opponent, a new scraver who swoops into the forge, aiming for Sephran this time.

"Grab as many arrows as you can!" Jax yells, and I can tell he's pulling any he can reach out of the fallen bodies. Overhead, thunder booms, and we all flinch, and then lightning strikes a tree beside the forge. Branches and leaves and wood all but *explode* around us with a crack of sound, fiery bits of ash flickering through the air.

"What keeps *doing* that?" I snap, trying to scramble to my feet.

"Me," says Tycho from somewhere behind me. He sounds a bit strained and breathless. "Are they still attacking the barn?"

"Yeah," calls Malin.

Wind surges, carrying snowflakes and still-flaming bits of wood from the first tree that exploded. My cheeks sting when either land on me. But thunder roars again, and another lightning strike hits near the barn. Then another. It's louder than normal thunder, each crash bringing a surge of energy to the air that makes gooseflesh rise along my skin. I hate it.

It's clear the scravers hate it, too, because they scatter away from the barn, taking to the air.

I look at Tycho, and the strain on his face is clear. There's blood on his hands and in a wide spray across his armor, and his eyes are all but glowing. He simultaneously looks like he's full of lightning himself, yet also like he could collapse at any given moment.

Maybe I should care, but I don't.

"Can't you hit *them*?" I demand.

"I'm trying," he gasps.

"I can," says Jax, and with that, he nocks another arrow.

And just like that, the scravers attack *again*.

We're badly outnumbered, and it's painfully obvious that we've never all fought as a unit, because there's no easy fluidity to our fighting. Most of us have never trained together, or even trained in the same *way*. There's no real trust or cohesion. At one point, Malin drives a scraver away with his sword, but it spirals into me, and I strike it with mine, but it leaves me open to the winged creature coming right behind it, talons outstretched.

From behind me, throwing knives streak through the air, embedding themselves right in the scravers' throat. *Snick. Snick.* The creature drops, twitching.

When I look, I'm shocked to see the *queen*.

She's in the doorway. She's a little breathless, but she already has a new set of blades in her hands.

"Stop looking at me like that!" she snaps at all of us. "You think I can have a husband like Grey and be defenseless?"

I laugh under my breath and turn back for the next attack—because it's coming. One of the Emberish soldiers dives for the bodies, pulling arrows and tossing them back to Jax. It seems useful, but I can already tell that this is going to be fruitless. It feels like we're holding them off, but we're really not. They're playing with us, only sending a few scravers to attack at a time, because they know it'll tire us out. No, it's more than that—they know it'll tire *Tycho* out.

And it's working. His strain is obvious. I can hear his breathing from here. Not just his either. I don't know how many arrows Jax has shot, but it's probably been a lot. He's drawing a seventy-five-pound bow at least, and his arm is likely on fire. There's a reason archers in battle empty a quiver and then retreat to be replaced by someone else. It's a miracle he's lasted this long.

The scravers can tell, too. In battle, you can feel victory in the air from both sides.

Right now, we don't have it.

"Get the queen back in the house!" Tycho snaps at Sephran. "Now!"

"I can help!" she snaps back.

But Sephran is already trying to maneuver her back in the house.

Callyn has drawn close to me. I'm not sure how I know, because I don't look at her. My focus is on the air in front of the forge, on the winged creatures that keep attacking. But it's like part of my heart keeps paying attention to her location, centering on the exact space she takes up in the universe so I can make sure she's safe.

"Alek?" she says.

I can read nothing from her voice. I hope I killed whatever gouged me under the ribs, because it hurts like *hell*. "Callyn?"

"Are they going to win?"

She says it so softly, but the question is piercing—especially because I really don't think we are.

But somewhere over the howling wind and the screeching of the scravers, I think I hear hoofbeats. It's only for a moment, and then it's gone.

And then thunder rolls through the sky, and I realize I must be wrong—it must be Tycho's magic. But if I'm right, it could be a second wave—of Truthbringers this time—coming to finish us off.

Lightning flashes. Another tree cracks and starts to fall. Then another. A third tree crashes right in front of the forge, rattling the ground and making us leap backward a little. The scravers scatter wildly, trying to avoid the falling limbs.

But then the thunder goes quiet. Tycho is breathing hard, and the wind is settling. I glance to my left. The queen is back inside the house—with Sephran blocking the doorway, sword in hand. He's out of arrows. So is Malin. So is Jax.

My gaze shifts to the sky. Between here and the barn, at least ten scravers are left. I have no idea whether others lie in wait in the woods.

I swallow. Callyn moves closer to me. I can hear her breathing shaking from here. Or maybe that's my own.

The air changes, and I realize the scravers have paused. Several of them hover nearby. They're watching us.

They know we don't have much left.

As if they can read my thoughts, the ones waiting by the barn take to the air as well.

Quick as the lightning he just drew from the sky, Tycho moves to my side. "Alek," he snaps, like I'm a soldier he can command. "Cover the queen. Now."

I inhale to object, but then I meet his eyes, and I read the bleakness there. I see his exhaustion. I feel the way the wind has dwindled. There's no more thunder, no more lightning. No more snow.

He doesn't expect to survive the next five minutes.

"If they take the queen," he says, "they've taken Syhl Shallow."

I give him a nod, then grab hold of Callyn's wrist. "You too," I say to her. "Come on."

I expect her to resist or to argue, but maybe she hears it in his voice, too. She scrambles after me.

Screeching erupts in the air, and it's so loud and piercing I nearly drop my sword. Callyn gasps beside me.

"There are so many of them," she breathes.

I can't look. I don't *want* to look. Panic is a living thing in my chest, gripping my heart with claws.

The queen meets me at the doorway. "Your Majesty," I say. "Move to the back of the house. *Run.*"

"We will stand and fight," she says to me, her voice equally fierce.

"Then you will lose your country," I say, and she blanches. I move to shove her back from the doorway, just as a shadow falls over the forge. Callyn sucks in a breath, jerking free of my grip. Her sword raises, and I don't even need to look to know. The scravers are descending all at once. Ice forms on every exposed surface from their magic, wind swirling through the space to lift my hair and cool my cheeks.

We're going to die.

I feel it with a certainty I've never known before. Not even the day I was attacked with Callyn. It gives my thoughts new clarity. Time slows. My breathing deepens. I shove the queen through the doorway and whirl to block, prepared to brace with my sword and dagger.

My eyes don't see scravers anymore. Just wings and fangs and claws. Certain death for Tycho and Jax. For the Emberish soldiers. For me and Callyn.

But then one of the winged bodies jerks in the air. Not once, but twice. An arrow appears in the side of its chest, and it falls out of the sky. Then another one falls, two arrows piercing its chest, too. Then a third, arrows slicing into its wings from behind.

The other scravers begin to change course, realizing they're under attack from behind, but there are too many archers—or too many arrows. Within seconds, the scraver bodies drop in front of the forge.

None of us even had a chance to swing a blade.

The sudden silence is louder than the thunder was. We're all still braced, weapons ready. No more snow swirls, the air returning to midsummer warmth. It's already melting in the lane.

And then, with absolutely no fanfare, a handful of Emberish soldiers slip out of the shadows between the trees on either side of the lane.

To my absolute shock, one of them is the king.

Beside me, Callyn gasps. Tycho says, "*Grey*," and he sounds stunned.

And then the queen is shoving past me, dropping her weapons in the dirt, all but scrambling over the fallen trees and the bodies of scravers and charred debris to get to him. The king strides forward, doing the same. A sob breaks free of her throat, and then she throws her arms around his neck. He catches her so tightly that *I* feel something in my chest clench, and my throat grows tight. Callyn must feel it, too, because she gives my hand a squeeze.

"Don't you feel it?" she whispers to me. "They shouldn't be apart."

"I do," I murmur—and I hate myself, but it's true.

The queen's voice is nothing more than a hitching breath against the king's neck, so we can't hear what she's saying. But it doesn't matter. The king's voice is low and sure and soothing, as if we're not surrounded by the remains of a violent and bloody battle.

"You're safe now," he's saying. "I'm here. I'm here."

Tycho has sheathed his weapons, and he steps forward. His expression is full of wonder and shock—but no relief. Not yet. "You *are* here," he says. He frowns. "You got my message?"

The king's brow furrows. "I didn't get a message from you. I got a message from Lia Mara."

The queen draws back and looks up at him. "And you came back."

"Of course I did." The king touches a hand to her face.

"But . . ." Tycho's frown hasn't gone away. "But how? How did you know we were here?"

The king glances back at one of the soldiers with him—and I recognize the young man who'd been with Tycho's soldiers this morning. "Fate put Leo right in our path near the crossroads. So we had advance warning." He looks at Tycho. "Though I could feel the magic in the air from ten miles away. I knew we were headed for trouble."

My own brow furrows. I glance from the king to the queen to the soldiers. "But Lady Karyl said the Truthbringers killed the queen's courier." I look to Tycho. "*You* said the queen's courier was killed, too. You said you found the body."

"We did," says Malin.

"I saw it," says Jax.

The king straightens, looking from soldier to soldier, then looks back at his wife. She holds his gaze for the longest time, and after a moment, he runs a hand along her jaw. It's a gentle movement, as if he can't help but touch her again. "Perhaps the queen can speak to that," he says softly.

She puts a hand over his and takes a long breath, letting her eyes fall closed. But when she finally draws back and turns to face us all, her eyes lock on mine. "I've been betrayed too many times. You, of all people, know this, Alek. I told you I couldn't trust anyone in the palace."

"Yes, Your Majesty. And I swear to you, I was loyal—"

"I know that now. But at the time, I wasn't entirely sure. Someone burned down Tycho's safe house last spring, so I knew someone would try to kill a royal courier—especially if I sent a message begging the king to return."

I frown. I still don't understand, and I'm sure it's obvious. "So it *wasn't* a courier who was killed?"

"Oh, no. It was. It was likely more than one." The queen's eyes flash with vicious vengeance, reminding me that she might be clutching at the king, but moments ago she was fighting the scravers right alongside us. "I considered your warnings, Alek. I considered how many times the Truthbringers had come close to destroying my family. I knew I would have to tread carefully, without fully revealing my actions. Not to you, not to Callyn, not to my advisers, not to my generals. Not even to my *sister.* So when I said I wrote a message and walked among the soldiers to choose a courier, I spoke true. But I didn't just send *one* rider to Ironrose Castle."

My eyebrows go up. I remember our conversation in the nursery, when she told me about Lady Elisa Ruhl, how Nolla Verin spoke for her. I remember doubting the queen's strength in that moment.

Lia Mara takes hold of her husband's hand, and her gaze is as hard as steel, reminding me why she's the queen. "Instead, I sent *four.*"

CHAPTER 35

TYCHO

The feeling of relief about the king's arrival is palpable, almost pulsing through the small clearing in front of the forge. Grey's soldiers stand at ease, and Callyn's expression has softened for the first time all morning. But even though we survived the scravers, there's no relief in my heart. Not yet.

Because this isn't over.

Jax moves to my side, and I realize he's claimed any arrows within reach. His bow is still in his hand, those arrows tucked in his palm. When I glance over, his hazel-green eyes haven't lost their worry, and his jaw is still set. Malin and Sephran are closer to the other side of the forge, but neither of them have put up their weapons. Alek might hate us all, but he's no fool either. When his eyes flick my way, I see the awareness there.

Grey met my gaze for one long moment while Lia Mara was clutching at him, and I know he can sense it, too.

Because Xovaar isn't among the dead—and the Truthbringers are undoubtedly still coming. Lady Karyl is likely with them, and she's likely well fed and well rested.

Unlike us: wounded and weary and exhausted.

I quickly scan the five men backing the king in the lane. They're vaguely familiar—all officers from the Emberish army. I glance past them toward the barn where Nakiis and Igaa waited out the attack. The structure took some damage from the lightning and falling trees, but it's still standing—likely because all the rain kept the wood too wet to catch on fire. I have no idea whether scravers were able to get inside.

I have no idea if they even survived. I haven't heard one word from either of them for the entire duration of the fight.

Wind swirls through the clearing, bringing a few snowflakes, the magic in the air responding to my emotion.

Am I still drawing from his magic? Does that mean Nakiis is still alive?

Grey must feel it, because his head snaps up, his focus sharpening as he looks at me. For a moment, it reminds me of every conflict over magic we've ever had, the way he'd question my judgment or order me not to use it. When I left Emberfall, we'd put our difficulties behind us, but that was before I'd taken control of Nakiis's power, and I have no idea how the king will react to *this*. He was already wary of my bargain with Nakiis. Without warning, the magic responds to my memories, flickering in my veins and sparking in the air. I brace myself, ready for his anger.

But Jax bumps me with his shoulder. "You should probably save all that for later," he murmurs.

Malin is close, and he glances over. He's grown fluent enough that he says, "Tell him a story. That usually works."

It breaks through my focus and makes me smile in spite of myself—and when I look back at Grey, I realize that there was no judgment in his gaze. No censure. It was all in my head, my own insecurities getting the best of me. The wind swirls into nothing, and I take a deep breath.

"Good?" he says.

It's not patronizing or condescending. It's not even an officer addressing a soldier. It's a friend—addressing a friend.

Any lingering tension in my heart eases. I nod. "More scravers may be coming," I say. "The Truthbringers definitely are. I don't know how much time we have." I glance past him again, hoping there's a whole regiment waiting just at the end of the lane. "How many other soldiers do you have with you? Surely not a full regiment, but—"

"None," he says.

My eyes go wide, and the wind kicks up again. Malin and Sephran both snap their heads around to look at me. Any relief they might have felt has vanished in an instant. Alek swears under his breath.

Callyn murmurs something to him, and I realize she's asking for translation. There's no missing the disdain in his tone when he reveals that the king practically came alone.

Even Lia Mara draws back to look up at her husband. "*None?*" she says. "You . . . you didn't bring anyone else?"

Grey looks at her, incredulous. "You said danger still lurked in the palace! That you had proof the Truthbringers were still spying. You said nothing of . . . of *this*." He gestures around, then runs a hand back through his hair. "Given the way I left, I thought it best if I didn't come through the mountain pass prepared for *war*. Clearly I was wrong." He sighs and looks back at me, then to Malin and Jax, lingering for a moment before shifting to the others. His eyes narrow a little, and it's a more appraising look, assessing readiness and resolve. He's always so *aware* of the soldiers under his command, so I know exactly what he sees: a handful of people who barely survived the first battle, and might not have much left to give another.

"Our arrows and blades were tipped in Iishellasan steel," I say to him. "We should pull what we can before the others arrive."

Grey's eyebrows go up. "How did you manage that?"

"Jax," I say.

Beside me, Jax inhales as if to offer more of an explanation, but the queen leans into her husband and says, "He's *very* useful."

Alek sighs heavily, but Callyn hits him in the arm.

Without hesitation, the king looks to one of his soldiers. "Pull the arrows and salvage any blades you can find." He turns to the others. "Drag the bodies into the trees and clear the lane." His eyes flick back to us. "Let's return to the bakery." He glances down at the queen, then looks to Callyn. "Fetch Sinna and Nora. Tell them it's safe—"

Callyn pales a shade. "They're not—" Her voice breaks a little, and she has to start over. "They're not here."

Grey goes absolutely still. This time it's *his* magic that flickers in the air, like a sudden burst of energy around his form. His voice is deadly quiet. "They're alone in the palace? Now?"

Callyn shakes her head fiercely. "N-no. We had to send them away—"

"They're safe," says the queen, but a desperate note in her voice reveals her own fear. "Grey—they're safe. We had to send them away from here. We knew what was coming. We told them to hide. Nora will protect her—"

"Nora is a *child*." He takes a step back, and his eyes are a little wild. I instantly realize he's going to abandon all of us to go after his daughter.

I stride forward and grab his arm before he can. "If you go after her, you will lead them right to her. It's *you* they want. *Your* magic. *My* magic."

"My magic," the queen says softly.

"And mine," says Callyn.

That seems to hit him like an arrow. Especially when I add, "Grey. It's the whole reason you *left*."

He jerks like he really received a blow. "And it still didn't protect them."

“Scravers are coming *here*,” I say. “Truthbringers are coming *here*. Nora got Sinna away. She’s safe. But we aren’t.”

He stares back at me, his arm tight under my hand. If he decides to leave, I can’t stop him. I *won’t* stop him. I remember his desperation when he lost the baby. I know how Sinna’s absence must be tearing him apart from within.

But he’s been a king for years, and he’s been a soldier and a guardsman even longer than that. Grey knows how to put aside emotion and fear in order to do what needs to be done—and he knows it better than anyone. He’s the one who taught *me*.

He does it now. “To the bakery, then,” he says sharply. “We’ll make a plan.”

“No,” I say, and even my voice is exhausted. “The barn.”

His eyebrows go up, and I add, “Nakiis.”

CHAPTER 36

JAX

An hour ago, Tycho had so much energy radiating from his form it was like standing beside a bolt of lightning. Now, he seems so drained that it's like walking beside the dying embers of a campfire. I know he's exhausted and hungry—we all are—but I wonder if it's more. I can tell he's worried about Nakiis, and I am, too. None of us have heard a word from Nakiis or Igaa since the battle began.

But as we walk down the lane from the forge, the king's soldiers are following orders, pulling arrows and throwing knives from the fallen scravers. I don't want an empty quiver, so I pause to pull a few for myself. We have so few with Iishellasan steel; they might as well be forged in silver.

"I'll catch up," I call to Tycho.

I'm startled when the king glances back and takes note of what I'm doing. "Ward," he calls to one of the men. "Hand over the arrows you've gathered."

I inhale to say it's fine, that I don't want to interfere, but I always forget that soldiers are used to following orders, and the man offers a handful of arrows before I can say a word.

I take them and thrust them into my quiver. "Ah . . . thanks," I say.

He gives me a sharp nod. "Yes, my lord."

"No, I'm not—"

But Ward has already moved away, onto his next task, dragging a body into the trees.

A flush crawls up my neck before I can stop it. Bemused, I stride down the lane to follow Tycho and the others. In the absence of the scraver's magic, the heat has swelled in the air again, bringing humidity back with it. All the snow already melted, leaving the lane a bit of a muddy mess, too. I'm glad for the thick tread on these boots, because I don't slip at all.

And with that, I'm struck by the fact that a year ago, I would've been slowly hitching my way down this same lane, praying my crutches didn't go skidding out from underneath me. I would've been avoiding my father's wrath and probably hiding in Callyn's bakery, wishing for my life to be different—all the while thinking nothing would ever change, and I'd spend my life here, bitter and alone.

Instead, everything changed, from the moment Lady Karyl showed up with that note. Or maybe it was the moment Lord Tycho walked into the bakery.

Was that fate, as they believe on the other side of the mountain? Or was it me?

Or was it a little bit of both?

The others have reached the barn, only pushing the doors open enough to slip through. A cool breeze snakes through the trees, making the leaves rustle, and I snatch two arrows from my quiver without thinking about it.

Lord Alek was the last one to head into the barn, and my sudden motion must catch his attention, because he stops and looks back, then scans the sky overhead, his eyes searching the trees just like mine.

But there's no screech in the air, no winged creatures. No wind anymore either.

He looks back at me, and I wait for him to make a snide remark about wasting time. But he doesn't. He just waits by the door.

Is he waiting for me? I shove the arrows back in my quiver and close the distance between us.

Like the rest of us, he took some damage during the fight with the scravers. One sleeve is torn, his arm dark with blood all the way down to his wrist, though he doesn't seem to be favoring it. Another wound at his waist darkens the tunic under his armor, though his trousers are dark, so I can't tell how much it bled. He's upright and glaring, so it can't be too bad.

When I reach the barn, I completely ignore him, moving to push past him without saying a word.

Alek reaches out to grab my arm. "Jax."

I whirl and shove him. He stumbles back, his eyes flaring wide in surprise.

Months ago, I wouldn't have dared. I probably shouldn't dare right now. He's the head of one of the Royal Houses. Despite everything I've done and everywhere I've gone, I'm still just a blacksmith.

But for the first time, I don't care.

"Don't touch me," I snap.

He steps forward. "Look, you stupid blacksmith. I'm trying to *apologize* to you—"

I shove him again, harder this time. He falls back in a way that makes me wonder if he's really injured, especially when it takes him a moment to catch his balance. But then he straightens, and a familiar annoyance lights in his eyes.

"Are you going to call Tycho to break all my bones?" he says, his tone low and mocking.

"You think I can't do it myself?" I shove him a third time.

He falls back a step, and for a second, I'm gratified. But then he surges forward, a fist swinging.

I block without realizing it, deflecting the blow and swinging a fist of my own. He's better than I expect, however, because he dodges and swings again, clipping my jaw before I can regroup. He gets close enough to grapple, and this time, I land a strike. I have a moment where I wonder if we're going to end up on the ground. Before we can, someone grabs hold of my armor from behind, and suddenly we're being dragged apart.

"That's enough," a voice is saying, but I can barely hear over the rush of my heartbeat in my ears.

I blink, and Sephran has a hand against Lord Alek's shoulder, holding him back. Alek's lip is bleeding now, and his eyes are dark and furious.

I have no idea who grabbed me, whether it was Malin or Leo, but I jerk free of their hold. It feels like my own lip is bleeding, and I swipe at it. My father knocked me around often enough that I don't appreciate the memory, especially since I forgot how much it *stings*. "What do you want to say to me now?" I snap.

He spits blood at my feet, the derision clear. "I'm sure you can guess."

I surge forward to take another swing at him, but I'm grabbed from behind again. The king speaks from behind me, his voice low and even. "Jax. I said, *enough*."

That shocks me still, jolting the fight right out of me. As if he can tell, the king lets go, and I turn slowly.

It wasn't Leo or Malin at all. *Clouds above.*

The king glances between us, his expression stony and unreadable.

I take a step back, then swipe at my lip again. "Sorry," I say in a rush. "I'm sorry." Then I repeat it in Emberish—as if the king isn't fluent in both languages. "I didn't—I shouldn't—"

He lifts a hand and I stop. My heart twists into a knot as I wait for him to snap or yell or order us all to go back to the forge so we're out of the way.

But his voice is mild as he says, "Come into the barn. We have a battle to plan." Then he steps through the doorway, leaving us to follow.

I hesitate, then follow. Sephran shuffles in after me, and I'm glad. I wouldn't want Alek at my back.

"*Tahlas*?" he whispers, and it makes me smile. I've hardly talked to Sephran since we fled the last town, and there's a tentative note to his voice.

"*Tahlas*," I whisper back, and he claps me on the shoulder.

But then we move farther into the barn, and we're struck by heavy silence. In the absence of the scraver magic, humid warmth has swelled to fill the space, because it smells like moldy straw and damp horse. But under all of that is the bitter scent from earlier: Infection. Sickness.

It's dark in here, shadowed with the doors closed and no lanterns to offer light. But as my eyes adjust, I realize Tycho has moved across the barn to drop to a knee beside the two scravers, who are now wrapped up together. The queen and Callyn stand nearby.

The scravers are both alive, but even from here I can tell that Nakiis does not look well. Overhead, it appears that the roof was damaged, because large sections have been torn out. I don't know if the other scravers did it or if Tycho's lightning did it—or both—but it's clear that *something* came through here. Nakiis has his head in Igaa's lap, and his hands are clutching hers to his chest.

As I watch, Tycho reaches out to rest a hand over his.

Then he looks up and meets my eyes.

I don't know what I see there, but I know it's not good.

CHAPTER 37

TYCHO

Nakiis isn't awake, but he's still breathing, and when I rest my hand over his, the warmth of his skin pulses into mine. His wings are limply splayed across the ground, but they flicker a little when I touch him. I knew the moment his magic started to fade during the battle, because it no longer felt like a blizzard lived inside my veins, and instead began to feel like the dwindling winter winds that bite at your cheeks just before spring.

I'm very aware of Grey and the others in the barn around me, and I'm sure he wants to discuss a battle strategy, but just now I can't think past the fact that taking Nakiis's magic caused this.

"Did I do this to him?" I say to Igaa, and my voice is hushed.

"No," she says, but I don't believe her.

Then Nakiis's voice speaks to my thoughts, though his eyes don't open. *—**I gave what I could, young magesmith. You needed it more than I did.***

I glance up at Igaa, thinking of the storms, the lightning, the magic that swirled through the clearing and held the scravers at bay.

I think of the way Nakiis didn't want to give me any of it—and in the end, he forced me to take it.

A hand touches my shoulder, and I look up to find Jax. He drops to sit on his heels beside me.

"Can you help him?" he says softly.

"I don't think so," I say, and my voice is rough and worn. I have to swallow past the lump in my throat.

"Can *I* help him?" Grey says from behind me.

"Can *we*?" says the queen. She's taken Callyn's hand, and they're all looking down at the broken scraver.

At that, Nakiis's eyes flick open. In the shadows, they're so dark, but they pick up a glint of light from somewhere.

—No one can help me.

"Can I give it back to you?" I say desperately. "This is my fault. There must be a way. Can I—"

"Tycho," Nakiis says, and his voice is barely more than a rasp. "Xovaar did this. Not you."

"But you didn't want to do this. You could've had more time. You could've—"

"We're all forced to make choices we don't want to make . . ." His voice trails off in a rasp, and he reverts to mind-speech. ***—Haven't you learned this yet? I feel certain your king has.***

I swallow thickly. My eyes feel hot.

"Xovaar is coming," Igaa says. "I can feel his power on the wind." She looks toward the barn doors. "I can hear the horses."

Nakiis's black eyes lock on mine. ***—Do not grieve yet. There is work to be done.***

The tone of his voice in my head has his usual irony, and it's enough to choke back my emotion, just for a moment.

But he holds my gaze, and I realize what he's not saying.

He doesn't have much magic left. The help he already gave was likely all he had to offer.

I give his hand a squeeze. "Thank you, friend," I say softly.

His clawed hands wrap around my fingers, surprising in their strength. "Keep her safe," he says, the words so soft they're barely audible.

"I will," I say. "I swear it."

His eyes flicker closed, and he lets me go.

I don't waste time. I look back at Igaa. "You can hear them? How far?"

"And how many?" says Grey.

"Less than a mile," she says, and my heart slams hard against my ribs. That's a matter of *minutes*. I don't know how much time I was expecting, but it was more than that.

"Captain," Grey is calling to Malin in Emberish. "Call them in."

But Malin is already at the door.

Alek has drawn close. "How *many*?" he repeats to Igaa in Syssalah.

"I have no way to count," she says. "Many horses."

Grey looks to Sephran. "How many did you face in Gaulter?" he says in Emberish.

"At least four dozen," Sephran says.

Grey looks to me, and I nod. "Armed," I say. "Mostly Syhl Shallow nobility and private soldiers."

"With Lady Karyl?" says Queen Lia Mara.

"And her magic," Alek says grimly.

Once the other Emberish soldiers make it into the barn, they all gather to stand at attention and await the king's orders. Grey's five, plus Malin, Sephran, and Leo. Jax and I stand beside the king and queen, with Alek and Callyn just to our right.

Fourteen of us to stand against fifty. Maybe more.

I watch Grey scan the people in the barn the way he did earlier. Assessing readiness and willingness. Leo looks all right, but he didn't fight through the battle. Malin and Sephran look rough and worn—but determined. Alek looks a little pale.

Grey's eyes stop on the horses, still tethered in the corner, then skip back to me. His voice is very quiet. "What do they want, Tycho?" he says in Syssalah. "Do they want to kill me?"

"Yes."

"It's not just you anymore," says Alek.

We both look over.

"It's anyone with magic," he says. He presses a hand to his side and winces.

"Do they know it's me?" says the queen.

He shakes his head. "They have their suspicions, but they don't know for sure."

"Do they know it's me?" Callyn whispers.

Alek reaches out a hand and clasps hers. "No."

But they know it's me. I swallow.

Grey looks at Igaa. "How far now?"

"Less than half a mile, perhaps."

He turns to the queen and presses a kiss to her lips. But it's only for a moment before he pulls away. His voice goes very soft. "I am very glad you sent word. You have my heart. Tell Sinna I love her." Then he looks to Callyn. "Take care of my wife and daughter." He looks to his soldiers. "Keep them safe," he says in Emberish, the words sharp like an order. "Do not follow me."

He turns away, heading for the horses.

Lia Mara sucks in a breath, but she slaps a hand over her mouth as if to stop herself from crying out.

My heart stops. I suddenly realize what he's doing.

And I realize what *I* have to do.

I turn to Jax, whose eyes are a little wide, his breathing a little quick. Before I can think about this too carefully, I press a kiss to *his* lips.

"You have *my* heart," I whisper. "Be safe."

Then I turn and follow Grey to the horses.

"Tycho," he says behind me, and there's sorrow in his voice, but anger, too. "*Tycho.*"

It tugs at my chest and nearly makes me turn back around. I think of what Nakiis just said. *Do not grieve yet. There is work to be done.*

He was right. We really are forced to make choices we don't want to make.

The Truthbringers aren't going to stop coming after our magic until they eliminate it. Maybe we've been prolonging the battle all this time, when we really should've been yielding.

My heartbeat is a roar in my ears, but I stop beside Mercy. She noses at my hands, looking for caramels, just like always. "I'm sorry," I whisper to her. "I'm sorry." But I'm not apologizing to her. Not really.

Grey takes one of the other horses. His eyes meet mine as he swings aboard. "Are you sure?" he says.

I don't have a voice, but I'm not sure of anything.

I do know I can't watch everyone I love die, just because the king and I have magic.

I can't watch him sacrifice himself alone.

I nod fiercely.

But then, when I swing aboard Mercy, I realize Jax has followed me to the horses, and he's pulling himself into the saddle of the third.

"Get *down*," I say, the words sharper than an order.

"They don't know who else has magic. This gives *them* time to get away. I'm going with you."

"No, you're *not*."

"No one can leave me behind," he snaps, quoting my words right back to me. "Not anymore. Never again."

I stare at him, my chest heaving. I don't know what to say.

In my silence, his feet find the stirrups and he arranges the reins like he's been riding all his life.

"Tycho," says the king. "Now." My breath catches. Everyone is staring at us. Callyn and the queen are together, clutching each other's hands. Alek is beside them. Malin is staring at me, and it's clear that he knows what we're doing. If I meet his gaze, I don't know if I'll be able to do this.

Wind swirls through the barn, and I shiver. It's not my magic.

Xovaar.

If I don't do this, they're all going to die.

"Go," says Jax, nodding past me. "I'll be right behind you."

I gather my reins, then move to follow Grey one last time.

The clouds have shifted, leaving the sky blazing with sunlight, bursts of bright blue visible through the tree branches. After the wild morning of rainstorms, blizzards, and lightning, it's bizarre to experience weather that's suddenly so peaceful. Honestly, it's bizarre to ride down the lane with Grey and Jax. I know we're expecting to surrender to a massive crowd of Truthbringers who want to kill us, but right now we're completely alone. It could be any other summer day.

Especially when Grey glances over at Jax and says, "You've grown into yourself, haven't you?"

Jax looks startled, but then he shrugs, as if abashed. "I—yes, Your Majesty. Thanks to the soldiers, I suppose."

"It wasn't just the soldiers."

Jax blushes.

But then Grey says, "I heard you beat Rhen at cards, too. That's good. He needs a little comeuppance."

Jax chokes on a short laugh. "Well. Just the once."

"I regret that I won't be able to see it myself."

I scoff under my breath. I can't believe they're having a normal conversation.

Grey looks at Jax, and a light sparks in his eye. "Tycho thinks we should be serious," he says, very seriously.

Jax affects a stern disposition. "Yes, Your Majesty."

I let out a breath through my teeth and flick my eyes skyward—though I suppose I do appreciate their attempts at levity. "Maybe I should just kill you both and get this over with."

Jax laughs under his breath. But then the king looks over at him. "Grey," he says, any teasing gone from his voice. He puts out a hand. "If we're going to die together, it should be on a first-name basis."

Jax's breath catches, but only for a moment. Then he puts out his own hand to clasp the king's.

"Grey," he says, and his voice is only a little breathy.

Then he lets go, and it's as if sudden emotion captures all three of us. For a moment, a wave of . . . of *regret* washes over us, and it's like even the horses can feel it. All three of the animals seem to want to whirl to return to the barn. I give Mercy's rein a twitch and urge her forward.

"All right," I say, fighting for the same levity, though I'm never the one to bring lighthearted humor to any occasion. "Go back to joking about our impending doom."

Grey looks at Jax. "What did it feel like to punch Alek? I've been wanting to do that for *years*."

Jax grins. "You should've let me do it *again*."

"Why do you think I let you do it the first time?"

That finally makes *me* laugh—but then my heart gives a tug, choking off the sound almost before it starts. This is the kind of moment I've always longed for, where family and friendship and love all twisted together in my heart . . . and now it's going to be over in a matter of minutes. In a matter of *seconds*.

I swallow.

"He was trying to apologize," Jax says, musing, and that gets my attention.

I look over. "To you?"

He nods.

Grey looks at him. "You didn't want to hear it?"

"*No.*" Then he grimaces. "Maybe I should have let him."

"Why?" says Grey. "Forgiveness is earned, not owed." He pauses as if he wants to say something else, but then he thinks better of it. The weight of unspoken words hangs between us, and it takes me a moment to figure it out.

Alek won't have a chance to earn forgiveness.

"Do we have a plan?" I say softly.

"I do," says Grey. "But if they have a scraver, they'll hear it."

A cool breeze winds between the trees, and then a voice finds us.

—Yes, magesmith. I will.

My hands grip tight to the reins. I scan the trees overhead, but see nothing. The woods are dense here, and it's midsummer, and the lane is narrow.

I first taught Jax to shoot an arrow just near here. I could close my eyes and remember that day in the snow, folding my hand around his, listening to the sound of his breath, feeling those first flickers of attraction and desire and being so unsure if I could trust my heart.

But I don't close my eyes. I keep them open, and I follow the king, and we reach the end of the lane, turning south to follow the road out of Briarlock.

Instead of an empty road, we find ourselves facing an army.

CHAPTER 38

JAX

The king has a plan. The king has a plan.

The words keep echoing in my head, repeating over and over again in a rapid panicked spiral until I can't think of anything else. I sure hope he has a plan, because this has to be more than four dozen soldiers. It seems like four *million* soldiers. My mouth has gone dry, and my hands are frozen on the reins.

But whatever his plan is will likely end in sacrifice. In death. That's the whole reason we came out here.

That's the whole reason I followed Tycho.

You have my heart.

After that, did he think I *wouldn't*?

My breathing is so loud I feel like everyone here must be able to hear it. I try to slow it down, but it's overpowered by my heartbeat. A cool breeze wraps around us, and I shiver.

Then I see the scraver, and I only missed it because it's right in front of me, between two horses. Dark red-and-purple wings, one of which hangs a bit crookedly. Fierce, blazing eyes. He's half crouched against the ground, but he's tall enough that he nearly reaches the horses' withers.

Xovaar.

A chain is wrapped around his neck, looped twice for good measure. From there, it drags on the ground, and my eyes follow the links until I reach the saddle of the next horse. Astride the animal sits Lady Karyl.

My eyes go wide. My thoughts stop spinning.

I don't understand what's happening here. I thought Karyl was working *with* the scraver. I thought that's what we were all afraid of—that she and this creature would use magic against *us* the way Tycho used his magic to help defend us against the onslaught in the forge.

Has Karyl captured it? Has she taken the scraver prisoner?

But why?

My eyes flick past her to the armed men and women at her back. It's not four million, not now that my brain is working, but it's easily a hundred. I may not be a soldier, but I've spent enough time among them to know that these people aren't anxious and they aren't worried. They're ready for battle, and they're ready to take the king.

The king has a plan.

I swallow, and my mouth feels like it's full of sawdust. I have to remind myself—again—that any plan is going to end with his family's safety.

Any plan is going to end in sacrifice.

"Lady Karyl," says the king, as if we're just casually encountering each other in the woods, not here to negotiate a surrender. "Or should I call you Lady Clarinas? You'll have to forgive me—I was never informed which name was truly yours."

"Either name will suffice," she says. "Have you brought your magesmith allies here to surrender?"

"I am prepared to discuss the terms."

"The terms." She scoffs. "There will be no terms. You have no leverage." Her gaze settles on Tycho. "I knew the other one would not be able to lend you power for long." She gives the chain a little tug. "Xovaar told me."

Xovaar says nothing.

Grey ignores this, looking past her. "You Truthbringers claim to reject magic, yet you now seem to welcome it among you." His eyes settle back on Lady Karyl. "Am I mistaken about your intent here? As you are a magesmith yourself now, aren't you here to negotiate a truce between us?"

Her lip curls, and a bitter wind loops through the forest. I have to bite back a shiver. "We were *forced* to use your methods," she says. "*I* was forced to use your methods."

"No one forced you to do this," Tycho snaps.

But Grey lifts a hand. "Are you going to rule Syhl Shallow, too? You'll steal the crown from one magesmith and put it on your own head?"

To my absolute shock, she looks him dead in the eye and says, "If necessary."

Behind her, there's a hint of unease. I don't *hear* anything spoken, but there's a little ripple through the men and women assembled there.

They don't like this, and it doesn't go unnoticed.

"They don't want a magesmith on the throne," says the king. "They hate magic. What will you do with this power once I am gone?" he says calmly. "Will you surrender yourself as well?"

"I will return the magic to this creature," she says.

"You *cannot*," Tycho snaps. "If we could give it back, don't you think we would have already?"

That hint of unease rolls through the crowd a second time.

Grey lifts a hand again. His eyes flick to the chained scraver. "You have him on a chain, Karyl. It certainly doesn't look as if you intend to *give it back*."

"I *will* give it back," Karyl says, seething. "I don't want this magic in my veins." She gives the chain a sharp jerk, and the scraver makes a small sound. Despite everything he's done, a spark of pity flares in my heart. "He is on a chain to ensure *compliance*." She glares at the king. "Surely you remember, Your Majesty."

"Grey never kept anyone on a chain," Tycho growls.

"*Tycho*," the king says fiercely, his tone full of warning.

"You *didn't*. Iisak was your *friend*. He was my friend. You have never used magic to harm anyone—"

"Silence!" Karyl snaps.

But Tycho isn't looking at her. He's glaring down at Xovaar. "I know your magic was stolen from you. I know you want it back. I know why you hate magesmiths. I understand now. But the Truthbringers are *not your allies*. She cannot give you back your magic. She cannot protect whatever scravers you have left. Just because they hate magesmiths as much as you do does not mean they are *on your side*."

"I said *silence*!" Karyl cries, and wind roars between the trees, bringing snowflakes. Everyone shivers.

But not Tycho. He hasn't looked away from the scraver on the ground, and for as much damage and heartache as this creature has caused, Xovaar hasn't looked away from Tycho.

"I know you hated Lilith," Tycho says, his voice straining over the wind. It's stinging my cheeks and burning my eyes. "I know what she did to Nakiis, and I know why you were afraid of Grey. I do. I swear to you, I do, Xovaar. But Grey didn't take your magic—he didn't even want it. Neither did I. There is not one magesmith left who *stole* their magic from scravers." His gaze narrows, and he looks at Karyl. "Well. Perhaps one."

"The end justifies the means," she says, seething.

"I rather doubt it." Tycho looks past the scraver at the Truthbringers. "You came to the palace with fire. You tried to kill the queen. Believe what you want, but if you had come to the king with your fears, he would have listened. Instead you brought threats and violence and death." Tycho looks back at Xovaar. The scraver's claws flex against the ground, and he bares the edge of his fangs.

Tycho doesn't flinch. If anything, sadness reflects in his eyes. "You sought out help from rebels and traitors and spies, Xovaar. Perhaps you found what you wanted, but I promise you this: if you had come to the king for help, you wouldn't be on a chain. If you had come to me for help, I would have answered."

For one blazing instant, the wind stops. The sudden silence is shocking.

Then Karyl loops that chain once around her fist, as if reassuring herself that the scraver is still under her control. Another wave of unease rolls through the Truthbringers.

But my eyes are still on Xovaar, who hasn't looked away from Tycho.

Brave, kind, caring Tycho, who somehow finds a way to discover empathy in every situation, even when he's staring death right in the face.

"You're losing your army," Grey says to Karyl, speaking through the silence.

"Oh, you think so?" Lady Karyl smiles, and her eyes are so dark. "You can say what you want to this scraver, but it doesn't matter. They hate him, too." Her eyes narrow. "I'm done listening to you all. So perhaps it's time to do what we came here to do."

CHAPTER 39

CALLYN

We've pulled back to the forge. Nakiis and Igaa told the queen that their presence might draw Xovaar and that we should hide elsewhere—or flee altogether. King Grey and his soldiers had horses, but it's still not enough for all of us, and I know the queen won't run while her husband is out sacrificing himself—if the soldiers would even let us.

But they allow the queen and me to lock ourselves in Jax's house with Alek, taking shelter behind the forge while they guard it from the lane.

And *that* allows us to sneak out the back, creeping through the shadowed woods and over the hill to watch from high ground.

From there, we're able to see the standoff almost the instant it happens.

The queen gasps, and Alek grabs her from behind, slapping a hand over her mouth before she can make any more sound than that.

"I'm sorry," he says, and his whispered voice is tight with strain—and empathy. "I'm sorry. You *must* be quiet."

She squeezes her eyes shut, and a tear escapes. But then she nods fiercely.

Alek lets her go. She crouches in the brush beside me. Her breathing is shaking.

"I don't see a scraver," she says. She glances at Alek. "I thought you said Karyl had a scraver."

"She does," he says. He frowns, then points. "It's there."

We peer between the trees, and I finally spot it. No wonder we didn't see it at first. The scraver isn't high above the horses in the trees. It's on the ground, a chain hooked to its neck.

I swallow.

"Tycho said four dozen," I whisper, staring at the mob on horseback facing Tycho, Jax, and the king. "Is that four dozen?"

"It's more," a male voice murmurs from behind us.

We whip around to find Tycho's soldiers have snuck into the woods, too. Malin, who was in the house with me and Alek, plus the other two. Sephran and Leo. Beside me, the queen looks from face to face, and for one brief moment, I can feel the hope radiating from her, as if she expects them to have a new plan that will change everything and save her husband's life.

But their expressions are grim, their eyes heavy with emotion.

"They did this to spare you," Malin says quietly. "Your Majesty—the king would want you to withdraw."

The queen blanches.

I think of what King Grey said to me—to *me*—right before he walked out of that barn.

Take care of my wife and daughter.

I take hold of her hand. "The captain is right. Perhaps we *should* withdraw."

"I will see." She grips my fingers tight. "I will see what they do to him." Her voice goes a bit breathy. "They haven't dismounted the horses yet. They haven't surrendered. They're talking. Perhaps Grey can negotiate with the Truthbringers for—"

Something snaps, and the king's body jerks, then falls from the horse.

Then it happens to Tycho.

And then to Jax.

Alek catches the queen again, clamping a hand over her mouth.

My heartbeat roars in my head, blocking out the sound of everything. I can't move. I can't run. I can't *think*.

They killed them. Just like that. *They killed them.* I knew it was coming, but somehow I didn't expect it.

And then, as I stare, the scraver launches into the air, its flight crooked and clumsy. But it screeches so loudly that I want to cower, claws outstretched, fangs bared.

"Destroy them," shouts a woman, the first clear voice I've heard.

And the scraver descends.

CHAPTER 40

TYCHO

The first time they hit me with one of these arrows, it was sheer agony.

It's no better this time around, especially since it knocks me off the horse. I'm distantly aware of Grey and Jax hitting the ground somewhere beside me. One of the horses spooks and bolts, because I catch a hoof in the hip before the animal gallops away.

Xovaar's screech fills the air, and I hear the chain rattle as he takes to the air. There's a low murmur from the mob of Truthbringers, but I've already drawn my sword, though I know I won't be able to fight them *all* off. Not from the ground, not from my back. Not at all. But my training is too thorough, my will to live too strong. Beside me, I'm not surprised to discover that Grey has done the same.

"I can't shoot," Jax is gasping. "I can't—"

"It's all right," Grey is saying. "It's all right."

Xovaar hovers in the air above us. He's at the end of his chain, his hands flexed, his talons ready. There was a moment I thought I might've convinced him to help *us*. But I suppose it's been too long. There's been too much harm.

"You will see," Karyl crows to the Truthbringers as the wind whips around us, stinging my eyes and stealing my breath. I wish Nakiis had more to offer, but any power he has left is barely a shimmer in my thoughts. "This scraver is under my control."

Xovaar shrieks again, and there's something desperate to the cry—as if calling for help, or shouting a warning. I've never asked Nakiis if there's a language to their calls, and I don't suppose I'll ever get the chance.

"Finish this!" Karyl calls. "Xovaar, *finish this*."

The scraver swoops down. I lift my sword. I brace for death.

But instead of driving those fangs and claws into one of us, the scraver launches himself at Lady Karyl, and he tears her apart.

CHAPTER 41

ALEK

As soon as the scraver starts ripping Karyl apart, Callyn whirls and presses herself against the center of my breastplate. The queen is beside me, gripping my armor, but she's still staring. She's gasping against her hand, almost keening at the violence of it. I catch them both automatically, but I can't do anything but stare. It's graphic and horrifying and quite possibly the most vicious thing I've ever seen.

Especially because the Truthbringers fill the creature with arrows before he's even done.

Within seconds, Karyl is dead. The scraver is dead. Their bodies lie in a mangled heap in front of the horses.

The Emberish soldiers have surged up beside me and Callyn and the queen. They all have weapons drawn, as if the fight has shifted, as if there's some possible way they can forge ahead and save their king.

But they can't. The king has still fallen. So have Tycho and Jax. Their bodies lie in the lane, too.

And there's still an army of Truthbringers to contend with. The queen's shaking breath is very loud in the silence of the forest.

"Callyn," I murmur. "We need to get the queen to safety."

But as I say it, horns sound to our west—and then to our east. I snap my head up. I haven't heard that sound in years. Beside me, the queen draws a sharp breath.

The soldiers exchange glances. "What is that?" says Sephran.

"Battle horns," says Callyn. The shock in her voice echoes what I feel.

"The army," I say.

"*My* army," says the queen. She swipes at her cheeks, peering between the trees.

The horns sound again, so close they're nearly on top of us. They sound as if they're coming from everywhere. Ahead of us, on the road, the Truthbringers are beginning to scramble. Their horses are whirling and bolting in every direction, trying to flee. It's been years since Syhl Shallow was at war, but most everyone of fighting age knows what those horns mean.

And then I see the soldiers pouring between the trees, ready for battle.

At the front is Nolla Verin, the queen's sister, shouting orders like a general.

"You are surrounded!" she calls. "You will surrender to the Queen's Army. If you run, you will be *shot*." She must see the bodies on the ground because she stops short and stares, then gestures. "Lieutenant! That's the king! Find the field surgeon. Get the—" She breaks off, draws a bow over her shoulder, and shoots. Fifty yards away, a Truthbringer drops to the ground. Without missing a beat, she scans the grounds, then looks back over her shoulder. "Nora! Show me where to find my sister."

Callyn gasps.

Because there, riding up behind Verin, is Nora, still astride Teddy, little Princess Sinna tied in front of her, just like before.

I let out a breath. "Your sister," I say softly, because I can't quite believe it. "She went to fetch Nolla Verin." I shake my head a little, staring. The queen has already begun striding forward, the soldiers following. I'm a bit light-headed, but I give Callyn's hand a tug. "Come on."

"Do you trust this?" Callyn says.

For a moment, my usual cynicism kicks in, and I want to be suspicious. But then I look at this massive militaristic response, and I realize that all of my suspicion was probably my own guilt all along.

"I do," I say. "Also, you were right. I should have listened to you."

She peers up at me in the summer heat. "I was right?"

I give her a smile. "Your sister was the key to surviving the battle."

But then I take another step, and my vision goes spotty.

"Alek?" she says. "Alek!"

I don't know if I'm falling or if the world turns upside down. All I know is that I give her hand a squeeze, and then the sky goes dark.

CHAPTER 42

TYCHO

I'm not dead, but there's a part of me that wishes I were.

It hurts just as much to dig the bolt out of my shoulder this time. Maybe more, because I'm mostly conscious the whole time—and I told them what Nakiis told me, that any flesh that touched the Iishellasan steel needed to be cut away if we had any hope of healing it. The king's wound is worse, from what I hear. I haven't seen him. I haven't seen Jax either, but someone tells me they got the bolt out of his abdomen. I ask if his wound is worse than mine, but no one can tell me.

Then they go to cut away more flesh, and I lose track of time.

A lot of time.

When I finally wake, I think I'm dreaming. I'm in Jax's bedroom again, and the space is bright with sunlight. Nothing is dusty, and the window is unboarded. We're sharing his bed, both shirtless, his hair wild and unbound across the pillow. His body is a warm weight against mine, his cheek pressed into my arm, his breathing slow and even.

But when I lift a hand to stroke it across his cheek, my shoulder aches. I gasp and set my hand back down.

For a moment, I lie there and try to orient myself. The world seems whimsical and not quite real, like perhaps I dreamed all of it, and this is still the first morning after I was shot while galloping away from the Truthbringers on Mercy.

I think of Nakiis, feeling for the familiar flickers of his wind and ice magic in my blood, waiting for a breeze to swirl through the room, all the signs that accompanied the new magic he lent to mine.

But there's nothing. I knew there'd be nothing. His magic is gone. I knew it the moment we walked out of the barn. I knew it when we faced Xovaar and Karyl and I thought everything was lost.

My throat tightens. *Do not grieve yet,* he said.

How about now? I want to ask. *Can I grieve now?*

But no. I have no idea what happened, and as usual, there's probably still work to be done.

I run a hand down my face. I glance at Jax, but he's still sound asleep. Is he injured? I have no idea. I'm mostly shocked that he's *alive.* I remember the moment the Truthbringers shot those arrows, the way the king plummeted from his horse. The way I dropped from Mercy.

When I move, I expect pain like the last time I was shot, but beyond the ache in my shoulder, there's none. I sit up, swinging my legs over the side of the bed.

Even with my motion, Jax doesn't move, so I look down at him. His breathing is slow and even, so I think he's fine—but he doesn't have the magic in his blood that Grey and I have. Would the Truthbringers' bolts have caused more damage? Or less, since the steel wouldn't affect him as badly?

I tug at the bedding lightly and discover thick bandages encircling his rib cage, and I swallow. He twitches a little in his sleep, and I don't want to disturb him, so I let go, rising to leave the room. A tunic is strewn over the back of a chair, and I have no idea whose it is, but right now, I don't care. I gingerly pull it over my head and make my way through the doorway.

To my complete and absolute shock, Noah is sitting at the little table in Jax's kitchen. A cup of tea is in front of him, along with a stack of parchment and a kohl pencil. He looks up when I appear in the doorway.

"Hey, kid," he says softly, giving me his familiar, gentle smile. "It's good to see you upright."

I stare at him. "What . . . what are you doing here?"

"I came with Jake."

My eyebrows go up. "Jake is here, too? What—when—"

"Not now. He had to continue on to the Crystal Palace." He frowns a little. "When he comes back, you'll have to ask him for all the details, because we've covered a lot of miles in the last few days."

My thoughts refuse to catch up. "What? But how . . . how are you here?"

"You sent a letter to Ironrose, didn't you?"

"I sent a letter, but—" I try to count the days in my head, remembering my code, the way I stopped to send a letter after we discovered the dead courier. But my head is still twisted up in knots, and it probably doesn't matter anyway. "Yeah. I did."

Noah nods. "Rhen knew your code meant there was a threat against the king—but Grey had already left. He sent a regiment after him, but we weren't fast enough. We made it here two days after the Queen's Army seized the Truthbringers."

There are too many surprises in that statement to process them all. "Two days?" I run a hand across my jaw. I peer at the doorway. "The army is here?"

"Not now. Grey ordered the Emberish army back to Ironrose. Most of them left yesterday."

Grey. I stare at him. "The king left?"

Noah nods. “He had to.” His voice is grave. “He was in worse shape than you are, but you know their position. He couldn’t afford for rumors to start. There’s been too much insurrection already.”

The sad thing is, I *do* know their position. I swallow. “How long have I been asleep?”

“You’ve been in and out for about a week.”

That hits me harder than I’m ready for, and spots flare in my vision. I waver unsteadily on my feet.

Noah stands, moving to my side at once. “You should sit down. Do you need me to help you?”

I shake my head, but I don’t resist when he takes hold of my arm and lets me lean against him. For a moment, I just stand there, feeling his steady support.

“I have a thousand more questions,” I eventually say.

He laughs softly. “I’m sure you do.”

“First, I think . . . I think I need to go outside.”

“All right.” He guides me toward the door. The summer heat hits me like a wave, and I inhale deeply. The lane between the forge and the bakery is quiet, and I don’t see anyone at all. I wonder who else is here. Surely it’s not just me, Jax, and Noah.

Then again, Noah said the army was ordered to disperse. If Grey was wary of rumor and suspicion, maybe it *is* just us. My heart twists a little. I remember that moment we were riding in the sunlight, joking a little, how family and friendship and love all seemed to come together in that moment. How deeply I longed for that. How much I *needed* it.

The king and queen returned to the palace. They have countries to rule. I have a job to do.

Always work to be done.

“I can walk,” I say to Noah, and he lets me go.

I wander out of the forge and into the soft grass to attend to human needs. My feet are bare, and now that I'm awake, I realize I'm rather desperately hungry. But I stare up at the sky and walk deeper into the trees, just feeling the air on my skin.

And then I realize what I'm missing: not just Nakiis's magic. My own.

Well, not entirely. The sparks and stars in my blood are still there. Just . . . muted. Glowing embers instead of the flare off a torch.

I try to draw at it, but it's sluggish, like the magic has been torn apart. No wonder my shoulder aches so badly.

—Magesmith.

I stop short, my heart leaping to my throat, my hand going for a weapon that's not even there. I'm barefoot in the woods. I have no bow, no sword, nothing.

But then I find Igaa on a branch overhead, and a moment later, she's on the ground in front of me.

"Igaa," I whisper, and against my will, my throat tightens.

In truth, I barely knew Nakiis. We weren't quite friends, but . . . but we were *something*. Maybe it's my exhaustion, but before I'm ready for it, my eyes well.

Igaa steps forward and wraps me up in her arms.

It's so unexpected that I don't react for a moment. Nakiis was so wary of me that I didn't even expect Igaa to come as close as she did. But her arms close around me, and then her wings do the same, until it's like being cocooned in warmth.

"I'm very sorry I couldn't save him," I say softly.

"He did not expect you to save him," she says. "He knew, Tycho. He knew."

"Did my magic die with him?" I say. In a way, I hope it did. It seems fitting.

"No," she says. "But his power was ripped away, after being bound to yours. Your magic is mourning, too."

That makes my eyes spill over, and I have to let go of her to swipe at my cheeks.

Igaa withdraws, her wings folding back into place. She doesn't cry, but she says, "Nakiis would lick those tears off your cheeks."

Her tone is so dryly ironic, just like his, and it makes me laugh, chasing away some of the emotion. "He probably would." I let my eyes flick up, scanning the trees. "Are you the last one?" I say. "Are you alone?"

"Alone?" Her eyebrows go up. "No. Not everyone followed Xovaar out of the ice forests—nor did they follow him *here*." She pauses. "Nakiis was not the only one who was wary of magesmiths." She scoffs under her breath. "If Xovaar had been less arrogant, Nakiis could have warned him of the dangers of allying with that woman."

"Why did he ally with her at all? He had to know she couldn't really give him back his magic."

"Oh, he certainly knew," says Igaa. "He likely intended to kill her from the very beginning. Xovaar and Karyl were not dissimilar. They both intended to double-cross the other. I simply don't think he was prepared for the agony that sharing his magic would cause."

Agony. The word nearly makes me flinch. But then I realize something else. "Xovaar was able to kill Karyl. Why didn't Nakiis kill Lilith?"

"Oh, Lilith was far more powerful—a born magesmith. Nakiis couldn't come close. Karyl was new."

I remember watching it happen, the way the scraver launched himself at Karyl, destroying himself in the process. "He had to know they would shoot him," I say. "He *had* to know."

"Oh, it was likely tormenting him," Igaa says. "Especially once he heard the truth in your words. Nakiis once said having your magic bound to another was like having your very being ripped away, over and over again, day by day."

My breath catches, because I understand that. Probably better than anyone. "Igaa—I'm sorry. I didn't know. I didn't know. I didn't mean to—"

She puts a hand out, against my chest, over my heart. "Tycho. Nakiis *knew*." She pauses, her voice quieting. "Truly. He *knew*. He had numerous opportunities to share his magic with Callyn or the queen. But he said if anyone would understand the cost, you would. Only you."

That makes my chest ache, while simultaneously settling something inside me. I put a hand over hers, holding it over my heart. "Thank you."

She nods.

I let her go. "Where will you go?" I say. "Will you return to Iishellasa?"

She nods, then sighs. "For now. There is so much fear, so much misinformation." But then her eyes brighten. "Though I have spoken to your queen. In time, we will discuss a way for us to travel through your lands without fear and hostility."

"That sounds like Lia Mara."

Igaa smiles, and her fangs make it more terrifying than it is friendly. "I like your queen."

"I do too."

Her wings flare, and she leaps into the air. No goodbye, no parting words, nothing.

Then again, Nakiis was never one for goodbyes either.

When I turn around to head back to the forge, Jax is waiting there by the corner, leaning against the tethering post. His hair is still loose, hanging over one shoulder, shining in the sun. Even with his ribs tightly bandaged and a little beard growth coating his jaw, he's still the most beautiful man I've ever seen.

"How long have you been there?" I say.

"Long enough. I didn't want to interrupt."

I stop in front of him, my eyes flicking up and down his form. "Are you badly injured?"

"No more than usual."

That probably shouldn't make me laugh, but it does, and then somehow it turns into a broken sound. Jax wraps his arms around me, and for the second time in five minutes, I find myself crying against someone while they hold me.

At least Jax won't talk about licking the tears off my cheeks.

But eventually my sorrow eases, and I rest my head against his shoulder and feel him breathe for a while. I'm still hungry, and I still have a million questions, but I don't really care. After the last few weeks, I think I could stand here in the summer warmth with Jax for a year and be quite content.

"I'm assuming *you* haven't been asleep for a week," I murmur.

"No," he says. "I've been watching over you."

That makes me flush and shiver simultaneously. "So you've met Noah."

"He'd be hard to miss, staying in my house."

I smile against his shoulder.

"I like him," he adds.

"I knew you would. Noah is wonderful."

"And as fierce as a lion," he says, with a hint of awe in his voice. "I don't think I've ever seen anyone stand up to the king like that—"

I lift my head. "Noah stood up to the king?"

"Yes. Why else do you think he left you here?"

My head thrums. Too much has happened, and I can't make sense of any of this. "What did he say?"

From the doorway, Noah calls out to us. "Tycho. If you're going to be up and around, you really should eat something."

Jax takes my hand. "Come on. There's a cow again, and some chickens. We have eggs."

I stare at him. "We do?" I clear my throat and shake my head. "Jax—what happened between Noah and Grey?"

"He said you had been through too much these last few months. He said you should be allowed to heal, without feeling the pressures of the palace or the nobility." Jax's hazel-green eyes search mine. "And then he said you should be allowed to choose your fate."

There was a time when this would have left me unmoored. I would have gone searching for my horse and ridden off to the Crystal Palace right this instant, because I'd be so worried I was making the wrong choice. That I was disappointing Grey.

But for the first time, my heart is steady. I don't feel an urge to rush anywhere.

I give his hand a tug, but it makes my shoulder ache, and I wince. Jax follows me anyway.

After a moment, I look over, because I am still curious.

"What did Grey say?" I ask. "When Noah made all these demands?"

Jax grins. "He gave me a bag of silver and said, 'Lord Jax, I commit him to your care.' "

CHAPTER 43

CALLYN

In what should come as a surprise to no one, Alek is a miserable patient.

Especially since he keeps refusing to allow *magic* to heal him.

"No magic," he said in Briarlock, when the field surgeon was cleaning the gouges and puncture wounds he must have been ignoring for *hours*. "No magic," he murmured to the queen, when they were stitching him closed, and the surgeon finally shoved a rag of sleeping ether over his face. "No magic," he said to me when he woke.

"*No magic*," he grunted when we rode in a carriage back to the Crystal Palace. I'm sure every bump made his wounds ache.

"I know," I said soothingly, using the same voice I used on Nora when she had a fever last winter. "No more magic. Never again."

But of course I used magic. I saw how filthy his wounds were when they cut away his tunic. I saw how pale his skin was. His dark trousers were soaked with blood. I couldn't believe how long he was standing upright. The damn fool is lucky to be alive.

I keep waiting for him to tell me he needs to return to his House, because I'm certain he has things to *do*, but he hasn't left the palace.

And I . . . haven't really left his side.

He's different now. He still has an edge, but it's not the same as it was before. It's little flares of vulnerability that I don't expect, like when Nora comes to see me, and he tells her a rather charming story about his childhood. It's the tenor of his voice when he speaks to the servants. It's the way he apologized to Verin for any suspicion, and it carried a genuine note that seemed to lighten the tension between them.

It's the way he speaks to *me*. No challenges. No jabs. No belligerence.

It's not quite softness, but I don't think I'd want softness. It's . . . it's ease. Comfort.

Then again, maybe he's just in a lot of pain.

After a week in the palace, he's well enough to walk in the gardens, though he complains about it the whole time.

"It's entirely too hot," he whines. "Surely we could have done this at daybreak, Callyn."

"There, there," I say, patting his hand. "I'll get you back for your nap soon."

He almost scowls—but then he laughs.

And then, without warning, he pulls me close and kisses me.

The sudden motion steals my breath, because I didn't see it coming. For all the time we've spent together since our moments together in Briarlock, he hasn't kissed me here in the palace, and my knees go a bit wobbly. I clutch at him.

Alek makes a small sound. At first I think it's passion—but then I realize it might be pain.

"Oh!" I say, letting him go at once. "Oh, I'm sorry."

"You're worth it," he says—very soft, very simple.

My knees almost go weak *again*. "I might actually miss you when you have to go home," I say.

His eyes widen a bit, and his tone turns serious. "I think you'll have me around for a while," he says. "That was quite a large army the Truthbringers amassed—and they know I turned against them in the end. Verin may have captured most of them, but likely not *all*."

That's sobering. "You think someone would come after you?" I say.

He nods. "I expect it, Callyn. We survived, but while the king is on the throne, this isn't *over*."

"So . . ." I stare at him. "What does that mean?"

"For the king and queen, I have no idea. But for me, I likely cannot return to my House. Not for some time." He gives an aggravated sigh. "Perhaps I'll have to settle in Emberfall."

He sounds so disgusted that I laugh, and I rise up on my tiptoes to kiss him. "Somehow you'll survive."

I meant for it to be a peck, but he catches my waist and makes it more. "Somehow I've made it this long," he says against my lips. "Those fools over the border *almost* have me believing in fate."

"Ah . . . at the risk of interrupting," the queen says from behind us, her tone a bit droll. She clears her throat.

I flush, then draw back, putting some distance between me and Alek. "Forgive me, Your Majesty." As I turn, I realize she's not alone. The king is with her, their hands loosely entwined.

The king hasn't left her side since the moment we returned to the palace.

"Ah, forgive *us*," Alek says.

"You're not the first couple to steal a kiss in the gardens," the king says, and the queen swats him on the arm. But he catches her hand and kisses her knuckles, and all the teasing melts right out of her expression. It's such a complete shift from the brutal political tension that existed between them for so long. For an instant, I wonder if *we* should give them some privacy.

Maybe it's not just Alek. Maybe we're all a bit changed after what happened.

"I was looking for you," the queen says to me.

"Oh!" I say. "Does Sinna need me—"

"No. Well—perhaps. As you know, tensions are still . . . very high. The king and I are planning to leave the palace for a time. With Sinna." She pauses. "And we were hoping you and Nora would consider remaining with us." She pauses. "To help."

Beside me, Alek goes very still.

My heart thumps. "For how long?" I say.

"For . . . six months," says the queen. She looks a bit pale. "Possibly . . . possibly a year."

"Possibly longer," adds the king—and they both exchange a meaningful glance.

I look between them. My mouth has gone dry.

"You're hiding," Alek says, and his voice is hushed. A month ago, his tone would have been full of accusation—but now it's just full of surprise.

King Grey frowns, then sighs. "Yes. Matters have changed, and we will announce a tour of Syhl Shallow and Emberfall. A chance to revisit our people. We will have couriers send word of our visits to distant cities, and we will arrange letters to and from Prince Rhen and Princess Harper talking about our adventures and the people we have met. Rhen has been acting as regent in Emberfall for quite some time, so that will continue . . ."

"And Verin will act as regent here," says the queen. "Until we can determine that the prejudices against magic have settled. I have spoken with Igaa. We are hopeful that we can spin a story that the scravers reclaimed their magic—though there is still so much fear to go around."

Alek studies them both. "But you will not *really* go on a tour," he finally says.

The king hesitates, and I realize it's possible he may not want to admit this to Alek—the man who once plotted against him.

But I know how much Alek risked to protect the queen in the end—and how much he may have lost, if he can't return to his own home either. Perhaps the king realizes the same, because he eventually says, "No. We will settle somewhere privately."

I look between them and wet my lips. "Where?"

"We would remain close to the palace," says the king. "We do not want to be too far from military force if we are discovered."

"Anyone in the Crystal City would know the queen," says Alek. "It's too much of a risk."

"Not that close," says the king. He looks at me. "We were considering Briarlock."

I gasp. "But—"

"It's small," says the queen, as if I'm about to protest. "And we aren't known there. Your bakery was set a ways off from town. We thought perhaps we could build a small house nearby—"

"You can *have* the bakery," I cry. Then I notice that she really does look very pale. "Your Majesty—do you need to sit down?"

"I'm fine, Callyn." She rests a hand over her abdomen. "I haven't been sleeping lately."

The king brushes a kiss along her forehead and murmurs something I can't hear.

"Why wouldn't you take residence at Ironrose?" says Alek. "Surely you could be better protected."

"Perhaps," says the queen. "But after everything that happened, I would rather be somewhere private for a time." Her expression turns a bit pained, and she looks up at the king. "I think . . . I think . . . we shouldn't spend too much time in the sun."

"Of course," he says gently. They turn back toward the palace.

I stare at them, confused—and worried. Is she ill? But then I think of the other moments we've sat together over the last few months, when she wouldn't eat, or she only sipped at her tea, or she claimed to be feeling off. I think of the child they lost, and how it drove them apart—and, once the king was gone, how desperately she wanted him back.

I remember when I first met them, how I was so intimidated by their roles, but once the royalty was stripped away, they were really just a young family struggling with grief and loss and doing their best to move past it.

Queen Lia Mara is leaning against the king now, walking slowly back toward the palace. Her hand is still over her abdomen.

To help, she said.

"Oh," I whisper.

"But why?" Alek calls, completely clueless. "Surely you would be safer at Ironrose—"

The queen turns, her expression aggrieved. But instead of snapping at him, she throws up on the king's boots.

The king catches her hair, drawing it back from her face in a practiced motion. He doesn't seem surprised at all. But he looks back at Alek, who's stopped short, his expression shocked.

"That's why, Alek," he says dryly. "That's why."

CHAPTER 44

JAX

For days, I wait for Tycho to ask for his armor. I expect him to strap on his gear, saddle up Mercy, and ride back to the Crystal Palace to accept whatever orders the king may have. I'd follow him, of course, but I'm ready for it.

But days pass, and he doesn't ask.

We tend the animals in the barn, and we shoot arrows in the woods, and we ride the horses on lazy loops through Briarlock. I can feel his lingering sadness, as if something has been ripped away—but I don't pry. Noah hasn't left, but he gives us space when we need it, and offers company when we want it. I learn why Tycho is so devoted to him, and why he was such a confidant when he was younger.

At night, Tycho and I lie awake in the shadows and talk, our fingers wound together. Sometimes we kiss, sometimes we do more, but mostly we simply exist together, with no pressure to do or be any*one* or any*where* else. Just Tycho—and just Jax.

When Lord Jacob eventually comes to fetch Noah at the end of the second week, he brings a cat in a wicker hamper.

"Salam!" Tycho exclaims in surprise, pulling the orange tabby free.

"He scratched the hell out of me," Jacob says.

Noah cuffs him on the shoulder. "But it was your *pleasure*," he says pointedly.

"Anything for T."

They stay for a few hours, and we share a meal and conversation, telling stories around a campfire that make me laugh, but only pull a smile from Tycho. When they leave, I wonder if this will spark Tycho's desire to return to duty—but it doesn't.

Instead, he pulls me into the house and spends an hour making me forget my own name.

When we wake in the morning, his cat is in the bed, curled against my shoulder, purring loudly.

"Traitor," Tycho whispers to him, and I smile.

By the end of the fourth week, we've cleared out the mess in the forge, and I've started doing odd jobs for random travelers who make their way down the lane. I haven't started seeking more business yet, because I'm waiting to see if Tycho intends to stay here, but I don't turn it down when work shows up.

Soldiers ride through one day, and we're surprised when Malin, Sephran, and Leo come up the lane—though they can't stay. They've been ordered back to Emberfall.

Sephran does give me a hug goodbye, and it makes me grin to see the daggers in Tycho's eyes when he watches it happen. We both promise we'll visit Ironrose when we can, but Tycho is so vague about the promise that I can tell he's in no rush to leave.

Sheer boredom leads us to repair the damage to Callyn's bakery, too, even though it'll likely have to be boarded right back up. I'll have to send word to ask her what she wants to do with the property.

By the end of the fifth week, we're both healed well enough for sparring, and we grapple in the woods. At first, it's playful, and I can tell Tycho's being cautious because he's not sure how much I've learned or how much either one of us has healed. But Sephran never went easy on me, so when he lightly brushes my arm to the side, I try to spin him and trap him in a maneuver Kutter once showed me.

Tycho knows it, though, because he responds instantly, slipping free and sending me to the ground to pin me there. It's so quick, so effortless, like he was born to do it.

I once asked him what he liked about soldiering, and I remember him telling me how much he enjoyed the weaponry, the drills. The training.

I'd match blades and spar from sunup to sundown if I could.

The purpose.

We're both a bit breathless, staring at each other.

"You miss this," I murmur.

"Not all of it."

We hear the creak of a carriage coming down the lane, and we both look. It's an older vehicle with rusty springs, being pulled by two aged geldings.

I sigh.

Tycho laughs under his breath. "Do you miss *this*?"

"Let me up. I can show you how to fix carriage springs."

But when we climb to our feet, we're surprised to discover that the carriage doesn't go all the way down to the forge. It stops in front of the bakery.

And then, as we approach, we're shocked when the door opens and it's not a random traveler who steps out.

Instead, it's the king.

CHAPTER 45

TYCHO

For an instant, I'm frozen in place, because there's no possible way the king of Emberfall just climbed out of this rickety carriage *alone* in the middle of Briarlock. Especially since the man is clearly Grey—but also . . . not.

Beside me, Jax does a double take. So do I.

The man who *looks* like the king has a thin beard. He's in a loose tunic and calfskin trousers, though there's a dagger strung at his hip. He extends a hand to the carriage, and a young woman climbs out—a young woman who looks like the queen, yet also different. Her hair is much shorter, and tied into a single plait that ends at the top of her shoulders. No royal robes, no rich fabrics, just a simple undyed linen dress.

After a moment, a little girl climbs out of the carriage, too. Her hair is tamed into twin plaits, but *this* is unmistakably Sinna. She takes hold of the young woman's hand and looks around. "Where's the snow?" she says lightly.

"Grey," I say softly. My heart swells with emotion I'm not ready for. I haven't seen him since the moment that arrow shot him off the horse.

For weeks, I've been feeling adrift and lost, and I thought I was grieving Nakiis, and I couldn't unravel the emotion. I was, but until this moment, I didn't realize I was grieving Grey, too. Not his death, but everything else.

Against my will, my chest tightens, and my throat feels thick.

But then Grey closes the distance between us, and he wraps me up in a hug.

I don't see it coming, and it's so unexpected that at first I'm not sure how to react. I've done it to him, but I'm not entirely sure I can recall one single time that he's done it to *me*.

After a moment, little Sinna tackles my legs, too, and I laugh under my breath.

But then I have to draw back.

The instant I inhale to say anything at all, Grey shakes his head. He takes a step back, then extends a hand. "My name is Hawk. It's nice to meet you."

Hawk. The name he used in Rillisk, when we first met.

I'm desperate to know what's happened that he would be here now, like this. There are no soldiers, no guards. Nothing. I swallow, then clasp his hand. "Well met, Hawk. I'm Tycho."

When he grips back, his fingers are tight, and then he lets go. He gestures to Lia Mara, who's a bit pale. "This is my wife, Mara. We'll be staying in the bakery for a time. Mara's cousin, Callyn, will be along in a day or so. She's helping a friend get settled in town."

I stare at her, too, as if I could understand all of this by reading the emotion on their faces.

In my silence, Jax extends a hand to them both, introducing himself as if we're all just meeting for the first time, and we didn't nearly die together a month ago.

"Are you well?" I say to them softly.

Lia Mara places a hand over her abdomen. "Very well," she says.

My eyebrows go up. *Oh.*

"My wife has been through a lot," says Grey—*Hawk*, I mentally correct myself. "We both thought it best if we found a quiet place to heal." He hesitates, glancing between me and Jax, as if worried that perhaps he's intruding. "Unless we should look elsewhere."

Jax takes my hand, winding his fingers between mine. "This is a good place for that."

I nod. "I'm doing the same thing."

Late that night, Grey comes to the forge, as I knew he would. He might be pretending to be Hawk, and he might have brought his family here to heal, but he's still the king, and . . . well, he's still *Grey*. When the light knock sounds at the door, I expect my heart to pound with apprehension, but I'm surprised to find that instead, I'm ready.

Jax pours tea, and we sit at the table, a lone candle between us. Grey tells us of the king and queen's "announcement" to spend a year traveling throughout both kingdoms—while hiding in plain sight, right here.

"Alek will live in town," Grey says. "So will Callyn and Nora—though they'll come daily to work the bakery with Lia Mara. But it will give them all some privacy—and an opportunity to listen for gossip."

"You have no guards, though," I say. "No soldiers. No . . . no *anyone*. What if you're discovered?"

Grey is quiet for a moment, studying me, and a line appears on his brow. But then he looks from me to Jax. "I hoped to ask you both to stay. You would know our secret, so you could ride courier to Ironrose or the Crystal Palace if necessary. Jax is already known to the forge, so there would be no new faces to explain in town. You're both skilled in battle, so with the three of us, we could adequately protect—"

I don't know what he sees in my expression, but he breaks off and sighs. "Forgive me. I promised to earn back your trust, and I have failed even this. You deserve your peace. I will send word to Malin and have him choose a small team. They can rotate with—"

"Hawk," I say, and he stops short. The name feels familiar and wrong all at once. I look at Jax, and he nods. "Of course we'll help protect your family."

Grey lets out a breath. The relief that crosses his face is so profound. Stepping away from the throne wasn't an easy choice for him to make, and in a way, I think this might be harder for him than when we rode out to sacrifice ourselves to the Truthbringers.

"Thank you, Tycho."

"For the good of Emberfall," I say, and I'm startled by the flare of emotion in his eyes. I put out a hand, and he clasps it tight.

But when he inhales to respond, Jax says, "No, I know this." Then he puts a hand over ours, reminding me again of that moment of friendship and family and love, and my heart gives a tug.

Jax smiles. "For the good of all."

ACKNOWLEDGMENTS

I'm on deadline, so I'm gonna make this brief.

(Not really.)

As always, I am so incredibly grateful to my husband, Michael. You know how busy I am right now, so I know you'll understand why I'm keeping your paragraph short. Thank you for everything, baby. I love you so much.

For more than ten books now, Mary Kate Castellani has been my incredible editor at Bloomsbury, and unfortunately we were not able to work on *Sparking Fire Out of Fate* together. Mary Kate, thank you so much for all of your help over the years. Your insight, compassion, and wisdom were dearly missed while crafting this book. If you ever have the opportunity to read this, I hope I make you proud.

Kate Sullivan of New Leaf Literary was my editor for *Sparking Fire Out of Fate*. Kate, it was such a pleasure to work with you, and I am so grateful for all of your time and efforts to make this book the best it could be. I can't imagine how challenging it was to step in for book three in a beloved series, but somehow you made it feel like we've been working together for years. Thank you for everything.

Suzie Townsend of New Leaf Literary has been my phenomenal agent for years now, and I don't know what I would do without her. Suzie, I am so grateful for your guidance, especially when things get tricky and complicated. I am so incredibly lucky to have you, Sarah Gerton, Olivia Coleman, Keifer Ludwig, and the entire team at New Leaf Literary on my side. Thank you all so much for everything.

The team at Bloomsbury is so incredibly dedicated with every single book! Huge thanks to Kei Nakatsuka, Lily Yengle, Erica Barmash, Faye Bi, Phoebe Dyer, Beth Eller, Kathleen Morandini, Valentina Rice, Diane Aronson, Jeff Curry, Jeanette Levy, Donna Mark, Hannah Bowe, Laura Phillips, Nicholas Church, Katie Ager, Emily Marples, Josephine Blaquiere, Barney Duly, and every single person at Bloomsbury who has a hand in making my books a success.

Huge thanks to my amazing Street Team! If you're a part of it, thank YOU. It means so much to me to know that there are *thousands* of you interested in my books, and I will never forget everything you've done to spread the word about my stories. Thank you all so very much.

Huge debts of gratitude for regular chats and moral support to Victoria Aveyard, Tanaz Bhathena, Maegan Bouis, Erin Bowman, Carissa Broadbent, Susan Dennard, Alexa Donne, Stephanie Garber, Reba Gordon, Amalie Howard, Isabel Ibañez, Danielle Jensen, Amie Kaufman, Christina Labib, Jodi Meadows, Jodi Picoult, Nicki Prau Preto, Siobhan Reed, Beth Revis, Sarah Rifield, Laura Samotin, Bradley Spoon, and Melody Wukitch, because I honestly don't know how I would get through the day without you all. I am so grateful to have you in my life.

This book was one of the most challenging books of my entire career for a multitude of reasons. I am deeply appreciative to the friends who had the time and patience to read my (very messy) work in progress, so tremendous thanks to Jodi Picoult, Reba Gordon, and Laura Samotin.

Back when I was in the trenches of trying to get this book written on time, I was trying to do writing sprints on social media. Someone asked if I'd consider creating a Discord server so the sprints would be easier to keep track of. I thought maybe ten or eleven people would join my Discord, so I was *shocked* when over a thousand writers joined! From brand-new aspiring writers to established career authors, from fresh debuts to major bestsellers, from indie to trad to hybrid, the Missed Deadlines Discord Server has become one of my favorite spots on the internet to hang out and chat while getting work done. It's not my community, it's *their* community, and I'm lucky to be a part of it. This book would not be in your hands without the ongoing support from all the other writers who were trying to put words on a page right along with me. (And yes, all are welcome. If you're a writer yourself, you're welcome to join.)

Additional thanks go to readers, bloggers, librarians, artists, and booksellers all over social media who take the time to post, review, tweet, share, and mention my books. I owe my career to people being so passionate about my characters that they can't help but talk about them. Thank you all.

And many thanks go to YOU! Yes, you. If you're holding this book in your hands, I am honored that you took the time to invite my characters into your heart. (I know I say this every time, but please know I truly mean it.)

Finally, tremendous love and thanks to my boys. You love each other so very, very much, and I am so incredibly lucky to be your mom.